Jennifer Loren

# Books by Jennifer Loren

## The Laws of Kings Series

THE LAWS OF KINGS

DETHRONING THE KING

## The Devil's Eyes Series

THE DEVIL'S EYES

THE DEVIL'S REVENGE

THE DEVIL'S SON

THE DEVIL'S MASQUERADE: THE POISON

THE DEVIL'S MASQUERADE: THE REMEDY

THE NEW DEVIL IN CHARGE

## The Finding Ava Series

FINDING AVA

RECKLESS

THE LONG ROAD

## Short Story

THE HAND THAT HOLDS MINE

# Prologue

*I*t is disturbing how quickly my life has gone from being so assured to so mystifying. What I thought I always wanted now seems so meaningless. As hard as I try to curse the doubts and those debilitating feelings overtaking me, I am still being drawn to somewhere else, to someone else. I find myself night after night dreaming of a man I haven't even met, dreaming of a life I never knew I wanted. Even during my nights spent with Jasper, my idol, my boss and the man who should be the one - *he* distracts me. My discontentment is forcing my usual runs through the park to become longer and faster paced as I sort out the details of my dreams and the shadowy man that vividly calls out for me. It was only a few days ago, I felt him or at least what I thought was him but - I was wrong. This new presence has nowhere near the same emotion of the man in my dreams. The watchful eyes are suddenly everywhere I go, I can hear them breathing in anticipation of my recognition of them but fear keeps me from seeking them out. I pretend I am only imagining the malice that has begun to haunt me but I can't help wonder if I am being pulled toward something wonderful or pushed away from something sinister.

# Chapter 1: Ava

*I* have worked my whole life striving to achieve that seemingly unattainable dream. Despite my barriers, I have been able to achieve all that I could have hoped for, that includes working alongside the one I have long admired the most, Jasper Andrews. He is inspiring and I have taken every opportunity I can to learn from him regardless of people questioning the elite projects that Jasper is assigning me too. No matter what they think about me, no one can question my work ethic or my dedication. In fact, Jasper has proven his confidence in me by inviting me to a board member dinner at his home tonight. I know this is my opportunity to prove myself, and hopefully an opportunity to pick my own team for the new city project. One person I already know for sure will be on my team is my best friend since eighth grade summer camp, Kyle. I met Kyle when we both fell in love with Billy Press, the summer camp's king of all sports. If not for the Billy Press fan club, and the late nights discussing his joyous athletic abilities, Kyle and I might not be friends today. Even though Kyle is from Georgia and me from Kentucky we stayed in touch until we attended college together, all the way to Columbia. We earned our Masters in Architecture and both are now working for Jasper and living on the cheap, the wretchedly cheap, in a cramped apartment above Mr. Wong's restaurant.

"Okay you pretty, redhead girl, you go and sucker those Charlie Browns' into giving us those promotions that we most certainly deserve." Kyle said kissing me on the cheek and sending me out the door with my *nice* shoes in a bag and my coat covering everything else to keep it from getting dirty on the bus.

My eagerness is building as I begin to count the stops and mentally pushing people to hurry, "on or off, make a decision - and let's go!" Timing is everything, and I do not want my first invitation to attend a party with the board of directors, to seem as if I have taken it lightly. After I get off at the last possible stop, I wave down a cab to take me the short distance left, giving me a chance to quickly change my shoes, fine-tune the rest of my outfit, hair, and makeup and all the while practicing my well-planned lines. I rehearse all the way to Jasper's building, through the lobby and up the elevator. One quick deep breath and I knock. Surprisingly Jasper answers, with drink in hand, looking casually sophisticated and smiling pleasingly at me.

"Ava, I am so glad you could make it." Taking my hand, he draws in close kissing my cheek while I notice the candles and the low volume symphony in the background. "You look beautiful as always."

I smile curiously, as I search for anyone else, "am I the first to arrive?"

Jasper after taking my coat leads me to the dining room and the table set for two. "I am afraid I was a bit deceptive in my invitation but I was too nervous to simply ask you to have dinner with me."

"Jasper, I don't think this is a good idea."

"It is only dinner, I promise. Please, sit we can talk about all your ideas and the possibilities for your future at the firm." Sitting down at the immaculately prepared table, I watch from the edge of my seat as Jasper pours us some wine. "You know I don't believe I have ever met anyone with so much talent and promise in my entire career."

"Thank you, but I thought tonight was about my career not about …"

"Ava, this is all about your career but I thought we could talk better alone and you could give me a better insight to what your goals are. You know I can't do everything, the firm is growing rapidly, and I need someone I can trust to help take the reins." My interest peeks as Jasper continues with questions and seeming interested in my every word. The night is unnerving but he never pushes for anything inappropriate, putting me a little more at ease and even more hopeful.

Over the next couple of weeks, I have lunch at expensive restaurants and travel to meet the firm's best clients. Jasper eventually asks me to help him present our latest design, which I did, helping win a high profile project for the firm. I celebrate with him - unreserved. The next morning is awkward and immediately regrettable. The "redheaded whore" title I have so easily dismissed now seems all so fitting. Still feeling his cold hands on my bare skin, I ease myself out from under his limp arm and try to make it to the door before he wakes.

"Where are you going?" Jasper asked sitting up in bed with a superior smile.

"I thought I … I really need to get home."

"Oh my darling, there is no need to rush out." Jasper jumps up putting his robe on over his naked body and putting his arm around me as if he has done this same routine for years. "Have breakfast with me and then I will drive you home so you can prepare for our dinner tonight."

"Tonight?" I look up at him puzzled, while I try to finger my tousled hair back into place.

"I will pick you up at seven. We have dinner reservations at Per Se tonight. And then." He turns to me smiling, "and then you can decide if you stay over again or not."

Breakfast was wonderful, dinner was beyond words, but Jasper's confidence is weakening me. I try to resist him, determined to keep our relationship, *professional* but with his always-charming poise, he reminds me of the future we can have together, like a dream I should have thought to have. Over time, I find my wordless acceptance has caused me to be deep in a relationship with my once idol, and my now boss. At first, he spoils me beyond anything I could have hoped for and I start to believe. However, the dizzying happiness comes to an abrupt halt when Jasper hires a new receptionist. Although, Jasper always reassures me just before he dismisses me for another meeting or another overnight trip. I can't believe my once strong and respectable persona is now nothing but a background fool.

ങ୫ଔ

*A* typical early morning, with my coffee and Kyle's head lying on my shoulder, allowing him a few more minutes of sleep until the bus gets us to our stop where we will make our way with the masses up to the twenty-second floor. The morning is over before I know it, the afternoon seems to have come and gone without me even recognizing, and suddenly people are fleeing for home. Five o'clock again … and Jasper walks by making sure to give me his usual exiting nod on his way out of town, still believing that our relationship is somehow a secret. Today is my birthday and Jasper promises to do something special for me when he gets back. I tried to look disappointed, but all I could think about is that it will be nice to have a night without Jasper's superior influences and enjoy Kyle's always -

energetic optimism. Speaking of the impatient devil, I can feel his frustrated eyes boring holes into my skull.

"I am not going to allow you to work late tonight. I don't care what you say." Kyle said stretching back in his chair making his glare, even more obvious. "Ava it's your birthday and we are going to celebrate tonight."

"I don't want to be tired for my meeting tomorrow, Kyle."

"We at least need to get a bottle of wine tonight."

"Wine?" I laughed. "Do tell, what goes with peanut butter and crackers or do we have any frozen waffles left?" I giggled with him.

"No, I ate the last one for dinner last night. Oh and we are going to have to pick up some more crackers from the cafeteria on our way out. As far as the wine, I think that a Merlot might be nice since we do have a creamy peanut butter. Or whatever they have for less than ten dollars because that's all I have until payday." He said pulling out his lint filled pockets.

"Oh you poor pitiful boy," I said pulling out a fifty dollar bill.

"Hey, where did you get that?"

"Jasper gave me some money to buy myself some flowers or any other dying organism that I might like to waste money on." I said with a sarcastic tone.

"Uggghhh, I don't get what you see in him but at least the jerk gave you cash and left town, the best gift of all." Kyle smiles.

"*Anyway*. I thought we could get some nicer wine with this and maybe a movie and use the rest to put towards our … *We have a dream jar.*"

"So you have decided?" Kyle asked with a vibrating expectation.

"I don't know for sure yet but it can't hurt to dream."

"I'll accept that for now but I know it's only a matter of time before I get to say, GOOD-BYE Mr. Jasper Andrews, and hello Kyle Brice and Ava Kelley Architecture and Design." Kyle said exaggerating his glamorous walk out the door. "Come on girl let's get out of here, these bright gray walls are starting to close in on me."

"I'm coming but I need to go by the library first. I want to do some research."

"Ava, Jasper already said he liked your ideas, don't over analyze what you have already done."

"I am not over analyzing. I simply want to be prepared for an important client."

"Well when it's my birthday, we are calling in sick and watching Lifetime in bed and eating cheddar popcorn all-day, because I'm worth it." He said waiting for me to agree.

"Of course you are, sweetie," I laughed kissing him gently on the cheek.

As soon as we get to the library, we both take to a computer searching for anything and everything helpful, Kyle a little less eagerly. Once I feel satisfied, I gather what I have found while Kyle throws a book on my pile of notes, about why not to sleep with your boss. "Funny." I said rolling my eyes at him and ignoring his laughter. Preparing for the cold, I overly bundle up, barely leaving enough room for my eyes to see where I am going and as expected, one-step outside and we both let out a frigid gasp.

"Let's go to the liquor store near that fancy little Italian restaurant, I love the smells," I yelled through the blistering wind and the layers of fabric.

"You're only going to torture yourself," Kyle said shaking his head.

"I don't care, at least this way I can dream my wretched dinner is a lavish Italian meal," I said earning a reluctant sigh of acceptance before we cross the street, huddled close together. I pay for the bottle of wine and wait outside for Kyle while he searches through the market across the street for an extra surprise birthday treat. I might have complained or even followed if not for the seductive aroma of the restaurant next door. Its torturous smells carry me away to a better place. With one last inhale, I take a short step back before hearing a screaming mob approaching me rapidly. With no time to prepare a safe exit, I curl around my wine and brace for impact. Unexpectedly, warm strong arms surround me and carry me safely through the hormonal girls.

"Don't worry they'll be gone in a minute," he said continuing to hover over me. I lie peacefully between his open coat and against his warm, taut chest, letting a new alluring scent fill my nose." Okay I think it is safe now. You okay?"

"What?" I asked feeling his rhythmic heart beat against his chest while mine speeds.

"Are you okay?" He stressed with a sarcastic chuckle.

"Yes, I think so," I said lifting my head only to be stunned into silence again by his deep green eyes and warm smile. The cold wind barely moves his expertly styled dark hair and his sweater gently highlights his athletic build but when his smile stretches across his handsome face, I imagine my heavy beating heart jumping from body into his.

"What the hell happened to you?" Kyle yelled reminding me of my scattered books and notes that are beginning to blow out of reach.

"Oh no!" I yell jumping from the man's arms to try to rescue my hours of work, managing to grab most everything in sight except the book Kyle got me, which the stranger hands me with the rest of my notes. I respond shyly, thanking him while unable to take my eyes off him, I can barely grasp what he is saying to me. *Just smile and nod Ava. Damn what is wrong with me! He said good-bye … I think. Say something you idiot.* "Bye." *Wow, that was impressive.* I watch him walk away as Kyle grabs my arm turning me back towards our apartment but I look back once more to see him doing the same before disappearing into the restaurant.

"Ava, do you know who that was?" Kyle asked.

"I think that guy called him Sean."

Kyle laughs, "no ridiculous girl not him, the other one, the one the mob was herding towards." Shaking my head, I can already foresee the informative celebrity news coming by way of dramatic explanation. "It was Ethan Grant, the actor, the hottest and the sexiest movie star I can think of and he …"

"Oh, well I didn't talk to him."

"No, but you sure did get close and personal with his brother, who I must say is not bad either. I hear Sean is getting ready to do a movie too, I can't remember what it was about though. Wow you are having one hell of a birthday," Kyle said hanging his arm around my shoulders.

"Yea, I guess I am. So what did you get from the store?"

A huge smile sweeps across his face as he reaches into his bag and pulls out a box, "macaroni and cheese, the name brand too. My best friend wants a lavish Italian meal and I will do everything possible to get it for her," he said as both our stomachs growl in anticipation.

CB80

*M*y meeting went better than expected and Jasper made good on his promise for a birthday dinner together. As usual, he is charming and sweet, even dancing with me at least long enough for him to convince me to come back to his place. His breath heats up with every item of clothing he removes from my body, his hands grasping me securely and confidently, while kissing me as if he owns me. The cold stiffness of it all is bringing up a harsh realization and my stomach immediately begins to churn with every grunting obnoxious pounding into my body and the feeling of his sweat dripping down between my breasts. He reaches his climax, finishing with no worries or regrets. I receive a simple kiss to the forehead for my assistance before he leaves me to clean up. I am allowed to sleep over, if I promise not to keep him awake because he has a hectic schedule to keep tomorrow. Instead, I decide to take his offer to pay for a cab ride home. *I prefer to go into work with Kyle anyway.*

&#x03A8;&#x0460;

**K**yle is gasping and huffing at me the whole ride to work this morning. "Ava you are one of the smartest people I know and somehow you have gone stupid over this guy,"

"You don't know, maybe it's something." Kyle interrupts me with a - *I see through your bullshit smile.*

"Well at least you got laid. Was it good at least?" He said as I give him a quick look. "It wasn't even good?" Cringing, I look away from my judge.

"Good morning Ava!" A security guard from the building greets me standing and giving me his full attention.

"Good morning ..." *What was his name? I think I saw him at last year's Christmas party. What was it?* "Spencer."

"You look beautiful today, Ava." Spencer says awkwardly fidgeting with his pocket change.

"Thank you," I said feeling the nudge from Kyle as we rush away to the elevators.

"What was that about?" Kyle asked.

"He helped me get rid of some guy that followed me in from lunch the other day."

"What guy?"

"Just a guy who wanted to take me out, he said he wouldn't take no for an answer, so ummm ... *Spencer* ... stepped in and told him to leave. It was nothing but he was sweet to step in and help me out as he did. I told him that he's my hero."

"Your hero, if he is your hero he will rid Jasper Andrews from your life." With an angry huff, I take an obvious step away from

Kyle. "Ava you know he is using you, he doesn't care about you. He knows as well as everyone else that you are the most talented person in this place and that includes him. Not to mention, you look great on his arm."

"He said he loves me." I said instantly regretting the stupidity.

"Loves you? Please, that man is too full of himself to love anyone but himself. Kick him to the curb Ava, you know that's what you should do. Stop trying to be respectful to a man who has not bothered to do the same for you," Kyle said leaving me to drown in my doubts.

I know Kyle is right about my relationship with Jasper, it is less of an equal partnership and more of Ava being the dutiful shadow. We argue all the time now, and Jasper is jealous of everyone I talk to but he feels righted flirting with anyone and everyone he meets with a skirt. I know he is cheating on me but the telling part is … I don't care.

ೕ৵

*R*ecently, Kyle has made some new contacts in Atlanta, a chance he says for us to go out on our own and today, I finally agree to go with him. *I cannot wait to move.* I had planned to tell Jasper tonight at dinner, although the rumors have obviously already reached his ears since he has asked to speak to me alone. Jasper manages to put me off until after everyone has left.

Inhaling deep before I walk boldly into his office, "Jasper I have everything ready for you. You should have no problem impressing them on Monday."

Jasper eases back in his chair and admires me with an obvious smile. "Why don't you come with me? We can leave tonight, spend the weekend together …"

"No Jasper, I can't."

"No?" He says getting up and taking my hand. "I was going to wait to do this but as usual you're stubborn." With his confidence shining through he kisses me, "Ava I want to marry you."

"What?"

"I know, not something you expected at all from me but I love you and I know you love me. We can do it this weekend in Paris, go to the meeting on Monday, and be back and ready to work …"

"Jasper, have you lost your mind? You don't love me, you only want me to stay here." I push his hands away and take a deep breath.

"Jasper, I am so appreciative for what you have done for me here but it's time for me to move on - Kyle and I are going to start our own firm. I was planning to tell you tonight."

Jasper with a harsh expression begins gathering his things, "you fucking bitch! With all that I have done for you, you are going to leave me!"

"Done for me? I have been doing your work for the last year. The clients have liked my ideas because you have been too busy fucking everything that you came across to deal with work. Oh don't look at me that way. Did you think I didn't know? Everyone knows and you love that they do. It is over Jasper. Let me leave, so we can end this respectably."

"Good luck with your little woodsheds in Atlanta, Ava." Jasper takes a wide curve to walk around me.

"You're leaving? You are going to leave me here." Jasper shrugs with an obnoxious expression. "Jasper it's raining and it's late, you know I can't afford a cab ... drive me home at least."

"I would Ava but it is late and I don't want to have to drive that far out of my way in the rain. But I don't want you to think I'm bitter about anything, so here, you can take my umbrella." Jasper hands me his designer umbrella and grips my face hard, "I will give you until Monday to change your mind." Like a fool, I stand silently watching him leave.

With Jasper's umbrella, I fight the cold rain while making my way home. Taking notice of everything around me along the dark streets, I become aware of a car slowly traveling behind me. I quicken my pace and the car suddenly pulls up next to me. "Ava do you need a ride home?" A familiar voice calls out.

Looking down in the car, I see the security guard from our building. "No, I'm fine Spencer, thank you though."

"You have to be cold. Get in. It's no problem, really."

After considering for only a few seconds, my frigid, exhausted body replies eagerly. "Okay, thank you," I said jumping into his car.

"So are you going out tonight?" Spencer asked.

"Jasper was supposed to take me out to dinner but ..."

"He doesn't deserve you, Ava."

"Well thank you, but it doesn't matter anymore I broke it off with him for good. Kyle and I are going to move out of New York and start our own firm." Before I can speak another word, Spencer's silence becomes noticeably awkward and cold. Suddenly he turns the car around. "Spencer, I live in the other direction."

"You need to see my house."

"No, I want to go home," I said fisting my hands and pounding on the seat, demanding my way.

"No! You need to see our house." He demands.

My body begins to shake violently as I try to calm, "Spencer, I would love to see your house sometime but tonight is not a good time but maybe tomorrow. I will call you and we can setup a time."

"You are going to love it. I even restored your old desk from college and put it in the study. Don't worry though, I removed that piece you were always hitting your knee on." He smiles happily, as a familiar haunting presence takes over him.

"Spencer! Let me out of this car now!" I yelled with every ounce of Irish fuel I have within me. Smiling a bone-chilling smile, he pulls over and I quickly grab the handle to the door ….

CR&ED

**M**y body feels heavy, as I force my eyes open to the darkness that surrounds me. Nothing seems familiar, not the smells, not the sounds, nothing at all. Panic forces me up, jerking my wrists back to the bars that they are tied to. I scream for help, until out of the darkness, a door lights up, and opens with a large shadow hovering within the threshold.

"Go to sleep Ava, no one can hear you here," Spencer said locking me back into the darkness....

# *Chapter 2: Sean*

*M*y father, William Benjamin Grant died almost two years ago now, and yet I still believe he is going to walk through the door any moment with his usual debonair attitude. He could have done anything with his life but instead he chose my mother.

They met when she was taking a break from doing Off Broadway shows and decided to take a chance in London. My father, who was never one for the arts, found himself tricked into seeing her play one night and as he said, "as soon as I saw her, I knew immediately she was my everything and I had to let her know." It was a little too fairy-tale for me but they believed it and they were married within a few months after meeting. My mother soon dragged him to New York, to concentrate on her career that is until Ethan, my brother was born. Then my father took over by managing several important political figures finances. He was great at managing money and exceptionally smooth. I always assumed that it was because of the accent, no matter what it was, Ethan and I idolized him. He moved us briefly to London, hoping to increase his business but we returned to New York when Ethan took an interest in acting. Mother insisted we move back to where she had connections to help him, and so we did, and my father never complained once. I wasn't sure that she ever appreciated what he did for her, until he died and then she barely spoke a word for almost a year. I left the military, Special Forces to take care of her while my brother was busy working on his next big Oscar winning role. Nevertheless, when my mother recovered, my successful older brother came to my rescue and helped me get my first acting job. It was nothing more than a couple of lines in a commercial, but it helped me get some minor roles in some movies, some were so minor that I was cut out of the films entirely. It has been a long and frustrating start, but recently I did a brief dramatic scene in which I somehow misplaced most of my clothes and now suddenly my agent can remember my name.

I am hoping the recent interest in me will also help Rebecca's career take off too. Rebecca Carol, an actress I met while filming a previous movie and who is now living with me in our comfortable one bedroom apartment. Rebecca is a gorgeous, tall, and brunette and laughs all the time, which I love. We are perfect together, except for one *thing* and I am not sure what that one *thing* is but I can't get rid of the feeling.

"Sean are you home?" Rebecca yells.

"In the bedroom."

"Why are you in bed?" Rebecca jumps on top of me laughing and smiling at me seductively.

"Waiting for you obviously," I said pulling off her dress. She lacks underwear as usual so there isn't much else to do but give her what she wants. Our typical ritual begins by me kissing her while grabbing a condom from my side table drawer. Her legs move up onto my shoulders teasing me until I find my way inside her, immediately she calls out to me. Her orgasms are abrupt and lately seem to be loud for the sake of being loud. I am not sure who she is trying to impress but I assume it has something to do with the newly, pretty, young tenant next door. The poor girl has been the victim of ridicule after Rebecca caught me helping her bring in her groceries. It was funny at first, even a little flattering but now she is constantly accusing me of cheating on her. All because she heard a rumor the girl is a hooker and takes in nightly visitors for fifty bucks. I cannot imagine it being true but Rebecca insists that it is and that I need to stay away from her. I agree to keep my distance for no other reason than to keep from arguing about it anymore.

After we are done, I ease out of bed and shower to go meet a friend but I can already hear her huffing complaints. "Where are you going?" She said with her piercing eyes.

"I'm going to meet Joel."

"Joel again?" She asked crossing her arms with a huff. *I am so tired of this argument.*

"Rebecca, I'm not discussing this with you again."

"Sean, you're my boyfriend! Why are you always hanging out with him?"

"Rebecca!" I yell back at her with emphasis, waiting for only a second for her to uncross her arms before kissing her tense lips and walking out the door.

While I wait for the elevator, our apartment door flies open and Rebecca comes storming out, "you know I can have any man I want, I don't have to put up with you."

"Put up with me?" I laugh at her demanding stance. "Go back inside Rebecca before you say something you'll regret." I said as the elevator door opens and standing innocently in front of me is our pretty, young neighbor.

"Hi Sean." She said shyly and blushing when I wink at her.

"Hi, Hannah. Nice to see you again." I said passing her and smiling wide at Rebecca's disgusted expression before she huffs at me and stomps back into our apartment. Her tantrum makes it easy for me to leave and find Joel waiting for me at the bar and already ordering a drink for each of us. Joel Castor, the son of one of the top execs, at one of the largest production companies going these days and he is my best friend. We are both struggling actors currently but Joel aspires to write screenplays and despite his father's claims to the contrary, he is too talented not to be successful.

As soon as Joel spots my frustrated expression, he immediately breaks out in laughter. "She gets mad every time you come out with me, is it something I said?"

"It's not you, it's any time I spend away from her."

"She wants to get married," I shoot him a wicked look of disgust. "Oh come on Sean, you know that's what it is?"

"Maybe, but we aren't ready for that." I said sighing and downing my drink quickly.

"Why not? You're living together what's the difference?" Joel said knowing he is only egging me on to stay out even longer and piss Rebecca off even more.

"I don't know, we discussed it at one point and even went shopping for a ring but it doesn't feel right, something's missing."

"I don't get it, she's hot, and she has a promising career of her own. She does go down on you doesn't she?" He smiles wide.

I spit my drink out laughing at him. "You're an idiot."

"Well damn, what more do you want?"

"I wish I knew, although it would be nice if my mother didn't hate her." Joel looks at me with a questioning expression. "Seriously, I tried to take them both out for dinner the other night and it was horribly uncomfortable. Rebecca hates that my mother wants me to come over for dinner without her and my mother thinks Rebecca is … I think the words she used was … *Evil Bitch*." I say as Joel laughs. "Don't laugh it's a mess."

"Well you know what they say, mother does know best." Joel said eyeing another desperately dressed girl coming through the door.

"Well I'm not ready to give up on her yet, I do love her … I think. Let's change the subject I'm getting depressed," I said downing another drink and laughing at Joel trying to stand in front of me so the girls notice him first.

"He's already taken girls, I'm the one that needs love." Joel remarked with arms wide open.

I am not sure what time I stumble my way back home but the locked bedroom door is a good sign that I stayed out too long. Too drunk to care and too drunk to argue with her, I crash happily into the jutting springs and torn fabric of our sofa. Within seconds, I am deep into my dream, a particular dream that has been seeking me out more vividly with each passing day. I don't know who she is, all I can do is get a sense of her presence and want her even more. This time I am determined to break through the cloud that surrounds her.

"HELP! Oh God please help me!" Hannah screams from next door.

"What the fuck?" Jumping up I run quickly to the door only to be met by Rebecca coming in.

"Sean don't. I saw one of her clients go in, you shouldn't get involved in that kind of mess." She said gripping me hard.

"Rebecca she's screaming?"

Rebecca tries to hold me in place. "No Sean, stay with me I'm scared."

"You'll be fine, lock the door, and call the police." I pull away from her and call for Hannah briefly outside her door before rushing in and pulling some guy off her. Hannah begins to curl around herself and cry. Her clothes are twisted and torn, and barely hanging onto her abused body. The man tries to fight me but I have no problem controlling him and putting him into the wall until the police come.

"Are you okay?" I asked Hannah, helping her up and letting her cry against my chest.

"I don't know what happened. I was sound asleep and next thing I know I wake up and he is on top of me. I didn't hear him come in or anything." She continues to cry while I check the unscratched lock. *She must have forgotten to lock her door, this country girl still has not gotten use to the city yet.*

Once Hannah is rushed off to the hospital and I make a quick call to her parents, I go back to check on Rebecca who is vibrating across our living room floor. "Are you okay sweetheart, everything is fine now, you don't need to worry. Hannah is going to be fine."

"I don't give a fuck about her!" She screams in my face. I carefully remove her from my face and give her a hard glare. "Sean you should have stayed here with me and not gotten involved. The police could have handled it."

"There is no telling what could have happened to that girl by then." I said shocked by her thoughtless attitude.

"I don't care … I was so scared something was going to happen to you." She says crying hysterically.

I pull her into my arms and kiss her, "I'm okay, everything is okay now. And I'm sorry I worried you, okay?" She nods pitifully. "Okay, now am I allowed back in the bed or am I still in the doghouse?" She shrugs causing me to laugh at her. "Well it's almost …," I said looking at my empty wrist. "Shit, I must have dropped my watch at her place. I guess I will have to call and ask her about it tomorrow." Rebecca grips me harder, crying even more hysterically, so I pick her up and carry her to bed.

☙❧

"**S**ean!" *Oh, fuck my head.* Rebecca hovers over me as I try to hide under my pillow. "Sean the guy downstairs made advances towards me. He was disgusting." I roll away from her hoping she will go away. "So are you going to do something?" She grabs my face, jerking it towards her abused expression.

"What would you like for me to do?" I said as she crosses her arms with a whimper. "What did he say to you?" *I hope it is not too serious so I don't have to go and kick this guy's ass because I really am tired.*

"He said he liked my outfit and then stared at me … hard." She said searching for the tears. *Not even close to serious.*

"That's flirting, not anything serious. Now leave me alone Rebecca, I'm tired."

"Don't you ever get jealous?"

"No, now go away." I said rolling away from her.

"You are so frustrating," She said sitting impatiently waiting for me to apologize as she vibrates the bed with her usual hyperventilating hysterics. "Funny how some guy nearly attacks me, could have killed me and nothing from you but as soon as that whore next door cries - you go running." I sit up to say something to her but as soon as I see her stick her chin out at me, I know it is useless, so I lie back down and turn away from her again. "I can't believe you are treating me this way and after I was nice enough to go and get your watch for you." She said laying my watch on the night table in front of me.

"Hannah's home, I thought she was staying with friends for a few days?" I asked confused.

"*No*, she is not home! I used the key she gave me in case she locked herself out. Why! Why are you so concerned about her?" Rebecca runs off crying and making sure to slam every door on her way out of the apartment. *I don't know what I said this time but at least it made her leave so I can have some quiet.*

CഇൠD

*I*t was only a few days ago that I auditioned for a role that may help jump-start my career. I knew it was a long shot but to my surprise, I got it and as soon as I get off the phone with the news, I rush home to tell Rebecca. "I got the part." I said blasting through our apartment door.

Her eyes widen as she jumps into my arms, "really? Are you sure?" I nod at her even wider smile. "Oh Sean this is wonderful, I can't believe it."

"I know. I hoped for something but I never thought …"

"So we are going to California?" She asked as my smile diminishes. "You are taking me with you aren't you?"

"You know we can't afford that right now and I won't have time to be with you anyway. I'm going to stay with my brother." Rebecca pushes me away, crossing her arms. "Don't be mad. What do you want me to do?"

"Take me with you." I shake my head. "Sean you know I have always wanted to move California, it could help my career too, and we can make so much more money." Rebecca said pulling me sweetly into her arms. "Baby please, it would be a chance for us to make all of our dreams come true."

"I would love to Rebecca but it doesn't change the fact that we can't afford it."

"We could if you would just ask your mother or even your brother for the money."

I pull away from her, wondering if I was wrong about her. "No." I said firmly to her already pouting figure. "We've talked about this before and I'm not going to again."

"Sean, you're being ridiculous about this. Your brother is on the cover of almost every magazine there is and your mother still has pull to help me too. If you are not going to ask for money then can you at least get them to mention me for a part? At least ask Ethan to get me an audition for that movie he is doing here in New York."

I stare at her as she begins teasing me, "I'll think about it." I said to her instant smile. She knows that I have plans to meet up with Ethan after his flight gets in tonight but unfortunately for her, I change our plans and meet him at Mom's so Rebecca will surely not want to come with me.

രൂ

"Sean have you looked over these financial reports?" Ethan asked.

"I have, have you?" I asked in retaliation as he rolls his eyes at me.

"So the new role is good?"

"Yes, I am really excited about it. Rebecca's not too happy about me going to California to film though."

"I told you women only make things complicated when they don't have to be."

"Right." Ethan's approach to women is *keep your distance*, they only screw things up. "By the way, have you talked to Mom?" I asked watching him for any sign of misery.

"Some. Why?"

"No reason." I said as our mother on cue walks in greeting us both with a kiss on the cheek.

"Sean said you wanted to talk to me about something?"

Mother does not even bother to look my way, "yes, you know I have been seeing this physical therapist since my fall at the gym."

"I told you Mom that place is not managed well. They let people run around out of the pool and they never clean it up. I'm surprised more people haven't fallen."

"Ethan, I have changed gyms so no need to worry anymore. Sean went with me and approved it himself." I nod at Ethan as he questions her truth. He even bosses her around. Neither one of them realize how much alike they are. "Anyway, I was hoping while you are home you can take me to some of my appointments."

"Sean can do that, Mom." Ethan snaps at her.

"I offered, but apparently I'm not … suitable." Ethan looks at me amused.

"Sean don't be ridiculous, I would simply like for your brother to meet my therapist."

"Why?" Ethan said apprehensively.

"Well because I think it's important for you to take an interest in your Mother's life." Mom begins to work up a tearful disappointment. "After all that time I spent helping you and now I want to brag about you and show you off to some of my new friends and you want to question me like I'm some kind of monster. I don't understand how you can dismiss me like this." I hold my breath trying to keep from laughing hysterically as she sniffles into a folded Kleenex from her pocket.

Ethan surrendering, throws his hands up in the air. "Holy …, fine mother … I will take you."

"Wonderful, I can't wait for you to meet Abbey," she said running out of the room.

"What just happened here?" I smile innocently as Ethan looks at me puzzled. "She's setting me up?" I nod. "Shit."

"Come on take me out to dinner, you'll feel better. There is this great little Italian place I have wanted to try." I put my arm around his shoulder smiling sheepishly as I guide him out the door.

"It better be good." Ethan said with a scowl.

"If not you can buy me some drinks to get the taste out of our mouths." I said smirking at Ethan's typical look of disapproval.

As we pull up to the valet of the restaurant, I see someone standing nearby as if she is trying to smell the billowing panels to the entry of the restaurant. I start to laugh at her until I hear the screaming mob coming after Ethan. I watch as the poor girl turns in their direction and immediately freezes in place waiting for them to trample over her. Running to her, I reach out quickly, pulling her safely out of the way while the restaurant takes Ethan in and after giving up trying to follow him, the mob vanishes. *Those crazy girls have been following him around since he got back to New York. I don't know how they know where to go.* Looking down at the bundled girl in my arms, I am only able to make out eyelashes and take in her invigorating scent.

"You okay?" I asked.

"What?" She responds seemingly dazed.

I huff a slight laugh. "Are you okay?" I asked.

"Yes, I think so," she said lifting her head and looking at me with the most beautiful sapphire blue eyes, sending my heart racing against my chest.

"What the hell happened?" A man coming out of nowhere said while flailing his arms at the girl. I let go of her and she leaves me to pick up her things. Bending down to help, I find an odd book and hand it to her watching her barely visible skin turn a charming pink.

"Thank you ... oh this was given to me as a joke," she said with a southern sweet voice that arouses me.

"Well you shouldn't screw your boss, it makes it hard to get any work done." I said leaning in close to her, taking in her scent one more time and whisper, "you're welcome by the way."

"So what happened?" Her boyfriend persists as I glance back at the annoyance.

"I'm afraid she was nearly crushed by my brother's stalking fans," I said staring into her stunning eyes.

"Sean, what are you doing, let's go eat?" Ethan yelled impatiently.

"You nearly got this poor girl crushed Ethan, give me a minute to make sure she is alright at least." I sigh barely making out the impression of a smile through her scarf. "Sorry he is a little stressed lately, I promise he's not always an asshole." She shakes her head, I think, it's hard to tell under all that fabric, she moves but it doesn't and it is cute as hell. "Well it looks like you are okay so I better get back to my brother before the veins in his head explode."

"Bye." She said so sweetly that I can't help smile.

"Try to stay clear of crazy mobs." I said and turn to walk back towards the restaurant but before I walk in I look back to see her blue eyes smiling back at me, a smile that I know will be embedded in my memory forever.

"What the hell are you doing?" Ethan asked holding his hands up in the air.

"Shut up, I'm coming."

Once I sit down at the table Ethan begins glaring at me, "What's wrong with you?"

"I'm thinking about that girl."

"What girl?"

"Shit Ethan, the girl I was just talking too. Are you going senile or something?"

"Sorry, I'm hungry," Ethan said ordering his food and sitting back with a sigh, "so what about this girl?"

"I don't know, I wanted to invite her to eat with us."

"So go ask her."

"I can't she already walked off with her boyfriend."

"She was with her boyfriend while you were flirting with her?" I huff at him pushing myself back from the table. "I'm just asking."

"Well stop," I said ignoring his rolling eyes.

"I don't understand why you are so dreamy-eyed over a girl you don't even know, who has a boyfriend and I thought you had a girlfriend?"

"I don't know Ethan, I can't explain it."

"You are so much like Dad." Ethan kicks my chair jarring me to attention. "That's exactly what Dad said happened when he met Mom."

I narrow my eyes at him, "I don't want to talk about it anymore." I said watching Ethan shrug before moving on to other issues. *I didn't even ask her name. Idiot.* Ethan's nonstop persistence about how I should live my life is starting to irk me. Before I say something unnecessarily rude to him, I walk outside hoping to ease my tension and hoping that she is waiting nearby. Standing outside, staring in the direction she left, I feel like an idiot. *Of course, she wasn't going to stand out here and wait for me. Who does that?* After a cold wind sends chills to my spine, I turn to go back inside but something sparkling from the ground catches my eye. I pick up a chain with a small locket dangling delicately from it. The chain is broken but the locket is fine and the pictures inside are old but undamaged. The sweet pictures of the happy couple inside and what I assume is their baby on the other is appealing to me and for reasons I don't understand I put it in my pocket. It is pretty, even though now broken for some reason it makes me feel better. For the rest of the night, I try to get the bundled girl out of my mind. Pretending that my newly found locket is hers, I will make sure to keep it hidden from Rebecca.

CR&

*W*hen it comes time to leave for California, I finish packing and begin searching for the locket I hid.

"What are you looking for?" Rebecca said entering the room with attitude.

"Damn it Rebecca! Give it back and you better have not done anything to it."

"HERE, here is your stupid necklace! It is old and ugly anyway. I hope your girlfriend loves it."

I take the locket from her sighing, "I found it, and I didn't buy it for anyone and I don't plan on giving it to anyone."

"Then why do you have it?" She said crossing her arms and pursing her lips.

*Fuck it.* "I don't know! Here I will throw it away - does that make you happy?" I toss the locket into the trash waiting for her forced smile. "I have to go." I grab the trash too, trying to look unbothered by the gleaming locket on top. "I might as well dump this for you on my way out."

"You will call me every day, right?"

"I don't think I am going to have time to call you every day but I will call you as much as I can." I said grabbing my bags and heading towards the door.

"I love you." She said cocking her head to one side.

"I love you too." I forced out of my mouth, kissing her impatiently.

"Sean, wait one second." I watch her frantically gathering items and returning quickly with a wide smile before taking the trash for my hand. Rebecca proceeds to dump out a container of yogurt, pasta sauce and some old milk before finally cracking some eggs on top of the trash. "That should do it, here you go. Make sure to tie it up nice and tight, I would hate for that mess to dump out." I take the trash from her hand and slam the door behind me.

⟪❧⟫

The time away from Rebecca, seems to have been good for us both. During our recent conversations, she manages a believable apology and some provocative discussions that cause a stir within me again. To ease some of my newly found guilt for leaving Rebecca behind, I ask Joel to look after her while I am gone. However, Joel has been either drunk or high during my last few conversations with him so I don't expect too much help from him. Joel's latest career making opportunity fell through and he has been on a downward spiral since. As soon as I return home, I plan to piece my friend back together as well as my relationship with Rebecca. I know what I want in my life and I cannot wait to see her again and plan our life together. Arriving home without warning anyone, I hope to surprise Rebecca with flowers and a special gift. I don't even wait for the elevator, I run up the stairs opening the door to our apartment eagerly, only to be greeted by two recognizable voices coming from our bedroom. I pause for some time, listening to the moans and the eager requests, but the determined fool that I am, I have to prove it to myself. Slamming the bedroom door wide open, I see Rebecca's legs hung around Joel's neck.

"Sean!" Joel yelled removing himself quickly from my girlfriend.

"Sean NO! Please, please don't be mad," Rebecca, cried.

"Mad, why would I be mad Rebecca? I'm just glad I didn't call first because I wouldn't have believed it if I didn't see it." I grab what little is still important to me before turning to leave.

Rebecca holds onto my arm with fierce resistance, "Sean please, he doesn't mean anything to me. I missed you so much that I broke this one time. We've been drinking, talking about you and …," She continues crying.

"This one time?" She nods as I look to Joel, casually leaning in the doorway of our bedroom. "You're lying. And I don't care enough to hear the truth." I pull away from her shaking my head in repulsion. "She's all yours friend … enjoy."

◌ଛଚ

*I* stayed with my mother for a couple of days before moving permanently out to California. I am not sure how long it took for the anger to subside or how long it took me to get over her but eventually, I moved on. Once my first big role came out in theaters the opportunities began rolling in and before I know it - I am in demand. I am able to buy a house I love, and hire Randy, my best friend from my military days to be my security adviser. However, the biggest change is Ethan asking to be my manager. He is ridiculously in love he says and detests the Hollywood lifestyle and prefers to let it go and raise a family with his new fiancé, Abbey, my mother's old physical therapist.

After much arguing with him and making sure that this is what he wants, I stand next to him and his beautiful bride watching him smile all over himself, like an idiot. He is going to regret this but for right now he looks like the happiest man I have ever seen in my life and for a brief moment, I am jealous of him.

# Chapter 3: Ava

*I* watch, frozen, as he mouths the words that will haunt me forever. I cannot run from him, I can't even scream, his presence alone controls me. No one is stopping him, the courtroom is full, and he is coming to get me - again. I search the entire room for anyone, someone to notice him coming at me. I don't want to go back there, I can't go back there with him. Trembling I feel his hands reach out for me. "NO!" I scream in a raging panic.

"Ava. Hey it's okay," Kyle says gripping me still. "Damn I knew it wasn't a good idea to let you go through these old boxes from New York."

Blasting through my back door Justin comes rushing in with Anna following shortly behind. "What happened? Are you alright?" He said rushing to my side.

"I'm fine, I'm sorry I must have fallen asleep and … it was just a bad dream." I said sitting up slowly and taking the glass of water from Kyle's hand.

"It's been years Ava, he doesn't even know where you are anymore." Kyle said reaching down and pulling out the newspaper article about the trial. "He's not getting out, I don't care what they say. No judge is ever going to put you through that again."

Anna sits beside me taking my hand, "you escaped him Ava, your safe from him now." I know her words are meant to be encouraging but she does not fully understand. I have only known Anna since hiring her to do our firms books, three year ago. Her role has grown to much more and so has our friendship but not enough to confide all the details to her.

"It wasn't the article," I said tossing the newspaper in the trash. "My grandmother called and said someone put flowers on my mother's grave, signed by him."

Justin slams his fists down on the table, "that fucking bitch mother of his! There has to be something they can do about her."

"They can't prove it was her Justin, we've tried." Kyle exhales. "Well you're going back to therapy."

"I'm fine Kyle, it was just a bad dream. I am done with therapy and talking about my feelings. As she said, I have the tools to deal with it and now I just have to use them."

"Sure, use the tools but I doubt she said stop coming to therapy." Leaning back into the sofa, I ignore his accusation. Even though he's right, she never said that but I can't talk about it anymore, so as soon as I was well enough to live somewhat normally, I quit going. What more does he expect me to do? I moved to Atlanta, we started our firm, I bought a house and adopted two young shepherds to keep me company. I am even able to let men touch me casually now, without wanting to scream, although I do not see ever being able to allow much more.

"Okay, well … Ava, Anna and I looked but we can't find the Schaller plans, can you take a look?" Justin asked.

"Sure." Justin takes my hand to lead me to the in-law house out back, where our small firm resides. His hand is warm and secure, I have always wondered about Justin since the day we met at his construction site, our first project together. I immediately noticed him, but only recently have I felt comfortable enough to allow him to hold my hand like this. It took months before I could look him in the eyes and even longer before I could shake his hand and not have to immediately shower and cry after. Not that he is any different from other men. Our courier still feels the need to put the signature sheet down and step about ten feet backwards from it before he asks me to sign it. Reminding me that with my fears, I need to give up on men and relationships entirely.

"You do seem better, Ava. I mean you can get close to me now, even let me touch you without cringing. It's like you're finally comfortable with … me at least," Justin said a little too hopeful.

"I trust you now." I said with a shy smile forced in the direction of his shoes.

"Do you trust me enough to go out to dinner with me?"

"Don't you have enough girlfriends to go to dinner with?" I laughed shrugging his question off.

"I'm serious."

Looking into his sincere eyes, "Justin I … I."

"Ava, it's just dinner. I won't even hold your hand." I want to say yes but I know I will end up canceling.

"Can I think about it some first?" The words leave my mouth with a hopeful sound but the true meaning of them still leaves the lingering doubt.

"I guess but could you try not to over think it … please. I promise to keep it innocent," he smiled sweetly.

Justin and I go over the plans for our next project and as he always does, he puts me at ease by not bringing up dinner and not pushing any needs he has on me. "Okay." I say quickly before I change my mind.

Justin looks at me awkwardly, "okay what?"

"I will go to dinner with you." Justin smiles wide taking my hand and letting go when Kyle enters the office.

"Ava, you have a call. They said it's real important." Kyle said raising an eyebrow at the sight he walked in on.

I nod and run to get my phone, "oh yes. How are you?" As I listen to news about a new project, I watch as Kyle becomes intrigued. "That sounds wonderful, I would love to. Yes you too." Hanging up I smile at my onlookers with pride.

"Was that who I think it was?" Kyle asked.

"Yes. Wow. I didn't think it would amount to anything."

"And!" Kyle vibrates.

"Okay I'm getting to it. As you know, I presented some ideas for that Cancer Center competition and well, they called a few weeks ago while you were on vacation and asked to meet with me. So I flew out to LA and I guess they loved what I had to say because they want me to fly out and talk about the details of getting the project started."

Kyle screams, "How big is it? Who is it for and who are you meeting with and I need … more information!" I place my hands on his chest and breathe with him until he calms.

Reaching into my bag I pull out the notes I had from my last meeting, "okay well it's a Cancer Center that is being dedicated to ummm … oh here it is, a William Benjamin Grant by his wife Mary Grant and his two sons …"

"Oh fuck!" Kyle screamed jerking at his hair with both fists. "Are you kidding me?" Slowly scooting away from him, I stare at him curiously. "You don't understand do you?" He asked me. "The two sons, Ethan and Sean right?"

"That's right, why?" I said to Anna's sudden gasp.

"Wow, Ava this is huge." Justin said smiling in unison with the other two.

"I don't think it's who you think it is. I met her and she is nice but I never once heard any mention of anyone famous being involved."

"Probably because they assumed the name alone would be enough to clue you in, honestly Ava you need to keep up with your celebrity gossip." Kyle huffs.

"Whatever, I guess we will know for sure after I meet with her and her sons in a few days but for some reason she wants me to meet her in Honduras."

"That's great!" Kyle smiled joyfully.

"It is? Honduras?" I asked.

Kyle walks over to his bag and takes out a magazine with a knowing smile forming across his face. "Because that's where Sean is currently filming his new movie," he said tapping his finger on the man that graces the cover.

"This is Sean?" I asked taking the magazine from him.

Kyle rolls his eyes. "Yes! He is so hot, I don't think anybody is any hotter than him."

"I guess he is but I'm sure he is just another spoiled celebrity," I said staring at the scantily clad man.

"You don't remember do you?" I shake my head slowly, as he sighs. "Avvaaa! Remember when he pulled you out of the way of that mob of girls going after his brother back in New York?" As soon as he said it, the images become clearer. Studying the man even more closely I try to connect this person with the one from my memory.

"When did this happen?" Anna asked.

"It was what five years ago? We were barely out of college and starving to death," Kyle said.

"Are you sure Kyle?" I asked.

"Yes Ava, it's him. I can't believe you don't remember, you talked about his gorgeous green eyes all-night."

"Wow. I guess I had built him into someone else and didn't think about him being … an actor," I said feeling uneasy about the possibility of ruining my memory of my Sean. "Okay, well now I'm nervous because I … I don't want to talk to him or … or anything, I just wanted to …." I toss the magazine back at Kyle with shaking hands.

"Calm down, I am sure he won't remember you and I doubt you will get to talk to him anyway and if you do, it will be a few minutes at most. You can handle it, it's not like you're ever going to be alone with him." Kyle said easing my tension some. "Okay let's get you packed. So do you have anything revealing?" Kyle says taking my hand with a dreamy-eyed expression and ignoring my sudden panic.

❧

**K**yle managed to pack many items I would have never considered taking, like a revealing blue dress that I am suppose to wear around Sean and Ethan for dinner. *I am not going to, I don't care what he says*. Not that it matters, I have yet to have a chance to wear it anyway or anything of the sort since arriving here in Honduras. Mary met me as soon as I got off the plane and days have passed and all we have done is tour around talking about everything but the potential project. We have talked all about my life though, how my father died of Cancer when I was young and my mother dying in a car crash shortly after. She already knew that I graduated from Kentucky and then received my Masters from Columbia but she even knows about my grandfather being a horse trainer in Lexington and that my grandmother is an artist. I don't know what to think about her, other than she is easy to talk to and reminds me of what I had hoped it would have been like with my own mother. Still I feel like I am wasting my time being here. If not for her paying for this exceptional hotel, I might be more anxious to leave. I however am lying here alone, in this ridiculously huge bed waiting for Mary to tell me what to do next, like the puppet and the puppeteer. This whole experience is strange.

When the phone abruptly rings, I jump quickly to answer it. Thankfully I get the information I have been waiting for, plus some other news I am not sure I am ready for. Mary has signed the contract to work with us and she has booked us a flight home with her son - Sean.

# Chapter 4: Sean

*M*y latest role is with my girlfriend, at least she was when we signed the contracts. I should have known better than to think I could make it through an entire production with the same girl. However, the location of the movie has made putting up with her worthwhile. We have completed this part of the filming as of today, and I am not supposed to be back in Los Angeles for a couple of weeks. As I sit on set waiting for the final word, my frustrations build up again and I do not understand why. It's absurd for me to feel this way but the last few days have been worse than usual. That strange draw is pulling me to somewhere else and I can't figure out to where. *I need to get away, clear my head. I need to go to my hideaway house in the Keys.* As soon as I leave here, I am going to force an escape and release the ridiculous greed that is obviously working its way through my veins. There is no way I am going to become that person I so desperately detest. My ex, Courtney, being one of them. She still believes we are meant for each other. I don't know why she cares, she doesn't stop looking at herself long enough to even notice if I am there or not. As soon as the crew starts packing up, I don't waste any time before jumping into my car, well my rented Mercedes, which is nice, but it is not my car. My car is back at home in California. A black Aston Martin DBS, my gift to myself after driving it in my last movie and realizing it gave me more pleasure than my last girlfriend did. Within the same day, I broke it off with her and drove my new girl home. If only women could be as easy to handle.

Pulling up to the lavish beach house, I immediately take notice of my mother's car. The chance of me being able to make a clean escape now, is slim to none. My mother insisted on being with my brother and me here. I thought she wanted to go see a new place, a vacation of sorts but Ethan thinks she is up to something. This means I need to stay clear of her until I can get away and avoid whatever she is planning. My mother is relentless when she gets something in her head. Like getting a Cancer Center built in my father's name. Ethan and I both jumped at the chance to donate money to the cause, anything to keep her busy. She has taken a bigger interest in our lives since my father died and it is driving us both crazy. Walking into the house I immediately spot my mother talking to Ethan. My only chance is to sneak to my room, grab my already packed bag and run out the door before she can get a hold of me and invite herself along. I can worry about a flight once I am free.

"Sean?" My mother called to me with an innocent desperation in her voice.

"Yes, what do you need?" I asked gritting my teeth as I walk slowly to the edge of the room.

"Sean, why do you always think I need something from you?" She smiled innocently at me.

"I don't always think you need something mother, I just do now because you are in my house waiting to pounce on me." Ethan walks to the sofa with a smirk on his face and a huge sandwich from my kitchen. This means I was right and I am going to have to check out the kitchen to get a sandwich for myself. I leave the room before she can say anything else and immediately make my way to the food. Ethan comes in and sits at the bar watching me as if he wants to tell me something. I assume he is trying to warn me but I am not sure what about. Before I can find out, my mother enters the room scanning both of us with suspicious eyes until she feels satisfied.

"Sean, do you have dinner plans tonight?" She asked.

"Oh there it is. I knew it!"

"What on earth are you talking about? I simply asked if you have dinner plans," she persisted with her innocence.

"And why is that mother so you can set me up with some girl that knows some friend of a friend of a friend of their cousins?" I said as my brother chokes on his sandwich and looks away from my mother's sullen eyes.

"No Sean, but I do think that you should meet the architect I chose for your father's Cancer Center."

"Mom I would love to but I am going away for a little while before I have to get back to California." I watch as the wheels begin to turn in her head. "Mom, I want to get away from everyone and zone out for a little while before I have to get back."

"So you're going to your hideaway house?"

*How did she know that? She is so scary sometimes.* "I don't want to be around anybody while I am there mother," I said as sternly as possible while trying not to hurt her feelings. Surprisingly she doesn't seem hurt at all but almost joyful by the thought, which terrifies me.

"Have you booked a flight yet?" I shake my head uneasily. "Well I have one already booked for later tonight to go to Miami. We can drop you off on our way if you like?"

"What? Wait, who's we? Drop me off on the way? What?" I rambled as quickly as the questions ran through my mind.

"I have already booked a flight for me and the architect to go back to the states and review some existing facilities. You can fly with us and when we get to Miami, you can drive over to the Keys. We will of course have to part ways since we will want to get on with our own plans." She said easing a little closer to eye me carefully.

*She sounds too happy for me to be comfortable. However, the plan sounds reasonable and the flight wouldn't be long, so whatever she has in mind can't be too bad and having something booked already does save me the trouble.* "We will part ways at Miami, correct?"

"Of course Sean, I think you deserve some time to yourself but now we can share a little time on the way. I barely get to see you. You are all over the world these days and if I had not come down here, I would not get to see you at all. I mean really Sean, must they shoot in Honduras? Could they not make a set so you could stay home and work? I need to make sure you are still eating and taking care of yourself. I worry so much about you traveling all the time, not to mention those distasteful women you are always managing to find and ...."

"Mother! Fine, okay, whatever you need or want I am happy to help you." I surrender.

"Wonderful! I will finalize plans and let you know the details later." She kisses my brother and me on the cheek before walking out triumphantly.

"You do realize she got what she wanted to begin with right?" Ethan asked.

"What? No she wanted me to have dinner with her and that architect person."

"Right, she wanted you to meet the architect and you are but instead of dinner you are going to be stuck on a plane with I am assuming ... *her*," he said with a sheepish grin.

"Uh no ... fuck," I sighed in defeat. "She is something else."

"Relentless," he said.

"So have you met this architect?"

"No, but since Mom flew this person down a few days ago she has been preoccupied until today. She is usually driving me crazy while you're on set."

"Huh, maybe we should hire this person full time?" I said with a wink.

"I will happily split that cost with you little brother."

"Plus all the food you have been eating out of my fridge?" I asked.

"No, that's part of my contract with you. You pay me to manage your life and I get to try all of your food to make sure it's right for your career," Ethan says grabbing an apple on his way out the door. "Have fun Sean, call me when you get back. I think I am going to take some time with Abbey. If Mom is busy following you around, then I should probably take advantage. Oh and I hope she's hot."

"Who?" I asked.

"Your future wife you are flying away with tonight." I quickly throw another apple at the laughing fool.

"Too bad I missed. Asshole!" I yelled after him.

∙ ❧ ∙

*I* was so anxious to get away, I had the driver come early to take me to the airport. Luckily when I arrived there were no signs of my mother anywhere or anyone else that may be flying with us. I boarded the plane analyzing the best seat to keep my distance from any possible conversations and sat in the middle, assuming my mother will make me move anyway. Although, I am in no mood for being setup with some girl, I do not have the time for, or the want to deal with. My mother is a sucker for these sad women trying to get to me. This girl isn't the first and I'm not sure how she pulled it off but I am going to have a private conversation with her as soon as I get the chance. She needs to understand that no matter how close she gets to my mother it won't get her any closer to me. *She's probably not even an architect.* I take a quick glance out the window before putting on my headphones and letting myself drift into a deep dream filled sleep. That blissful presence has become more and more present in my dreams these days, only now I can even smell her sweet scent.

"Ummm, excuse me. Um Sean, I mean Mr. Grant. HEY!" I sit straight up pissed off and jerking my headphones off before eyeing the interruption. A redhead, has to be the architect. *A redhead? Really, mother? I have never dated a redhead in my life. Well except for Rachel who was a lot of fun but I quickly found out she wasn't a natural redhead.* "Do you talk or are you just going to stare at me?"

She is already annoying me, "what do you want?"

"I am truly sorry to bother you …" She spelled out slowly. "But I was wondering where your Mother is?"

"What do you mean?"

"Well we have taken off and she isn't on the plane."

"What?" I asked standing up to verify. "What do you mean she isn't on here?" I said checking the seats in front of us and behind us. "She couldn't have? Unbelievable!" I yelled hitting the call button for the pilot.

"Yes, sir?"

"I believe we have left one of the scheduled passengers behind," I said knowing the intention is probably correct.

"If you are referring to Mrs. Grant, she called and said that she was unavoidably detained and to take off without her. She said she would find another flight at a later time."

Rubbing my hands over my face, I let out an exasperated chuckle. *How in the world did I let her get me into this?* "Did she say when she was taking another flight or where she would meet us in Miami?" I asked hopeful still.

"No sir," he cleared his throat before his muffled chuckled left his mouth. *He must have a meddling mother too.*

"Thank you," I said gritting my teeth and agonizing until I realize she is staring at me and waiting for an answer. "I'm sorry but my mother isn't coming … on this flight anyway. Do you know where you two were supposed to go in Miami?"

"Miami?" She asked looking puzzled.

"Yes Miami, what were your plans when you got there?" *She's not too bright.* "You were going to tour some Centers and meet with some people to get some ideas."

"I have no idea what you are talking about, I thought I was going back home to introduce her to the rest of my team."

"You live in Miami right?"

"No … Atlanta," she said looking at me even more confused.

"Then why the hell are you going to Miami?"

"I have no idea! I didn't make the flight plans. I was told to get on this flight so I could get back home." She yelled back at me.

"Ahhh damn. Well it looks like my mother made plans that neither of us knew anything about but no big deal when we get to Miami I will make sure you get to Atlanta from there."

"Why would she make plans without telling us?"

She probably deserves and explanation but there is no easy explanation for this. "It's what she does. I can't explain it."

"Well since we are in this together then, my name is Ava. Ava Kelley," she said reaching her hand out across the aisle to me. Now I am beginning to wonder how much *Miss, so called Innocent*, didn't know about this plan.

I eye her hand suspiciously, "I don't mean to be rude, but I got on this flight to get away from people. I am sure you are a real nice person and I am sure my mother got your hopes up that we might hit it off or some shit but I am not interested. Maybe I will take a picture with you once we get to Miami but I would really like to zone out over here and without a lot of conversation. Do you think you can do that for me sweetheart?" I said sinking back into my seat and drifting my gaze back to the seat in front of me until I realize she never replied. With a slight tilt of my head, I gaze back at her to see if she has passed out over her disappointment but instead she is eyeing me with an evil vengeance. "Are you okay? You're not mental are you?"

"Who the hell do you think you are?" She yelled but as soon as I open my mouth to tell her, she stops me. "Yes, I know who you are but I really don't give a shit who you think you are because no one can possibly be that wonderful. I was trying to be nice but I certainly do not care to talk to you either. I have never met anyone so full of himself. What do you think every woman on the planet will abide by your every wish because it is you? And take a picture with you? Are you kidding? Haven't you had enough pictures of yourself taken?" I roll my head back with my eyes. *Great. She is fucking crazy.* "Don't you roll your eyes at me, you conceded ass."

"What the fuck lady I just wanted some privacy and I didn't want you to get your hopes up that I might find you hot and have sex with you." At once the death rays from her eyes singe my skin. *She is obviously fucking nuts!*

"Oh! Well thank you, I feel so much better now that I don't have to worry about whether Sean Fucking Grant finds me HOT and doesn't want to have sex with me. Well let me put your mind at ease *Sean.* I don't find you good looking enough to care what you think about me and I certainly don't find you charming enough and there is no way in *hell*, I would ever consider having sex with you. So don't you worry princess, I don't have any desire to have another conversation with you ... EVER!" She said with a final exhale.

*I hope she doesn't think that is a turn on because crazy is never a turn on.* Suddenly the cockpit door flies open and out comes, Bronzer-boy, sticking out his chest and smiling his excessively whitened teeth to a maximum. He approaches looking to impress. I am in no mood for this, a want to be actor I am sure.

"Hi, I'm one of your pilots Kevin Walker but only copiloting today though. Trying to take it easy from all my flights for some important government officials that I can't disclose – no matter what you do to try to get me to talk," he laughed to himself. *Seriously?* "Anyway, I thought I would come an introduce myself and let you know if you need anything ... please, please let me know." He stressed looking directly at her. *He is trying to impress someone all right but it's not me.*

"Thank you, but I think I'm fine right now," she said so southern sweet it causes me to look her way.

"Are you sure?" His eyes stroll from her face and all the way down to her toes while twirling his tongue in his mouth. *This guy is unbelievable.* "If you like you can come up in the cockpit and see how we fly this bird. We aren't supposed to do that but you look like you can keep a secret," he winks at her. *I'm getting nauseated.*

"I ... I don't think so but thank you," she said squirming in her seat, seemingly to look for a window to jump out of.

"You're welcome to sit in my seat. I will make sure you're comfortable," he says propping up one leg against the arm of the seat and flashing his broad white smile.

*Coughing, choking loudly.* "Sorry, a thing in my throat." I gesture towards my neck as they both look in my direction.

"So, what do you think?" He did not even hesitate to continue. *I am starting to feel sorry for her.*

"Thank you, but I think I am going to stay here. I am really tired," she said emphasizing each word to his obvious displeasure.

"Okay but if you change your mind," he smiles making some ridiculous double finger-pointing gesture towards her and then back at himself. Grimacing I sink my head into my hands.

*I need a drink, although I don't think there is enough alcohol in the world for this shit. Of course, there is also no one here to fix me one thanks to my mother. Except her.* I look over at the redhead, who is doing her best to ignore me. "Miss, do you want a drink?" She does not even budge in my direction. "Hello."

"I guess," she speaks softly into the window.

"Yes?"

"Yes. That would be nice." She finally rolls her eyes towards me.

"Good, the bar is in the back will you get me one while you're up please?"

"Why should I get it?" She sits up straight, angry all over again and starting to amuse me.

"Because you are clearly working for my mother, which means you are working for me too, right?"

"Does everyone do what you want?" She squints an evil glare in my direction.

"Usually," I wink at her with a smile. *The smile always works.*

"What do you want princess?" *I guess she can be useful after all, not to mention entertaining.* I yell out my order as she approaches the bar in the back.

"I don't know if any project is worth this, he's crazy and probably an alcoholic too," she mumbles.

"You keep talking shit about me and I am not going to let you take that picture with me." I turn seeing her bringing me a glass and hesitating with it over my head - a little too long. "Are you going to give it to me or are you too captivated by my incredible good looks?"

"UUGgghhh! Unbelievable," she grumbles handing me the glass. "I should have made you wear it."

"I knew that was what you were thinking but to answer your question, I look good wet too." Her reaction is entertaining as hell and I am waiting for her to respond but she keeps stopping herself with frustrating sighs until she seems to decide on ignoring me again. "What was your name again?" She turns even tighter to the window away from me. "You know it's rude not to look at somebody when they are talking to you."

She turns quickly, setting me back in my seat, "I thought you didn't want to talk to me?"

"That was before I knew how much fun you are."

"What do you want, because I don't want to talk to you?"

"Oh don't be that way, I am still going to take that picture with you." I laugh at her snarling unappreciative sounds and lean back into my chair, putting my headphones back on. The flight will be over soon and I will make sure she gets home safely and for making me laugh, I might kiss her good-bye too. I exhale deeply thinking about my awaiting getaway until I am jolted out of my seat and with a quick glance out the window, I realize we are running right into a storm. The door to the cockpit flies open and the pilot approaches us urgently. *This is not good.*

"My name is Gavin Samuel, I am your head pilot. I am sorry to tell you that we will not be able to make it to Miami tonight. We need to turn around and go back. The weather has taken a quick turn for the worse because of a hurricane changing what we thought was its intended direction. I am sorry but it was a decision I had to make."

"When do you think we will arrive back?" I asked.

"Unsure at this time, the weather is creating a difficult scenario right now but we should be out of it soon." He runs back to the cockpit slamming the door behind him and causing it to slam right back open. The girl is gripping the arms of her seat so tight her knuckles are turning white. I lean towards her to try to reassure her when a loud bang with a simultaneous jolt hits outside the plane. *So not good!* The pilot begins screaming his request for assistance. "Alright I see you. We will need to land immediately?"

"All is clear. What's the damage?" A voice roughly came over the speaker.

"We are losing fuel rapidly, the landing is going to be rough."

"We will organize some emergency assistance …"

*Organize emergency assistance, where the hell are we landing?* The plane plummets and before I know it, we are landing in an awkward twist. With the plane skidding sideways down the runway, the entire contents of the plane fly around us, trees smash into the windows, and someone screams so loudly, it hurts me. *I am not sure what hit me or how many times but my drink is gone and I REALLY need it right now.* With a crashing slide we stop. I begin to breathe again and sit up slowly only to see Bronzer-boy run out of the cockpit screaming and heading for the door of the plane. He jerks the handle of the door open and flings himself down a chute that he barely gets up before jumping. *Wonderful he's not only a moron he's a jackass too.* There is smoke everywhere and more of it coming but I am not sure from where. Undoing my seat belt, I get up to see the girl out cold and I realize Bronzer-boy must have been the screaming girl I heard. "Ava." *Was that her name?* "Miss are you okay?" I cradle her face in my hands carefully waiting for her to respond.

"Help! Help me please," Gavin yells from the cockpit, I leave the girl and go to him only to find his leg sandwiched between parts of the plane.

"How am I supposed to get you out of that?" I asked looking frantically for something to pry his leg out.

"There is an ax behind that door, cut the top piece beyond my foot." I grab the ax, and after a couple of vigilantly projected swings it comes loose, and I am able to slide him out and help him to the exit. "Wait is she alright?"

I look over at the still unconscious girl. "I think so but don't worry about it, I will get her." I help Gavin out before returning to the girl. The smoke is getting worse and I am still not sure where it's coming from. "Ava? Ava?" Still nothing. "Perfect! This day just gets better and better. All I wanted was to get away, some time to myself, that's all I asked for." I mumble to myself while carrying her off the plane and to several fast approaching vehicles. "So Mom, your plan worked like a charm. Your baby boy nearly died in a plane crash. No problem though, luckily I managed to get off before the plane exploded and hey I thought I would grab my future wife you found for me on my way out. What a nice story to tell our kids." I said looking down at the girl lying against my chest and still unconscious. "This is so fucking absurd!" I yell as people surround us and someone takes the girl from my arms. Looking back at the unrecognizable plane I watch as the building the plane ran into burns and collapses, falling down the cliff into the docks below. What little hope I had for an escape off this island, is now destroyed. "This is so not good."

# *Chapter 5: Ava*

**M**y head spins as soon as I open my eyes. I cannot place where I am, it must be a dream. I am in a white room, an exceptionally white room. *Am I dead?* I sit up taking in my surroundings. *Can't be dead, I don't think death has a receptionist.* As I am trying to focus, the door opens and a tall dark man in a white coat approaches smiling.

"Ms. Ava, I am Dr. Bode. How are you feeling?"

"Confused and my head hurts a lot. Where am I exactly?"

"You are on Wilton Island a corporation owned island. We are strictly a sugarcane producing island, we don't get too many visitors here, especially not the way you and your friends dropped in."

"Oh yea, the plane," I said leaning back and shutting my eyes. "Oh crap, we survived. What happened to the rude actor guy and the pilots?"

The doctor clears his throat with a wide smile. "One pilot has minor scratches and bruises from jumping off the plane before the chute was fully expanded. The other has a broken foot and I am assuming the rude actor you speak of is Mr. Grant and he has some minor scratches but other than that, he is fine. He is the hero of your group, making sure everyone got off the plane and all." My expression turns to shock as he laughs at me. "Yes, he cleared Mr. Samuel's leg and then carried you off the plane himself. Quite brave I think, especially for a rude actor," he chuckled.

"He didn't have to carry me did he?" I asked watching him nod. "Oh that's so embarrassingly awful."

"Well I don't know about that but I can give you some medicine for the headache. All your tests came back fine so we can let you go whenever you're ready."

"Let me go? Go where exactly?" I asked searching for a window to look out of.

"Well I believe that's what will be discussed with you shortly. We are a small island and most of our available beds are taken. All we have left is the two cabins the research team uses when they are here.

They shouldn't be back for a few months so they should be fine but with only two … you will have to share."

Sitting up straight with my eyes wide open, "share?"

"Well yes, it's best anyway I would prefer you not be alone since you hit your head." I slump over into my hands. "The nurse has some medicine for you and some clean clothes. Let me know if you need anything, my number is in the directory in your cabin. I hope you have a better rest of the night."

After hearing the doctor leave, I bury my face into my hands. "This is not happening!" I cried punching the bed in front of me with both fists.

"Come on Kelley, it's not that bad … you got me," his voice smug as always.

I gasp looking up at his sarcastic smile, "oh no, don't tell me. There has to be someone else I could…"

"Who? You want to room with Bronzer-boy so he can find new ways to get you to sit on his lap?" Sean says with a less than humored expression.

My stomach churns, "no, but what about the other pilot he seemed nice and shy. He wouldn't even look directly at me when I got on the plan?"

"Yes, but apparently he loves his wife and he doesn't want her to cut off his balls when she finds out he slept in a cabin alone with you. I don't particularly want to spend my time with Bronzer-boy anymore than you do. Listen, I am not too happy about it either but considering it could be a lot worse."

"How?" I fall back into the bed pouting.

"I am going to pretend you didn't say that, you're hurting my feelings. Look, we can stay up all-night and talk and play games and do each other's nails and hair and all kinds of fun stuff." I look over at him in questioning disgust as he shivers clapping his hands together like a little schoolgirl with a mocking smile before immediately changing his tone to disgust. "Now get your ass out of that bed and let's get the hell out of here, I'm tired," Sean said storming out of the room.

I walk slowly towards Sean, carrying a change of clothes a nurse gave me for the both of us. He looks as though he is as tired as I am. When he sees me, he holds out his hands like he has been waiting there all-day for me. *Jackass - as if he's the only one having a bad day.* Demerae, our driver for the night, and Jamaican it seems by his accent, as well as most of the people we have met so far. I guess he is nineteen at best, sweet and energetic, hyper or maybe it is the excitement of crazy people crashing on his island. He drives us to our cabin through the pouring rain and rough winds. I sit in the back of the tiny truck listening to Sean talk to Demerae but when they get to the routine of meals for the next few days, I snap out of my daze. "Stop!"

Demerae slams on the breaks and they both look back at me wide-eyed. "Did you see something?" Demerae asked.

"Meal plans? How long are we going to be here?"

Demerae rolls his eyes and continues driving down the road. "It looks as though there is a second hurricane forming and the two together have us apparently sandwiched in here for a while. We cannot leave until the weather clears up and they are able to get the supplies they need to clean up the damage that has been caused to the runway and the docks. But we are safe here, outside the rough waters it's mostly a lot of wind and rain," Sean said forcing a smile before turning away to look ahead at the makeshift road. Sinking back into the seat I consider what the upcoming days are going to be like. *Misery is obviously ahead, pure misery.* Demerae pulls in beside a small cabin with a large covered patio. It is almost like something you would stay in at a secluded resort but unfortunately, that is not the case. Demerae grabs a bag from the seat beside me and leads us through the front door, Sean following holds the door for me with an obnoxious smile. It is one big room with a quaint sitting area, a wooden desk, a chair, and a chest with a mirror directly across from the small rustic bathroom. My eyes follow to the other side of the room where the single bed sits, with its four posts and netting. It looks small but maybe because the room is starting to spin around it.

Demerae grabs hold of my arm, "wow. You look white, you might want to sit for a second. You have some extra food and drink and some other things you might need throughout the night in the small fridge near the desk. The bath only has a shower but the pressure is good. There is a directory on the table if you need anything else." He says while opening the windows and turning on the rhythmic ceiling fans before heading towards the door. "See you tomorrow. Oh and I recommend the netting it helps with the bugs. So you might want to figure out something so you can share that." He seems to understand the one bed is not something we consider an easy agreement between us but he doesn't stick around to help us work it out.

"Are you going to get a shower because I would like to?" Sean asked ignoring the bed issue.

"Please," I said handing him the extra clothes they gave me before we left.

He pauses to look me over."You okay? You do look pale?"

"I'm ... I'm fine. I need a few minutes to catch up with the events is all," Sean stares at me for a few seconds longer before eventually nodding and continuing to his shower.

When it is my turn, I melt under the pressuring water, and even though it stings a bit on my wounds, my stiff muscles are grateful. I take as much time as possible in the bathroom, avoiding the bed and him. I am so exhausted and I want to crash into bed and not worry about it but I know my mind will not let me do that. I haven't let a man even kiss me since.... *If he were a gentleman he would not even suggest us sleeping in the same bed together. Surely, he is reasonable. But he did carry me off the plane. He just picked me up and carried me! How can I kick him out of the one bed? No, I should get the bed tonight I was the one injured. I would obviously allow him one of the two pillows and some blankets to make a bed in the floor, since there is not a sofa or chair he could easily sleep in. The floor should be fine, he will have plenty of room and we can alternate nights. I am not ungrateful or unreasonable.* I inhale, sticking out my chest confidently. *Ava you walk out there and tell him how it is going to be, do not let him bully you.* "Sean, I think we should alternate the use of the bed. It is the proper thing to do, and if you don't mind me taking it tonight then I will be more than happy to let you have it tomorrow night." I walk out of the bathroom sure of myself, until I see him lying in the bed with the netting already closed around his side. He lays on his back shirtless and almost asleep. My flawless argument with the bathroom mirror is beginning to falter.

"Sean?" I said weakly.

"Will you please get in bed and we can talk about whatever it is tomorrow."

"But ..."

"I'm too tired to even try anything, I promise. So *please* get in bed and go to sleep," he said not even bothering to open his eyes.

I look at him, then at the bed and after putting on another layer of clothes, I exhale and climb in next to him. I pull the netting around me and move as close to the edge of the bed as possible. *Great argument Ava, I think you almost had him there.*

Despite Sean's presence, I fall asleep easily, exhaustion having more control over me than my fears. However, it isn't long before the fears creep back in and so does the voice. The darkness suffocates me as I watch the door light up around its edges. I pull and tug as hard as I can to release my hands, panic taking over as his shadow surges towards me. I want to scream but I can't breathe as he holds me down with him, caressing me like his lover. No matter how much I beg he will not stop. *You're fearless, stand strong against him.* I kick away from him proud of my strong stance as I watch him cringe into anger and come at me with desperate determination. The constant blows to my body come swiftly, until I go limp and watch as he becomes excited with control. My clothes are ripped from my body as he resumes controlling his lover with forceful hands and smiling wildly with every grunting push. Stop him Ava. *Stop him! SCREAM DAMN YOU!* "NO! STOP! NOooo!" I screamed.

"Ava!" Sean screams at me. My eyes open out of my dark nightmare, fighting. "It's okay," Sean, said cradling my face with concerned eyes. "Dreaming about the plane crash?" I nod softly with broken breaths. "Yea me too, but we are safe now. And we won't be here forever, I promise." My body eases with his words. My trembling hand reaches out to touch his that is still holding softly against my cheek. He watches me silently as I hesitate to touch him several times before finally resting against his warm hand without a single quiver. I look up into his eyes - recognizing them. I try to breathe enough to speak but before I can, he rolls away from me without saying another word.

# *Chapter 6: Sean*

*N*othing but crazy dreams, I had hoped that all of yesterday was a dream but then I woke up and reality set in. *Damn. Now I'm awake, wide-awake, what am I going to do now?* I can feel her roll over towards me, letting soft red waves of hair fall across her face. Before I can stop myself, I sweep them back off her face with the sides of my fingers. Luckily she doesn't wake up. *She had her hair up before. Right?* I hadn't noticed anything but the color before. She is sleeping so peacefully, her sweet face expressing nothing like our previous conversations. Taking my fingers around the edges of her soft face, I remove some lingering stray hairs while watching her full lips make slow motions. *I'm feeling disturbingly pathetic suddenly.* Leaning back on my arms I try to refocus my attention to more appropriate matters but with a soft whimper she jerks suddenly next to me.

*"NO! STOP! NOooo!"* She screamed.

I jump to her immediately, "Ava!" When she opens her eyes, she stuns me with such intense fear showing deep in her eyes. I try to comfort her with a sincere smile but I become captivated watching her trembling hand taking minutes to reach mine. When her eyes look up into mine, I get a strange familiar feeling. I am not sure if she is a groupie so obsessed by me or … I don't know. Unsure of what to say or do next, I roll away from her silently, hoping to fall back asleep.

Dreams come rushing into my mind, dramatic and enriched with senses beyond what I have ever experienced. I don't understand what is taking over me but I am enjoying touching, feeling and being caressed by the intoxicating emotions my mind is creating. I exhale softly bringing it in closer, while searching for the softness and sighing with satisfaction when I find it. Finally being able to take hold of what has been taunting me in my dreams for so long, I wake myself up and immediately gasp at the site in front of me. *She is going to knock the shit out of me.* I try to untangle myself from the girl I barely know when her hands suddenly appear. Caressing my chest and my head she sends my mind elsewhere. Feeling her breathy moans against my skin and her tender lips trailing along my neckline, my eyes begin to roll back in my head. *Fuck, she's driving me crazy. I need to stop this.* Instinctively I grip what is in my hand and realize that is her bare ass. My lips prepare as hers are working their way towards mine.

"Ohhhh Sean." She moaned. *She's knows damn well what* she is *doing. Fuck it.* I press my now hard as hell erection into her freely, pulling her ass up into me more but pausing when she gasps and stops moving. I sit up cautiously seeing her bright eyes. "Don't panic please, I woke up like this too. Nothing has happened, it's all still innocent."

"Is that your hand on …?"

Carefully I pull my hand away from her ass. "Sorry, innocent except for maybe that but I didn't see anything or even try anything. I promise."

"Well then can you get off me?"

*Wonderful, now I am a freaking pervert.* "Yes, and again I'm sorry." I try to move but her legs are locked around me and holding me down on her. I huff raising my eyebrows at her as her glare changes to embarrassment. "Do you mind letting go of me so *I can* get off you?"

She removes her legs slowly and without looking my way sorry."

"Uh huh." Moving away from her, I sit up trying to calm myself back down before I get up.

"Umm I'm sorry, I'm not sure why I would have been like that. I didn't mean anything," she said fidgeting with the blanket.

"Don't worry about it, clearly you weren't the only one doing, I mean not doing but … or … being like that, however we got like that." *What the hell did I just say? I said it and I don't even know.* Her face turns puzzled as she searches the room obviously trying to figure out my ramblings too. *Wow all those years of being smooth and suave and one plane crash and I am Forrest Gump.*

"Do you mind if we forget this ever happened?" She asked.

"Deal." I responded eagerly with a nod, while taking notice of what she is wearing as she gets out of bed. You can barely see her. *Is she wearing two layers of clothes?* I relax knowing it must have been the dream because she isn't doing anything for me in that. "Supposedly there is breakfast at some community cafeteria this morning, let me know when you're done and I will walk you over," before I can even think another thought she darts out.

"I'm ready, let's go!" She stares at me wide-eyed and eager.

"That was quick. Can you give me a second?"

"Sorry, I'm really hungry. Your mother said we ... well you probably know."

"Yes, I know. Sorry about my mother by the way, she likes to meddle into my personal life."

"I like your mother she's sweet." She said before pausing, "your personal life? I don't understand?"

"You mean you hadn't figured it out yet?"

"I mean I wondered why she wanted to know if I had a boyfriend. Why it mattered what kind of men I usually like but I thought she was being sweet not that she would ever consider me for you. I mean you're ... you're ..." She stopped abruptly blushing.

I laugh at her attempt to try to be polite. "I am what? A jerk, an asshole?" *And lately a pervert.*

"No you're a celebrity, I'm not anybody. Why would she ever consider me for you?"

"Well my mother has this idea that with her help my brother and I can find the love of our lives. My brother is married now, so she is concentrating on me and she doesn't think Hollywood has anyone that is right for me." Ava suddenly comes running at me and I am not sure what her facial expression means. "What?"

"Your mother likes me!" She glows excitedly.

"What?" I asked staring at her excited expression.

"Well I mean she thinks I am good enough for you. I have never had anyone's mother think I was right for her son. It's so sweet and it makes me feel good that she thinks that way about me, you know?" She said shrugging with an innocent smile. *I am totally fucked.* "It makes me feel good that's all. Don't worry Grant, I am not going to fall in love with you all of a sudden. Gees you are so uptight."

*And you're annoying as hell.* "I wasn't worried and so she likes you, it doesn't bother me. This is a strange conversation, let's never bring it up again?" I get up meeting her smiling face with a scowl.

"Okay but when we get married your mother can come visit us anytime she wants." She winks at me laughing.

I shiver causing her to laugh harder as she walks away from me. Once I finish getting ready, I find the annoyance patiently waiting for me with that stupid grin still on her face. "Come on and wipe that stupid grin off your face." Holding the umbrella up for us, she continues to giggle and make ridiculous comments. "I'm going to push you into the rain if you don't stop," I said glaring at her biting her lip to keep from laughing.

"I'm sorry," she pouted. "Sean?"

"What?"

"What's your favorite name?" I glare down at her waiting for it. "I was wondering about possible baby names. You should have some say in our children's …" She starts laughing and I push her out from under the umbrella into the rain. "UGGhhhh, Sean!"

I laugh with pure delight watching her slip and slide in the mud, "I warned you." I continue to smile watching her walk casually back under the umbrella with her clothes stuck to her body from the rain. She growls at me as she crosses her arms and walks silently with me. "Are you mad at me now?" She ignores me, "don't worry you look almost as good wet as I do … almost."

"You are such a jerk," she said causing me to laugh harder.

We reach the cafeteria and Ava obviously starving rushes to the door in front of me, thankfully, since her wet clothes are stuck to her body and clearly showing every curve. Now I know why I must have been subconsciously drawn to her ass this morning. I follow her closely through the line, "you don't want that one." She looks at me as I shake my head at the apple she begins to take. "No the ones in the back are much better, fresher, plus you don't know who touched that before you." I said shivering a sour expression. With a sigh, she leans over and reaches for one a little further back. "No further back, yea that's good." I take my time eyeing her as she reaches and stretches her ass further out to me.

"I don't know why I listened to you, this one doesn't look any better Sean, and I'm going to wash it off anyway."

"Are you kidding this one is way better." She gives me a suspicious look and I simply smile innocently. *It was better for me, at least.*

# *Chapter 7: Ava*

*U*pon entering the cafeteria, everyone turns immediately to look at us, making me nervous. Thankfully, Sean is with me and guides me to a service line of food. He hands me a tray directing me to go first. I return his gracious smile happily. *Maybe he isn't too bad.*

"Ava! Ava over here!" Kevin called out motioning for me to sit with him and Gavin. I turn back towards Sean who is following me and looking guilty suddenly.

"I'm going to sit with them." I motion towards Kevin's table.

"I'll follow you," he said with an innocent glow but I narrow my eyes at him. "What? I didn't do anything."

"Ava, you are looking beautiful this morning," Kevin said eyeing me with a low grunt while Sean groaning, sits down beside me.

"I don't think I am making any major fashion statements, Kevin," I said knowing he is more excited about my clothes sticking to my body. *Which is probably why Sean looked so guilty too?* I glare at him eating happily next to me. *Gracious my ass.* "How is your leg Gavin, feeling any better?"

Gavin motioned to his crutches, "I am getting along. It could have been a lot worse, especially if Sean hadn't helped me off. Thank you by the way Sean, I never got a chance to tell you with all the excitement."

Sean waves him off, "no big deal."

I introduce myself to the other two people at the table and am able to learn more about them and the island. The impressive looking Jamaican is Khenan Williams. He is in charge of the island, keeping things in order as he summed it up for me. Khenan's presence immediately commands respect, his position was clear before I even asked. Khenan's wife, Ashlen, is a pretty Jamaican with a commanding presence of her own and one that Khenan respects more than any other. Their eldest son our taxi driver from the night before, Demerae just turned twenty. Their daughter Breanna is sixteen going on twenty-five and giving her father digestion problems already. Their third child, Alizabeth, the baby of the family, Khenan has to pause to consider an explanation before telling us about him.

"Alizabeth is an entertainer," Ashlen said with a smile placing a hand on Khenan's arm.

"An entertainer, is that what we're calling it? Huh. Be careful Sean, if he finds out you're here, you may never get rid of him," Khenan said motioning in Sean's direction.

"Consider me warned but I look forward to meeting him anyway." Sean said with a laugh.

"Well in that case, you will probably find him in the gymnasium shooting hoops. When he isn't trying to thank the academy for his award he is usually winning championships with last second shots," Khenan said with a proud smile.

"Oh hoops! What do you say Sean? You, me, one-on-one?" Kevin said standing up pointing at Sean animatedly.

"I don't want to do anything with you, especially not one-on-one." Sean groans back at him.

"Come on! After breakfast, it will be fun?"

"So this is a sugarcane island. I understand it is owned by a company, is that correct?" Sean asked glimpsing at Kevin folding his arms in disgust.

"Yes, well the company bought the island to mainly harvest sugarcane. The island isn't big enough for much else, no one wanted to build homes here because the views are not good and it isn't right for any resort. Our waves are not right for any water sports and our beaches are mostly rock, we only have one small beach that is even halfway decent. It is the best answer for unused land and for people who need work in the area. The conditions are perfect for harvesting sugarcane and the company can use the island to do research for alternative fuels. With so many families living here year-round, they subject us to alternatives constantly but we get to live here free and make decent salaries considering the benefits. We know everyone here, except during harvesting when we have seasonal help come in and harvest. They stay in something similar to a military barracks, it is closed down when not in use to save money. We send the kids to private schools off the island, except for Demerae who is taking a semester off from college to earn more money to help pay his way."

Khenan went on telling us about the other families and each of their positions and responsibilities on the island. It is a small community with each person having a specific purpose to help keep the next person or job working properly and safely, their success is impressive.

With everyone finishing off their last bites, Khenan kisses his wife and excuses himself to get to work.

"Okay Sean, come on let's go play ball. What else better do you have to do? It is raining like hell outside. There aren't any supermodels on the island for you to screw, so what do you say?" Kevin whined.

"Kevin please find someone else to annoy." Sean motions to the open room as he dismisses Kevin once again.

"You're scared." Kevin taunted him. Sean leans back in his chair pretending to be interested in something else."You're scared."

"I'm not scared of you Kevin," I said, instantly feeling my cheeks turn red as everyone at the table turns to look at me with shocked eyes.

"You want to play Red?"

"Sure, why not, I am after all a Kentucky girl. I know more about basketball than you ever could," I said with a lot more certainty in my voice than I thought was possible. I haven't played since college but I should still be good enough to beat him at least.

"Kentucky girl, figures." His gawking makes me nervous suddenly as I glimpse Sean's questioning eyes. "Sure Red, I would love to play one-on-one with *you*," Kevin said licking his lips. *Now I know why Sean wouldn't play him, maybe this was not the best decision on my part.*

"You know what though, I need some sneakers, dry clothes and something to hold my hair up and I don't know if I have anything available right now."

"You can borrow whatever you need from Brianna and me," Ashlen said.

"Oh. Well, then I guess I will meet you at the gym … in thirty … Kevin." I leave the table following Ashlen while Sean looks at me as if I just declared myself insane.

# *Chapter 8: Sean*

*W*hile walking to the gym with Gavin and Kevin, I'm still trying to figure her out. *She must be out of her damn mind. She wants to play with this guy? Does she like him or something?* I look him over for anything that might be appealing to her, "Bronzer-boy," I whispered to myself. *There is no way she … any woman could find something about him appealing.*

"Kevin, have you ever managed to get a girl," I asked.

"Please, I get more women in one night than you dream about. I know exactly how to work their body and turn them into my playthings. Mostly I like the clubs the alcohol helps me cut out precious time trying to seduce them and get right to the bedroom, car or restroom, whatever is convenient."

"Alcohol, I think I would put more stock in that rather than your moves," Gavin said with a mocking smile.

"Whatever you're all just jealous because Red chose me."

"What?" I yelled in shock. "Chose you? She only wants to waste some time playing a game."

"A game so she can get close to me. And when we are done, she is going to want more and I will have to give it to her of course. Actually would one of you mind vacating the room for us tonight?" Kevin said as my whole body begins to heat up, I am not even sure what it is I am feeling but the overwhelming urge to punch him is becoming clear.

"No, Kevin we are not giving up either room. I think you are expecting too much. I think she just wants to play the game not start some romantic affair with you," Gavin persuades the fool.

"Who's talking romantic affair, I only want her for one night. She is hot, did you see her legs and perfect body and the red hair? She's fucking hot. Of course, one night with me, and she will probably want more. I promise just one night though, if you two bunk up together and let me have some alone time with her tonight. Then you can have your chance at her Sean, what do you say?"

*I am going to hurt him.* I lunge towards him as Gavin holds me back. "How about we wait until she asks for us to do the same," Gavin says to Kevin's nodding acceptance.

As soon as we walk into the gym there is a sudden craziness amongst the three boys playing ball. "Sean Grant! Holy Shit, I can't believe it's you." Alizabeth I assume comes running at me with his hand out.

"Alizabeth right, nice to meet you," I said reaching out for his hand.

"Yea, wow I can't believe you're here. Are you guys playing ball?"

"Actually we are waiting on one other person and she and Bronzer-boy over here are going to play against each other." Kevin huffs at me as he grabs a ball.

"Bronzer-boy!" The three boys chant in unison while smacking each other's hands.

"So B-Boy over there is going to play against a girl?" Alizabeth asked.

"If she shows." *I am hoping she doesn't so I can feel better about her sanity.*

"Play him? What is she desperate?" Andy one of the other boys inquired while shaking his head at Kevin trying to be smooth shooting balls.

"I don't think so," I said but before I can explain anymore, Alizabeth changes the subject and starts asking me about every movie I have done and showing me some of his character impersonations. We move to the bleachers as the boys entertain Gavin and me with their antics.

While we are talking Paul's face freezes, "dammmmmnnn!" He said cocking his head back in an exaggerated position. Alizabeth and Andy turn as well before nearly knocking each other over as they sprint away. *Sigh. She showed up, she is officially insane.* I turn seeing them fight to see who can talk to her first, while she talks and laughs in her sweet southern voice making them even crazier. She walks casually over with her ponytail and sneakers. In a pair of shorts and a plain white t-shirt that barely covers her stomach and at times allows a glimmer of her small belly button piercing to sparkle brilliantly. My eyes become fixated and barely notice Ashlen coming over and sitting near us. *This is not the girl I woke up with this morning.*

"So Red, are you ready to get schooled?" Kevin drools at the opportunity awaiting him.

"Sure, whatever," she said laying some of her things on the bleacher below me.

I reach out for her, "are you sure you want to play with this guy?" She should not be subjected to him, his mouth is watering at the mere sight of her.

"Don't worry, I got this handled," she said with a cocky tone. *Okay. Lunatic.*

"We may have to find a hose to get him off her," Gavin said looking at me to see if I agree and I do. I don't know if I want to watch this but I am afraid to leave her alone with him.

"You take it out first Red." *Oh, this is not good.* I watch through my fingers as I lean down on my knees. Ava catches the ball from Kevin, and dribbles it out. *Well at least she can dribble.* Kevin breathing heavily is already on her and then suddenly he is standing alone. Ava shot from the other side of him. *Swish!* The crowd simultaneously gasps. Kevin blaming it on his shoe is not giving her much credit. I however, remove my hand from my face and sit up a little straighter. He starts dribbling, trying to lose her but she swipes the ball in mid-dribble and moves quickly to lay it in, yet again. *I was so wrong, this looks to be very entertaining.*

The game continues, Kevin manages a few shots, although she doesn't give him many. Once I realize she indeed has this handled, I start to relax and pay more attention. However, I find myself paying less attention to her skills and more to the muscles in her legs and how they curve and pulse up and down with every change of direction. The sweat glistening as it rolls down her neck to her chest, causing her shirt to cling to her skin. With every shot she takes it causes her shirt to creep up a little further. Excitement pulses through my body every time she jumps to shoot, I don't even pay attention to see if the ball goes in. *I have never enjoyed basketball so much in my life.* The game is down to Ava needing one more shot to win. She dribbles the ball taunting him and me for that matter, licking the tips of her fingers and smiling with a devilish sexy grin. She dribbles turning her back toward him, her long muscles flexing in her legs spectacularly. My mind is blissfully entertaining itself when he slams her to the ground, steals the ball and lays it in the basket himself and scoring with a cocky grin. I jump out of my seat with clenched fists.

Gavin grabs my arm. "Don't, he isn't worth it."

"What's wrong Red can't take the pressure? Do you want to cry?" Kevin taunted.

"My ball," she said confidently.

"Sure here you go sexy."

Ava takes the ball and begins to dribble, watching him as he laughs at her. Suddenly she smiles back at him and bullet tosses the ball at his crotch recovering it off the bounce and taking her shot. *Swish!* Game Over. The crowd applauds her with great pleasure. "What's wrong Kevin can't take the pressure?" Ava mocks him as he rolls on the ground in agony. Everyone congratulates her before most reluctantly check on Kevin and escort him to the medic.

"Well dear that was fun to watch, I wish Khenan could have seen it. I know you said you played in college but I was still worried about him being so much bigger than you are. He didn't hurt you when he knocked you down?" Ashlen asked.

"No, I'm fine," Ava smiles still enjoying her victory.

"Too much fun. But I do have some things I need to get done today so I will see you both later?" Ashlen asked waiting until we both nod. Ashlen turns towards me, "see our girl didn't need for you to defend her."

"Apparently," I smile at Ava.

"Well good-bye dear I will see you both later." We nod towards her as she leaves us awkwardly alone.

"You want to play?" Ava asked looking innocent.

"Hell no, you scare me."

"Do you even know how to play?"

"Are you trying to taunt me Kelley?"

"I'm just asking but you probably don't know much about basketball do you?" She taunts with her charming smile.

"No, I guess it isn't my best sport, I played soccer, but I wouldn't say I don't know anything about basketball. You probably need to learn more about me on my web site, you will find it under *"Interesting Facts About Sean","* I motion with my hand to emphasize the process.

"*Oh dear.* Well I like soccer but it's not basketball," she said dribbling the ball away from me.

"So you're a ringer," I said, thankfully, bringing her back towards me.

"A ringer? What do you mean?"

"You pretended not to be any good and this whole time you played college ball?"

"I didn't say I wasn't any good. I did get a scholarship to play."

"Oh now you got a scholarship to play."

"Yea, well I still never said I wasn't any good, you assumed I wasn't."

"I guess we did but he is taller and bigger than you. No matter how pathetic he is, I was worried about you."

She jerks her head up suddenly, "you were worried about me? Why?"

"Why? Because he's a slime ball, I couldn't figure out why you would want to play against him. I thought you might like him or something or maybe you hit your head too hard and it knocked out any common sense you might have had." Walking down the bleachers, I take the ball from Ava, catching her eyes briefly before she shies away.

"Like him? Definitely not, I thought it might be fun is all. Although I admit, I did not think it all the way through. He is sleazy, all that heavy breathing almost made me forfeit the game."

"Well that makes me feel better. I can't imagine my mother picking a girl for me that would like that." I dribble towards the basket, pull up about seven feet out, and shoot. It goes off the backboard and barely hits one side of the rim. I watch it bounce away shaking my head. "See you are right."

"It's your wrist, you're not letting it roll off your fingers right. Look." She grabs my hand putting her back towards me as she plays with my hand and fingers. "Sean! Are you paying attention?"

"Yes, my wrist, fingers. Got it."

"Okay now try again."

"I am not sure I do get it, show me again."

She exhales exhaustively taking the ball from me, forcing me to watch her do it rather than being shown hands on again. "Okay now you try."

I take the ball and try again. It works, not nearly as pretty as hers but it goes in. "Well look at that, huh. Do you know any other great tips? Coach."

"What would you like to know?" She says putting her hands on her hips, making her diamond piercing visible again. *What the hell was I saying?*

"Why don't we play and I will learn from you that way." I said shaking off my fixation.

She shrugs, "okay."

Standing directly in front of her, "is this good?"

"You don't need to stand so close." She said pushing me away. I move right into her path before focusing in on her blue eyes that suddenly smile at me. My head starts spinning and I forget where I am. When she backs away I grab onto her before she can get away from me but her foot slides as do we both. Falling to the floor I manage to catch myself with one arm and hold onto her with the other. She falls with her hands on my chest, straddling me and breathing heavily in my ear. Leaning away from her, I watch her open her eyes and look at me with those big blue eyes again and their even more amazing up close. *There is something oddly familiar about …* "You okay?" I ask shaking off the strange sensations.

"Yes, I'm fine. I don't …." I look down at her pouty lips and without even realizing I start to lick mine. With her eyes now focusing on me, I move in, cradling her face closer to mine until we exchange breaths. Gently, I graze my lips across hers.

"Sean, hey Sean!" Demerae called out as he enters the gym. Ava leaves my grasp and I am left looking dumbfounded and lost. "Hey Sean what happen? Ava kick your ass in basketball too?"

"I can't seem to keep up with her," I said, finding her staring at the floor on the other side of the gym.

"I thought maybe you might want to come see some cool stuff."

Exchanging some uncomfortable glances with Ava, "I would love to Al."

"Great." He motions towards Ava. "You can come too if you want but it's mostly guy stuff. We have rain gear but it gets pretty muddy," he shrugs.

Ava smiles at him." That's okay Al, I would like to go explore on my own for a little while anyway." She catches my eyes and smiles weakly. "Bye Sean, I had fun." I nod watching her dash out the door.

"Do you think I hurt her feelings?" Al asked.

"No, I think she will be just fine."

"Alright, well here is a rain jacket with a hood. We have boots and stuff in storage. We are going to get real dirty."

"Where are we going?" I asked concerned about all the necessary gear.

"Three wheeling! It's fun, especially in the rain and mud."

# *Chapter 9: Ava*

The rest of my day, I spend trying to put my fall into Sean's lap out of my mind. Thankfully, our bags were rescued from the plane and I can get my clothes cleaned and unpacked into one side of the chest within our shared room. However, I was hoping the process would have taken up more of my day. As nice as the cabin is, it can be lonely when you don't have anything to occupy your time. There has to be something to read or get into somewhere in this place. Scavenging through drawers and closets, I find more odd things than anything that might be helpful in solving my boredom. Although the bottles of liquor might be helpful if nothing else becomes available. The rain is settling down some, maybe I can take advantage and go for a run, rain or no rain it's better than sitting around here all-day. I find a jacket and make sure to leave Sean's bag where he can find it easily and run out the door relieved to have the opportunity. The run is exhilarating and the slow moving rain is tolerable, soothing even. My thoughts however, are swirling through my head unbearably. *Feeling his breath against my skin and the gentle caress of his lips. I didn't even know I was capable, not to mention this morning. What was that?* My steps pick up as an excitement rushes through my veins. *Maybe I am not such a lost cause after all. Maybe that date with Justin will not need to be avoided anymore.* His letter he gave me before I left was heartbreaking but now maybe not so much. I can remember every word as if he branded it into my skin, I read it so many times.

*Ava, Please be careful and come back safely. I'd like to say stay away from that Sean guy but considering, I am sure that is a stupid request. Don't worry I am sure everything will turn out the way you want it to, if not I am here waiting for you and I haven't forgotten about our dinner plans to celebrate.*
*– Justin*

My smile escapes but is quickly dulled when I realize I will have to face Sean later tonight. *No matter what he expects I cannot do it or at least I don't know if I can, no matter if I would want to or not. Do I want to?*

*Why does it have to be so complicated? I will simply keep my distance and make light conversation with him until it is time to leave. We can't possibly be on this island much longer.* I finish my run with a reasonable conclusion and return to the still silent cabin. A quick glance around and I notice his bag missing. *At least the princess knows how to do his own laundry.* Hoping to enjoy a hot shower before he gets back, I gather some necessities and escape to the bathroom. After a couple of tries of flipping on and off the light, I am still left frustrated and in the dark. "Great, now what?" *I do not recall any bulb replacements during my scavenging earlier and I do not see how I can take a shower in the dark. It's pitch black in here with the door shut. Well it is not as if you can see into the shower from the door, but it is an open shower. Surely, Sean would not try to come in with me obviously in here.* Trusting a man I only met yesterday, I leave the door open, remove my clothes and step into the steam, hesitating for a second to move my towel to an easier reach. The heated water rushes over my body and I accept it with a welcoming sigh.

# *Chapter 10: Sean*

*I* am struggling trying to keep my balance up this path, the storm is picking up and the wind is getting more forceful by the minute. I walk into the cabin letting out a deep exhale, relieved that I do not have to face her right now. Although, I wonder why she left the bathroom door open, there is steam rushing across the floor and out into the rest of the cabin. *What the hell is she doing?* I open the windows so the steam will clear out, grab my now clean clothes and sort them to put them in the chest. I open the smaller drawer on top first to put my socks and underwear in, only to see that it has already been claimed for her small, frilly, girly underwear. I shut it quickly before my male wandering mind gets the best of me. *I have been perverted enough for one day.* I open the drawer next to it carefully until the emptiness inside is clear. *At least she is considerate.* While finishing packing the last drawer, I look into the mirror above and sigh at the sight of myself. *I am an absolute mess. I thought I got most of it but this stuff is sticking to me like glue.*

"Mmmmmm," Ava moaned from the bathroom. *She obviously didn't hear me come in.* I laugh realizing how embarrassed she is going to be when she realizes I am here. "Ooohhhhhh," she moaned again.

In one split, uncontrolled second, my eyes dart to the side of the mirror and I see her. The mirrors are perfectly opposite and perfectly clear now that I opened the windows. I try not to let my eyes slip. *Turn away Sean.* I close my eyes tight, only to open them to a full sight of her, leaning her head back, letting the water run down her face and catching on her full lips. She turns washing the shampoo from her hair, allowing the soap to run out and down her back and over her ass. Gripping the edge of the dresser and sweating, I watch the soap continue to wash down her body highlighting every curve and soft spot I have not even thought to imagine, yet. She tilts her head from one side and to the other running her fingers through her hair, down her neck and to her chest, cupping her breasts with soft exotic sighs. The lines of her body, gorgeous and wet hold me in place and cause me to breathe heavier as my eyes freely wander down her stomach to her delicately shining diamond and then down. My body begins to shake as I fight my own urges and desires to run away. *What is she trying to do to me? She is doing this on purpose, leaving the door open knowing I would put my clothes up in here.* I hold my hands tight to my face. "Fucking bitch!"

"Sean!"

"Yes?" *If she asks me to come in there, I am definitely not going. Unless she is hurt or needs ... something.*

"Oh, I thought I would hear you come in but I guess I wasn't paying attention. Sorry about the steam but the light was out in here and ...," she begins rambling as she steps out of the shower naked and wet. She grabs a towel to rap around her while I dash to the other side of the room and away from the mirror.

"Take your time." Thinking quickly I try to calm my erection down, before she sees me. *What is with this girl?* I pace concentrating, *old grandmas, car accidents, fucking mangled bodies by horrible car fucking accidents. Shit, all I can see is her by the fucking mangled bleeding body ... naked and wet. This is not helping.* She is coming out here. *Think Sean.* "Ava I will be right back, I need to go ... go and ... I will be right back." I dart out the door running out into the rain and up the path trying to breathe in deeply while listening to the rain, the ocean, and the soft sounds that surround me. I need to stay away from her before I cannot control myself anymore. Then I would have to explain to my mother why I fucked her architect. I made a similar mistake once, screwing the daughter of one of my mother's friends. I never spoke to the girl again, my mother ended up hearing all about it, and therefore, I had to hear all about it for months. It didn't even help when I innocently explained that I barely remembered any of it because I was too drunk at the time. I offered that girl a picture but she took it happily.

Darting out of the way of a fast approaching truck I shield my eyes from its blinding lights. "Sean!" Demerae called out.

Running to his truck, I jump in eagerly. "What are you doing here?"

"Another storm has formed so my Dad sent me over with some food for you and Ava. He said he didn't want anyone out with this wind, it's not safe for anyone to be walking in these conditions. Were you walking over already?"

"I was, but I guess I'm not now." I slumped down.

"Well here is your food, there is enough for a couple of days. Call if you need anything, there is always someone at the main office. Nothing like hurricane season," he chuckles while I groan.

*Somebody really fucking hates me.* "Thanks," I said taking the packages before getting out of the truck. I wave him off staring at the door to my hell and so as any good devil does I walk up the steps, breath in deeply, drop my head, and accept my fate. *This is so NOT good.* Upon entering, I put the food on the coffee table as Ava comes into the room. *Thank you God, she is fully clothed.*

"Hey, what's that?" She asked as her cheerful smile begins to diminish.

"Apparently the wind is too bad for us to be outside wandering around. So they sent us food and told us to stay inside until further notice." *I probably said that too sarcastically but I don't care.*

"Oh," Ava said looking down to her feet.

"Are you done in the bathroom? I have mud and dirt all over me from three wheeling today."

"It's all yours."

I walk past her towards the bathroom and flip on the light. "The lights out huh? Funny how it fixed itself!" I shut the damn door and shake my head at the mirror that taunted me earlier. *She had to know I could see her. What was she doing moaning and rubbing like she did?* I step into the shower still baffled by her actions. *She had to know. Why did she leave that damn door open, because of a light that is not broken? So she could trap me with her she-devil body wash that's why.* I pick it up flinging it back down in disgust. *She put her clothes up in that same chest she had to know you could see into the bathroom mirror from there. She had to. I am not having sex with her, my mother will kill me.* I rub my body with soap, images still passing through my mind making it harder to stay focused on my anger. *She did look incredible. I should have walked in there with her and let her watch me undress before fucking her in the shower. Damn that would have been so … wow. My mother put me in this situation, she is the one that encouraged me to be with this girl. It's not my fault that we crashed and have to sleep next to each other. What does she expect me to do, ignore her? If I get laid tonight then it is her own damn fault. I won't apologize. In fact, I am going to enjoy the hell out of it.* With a renewed spirit I shut the water off and quickly make myself presentable, maybe even a little better than presentable. Checking myself in the mirror and making sure my shave is perfect and my clothes fit nicely, I walk out, finding her sitting in her chair waiting for me, covered head to toe in clothing. *What the hell is with this girl, I'm dressed to encourage sex and she is dressed to discourage it and any other kind of contact? I don't know what the hell to do now. Damn I need a drink, there has to be something around here.*

"Is this what you're looking for?" She says holding up a bottle of vodka.

"Where did you find that?"

"It was in the bottom desk drawer, there is plenty."

I grab the bottle from her, "you're already drinking?" I asked wondering how much time I have before she becomes an undesirable mess.

"I think I have earned as much right as you."

Making myself a drink, I sit across from her while she sorts our dinner in front of us. After some time of silence, she pours herself a small drink and gives me a soft smile. I smile back feeling the uneasiness settling down, "so you live in Atlanta?"

She looks up seemingly surprised that I am talking to her, "yes. I do."

"You said you where a Kentucky girl when did you move to Georgia?"

"After I went to college in New York and worked there for a while."

"So why did you leave New York?" I asked trying to picture her body under those big baggy clothes.

"Ummm, I needed a change," she said softly.

"What kind of change?" She stops eating, sinking into her chair. "What, did you get fired or screw the wrong guy? I asked fantasizing about how I hope the night will end.

"NO. Well I did have a relationship with my boss but ..."

"You? Figures," I laugh watching her fidget nervously. "Don't worry about it, everyone makes mistakes right?"

"It's not what you think."

I raise my eyebrows at her, "so you weren't cleaning his desk after hours?"

"You are so disgusting," she said getting up.

Reaching out I grab her wrist, "I'm sorry, come on sit. Tell me about it, seriously"

"There isn't much to tell. It wasn't the best decision on my part and as soon as I realized it, I broke it off and he ..." Her mood shifts suddenly as her mind obviously wanders elsewhere.

"He what? Don't stop there the story is just getting good."

"He left me alone when I needed him the most. But it didn't matter my best friend Kyle and I wanted to start our own business anyway and there happen to be some opportunities in Atlanta that helped us get started." *Well that story went nowhere good.*

"Aren't you hot in all that?" I said waving my hand up and down at her body.

"Ummm yea, a little, but I didn't know what would be appropriate."

"Appropriate? You mean appropriate for sitting in a cabin alone with me?" She nods. "Don't worry about it, get comfortable. I promise I don't mind or care"

"Maybe before we go to bed," she says nervously.

"Sleeping with me again tonight are you? Maybe this time you can end up on top." I joked but her wide eyes nearly come out of her skull. "Only kidding, calm down. Damn." She curls up in a ball in her chair covering herself even more. "So tell me more about you." I listen to her sweet voice as I gaze over her body, making mental notes of things I want to do to her, places I want to concentrate on.

"What the hell are you doing?" She asked suddenly.

I jump at the sound of her voice. "Nothing why?"

"You look like you were having a little too much of a good time. Do you need for me to give you some alone time?" She giggled through her held down bottom lip.

"No. Keep talking." I huffed.

"No, it's your turn to share. Tell me about all those supermodels you have dated," she asked me with sincere curiosity.

"Which one in particular, there has been quite a few?" I stick my chest out like the man I am.

She laughs, "oh my gosh, only wanting some dirt stud. Don't get too excited about yourself again."

"Again?"

"The plane."

"The plane?"

"Yea on the plane, you acted like I should lick your boots or something."

"Lick my boots? No wonder you don't have a boyfriend. Do you go around licking people's boots very often?"

"No, it's a saying."

"I haven't ever heard of it. I think you made it up."

"I did not, my grandfather uses it all the time."

"Your grandfather, well that makes since then." I laugh at her while she growls folding her arms and looking away from me. It is comical and cute as hell, especially the growl.

"Okay I get it, I treated you like an annoying groupie."

"Yes," she said turning towards me again.

"Well I'm sorry, I shouldn't have acted like that."

Her face brightens, "thank you. Okay so tell me."

"Which one do you want to know about?" I asked smiling at her with more want than I care to admit at this moment.

"The last one, she was so beautiful why in the world did you break up with her?"

"She's too into herself and she isn't that smart honestly. She bored me to tears, not much behind the good looks." *And she certainly does not have your body.*

"I'm surprised you didn't find her sexy enough for it to even matter that she's boring."

I reach for my glass and pour another drink. "Honestly Ava, I haven't met anyone as sexy as you." I stop to wink at her before taking a drink. "Ava?"

"I heard you," she said folding over herself again.

"I was joking with you Ava. I didn't mean to upset you."

"You were joking, so you don't think that about me?"

"Honestly, I haven't thought about it." I ease out the next statement carefully, "I guess, you have sexy qualities about you."

"Like what?"

"Can we change the subject? I do not feel comfortable with this conversation. This happens to me a lot with you I've noticed."

"Please tell me, I promise I won't fall in love with you and become an annoying groupie." She says sitting at the edge of her seat and staring at me fixedly.

I gaze over her, "that piercing is nice."

"My diamond?" She asked lifting her shirt to show it.

"Yes, what's the story with that?"

"It made me feel like I had taken back control of my life." *Not sure, what she means by that but it doesn't look like she is going to explain it.*

"Why the diamond?"

"My friend Kyle picked it out, it's a little too showy for me but he said it would drive guys crazy for some reason," she said as if she doesn't believe it herself.

"Well it does, I would say that's one thing about you that drives men crazy." *It drives me nuts. I am not even sure why, I hope she doesn't ask.*

"What else?" She sits up straight eyeing me a little harder. *Okay you asked for it.*

Sitting my drink down, I get up to lean down over her while she scoots to the opposite side of her chair. "What are you doing?" I laugh.

"What are you doing?" She said watching my hands carefully.

"Sit still for a few seconds please … trust me." I wait for her to unclench her jaw before caressing her face in my direction and gaze over her face appreciatively. Her breathing becoming heavier as I sweep my fingers gently over her cheek. "Ava you have the sweetest face and the most hypnotizing sapphire eyes and your hair." Running the backs of my fingers down one side of her face gently and pushing the edges of her hair to one side, I take a soft breath against her neck. "Your hair is more beautiful than any sunset I have ever seen, not to mention your full, soft pink lips," I said tracing my finger around her chin and grazing the outer edge of her bottom lip. Pleased with myself I sit back in my chair enjoying watching her gasp for breath. "Not to mention your incredibly sex body." Her eyes widen. "Happy?" Getting up smoothly, I move back to my chair and take a drink, watching her. *Now if I did my job right she will be in my lap straddling me in no time.* I adjust expectantly, "Ava? Sweetheart, are you okay?" I ask rubbing my smile away so as not to look too obvious.

"Do you know we met once before?" She whispers.

"What are you doing?" I ask confused.

Her shoulders sink with a cock of her head, "I was trying to tell you about when I first met you."

"I don't understand what you're talking about? When you first met me?" *Nor why you are talking at all and not over here in my lap.*

"In New York." I shake my head as she continues to explain her story to me. "We both lived there at the same time. You probably don't remember, I am sure you don't remember seeing me since I was so covered up but you rescued me. You pulled me out of the way of a mob of girls trying to get to your brother." She gulps as my smile disappears and the confusion turns to anger. "I was standing in front of an Italian restaurant," she pauses looking away from me. "That place always had the most incredible smells," she said closing her eyes and taking in a breath with a smile. "Silly but we were so poor then, all I had was my fantasy food." She finds my eyes again and pushes her lips into an innocent smile. "You don't remember do you? It was a few minutes but when you pulled me out of the way, you held me so tight and when I looked into your eyes they were so." She says with a dreamy expression. "Wonderful and warm. I couldn't believe how incredible one moment could feel," she looks back at me and pauses to clear her throat. "Anyway I wanted to tell you that," she shrugs without looking at me.

"Why?" I asked harshly.

"Because you said all those nice things about me and I wanted to tell you something nice about you. You made me feel so good that day, I thought you might like to know that it meant something to me. The moment anyway not that I am trying to make it more than what it was but that encounter got me through some really tough times." She shrugs again looking at me with a wary smile. "And now you carried me off a burning plane. How crazy is that?"

"What do you want from me?" I seethe at her.

"Nothing."

"Then why are you telling me this … story?" I asked waving my hands at her.

"I told you. I thought it might make you feel good that you were a part of a special moment for me."

"You are such a typical fucking groupie!"

"I'm not a groupie. I have not seen you since then or even tried to. I barely remembered that it was you until Kyle reminded me. You weren't that famous then. You were a regular person like me and that's how I remembered you until I was reminded that it was … you."

Huffing, I stand waving off her obvious attempts. "Whatever."

"I'm sorry I didn't mean to make you mad. I promise I don't expect anything from you."

"Fine." I said sitting back down and pouring another drink. She rips the bottle from my hand and pours herself and even bigger drink. "Should you be drinking this much?"

"If you're drinking then I am too." I sit back eyeing her with disgust. "You know you don't have to be such and asshole about it. I didn't expect it to mean anything to you," she said tearing up.

"Mean something to me! Baby I don't even know what you're talking about. Do you know how many times my brother was chased by mobs of girls? I probably pulled a hundred different girls out of the way," I steamed, while Ava curls over herself yet again, and downing everything she has. "Fuck, are you going to cry now?" Tears stroll down her cheeks as she shakes her head. "Ahhh damn it! We were having such a nice time. Why did you have to go and ruin it?"

"I didn't know that I was," she whispered.

We sit in silence for a time, both drinking what we can to get on to the next moment. "Listen I'm sorry I yelled at you but you wouldn't believe how many girls make up stories to try to persuade me to be with them or take them out or whatever they are after me for."

"Well I'm not making it up and I didn't tell you to persuade you into anything," she whimpered.

"Fine. I believe you."

"Besides the moment might have been nice but it wasn't perfect. I ended up losing my locket that night."

"Your locket?" I asked unable to look at her.

"My mother's, it had pictures of her and my father before they died and then me as a baby," she said unknowingly striking me hard. "Not that you care but her name was Lillah and that locket was all I had of hers and … oh forget it!" She snapped at me. Her blue eyes suddenly meet mine and my heart jumps, like it hasn't since.... "You know what you're right it is hot in here, I think I will change." I stare blankly at her, everything I was planning for tonight is suddenly off the table. *I don't want anything to do with this girl.* Ava returns wearing an outfit that suits her body much more so than the previous. *Why didn't she put that on before?* I lean down lowering my head to look at anything other than her. Out of nowhere, she reaches over touching my hand. "Sean, I'm sorry I didn't mean to make you uncomfortable."

*I can't breathe.* "Ava I'm going to bed," I said getting up quickly but I am not able to take more than a few steps before she grabs my arm.

"Why? Did I upset you that much? I am sorry Sean. I didn't realize. I was only trying …" I take hold of her face causing a stillness between us that allows me to see her for the first time. My heart continues to pound its way out of my chest as she stands in silence watching me gaze over her, trying to understand what I am feeling.

Without thinking, I move in until I feel her sweet breath against my lips. "It can't be you," I whispered into her mouth taking in one lip between mine and then the other. My heart easing its desperate escape, as I go deeper into her mouth, craving even more with every soft touch she returns. My mind explodes and I pull away from her abruptly. "I'm not going to have sex with you Ava. I'm not doing it." I said turning away from her. *No. I don't feel anything. I am not having anything to do with this girl, it's not possible ... it's a lie ... NO!*

"I didn't ask you to. You kissed me!" She yelled as I pace away from her. "I don't understand you, you're like an emotional roller coaster. I can't figure you out at all." Continuing to ignore her, she becomes even more emotional. "You are so exhausting no wonder you drink. Have sex with you? Which one of you would that be?" She smacks my arm gaining my full attention. "Damn you Sean, talk about messing up a nice night. Well that was all you *baby*, not me." She is silent almost long enough for me to turn around and apologize. "I'm going to bed I have had enough of this." She said huffing her way into bed, while I turn out the remaining lights. "Not that one!" She yelled at me. "Please." I shrug catching her tear-filled eyes shyly pleading.

"I'll leave it on. No big deal." I crawl in next to her as she clings to the opposite edge. "I'm sorry Ava, it is my fault." I am not sure if she heard me since she doesn't respond. *I hope she doesn't expect me to say it again, because I'm not. She heard me. The most annoying woman I have ever met. I don't even know why I care whether she's mad at me or not.* I spend the rest of the night tossing and turning in the uncomfortable bed. I am not sure how much time passes before I hear her soft murmuring turn into tense flinching. I sit up seeing her lip quivering and her fists clenched.

"I don't want to be here. I want to go home please. Let me go, please let me go," she whimpered getting more hysterical by the second. "NO! No, you're hurting me. STOP!" She screams hysterically fighting me to get a hold of her.

"Ava! Ava ... Ava." I wrap my arms around her, holding her and kissing her cheek until her eyes open filled with tears and that same desperate fear I saw the night before. "It's okay it was just a dream." She shakes her head. "Yes it was. It was only a dream. A bad dream." I clear the tears from her face as she stares at me pitifully. *I am not sure what she wants or even needs at this moment.* "It's okay, no one is going to hurt you – not while I'm here."

CX80

**T**he night brings all new thoughts and exhausting dreams, only to be followed by another day of being restricted to the cabin. Ava and I spend as much time as possible avoiding talking to each other, it is an impossible feat.

"I can't take this anymore. Will you talk to me about anything? Something at least?" She finally begs me.

Sighing I sit down and look up at her for the first time all-day. "Where did you go to school?"

"Kentucky first, I had a scholarship to play basketball there and then I got an academic scholarship to do my postgraduate work at Columbia."

I stare at her. "That's impressive."

"I guess, it wasn't easy though. What about you? Did you go to college? And before you say it, no I didn't read up on interesting facts about Sean."

Laughing at her smartass comment, I ease into my seat a little deeper. "You should you know it's quite ..."

"Interesting?" She said with a smile.

"Alright smartass, I graduated from VMI before heading into the military," I said finding a ball and tossing it into the air.

"Army?"

Nodding, "Special Forces." Her eyes widen and suddenly I feel good about impressing her. *Damn Sean, get a grip.*

"Did you leave to get into acting?"

"No, my mother needed help after my father died and once she got back on her feet I needed a job. So my brother who was already deep into it encouraged me. Of course, my mother encouraged us both."

"Did your mother want to be an actress?"

"She was actually. She was doing plays when she and my father met. She stopped when they got married and I guess now she lives the life through us."

"Do you think she regrets quitting?"

"I don't know. I've always wanted to ask her but I never have."

"Your brother? Does he like acting?"

"He stopped doing it when he met his wife, he didn't want to live in front of the cameras anymore. Now he's my manager."

"How does that work having your brother run your life?"

"It was weird at first but he knows me better than anyone, so he usually takes care of things before I even have to ask. Plus, I know I can trust him, it's not always that way."

"And you, you love what you do?"

"Most of the time I do, there are a few things that I could do without. I love becoming the character and exploring other lives, experiencing other experiences. I don't have to go to work every day and do the same thing for the rest of my life. At the end of my day, I still get to be me no matter if I just battled aliens or I stole a car and ran from the police. I get paid to do the craziest things and not get into trouble for doing them." I smile as her face brightens with every question I answer. "What about you?"

"Somewhat similar, I always get to do something new, mostly anyway. Same surroundings but the projects are always new. I get to take what was nothing and create an experience, create a feeling or a song," she laughs when I look at her strangely. "I am always inspired by something, whether it's a color or a song or the way petals on a flower cross one another in just such a way to be interesting. Kyle says I am passionate, I guess that is true but I don't want to look at the same things everyday and never notice all the uniqueness about every detail within them. I don't want to miss anything."

"So how big is your firm?" I asked eager to hear her speak some more.

"I have a couple of people working with me. Kyle who handles everything that I do not, he is my lifesaver. We have been best friends since before college."

"You and Kyle ever date?" I asked glimpsing at her from the corners of my eyes.

"Me date Kyle? Oh no, I am nowhere near Kyle's type," She laughed. "No he is into other avenues other than me," I nod understanding. "Then there is Anna, who answers all my phones, keeps my books and other jobs not directly related to the work itself. You should meet her, although that's probably not a good idea because she will probably try to become your sex slave."

"Really? Is she hot?"

"Sean!"

"You brought it up. So where is this office that my sex slave works at?"

"Stay away from her Sean." She eyes me biting her lip to keep from my smiling. "I turned an old in-law suite in the back of my house into an office. Gutting most of it to make one big room but it works well thus far."

"How do you get projects?"

"Word of mouth, past clients, things like that mostly and of course, Justin. I would have never been able to keep it going if it wasn't for him," She said smiling and seemingly remembering him fondly.

"And how does Justin help you exactly?" I hold up tossing my ball waiting for her reply.

"He's a contractor. A good one and we usually go after projects together. We met on my first few projects and then he started mentioning me to new ones and he helped me build out my office. He's incredible, better than I deserve that's for sure," she sighs playing with her hands.

"So he likes you?"

"I don't know," she shrugged.

"He likes you, a lot from the sound of it," I said smacking the wall hard with the ball.

"Maybe but he has so many girlfriends I don't think he has the time to be worried about me."

"Oh so Justin is supposed to be some kind of stud huh?"

"Yes." I glare at her as she sighs dreaming in another direction. "He has the most incredible muscles from working out in the field all the time, great tan, sandy blond hair and his smile …" She continued her gushing, nauseatingly before I have to interrupt the love fest.

"I got it!"

"You asked?"

"I wish I hadn't. So why haven't you married prince charming already? And don't tell me because he hasn't asked because I am sure he would love to?"

"Well when he kissed me…" I sit up straight, eyeing her entertained smile. "I'm joking. Gees, you act like you are jealous or something."

"I'm not jealous Ava, I am certainly not jealous of … Justin." I throw the ball a little harder fantasizing a particular face on the wall. "So what about your parents?" *She thinks I didn't see her roll her eyes at me, I don't know what that was about but she better stop.*

"My father died of cancer when I was real young and my Mom died in a car accident when I was five. I lived with my grandparents mostly in Kentucky." I watch as she twists slightly in her chair and then catches me staring at her. "So what do you think of your brother's wife, you don't talk about her much?"

"Abbey? She's fine, she makes my brother ridiculously happy so it's hard not to like her." Ava and I both reach for the bottle from the night before. "You want a drink?" She nods, holding out her glass. I pour us both one as we continue to talk at least until Ava decides that we need music. *I am so glad she found somewhere to play her sickening iPod, maybe the power will go out.* At least that was my thoughts until obviously affected by the alcohol, she starts dancing and singing to the music. Bored beyond reason, I have no choice but to watch her hips sway and her body bounce to every beat as she sings her favorite part of each song. *Why does she keep doing this to me? I am living a sexless nightmare.*

Before I can run into the storm screaming, she sways to me with her fake microphone and points it in my direction, "no," I said looking opposite her. Again, she points it in my direction leaning over into my lap. "I think that's enough alcohol for you."

"Come on Sean as least dance with me, do something besides sit here and brood all-night." She pulls on my hands to get me up and again I shake my head. "Come on, if you don't know how I can show you."

"I know how to dance."

"Prove it then."

"I'm not doing that kind of dancing and certainly not to this music." I stand with her as she holds onto my hand.

"Why?" She asked as I cross my arms. "Fine, pick whatever you want."

Immediately I change out her iPod for mine and to something a man would dance to and not feel stupid. "Now you come here." Taking her hand I twirl her around to me and caress her into my movements. I nuzzle my face into her hair until I can't handle it anymore and have to twirl her away bringing her back to me again after I calm. That works until she lays her head against my shoulder and moves her hand slowly up my chest and to the back of my neck, pushing her fingers through my hair. Comfortable and content, I allow my fingers to trail up and down her sides and through her hair. She sinks deeper into my arms letting me hold my head against hers. The warmth of her hands pull me into her with every motion we make against each other, drawing my lips to hers more and more ....

Suddenly she pulls out of my arms. "Maybe we should do something else," she turns the music off before returning to her chair.

"How come we have to stop when you say so?" She curls up ignoring me, with another drink. *That's going to help.* "You better be careful with that, you drink too much, and you're going to be begging me to have sex with you before the end of the night," I smile at her disgusted expression.

"You have some ego!"

"It's true and you know it," I said taking a drink. "But don't worry, I'll turn you down and make sure you get to bed safely but I would prefer not to have to."

"Why because you want me that bad?"

I eye her harshly, "you know you could try to be nice to me, be kind to my ego somewhat. Despite what you think I'm not completely heartless."

"Boost your ego? That is the last thing you need Sean Grant. Your ego is in perfect condition."

"Come on say something nice to me. You can do it, I believe in you."

She glares at me before straightening with a confident smile. "Fine, I like your tattoo."

"The one on my back?" She nods standing up to meet me with a smile. I raise my shirt over my shoulders and turn to show her my upper back. Before I can prepare she begins tracing it with her fingers, sending arousing sensations through my body.

"What does it mean?" She asked continuing to caress my back gently with her fingers.

I glance over my shoulder at her concentrated eyes. "The eagle represents my country and my military career and then he carries an American flag in one talon, for my mother and a British flag in the other, representing my father. The three together represent me as a whole." Getting more aroused with each touch, I pull my shirt back down and face her, "what else do you like about me?"

"No, I'm supposed to tell you something nice about you, not what I like."

"Either way." She rolls her eyes at me as I smile stepping closer to her.

Suddenly she slinks away stretching and yawning, "you know it's getting late I should get to bed."

*Unbelievable.* "Oh no you don't," I follow her reaching for her waist and turning her around to face me before she can hide behind the netting of the bed. "Talk, it must be good if you're running away."

She bites her bottom lip and falls against me. *Damn alcohol.* "I'm not running away." She lifts herself up on the bed falling backwards and I follow hovering over her as she begins to giggle causing me to laugh.

"Tell me."

Ava runs her fingers through my hair, mocking my request. "Oh Sean, you are so hot, I love your dark sexy hair," she said moving her fingers to my face, tracing my features while still amused by the situation. "Oh and your hypnotizing green eyes, your handsome face and oh these incredibly kissable lips." I pause as she continues moving her hand down from my lips to my chest. "And your ripped abs make me crazy." Caressing my stomach, she focuses on every line. Her hand lingers and not waiting for her anymore, I take my damn shirt off and return her hand where it was, silently she watches her hand move against my body. Taking in a single breath, I move my hand to her stomach rubbing her belly button through her shirt with the back of my fingers causing her to inhale. Feeling for the end of her shirt, I trace my fingers underneath it and across her stomach gently. Her eyes close as I move my fingers up, until I find her diamond, tracing around it and across her stomach. I hesitate until Ava moves both of her hands to my chest and feels me more aggressively.

"Ava," I whispered. And those beautiful blue eyes look up at me big and bright and that is all I need. I run my fingers across her cheek, licking my lips before taking in her soft lips and moving over top of her. She responds with wet, pressing lips. I brush my tongue across her lips and encourage her to open her mouth for me. She does and I go deeper, massaging her tongue with mine, drawing her into me more. Her hands wander my body freely while her leg moves up over mine. She arches her back and moves up further on the bed and at the same time presses her body into my intense erection. Whether on purpose or not she forces out my groan for her, "I want you." She grips the back of my head moaning and breathing heavily. *Damn, I want her so bad.* My hand wanders further finding her breasts, tracing the edges of her bra before becoming impatient and pushing it away, taking hold of her supple fullness completely - unexpectedly, she jumps up and away from me. Holding my hands up, "I'm sorry, if I got carried away but I thought that you wanted me to."

"No, it's not you, I wasn't expecting … that," she folds her arms over herself as she puts her bra back into place.

Frustrated, I fall back into bed as someone starts knocking at the door. "Now what?" I get up and take Ava's face in my hands, trying to look into her shying eyes. "I'm sorry, okay?" She nods at my apology, letting me walk away to get the door. Demerae wide-eyed and anxious meets me at the door.

"Some kids were smoking in one of the crop sheds and it caught on fire and now the wind is causing it to threaten the main work house," he said in a panic.

"Ava lock up and I will be back later." I put my shoes on and take the hard-shelled jacket from Demerae. Arriving quickly we get instructions and work together putting out the blaze. The wind made it difficult but I stick around until they have everything handled and then trudge back to the cabin exhausted. As I approach, I see someone staring into the windows of our cabin.

"Avaaaaa." Kevin yelled as he peaks through the windows.

"What the fuck are you doing?" I yelled at him.

Kevin turns to me immediately looking guilty, "back already Sean?"

"I thought you were helping with the fire, what are you doing here?" I asked him feeling my muscles tense up.

"I was worried about Ava and it looked like you guys had it handled so …"

"Ava? Ava's fine, she's inside safe. We needed your help with the fire!"

"But the power went out and I was afraid she might be scared or try to fix it herself, so I came over to be with her until you could get back…" I stare at the lying piece of shit fisting my hands.

"How did you know our power went out?"

"What?" He said darting his eyes around me searching for an escape.

"Get the fuck out of here." Kevin tries to move quickly around me but I grab him pulling him back close to look him in the eyes. "And stay away from Ava. Understand me?" He nods and I let him run away. I walk into the pitch-black cabin cursing under my breath until I hear her crying. "Ava?" I search trying to find her with the flashlight they gave me to get back. Her figure highlights in the corner of the shower, curled up in a ball trembling and crying hysterically. "Ava what happened?" I crouch down to her only to be met with flailing hands and arms.

"NO! Let me go!" She screamed at me.

Shocked I call out her name trying to get a hold of her arms and holding them until she breaks down in my arms. "What happened?" She shakes her head burying her face into my chest. "I'll kill him if he hurt you. If I had known, I would not have let him leave. But I will go get the prick right now and …"

"It wasn't Kevin."

"Then who was it?" She shakes her head pulling away from me. "Who was it Ava?" She sits silent, rocking in place. "You're not going to tell me?" Watching her shake her head again, I sigh. "Was it anyone on this island?" She shakes her head one more time before I pull her into my arms and let her cry against my chest until she calms completely. "Do you want to go to bed or do you want me to stay with you a little longer because I would like to get a shower?"

"I don't like the dark," she whimpered. I hand her the flashlight. "What are you going to do?"

"Unless you want to take a shower with me I guess I will have to feel my way around." I said helping her up. "I'm going to leave this door open to get some light in, so don't come in spying on me." I said against her ear, earning a slight smile. "Are you sure you're okay?" I ask holding her against my chest until she nods. "Give me a few minutes and I will be out to protect you from dumbasses trying to get in." I get my cold fucking shower, no thanks to Kevin, I am sure of it. Afterwards, I find Ava sound asleep outside the bathroom holding the flashlight for me. "Ava Kelley, I don't know if you're crazy as hell or adorable or both, which is more my luck." I take the flashlight and pick her up putting her in bed and the flashlight on the bedside table directing it away from the bed but leaving it on for her. Exhausted and eager to crash into bed, I make my way into my side of the bed and find a comfortable position before I suddenly feel her crawl up against me, and hold onto me. My exhausted body suddenly comes alive again.

# Chapter 11: Ava

The next morning, I awake in the middle of the bed alone and find him sitting in his chair staring at the wall. "Why did you let me sleep?"

"I wanted some time to think." His tone is harsh, his entire body shaking, he avoids looking my way.

"About what?"

With a sharp glare, "about you!"

"What about me?"

"You know damn well what I'm talking about." I shake my head and he immediately jumps up hovering close as he motions with his hands. "Ava come on, what happened last night and why are you having nightmares every night?"

"The plane crash," I shrug looking away from his judging eyes.

He laughs sarcastically, "the plane crash?" I nod. "The hell it is! Ava say whatever you want but don't fucking lie to me. Tell me what is going on with you? Or better yet tell me what this fucking letter is about?" His furious figure stands waving my letter from Justin in my face.

"Where did you get that?" I snapped snatching it from his hand.

"It doesn't matter, tell me why I am such a key part of your trip."

"You're not!"

"NO? Then why does that fucking letter say that I am?" Confused, I shake my head and he rips the letter back to show it to me, "It says right here …," he points to Justin's words as if they make sense to him.

Tears building up, "you have no idea what you're talking about. What he is saying has nothing to do with you."

"Then what does it have to do with Ava? Because to me it looks like you planned this whole time to get to me somehow. And you worked my mother perfectly to do so." My body tenses as I take my letter back and walk away from him, with sadness, I don't understand. Sean pulls me around to look at him, "you took advantage of my mother to get to me and that story about how we met the first time; it was all a lie wasn't it? I don't know how …"

"I would never do that!" His anger deepens into his eyes. "SEAN!" I jerk away from him, tears flowing rapidly down my face as my body shakes with dread.

"Tears aren't going to help, Ava," he said holding my face up to look at him. "I don't care why you did it but you better believe it's not going to work. I'm not going to be with you, I'm not going to give you money for anything and you better fucking believe I am not …"

"I was RAPED!" I screamed at him. His wide eyes back off at once. "Oh now you're not so tough are you? You conceded fucking ass! That letter has nothing to do with you. He wants me to go out with him and he said what he said about you because I haven't let a man touch me since it happened." Breathing in deeply, I calm as I stare into his horrified green eyes. "You see it's funny, ha-ha. Ava doesn't let men touch her so good luck with Sean Grant, one of the sexiest men alive, oh wait we are talking about Ava so it's more like a miracle is what's called for." He shakes his head hesitantly at me. "Only the real joke of it all is that you're the first man that can touch me and not make my skin crawl. How incredibly FUCKED UP is that? Of all people, you are the one man that I am comfortable with. But don't worry, chances are that it only goes so far. There is no way I will ever be able to trick you into bed because I'm too scared. To scared to take my clothes off and lie down in that bed and let you fuck me." Wiping my tears away I look back up at him, "but you know what? You are right about one thing, I do want to. Oh like you don't know. I wish I could fuck you Sean, because maybe if I can with you then I can let someone like Justin, who cares about me make love to me like I have dreamed about for so long. Maybe I can let him love me and I won't be alone anymore." I pause regaining my voice again. Patting the letter against his chest, "you keep it, because it obviously means more to you than it does to me."

"When did this happen?" He asked suddenly.

I stare blankly at him, "why does it matter?" His defeated expression seems desperate for an answer. Forcing a smile and focusing on him with a brave face, "it happened a few days after I met you in New York. That's why I told you that story and why those few minutes with you meant so much to me because that was the last time I felt normal." The emotion grips me as all the pain and memories come rushing back.

"Ava, I am so," he said reaching out for me.

I close myself off from him, "don't touch me. Don't ever touch me again." I said rushing back into bed, burying my face into the pillow to hide my tears from him.

"I don't blame you at all, but will you at least let me apologize?" Sean said tugging at my shirt as he tries to get me to look at him. "Please Ava, I feel like ..."

"I don't give a shit how you feel, leave me alone. Hopefully we won't be on this stupid island much longer and I won't have to see you ever again."

His pitiful expression is breaking me. "I'm so sorry Ava. I really am. I know it doesn't mean much but you don't know the kinds of people I have to deal with sometimes and I know that's no excuse but I ...."

"Leave me alone."

"Not until you accept my apology"

"Fine it's accepted. Feel better?"

"Not really," I shrug at his answer.

"Demerae is going to be here soon to pick us up for breakfast." I say trying to get around him but he grabs my hands quickly and forces me to look into his sorrowful eyes, feeding my guilt for being still angry. "Ava please, I'm so sorry. I didn't know, if I had then I would have never hurt you like that. I would never let anyone hurt you. Please believe me. I will do whatever you want to make it up to you." *He has no idea about what hurts!*

"Anything I want?" He nods expectantly as I seek my revenge for my hardened pain. "Then go back in time and keep that psycho from raping me so someone other than *you* can touch me." Sean drops his hands without a word. "Sean ..." His pain filled eyes rip me apart. "No, Sean I didn't mean that." I said reaching for him but only manage to be left standing alone.

"I'm going to walk to breakfast," Sean said avoiding my hands once again and walking out the door without another word spoken.

Demerae picks me up and drives me to breakfast - everyone is there, but him. My eyes are beginning to blur staring at the door waiting for him to come through it. After everyone leaves, I stay a little longer, waiting, only to be disappointed.

With the weather lightened up for a little while, I thought the small beach I was told about, might be a nice break. Ashlen offered me one of Brianna's bikini's that she bought for herself but was forbidden to ever wear and after I put it on, I know why. The bikini is smaller than I would ever think to buy for myself, a turquoise string bikini with carved wooden tassels provocatively hanging down between my breasts. It is masterly designed but only the most confident person would parade around in it. I of course, cover up the racy suit with shorts and a t-shirt before proceeding down the trail to the expected secluded spot.

CB8O

The beach is not big but the water is clear, warm and without another soul anywhere near and that is all I need. I slip out of my clothes and pack them into my bag before wadding in and letting the tender waves break against my back and the sand wash over my toes, rejuvenating myself as I watch the distant storm. My tranquil setting lasts for a few minutes before engines gearing down the path nearby unsettle me. They speed and slow and speed again as they curve the path leading away from me. I sigh in relief with the renewed silence until one returns. I close my eyes willing whomever it is to keep going but no luck.

"Hey Red. I like the suit, it works well on you," Kevin called out, eyeing me and adjusting himself openly.

"Kevin where are the others … I thought I heard them?" Noticing him slyly kick my bag of clothes further away from me, I quickly search for alternate escape routes.

"Oh they are enjoying playing on those machines but I thought maybe you would want some company." He said jerking his clothes off down to his boxers. "I hope the water is warm." His approaching nearly nude body sends violent chills up my spine. I slowly back away from him. "Where are you going?" He rushes towards me and barely misses grabbing me as I move even deeper. "You sure do look good but you might want to be careful before you step off too deep. Here let me help you."

"I think you should go find the others Kevin, I really want to be alone," my shaky voice discloses my fast approaching fear and paralyzing weakness.

"Alone huh? You don't sound too sure. Well I'll be quiet, you don't have to worry about me. I'll just enjoy the view." His eyes trace my body down through the clear water. With a startled gasp, I step back too far and fall off the ledge deeper into the water. With eager expectations, Kevin lunges, grabbing me and pulling me tight into his arms where his loaded breath clouds my face. "You better be careful there." His hands hold flat and hard against my body with his excitement growing and protruding repulsively into my thighs. "MMMmmm you smell good," he moaned nuzzling his face into the crook of my neck, grazing his sun-chapped lips against my skin.

My body shakes until my sight blurs, "please Kevin, I want to go, I don't want …."

"Hey do you know I have been thinking about you since I first saw you get on the plane? After we crashed and you ended up rooming with Sean I thought for sure I would never get my chance with you," he pushes into me breathing heavily into my ear. "But here we are and I can't wait to taste those lips of yours," he said leaning in and forcing his lips to mine.

"No! I want to go!" I yelled at him slapping the salty water into his eyes, forcing him to release me. I run reaching my towel and getting one fisted grip before he falls on top of me.

"Ava this bikini is so sexy, you can't blame me for wanting you. You had to know what you would do to me in this. It's only fair that I get to enjoy it," he says tight into my ear while I struggle against his pressing body, his wandering hands, and loathsome, wet mouth.

His experience is obvious as he holds me in place giving me no options to take advantage of. "Kevin let me go or I am going to start screaming."

"Scream, I might even like it." Forcing me on my back and pressing down on me with his exposed, hardened excitement digging into me, causing daggers of panic to shoot into my veins as equally panicked screams escape my mouth. Ignoring my protests he covers my mouth and continues his attempt to persuade me as I jerk my head from one side to the next, freeing myself from his forceful hand. "NO! LET me go!" I screamed, slowly weakening by my overpowering dread.

Kevin places his hand back on my mouth with so much pressure my head whips backwards into the ground with a loud thump. "Stop fucking crying, you're ruining this for me! If you would just relax and enjoy it."

Fighting his hands and weight, he forces my face down into the towel and then suddenly he lets go of me. I open my eyes to see his mouth wide and gasping for breath as hands choke him into a strained stand. "I thought I told you to stay away from her." Sean's powerfully directed words singe Kevin's face as he pleads with the hands controlling his life. "Do you know what I could fucking do to you right now?" Kevin nods before landing on the ground choking on the air he swallows back into his lungs. In awe of my rescue, I watch dumbstruck while Sean leans down to me and looks me over with tender hands. "I didn't mess up saving you this time did I?" I shake my head with an emerging smile.

Kevin stands abruptly and kicks Sean in the back and then repeatedly in the side. "Stop, you're hurting him!" I yelled jerking at Kevin's arm.

"Ava, get back I'm fine," Sean said holding his ribs but getting up strong. Kevin knocks me backwards, watching Sean motion for him to come at him again. With a laugh, he runs towards Sean - and his fists, falling to the ground with a heavy thud. Rubbing his bleeding face, Kevin gets up staggering but ready to square off with Sean once again. "You don't want to fight me dumbass." Kevin still staggering begins circling away as Sean takes my hand and carefully maneuvers me out of the way with his muscles flexing and jaw tensed.

"Wow! Are you really concerned about her? I don't understand you at all Sean, you can have any girl you want, you can't possibly be this angry over one. That pussy must be good." Kevin barely gets a full sarcastic chuckle out before he is on his back and seeming shocked at the fervent rage that is cursing his body. The beating is hard to listen to but even harder to watch.

"Are you understanding me now, you disgusting fuck?"

"Sean stop!" I screamed.

"Sean let him go! You're going to kill him!" From out of nowhere, Demerae rushes to Sean and drags him away from Kevin's bloodied and swollen body.

Alizbeth runs in with Paul - mouths wide open, "what the hell is going on?"

"Alizbeth call Dad and get this stupid ass out of here," Demerae demanded.

"Sure thing," Al agreed as he takes in the sight fully, helping Kevin up and pushing him back towards the path.

"Wait, I have to get my clothes," Kevin said scrambling to pick up his scattered clothing.

"I wouldn't fucking worry about your damn clothes. Get the hell out of here!" Demerae screamed, using his entire body against Sean's chest.

"I am getting my shoes and shorts at least, I can't ride that machine without them," Kevin leans down near me grabbing his shoes and causing a stir when he makes a cynical attempt to kiss me good-bye. Sean immediately edges forward sending all three boys at him. "Keep him away from me!" Kevin yells leaping back on his heels.

"Fuck!" Demerae tenses fighting Sean and his fisted hands back. "Keep him away? You are a seriously special kind of stupid. I should let him go so he can put you out of your damn misery. Get the fuck out of here already!" Kevin limps back to the path with Al and Paul following shortly after. Demerae slowly lets Sean go and steps away with a long exhale. "I am going to follow them. I know he had it coming but you need to let it go now," he said focusing on Sean with eyebrows raised, waiting for his acceptance. "My Dad will deal with him, trust me." Sean nods, slowly relaxing his fists. Demerae sighing, rubs his head with his hands. "You stay here and look after your girl, she's still shaking like a leaf," he said gesturing towards me. "Give me a few minutes to get him restrained and to my Dad, then you can take her home. Enjoy the water for a little while and calm down." Demerae with his hands on his hips exhales once more before making his way back up the path.

It is silent, as I hold my breath waiting for Sean to look at me. I watch him closely as his eyes slowly meet mine. Without thinking I run into his arms. "Stop crying, everything is going to be fine now." Holding tight to him, I wipe the trickle of blood from his mouth and smile warmly up at him. "Does this mean you have forgiven me?"

"Should I?"

"Yes. I nearly died trying to get to you. I cannot control those damn three-wheelers well at all in a rush. I think I ran into every tree and thorny plant alive. I almost fell off at the turn," he shakes his head laughing at himself. "You would have laughed hysterically at my clumsiness, it was terrible." I realize what he has done for me and so for the first time in a long time, I take control of a man, by pressing my lips to his and caressing them as appreciatively as I can manage. I wouldn't be surprised if he pushes me away but instead he is pulling me closer, holding my head close to his. Feeling his heart beat rapidly against mine, I am sure I can move but I am not sure I want to. I can't remember the last time I was held like this and didn't want to run away. "Can I swim with you?" He asked with gentle kisses and soft touches. I nod and enjoy watching him remove his clothing piece by piece until only his simple fitting designer boxers remain, quite a contrast compared to Kevin's prepackaged baggy ones. Entranced by the cut of his body, I am barely able to realize his hand stretched out to me, the smoothness of his skin and especially his perfectly structured hipbones setting just above the seam of his boxers. "Are you coming beautiful?" Taking me by the hand, he leads me into the water, wrapping one arm around my waist and picking me up into his arms effortlessly. My body curls around his as if it is made to do nothing but. I press my head against his while we float in the water, kissing and caressing and finding peace within each other's eyes and soft smiles. Running my hands over his body, pushing away each droplet of water down and off his skin stirring up a heat within me that is becoming too hard to control, little by little I let go even more. "Ava, sweetheart this is starting to go in a direction that I don't think you want it to. Why don't we take a break before we both get carried away?" Before I can respond he sits me down with a heavy sigh. He dives forcefully into the water, his back muscles flexing concurrently with his arms.

Even with the break, I can't let go of my renewed joy. Letting my fingers rake through the water and my body sway to a favorite song in my head, I move further and further towards the beach. Stopping short of the edge and letting my toes sink during the drifting tide until a soft sigh releases behind me. "How long have you been there?"

Stroking his hands over his head, pushing the remaining water out of his hair and down his back, "miss me?" He asked winking at me as he passes to go lie down on my towel.

"That's my towel you know and you didn't answer me."

"I can't hear a word you are saying," he yelled stretching out.

Dripping on his body with crossed arms, I start to speak when he opens his eyes smiling his assured smile at me. "That's my towel, you know?"

"I'm sorry did you want to lay here?"

"You knew that's where I was headed."

"I didn't actually but I am sure we both can fit," he said motioning to his side. Uncrossing my arms, I lie down beside him stiff and uncomfortable until the feeling of his fingers trailing down my stomach causes a rugged breath to be released from my lips. "Does this bother you?"

"No, I'm fine." *Breathe.*

His fingers move in caressing patterns up to my breasts, finding the wooden tassels that hang between them and playfully fumbling with them between his fingers while allowing one finger to trail along my skin. "These are incredible," he said meeting my eyes briefly. "Yes, I really ... really like these," he moaned stroking with more purpose.

*Breathe Ava.* "Yes I think the wooden tassels add a nice accent to the turquoise color of the suit." I mumbled. *Oh my God, I am so lame.*

With a light chuckle he leans down to my ear, nudging the edge, "I wasn't talking about the damn wooden tassels, Ava."

*Gasping.* "Sean ..." His lips meet mine, cradling them to his mouth.

"Thanks for the dance by the way but next time wait for me, I like dancing with you." A single moan escapes my mouth as he leans down kissing the water off my skin from between my breasts. I pull his face back up to mine taking in his succulent lips while his strong hands continue to explore me. Grazing my nipple he waits to see if I will protest but I take him in closer. Kissing him deeply, I enjoy his soft groans as he palms my breasts completely, massaging each one after the other while he carefully repositions between my legs.

His hands squeezing and at times searching just under the edges of my top, I begin to feel those once lost desiring feelings again. "You are driving me crazy."

"Am I?" He said with great satisfaction. "Do you think you can handle going a little further?" I nod and he releases his arm pushing down on me slowly, letting me feel him between the two pieces of thin fabric that separate us and causing me to gasp sharply. "Ava?"

"I'm fine," I said torn between extreme pleasure and intense fear.

"No, you're not," Sean moves away from me quickly.

Grabbing a hold of him, I try to bring him back. "Sean I am."

"Ava, if we go on much longer I am going to strip you naked and take you right here and I know you're not ready for that." He gives me a stern look to let me know he isn't arguing about it and lies back on his arms, his erection standing proudly. The presence is hard to ignore and my curious wandering eyes find it even harder to overlook. Sean begins laughing, "Are you checking me out?"

I look back at him in shock. "No!"

Mocking my shocked expression, "yes you are," he said sitting up next to me so I cannot ignore his cocky attitude. "I guess it's only fair since I have been doing the same to you."

"You have?" He nods with a smile, dragging me in front of him and leaning me back against his chest.

He sighs resting against me. "See this is much better. By the way, where did you get this bikini?"

"It's Brianna's, it is a bit too small. It's bad huh?"

"Bad? No. It is ummm … something though, not much of something but certainly something I'm glad I got to see."

"Well I didn't have much of a choice and I assumed I would be out here alone, not …"

"Not out here starting a riot?" He laughs softly in my ear.

"No, that was not my intent." I laugh, while being held securely and safely in his arms.

"How is it that I can hold you like this, if no other man can?"

"I think I know but I am not sure if I want to tell you," I said running my fingers between his. "It's embarrassing but especially after you accused me of being a groupie."

"I didn't mean that and I wouldn't think that now, so tell me … please."

"Well the night when you pulled me out of the way of those girls," I pause catching his eyes as they watch me closely. "That moment with you, something sparked in me and I don't know what it was exactly but it was such an incredibly, wonderful feeling, that I held onto it, hoping that I would see you again someday. I held onto it even tighter while he held me captive in that dark room."

"He kidnapped you?"

I nod nervously. "He stalked me until he got his chance to take me. I woke up in that dark room for nine days and all I had was that moment with you to hold onto, that … feeling … is what gave me the strength not to give up."

Sean clears his throat with a harsh struggle and leans his head against mine. "How did he … how … I don't know what I am trying to ask you. I don't want you to tell me more than you are comfortable doing but I can't help be curious."

"You want me to tell you everything?"

"It's none of my business."

Holding tight to his hands, "he first took notice of me when I was going to Columbia and when I got my first job he managed to get a job in security for my building. So, he saw me every day and I barely noticed him. I didn't even realize that he had worked at my school too until the trial. He followed me all the time, he knew where I lived, he knew who I went out with and when. When he could buy a place far enough out of the way, he thought he could convince me to move there with him so we could make a life together without interruption. But once he found out that I was moving away he became desperate and one night when he was following me, he offered me a ride home. It was raining horribly and it was late and I was already so upset after I broke up with my then boss that I wasn't thinking about anything other than getting home." My hands begin to tremble until Sean takes hold of them.

"You don't have to tell me anymore."

"I can't believe how stupid I was to get into his car, to trust someone I barely knew just because I saw him every day and knew where he worked."

"Most people would have done the same." Shaking my head, he whispers reassurances in my ear.

"He drugged me Sean." I feel the tenseness in his arms and without even realizing I continue releasing the pain from my shoulders and on to his. "I woke up tied to a bed in a pitch-black room and for a while he left me alone, mostly, he would bring me food and tell me how happy we were going to be together. Every day he would tell me that I was going to love him and appreciate what he was doing for me. I got so tired of hearing it that one day I got angry and threw my food at him and screamed at him that I would never love him, that I hated everything about him." Breathing in deeply, "and then he went crazy. Punching me and hitting me with his gun, all the while screaming at me until I was too weak to fight him anymore and that's when he decided he wanted more. He pushed me down, cut my clothes off me with a pocketknife. I screamed and screamed, begging him to stop but he had this perfect image in his head and thought we were having this beautiful time together. He held me in place while he …" Closing my eyes I grip Sean's hands and feel his lips against my head. "It happened again and again, or whenever he felt righted to do so." Sitting up and looking into his eyes, "I remember thinking of you and drifting as far away as I could in my thoughts until I heard his pocketknife drop out of his pocket, he didn't hear it. He left me in the dark all the time so whenever he would come in, the light behind him would blind me. After so many days, I had become aware of the sounds around me. As soon as he left me, I searched through the dark for it and when I found it, I cut myself free. I am not sure how many times I cut myself until I found a 2x4, four of them holding up my tiny bed in the frame. I took one and waited by the door for hours and hours. When he finally came in the door, he opened it shielding me from the direct light and for one brief second, I could see him - perfectly. Once he fell, I ran - blind. It had to be the brightest morning ever. I stumbled around finding a coat and when I put it on to cover myself I found his keys and cell phone within the pockets. I did the best I could to feel the keypad and figure out the numbers, dialing carefully 911 only problem was I didn't have any clue where he had taken me. Spencer was screaming and banging trying to knock that door down so I felt my way outside and to his car. Somehow, I drove trying to recognize what felt like a road and what didn't, managing to get down the road far enough that a cop happened to see me. He thought I was drunk."

Turning around I position myself around him forcing him to look at me. "I have thought of you and that feeling every day since. Only I never imagined you being an actor, only the man that rescued me one night and made me feel wonderful in only a few brief minutes."

"Maybe if I had asked you out or … I don't know, if I had done something, you would have been with me that night."

Shaking my head, I take his face into my hands and force him to look at me. "I was wrong to say that to you Sean. It wouldn't have mattered what you would have done, he would have found a way. He's too obsessed and crazy."

# *Chapter 12: Sean*

*I* would have stayed on that beach forever, holding her and kissing her tears away but the black clouds rushed up on us and gave us no choice but to return to the cabin. Luckily, we are able to push the dark memories and dark clouds away and enjoy the rest of our day by nearing the line of no return but still, never crossing it. It's not easy stopping myself but her appreciative smile fills me with enough pleasure.

The next morning the storm calms and Ava is ready to go for a run and apparently so am I since I'm not willing to let her go alone. No matter how calm the weather is now, the mess that's left from last night could still be hanging in the trees waiting to fall on her head. I follow behind her but for more than one reason, she is simply too enjoyable to watch. We run for some time until we disagree on what direction to take. Eventually I give in but after running off a clear trail into some wild growth, I ask her if she is ready to turn back, only to be ignored. "Ava! I think we are getting too far away from the main trail."

"But I haven't gotten the chance to explore like you have."

"There is nothing for you to explore this deep into the island, except trouble. You don't know what the damage is back in there and we are too far away for anyone to find us." I watch as she expresses a typical annoyance with me. "Did you just roll your eyes at me?"

"Sean, I want to see if I can find that waterfall Ashlen told me about. It's supposed to be real …"

"No Ava. No, we are not going any further. You're going to end up getting hurt, now come on let's go back."

"Don't tell me what to do. Go back if you want to but I'm continuing."

"Ava!" I watch her turn away from me and continue as if I never said a word. "Fine! Go. But I'm not going to follow you anymore, I don't care." She did not even hesitate, running off like I never said a damn word. Standing in place, I fight with myself until deciding to stomp my way back towards the cabin.

"SEAN!" Ava screamed and I cannot move fast enough, only to find her with a deceptive expression and no clear injury. "Why were you screaming?"

"To see if I could get you to come running for me. You must really like me, I have never seen anyone run so fast," she wiggled in place biting her proud smile.

Narrowing my eyes at her, I nod my head in acceptance and approach her slowly. "Okay that's it I'm taking you back, stripping you naked and kissing you all over." She steps back from me giggling and smacking my hands away from her. "You might as well accept it, you're coming with me ... now." I lunge forward throwing her over my shoulder.

Immediately she begins smacking me on the back and giggling hysterically, "Sean no, put me down!" Flying through the cabin door, I throw her on the bed and give her a look of determination. While still laughing she scoots away from me slowly. "Sean no, you stay over there."

"I don't think so," I said confidently before removing my shirt.

"No," she makes a move off the bed as I grab her by the waist and drag her back to me. I remove her shoes and pull her shirt off over her head. "Sean," she breathed.

Eyeing her breasts and her easily strippable bra, "one finger flick and these types fall off easily." I wickedly play with the edges of the snap. Looking deep into her smiling eyes I edge her tight pants partially down waiting to see if she will protest. She doesn't and I quickly toss them aside. Her eyes set on mine, are obviously curious to my next move ..., and so am I. We have never gotten this far before, we have talked about it exhaustively but never has so much clothing been removed from her body, by me anyway. "Baby I don't want to do anything you're not ready for." With a wary expression, she leans back and calls me to her with one finger. I take hold of her soft, wet lips and ease down between her legs. "I want you so bad Ava," I whispered into her mouth and take her hands into mine, kissing them each before jerking my pants off. Pushing down against her, I feel her so well that I have to gasp for breath while trying to remind myself to go slow. I cannot get enough of her delectable lips or her tender tongue. *I want her so fucking bad.* My hand wanders down to her thigh tracing the delicate edges of her panties over her ass and to the inside of her thigh, tugging gently, I force sharp gasps from her mouth. "It's okay, I'll move slower." She shakes her head and lets her hands slide down my back and under my boxers gripping me fully as she reaches for my lips passionately. *I am about to lose my mind here.* I reach down between us grazing her with my fingers and whimper a begging moan, "Ava … pleeease?" With heavy breaths, she looks at me with uncertainty. "Ava, I'm not going to go any further unless you say it is okay, I promise but pleeease."

"Can you give me a few more minutes?" She asked innocently.

*She's going to kill me.* Groaning, I smile affectionately, continuing with tender touches and soft kisses and controlled wandering hands until finally she holds my face still. "Now?" She nods and if I thought I was excited before, nothing compares to this moment. I feel for my bag under the bed, sifting through pockets for condoms and grabbing a hand full to her nervous surprise. "We don't have to use all of them … right now at least." Her instant smile relaxes both of us and brings us back into the moment. "You're so beautiful," I said, gently pressing my lips to hers. With permission I find it easy now to work slowly over her body and make my way to her bra straps, sliding them seductively off her shoulders with my mouth. Suddenly with a loud thump, someone jumps onto our porch and begins knocking on the door. "What cock blocking prick is that?" I mumbled. Ignoring the nuisance, I move back to Ava but to my harsh disappointment, she pushes me away.

"Shouldn't we answer that?" She asked.

"Nooo!" I mouthed harshly.

The mother fucking knocking asshole persists as I silently argue with Ava. "Hello! Sean - Ava?" Demerae called out. "Okay. You can ignore me but I was told to stay here until I talk to you both."

Persuading Ava with my patented mood enticing kisses I wonder if I should get up or make the poor bastard wait until after I get what I want. I briefly consider both and decide I do not care about his time. However, Ava's eyes say she has decided differently.

"Sean, I think we should answer the door."

"He can wait until after."

"After what? I'm not going to have sex with you while he stands out there waiting."

I plead and whimper like a lost puppy to her but there is no give. "Fine!" Gritting my teeth and mumbling harshly I find my pants and put them on carefully over my now clearly obscene cock, glancing at her as she snickers at me behind her hands. "I'm so glad you find my pain amusing." I grumble my way towards the door.

"Oh Sean, I don't want you to be in pain. Answer the door and find out what he wants and then you can come back to me." She smiles seductively sneaking under the sheet and sliding her bra off and letting it fall to the floor as the thin sheet floats down to her bare breasts highlighting them for me. Instinctively I move back towards her. "No Sean. The door first or you get nothing."

"Door. I will get the door," I mumbled with a focusing grunt.

"Get the door Sean." Sighing I opened the door to Demerae's goofy grin.

"Bad time?" He chuckles.

"Is there something you need?" I asked impatiently.

"Yes actually," he smiles wide at my obvious disgust. "Okay, well I was told to give you this information come hell or high water, so here I am. You don't mess with my mother you know." I wave him on to continue, while glancing back at Ava lounging seductively under the sheet.

"HELLO Sean," Demerae said pulling me out of my wet dream.

"WHAT!" I yelled concealing part of my body with the door.

"I said! The weather is suppose to clear up tonight and my mother has decided to have a barbeque."

"Great, thanks," I said shutting the door.

Demerae sticking his foot in the threshold, "no! Sean. I am supposed to let you know what time to be there and a few other details that I have to tell Ava," he said with his Cheshire grin. *Asshole he knows what he is interrupting.*

Ava jumps out of bed and gets dressed and I glare at his snickering figure as she comes around the corner, ducking under my arm to greet him." Hi Demerae."

He looks at me with that same stupid grin. "Ava, you are here. I thought Sean was alone, he seems so excited, I mean eager to get back to what I assumed was some self-reflection time."

"That's hilarious asshole." I grumbled under my breath.

Ava elbows me and Demerae nearly chokes holding back his laughter. "Okay so here it is? I am supposed to let you know to be there at 6:30 and that …" He pauses looking at me while backing away. *That can't be a good sign.* "Well Ava is suppose to come with me. And here is the letter my Mom wrote to explain to her why." He rambles the last part quickly as he practically throws the letter at Ava to stay clear of me.

Ava walks back inside to read the note. "Do you understand what you are doing to me right now?" I whisper to Demerae.

"I feel for you, I really do but my mother is scarier than anything you can do to me."

"Are you sure?"

Ava steps underneath my arm again, "okay Demerae, give me a second and I will be right with you.

"What?" I asked darting my eyes between them.

"Ashlen wants my help setting up, so I need to go now. I will see you later." Ava explained putting her hand against my chest and ducking back into the cabin.

"What?" I said watching her gather items to take with her. Turning towards Demerae, "what?"

He shrugs. "I don't know, honestly, I don't know."

*Great*, I lean into the doorframe and try to relax before I slam the door shut and lock her in with me. "Hold on one second." I said to Demerae and shut the door. I turn inside watching Ava gather a bag full of stuff. "What are you doing, moving? If you don't want to have sex just say so but don't leave."

She turns to me with a surprised smile, confusing me even more. "I'm not leaving to keep from having sex with you. Why would you think that?"

"Because you're packing and leaving."

"I'm only taking a few things to get ready with tonight. I will come back here with you tonight, I promise," she rolls up onto her toes kissing me sweetly on the lips.

"Ava, do you have to go? Can't you go with me later?"

"I promised her Sean, I have to go. She wants to show me some recipes and," she shrugs her shoulders. "It's a girl thing, you wouldn't understand. I'm sorry but I'm glad you want me to stay with you and after all that time you spent calling everyone you know trying to get away from me," she laughs.

Raising my eyebrows I take a step back from her, "how do you know that?"

"It's a small island Sean, people talk and especially when they find us the most interesting thing to happen here in awhile."

"Ava, I wasn't trying to get away from you." I said as she folds her arms. "Well I didn't call everyone I know, just my brother, who I could never get a hold of and maybe my mother too. Who decided it was best and safer if I stay here. Like that was a surprise. It was frustrating and I only did that right after we crashed here and after I found out I was going to have to share a one-bed cabin with you. Tell me you wouldn't have freaked out too?"

"You're right I would have, I did. But I have to go now, I promise I will see you tonight. I will save you a dance this time if you want." She kisses me with an encouraging smile and takes me by the hand walking with me back to the door.

"Okay Demerae, let's go I have what I need." I pout heavily earning only a smirk and a giggling kiss. "I will see you later?"

"Sure," I said defeated.

"It's a lot of fun Sean, lots of great food, music, and dancing and …" He trailed off once he notices my deep disinterest.

Standing in the doorway, I watch Demerae drive off with my girl. *Interesting, now what?*

CR&CO

*I* waited about as long as I can possibly stand it before making my way to the party, arriving early enough to help Khenan hang white Christmas lights around the perimeter of a dance floor and tables. When we finish the decorations the mouthwatering aroma in the air begins making my stomach growl. As I sniff the air, I see Ashlen making her way to the food tables with trays of even more food. "Do you want some help with that?" I asked searching for others inside the house.

"No thank you, I think we have everything handled." Ashlen said with a smile before darting back into the house. *Okay, nice talking to you too.*

Gavin comes hobbling in on his crutches to take a seat near me at one of the many tables. "I heard you had some excitement the other day," Gavin laughed.

"Oh right. So where is my friend?"

"Khenan put him in their jail here until they can transport him back to the main island. Dumbass took a swing at him – broke his hand, of course. Come to find out he has some warrants out for his arrest. Three girls came forward and said he forced himself on them."

"I'm shocked." I said shaking my head.

"I hate what had to happen to get him out of here but I can't tell you how happy I am to have the cabin to myself," Gavin sighs with an expressive smile.

"Did I hear my name?" Khenan said taking a chair next to me.

"Khenan, how are you?" Gavin asked.

"I'm good. My women are acting a little weird though. It always scares me when they are up to something."

"How do you know they are up to something?" I asked humored by his fidgeting stress.

"Trust me, you always know. Be prepared, I don't know what it is but be prepared"

"That bad huh?" I laughed.

"Scary bad." He shakes his head looking back at the house as if to stare right through the walls at them. "You boys are in for a real treat though, my wife has put together some incredible food and it looks as though it's ready so let's get started no telling when the girls will be out here." Like a ravenous bear, Khenan rushes towards the food tables.

We gather back around the table with plates full of a food and digging in with no audible words. *The food is so good, I don't know if there is anything that could tear me away from this.*

"Wow is that Ava?" Demerae asked.

I follow his gaze seeing Ashlen walking over with Ava close behind, wearing a deep blue dress that has everyone taking notice. I gaze admiringly, from the heels at the end of her gorgeous legs to the soft red waves floating around her beautiful bright smiling face, her seductive approach erases my every thought. I stand up as everyone greets her and then with muffled amusement, watch me stare at her in awe. *Not the best time to feel like an idiot Sean ... speak.* She sits her plate at the seat next to mine, waiting as I pull out her seat for her. Smiling at me, she causes the most moronic grin to come across my face. I try to eat but find myself catching glimpses, memorizing every part of her while trying not to be noticed doing so. When a breeze comes blowing through, her hair *whisps* near my face and seduces me all over again.

Khenan leans over to me. "I think whatever they have been planning today ... is about you." He raised his eyebrows at me, nodding in Ava's direction. I shake my head but he nods assuredly.

"So Sean, what do you think of Ava's dress? She was afraid it wasn't a good color for her but I think it's perfect with her eyes." Ashlen asked bringing me out of my cloud of confusion.

I look up at Ashlen and follow her eyes to Ava and that blue dress.

"It goes nicely with her eyes right?" She pushed.

I pull myself together enough to look up into her eyes, those gorgeous deep blue sapphire eyes are even deeper tonight. "It's perfect." I managed to say watching her smile wonderfully at me.

"Thank you," she said in that sweet southern voice of hers.

"You're welcome." I gush.

Demerae makes his way to the DJ stand and begins playing music as people are finishing their meals.

"Hey Sean," Alizabeth said approaching in his finest suit.

"Hi Al, what are you up to?" I asked finding amusement in his sophisticated attire for the night.

"Well I thought I would come over and ask this beautiful lady to dance," he said holding out his hand to Ava.

She smiles sweetly at him, "I would love to"

Al acting a complete gentleman escorts her to the floor and takes her hand respectively. Spinning her and dancing so politely that more people than myself find it humorous. Ava however, is enjoying every second, laughing with him and respecting him right back with every effort to move along with him. As more people begin to dance the more I have to move to be able to see her. Ava spins around laughing and smiling at me, making me as anxious as a schoolboy waiting for his turn.

Ashlen nudges my arm with disapproving eyes, "are you going to stand there all night like a fool or are you going to go grab that girl and dance with her?" I laugh at her motherly encouragement.

"Al would it be alright if I cut in?" I ask winking at her.

"Sure, she's all yours."

Taking her hand, I slide my other across her body to the small of her back, pulling her in close I bury my face into her soft curls, inhaling her enchanting scent. With her hand on my chest and her head on my shoulder, we move gracefully together. I spin her out watching her twirl and laugh, making me crave her all over again and forcing me to bring her back to me even closer than before. As the night continues, the rest of the world disappears while my heart and mind spin out of control. I stylishly dip her back, holding her close and trailing my lips up her neck to her ear, "I can't take my eyes off you. You look so beautiful tonight." Looking up at me through her long lashes, she does not even try to tame her perfect smile this time.

"Thank you, this is the best night I have ever had Sean."

"The night isn't over yet, sweetheart," I smile as Khenan huffs at the stragglers in his yard.

"Okay people party is over, time to go, be safe and see you tomorrow." Khenan yelled.

"I guess we should go," I said taking her hand and leading her back to our cabin.

# *Chapter 13: Ava*

*H*is hand strong and warm, gently folds around mine while my mind races with thoughts and desires. *I am not sure if I should jump him and rip his clothes off his hard body or strip naked and wait for him or offer to play cards with him until we get tired and go to bed.* It is amazing how many thoughts can pass through your head in such a short walk, none prepare me for when the cabin appears in the distance. The moonlight shines on the tiny, wooden cabin, like a blazing spotlight on my awaiting decision. Sean glances over at me with a tender smile, twirling circles on my hand with his thumb and for a brief moment, I forget what I was worried about but only for a moment. As soon as we step into the cabin, I feel lost and take in the room as if I have never seen it before. Sean shuts the cabin door behind me and I can feel his eyes on my back. "So … are you tired? Do you want to go to bed or get something to eat or …" I ramble on with his hands warming my body and his breath heating up my neck.

"Are you nervous?" I shake my head but his once brilliant eyes begin withering with each passing second that I remain silent.

"Sean I … I."

His exhausted sigh ends with an even weaker smile and a gentle kiss on my forehead. "Don't worry about it," his hands fall from my body as he turns away.

Silent fears begin charging their way into my brain. "No." I murmured gazing up at his waiting eyes. "No Sean. I don't want you to go."

"I'm not going anywhere sweetheart."

"I mean I don't want you to stop touching me."

Taking my face into his hands, "Ava what do you want me to do? Tell me and I will do it. I'll do whatever you want me to." His warm lips press tenderly against my cheek, "but I can't read your mind Ava." His hands deepen into my hair, "you have to tell me what you need."

I feel the words waiting to come out as my fears battle with each other until I see his loving green eyes reaching for me, "I want you. I want what you want Sean. Now, I'm ready."

"Are you sure?"

"Yes," I nod stepping into him and drawing in his lips. "Please." With one hand sliding up my thigh he lifts me up against the wall pushing his body up against mine, his tongue tasting my lips until I welcome him into my mouth. Everything in my body is heating up from his supporting hands, wet lips and his rapidly growing hard excitement between my legs. Sean pauses removing his shirt and allowing me to set him back from me while I take the initiative and undo the tie around my neck for him. Slipping my dress casually down to the floor, becoming more excited as I watch him lick his lips and take in my body fully. Finding his way back to me, he does not wait another second to release my bra. I manage a single breath before his mouth is on my breasts, sucking, palming, and groaning his respects for them while he swirls his tongue around each nipple with emphasis. With my back pressed hard against the wall and my hands cradling his head to my breasts he slowly releases my hold making his way down to his knees. He tongues my diamond with a smile as his fingers trail underneath the edges of my panties, sweeping in soft motions and sending waves of intense tingling sensations to my core. The intensity increases when his mouth moves lower, tonguing the laced boundaries and looking up at me with wanting eyes. Our eyes stay locked as he slides my remaining garment down my legs, setting my thighs on fire. With full palms, he continues back up my body with his mouth and tongue leading the way - setting my whole body a blaze.

"You are so beautiful, Ava," he says as he memorizes every part of me with his slow wandering hands. I stand frozen watching him admire me and kiss me tenderly. "Do you still want to do this?" I respond eagerly earning a soft kiss. He caresses my face gently with the back of his fingers and breathes heavily against my skin. Taking a step back from me and watching me closely he takes hold of his pants, undoing his belt, and sliding it out of the loops with a *whish*. He continues to watch me as I bite my lip, holding back my heaving breaths of anticipation while he slowly undoes his pants, the button, the zipper, each moving with a sound that sends speeding vibrations up my legs.

His sudden hesitation causes me to look up at him with frustration, "don't stop."

"You do it then," he says holding his hands out to his side waiting for me. Eyeing his bulging pants, I close my eyes and take hold of him. Forcing my hands down in between his underwear and his soft torrid skin I feel the heat through my palms. "I want you," he whispers against my skin, encouraging my hands to glide down further into the heat. Watching his throbbing bulge extend closer and closer to my hands, I guide his clothes over it, down his legs, and off him completely. Encouraging me with his stance around me, I begin wandering over his body, taking hold and feeling his wanting groans rippling through his every muscle. "Come here," he says picking me up easily into his arms and carrying me to bed, his lips taking in mine while he positions me to his needs and fueling my body with full and respectful hands. The weight of his body heavy on mine and his throbbing presence between my legs, all of which sends faint signals of distress until he breathes my name freeing me of my fear of him for good. He allows me to freely comfort him, tracing his muscles with my fingers and hands, following the glistening beads that flow down his back. Feeling every part of him fully against me, I pull my legs up around his waist, "do you want me Ava?"

"Yes." I breathe into his awaiting smile, feeling the hardness work its way inside me until filling me up tight and relieving me of a long awaited exhale.

"Are you okay?"

Opening my eyes, I smile exuberantly at him, "oh yes, I'm better than okay." Reassuring him with passionate kisses, he resumes. Feeling up his arms, down his back and taking hold of his tight roundness with both hands riding its movements while pleasure filled moans escape my mouth with every thrust and every ear-filled whisper of admiration. While curling around each other, I take the time to memorize the feeling, this moment with him. For the first time, I feel empowered again and I sit up on him, taking him in deeper, enjoying the satisfactory groans from his sexy mouth. He calls out to me against my breasts, caresses my lips, strokes my hair, and thrusts up into me with delightful respect. Looking deep into his eyes, searching and feeling what I had thought had been lost, desiring what I thought never to be. The pleasuring sensations increase with every movement he makes and every desire he requests from me. A single thrust and my body quivers and my head falls back. I stare blissfully up at the ceiling fan that rotates its dizzying circles. The room continues to heat up and my body glistens in the moonlight as he holds me up and helps me enjoy every inch of him. Slowly he brings me back down on the bed pulling my legs up a little further around him. My eyes flutter and my legs tighten while steady orgasmic waves turn to cyclones of concentrated pleasure. I grip him with moans and desires of my own and call out his name in stunning ecstasy. Groaning against my lips he watches as my head falls back and my eyes close and my body quivers in pleasure from head to toe, going limp with a breathless smile.

Sean taking complete control grips me closer, moving his body with purpose, groaning forcefully and sending constant vibrating sensations between us. When his body finally stills and his moans turn to soft whispers he cradles me to his chest. "Ava that was amazing," he exhales, kissing me with an exhausted smile.

"Really?" I smile at him with an excitement that I can barely contain.

He laughs nudging his lips against mine. "Yes sweetheart. You're amazing."

Gripping his neck and holding his lips to mine, "you're not bad either."

"Not bad? Baby I am fucking unbelievable," he says causing me to laugh as he persists about his talents. "I love to hear you laugh. You're even more beautiful when you smile." I try to fight my smile but he will not let me with his tender lips and encouraging whispers. "Alright beautiful I will be right back." I nod watching him walk away, gazing over him from head to toe and back again. My body still tingling wants him again. Shaking off my daydreams, I gingerly make my way out of bed and find some comfortable clothes to wear to bed, only changing my mind twice as I make sure to find something that will not turn him off completely. "What the hell are you doing?" He asked taking hold of my waist.

"What? I was going to get cleaned up for bed," I shrug holding out my hands in confusion.

Shaking his head at me, he tugs at the ends of my simple but form fitting t-shirt. "This. What are you doing with clothes on?"

"I thought we were going to bed. Why do you want to do it again?" I asked feeling the anticipation beginning to creep up from my toes.

Laughing at me, he nudges my chin with a touch of his finger. "Ava, it's only been a few minutes, give me at least a few more, baby. And yes, we are going to bed but you are not wearing clothes to sleep with me tonight. I have seen it all and there is no sense hiding it from me now."

Rolling up onto my toes and steadying myself against his chest I look up into his eyes, "but Sean I always wear clothes to bed, it's not that I am hiding from you … baby … that's just what I do." I kiss him lightly on his lips and roll happily back down off my toes.

"What was with the cute toe stand? I hope that wasn't supposed to intimidate me because it was way too cute," he said wrapping his arm around me and taking hold of my butt fully in his hand. "Now I expect you naked and in bed with me in five minutes." Abruptly he pulls me in close and tastes my lips. "Got it?" He lets go of me, smacks me on the butt and laughs at my shocked gasp. "You better not have anything on when you get in this bed or I am going to rip it off you. " He yelled out to me as he cleans up our bed.

I simply do not have it in me to obey on command. At first I was not sure what I was going to do, but then I remember something I had found during my scavenge earlier through the cabin. I wait until his huffs become more directed and impatient before meandering out in front of him with the largest, puffiest and certainly the ugliest green coat I have ever seen. With a knowing smile, I fight my laughter at his expected exasperated expression.

"What do you think?" I said twisting and turning to give him a full view.

His stern concentrating eyes take in more than an eyeful before narrowing at me. "Where in the hell did you get that?"

"I found it when I was being nosy the other day, it must be one of the scientists that stay here. I think they come down from Michigan in the winter. Cool huh?" I nod with a slight smirk.

"It's hideous."

"Really, I rather like it. I think I am going to wear it to bed."

"No Ava. Don't you get into this bed with that thing on. I'm warning you," he said watching me walk slowly towards the bed, pull back the covers, and glance at his stiff awaiting posture. "Don't you do it, I'm not playing with you." I ease my way into the bed exaggerating my movements, lifting my foot and then touching the bed lightly, up again and I let it hover over the ruffled sheet while his hidden expression gives him away. He forces his laugh in the opposite direction and I take the opportunity to jump in laughing aloud, as he quickly takes hold of me and tugs at the zipper of my coat. "This coat is so big I can barely find you in it." He laughs struggling with the zipper and fighting my hands to get control. "This damn thing won't move!" He yelled laughing harder at the busted zipper.

"Good, I am keeping it on all-night!"

"The hell you are!" He said taking his hands off the zipper and feeling underneath the coat. "I will pull you out of this thing if I have too." He tickles me to get me to release my grip until he is able to pull the coat right over my head. "Finally!" He leans down kissing my stomach and dragging his smiling face up slowly between my breasts to my awaiting lips. "Now this is much better."

Huffing I surrender into his arms, "fine, you win."

"That's right I win and you should remember that."

◌₃₮◌

*T*he sun rises bright and beaming through the cabin's windows making it too tempting to pass up. Carefully I maneuver out from under his arm leaving him naked and safely tucked in bed with a kiss before my early morning run. My body feels so renewed and so alive this morning that I think I could run to Atlanta from here without even touching the water along the way. However, my early excitement soon gives way to fear and my joyful run turns into an investigation of the airfield, confirming my suspicions. The airfield reconstruction has already begun and is close to being finished from the sight of it.

"They're almost done," I turn to see Ashlen smiling a concerned smile.

"Maybe another storm will come or maybe we can call Sean's mother and have her send another plane to crash," I cringe with a sarcastic laugh.

"You have to go back to your lives sooner or later." Ashlen sighs at my tense expression. "You are going to continue seeing each other after you leave?"

"We discussed it, he wants me to move to Los Angeles but I can't leave my firm and with his filming schedule he wouldn't have time to see me much anyway. Not to mention, I can't afford to live out there alone and he nearly had a panic attack when I asked about living with him. Not that I expected him to act any different, I am not ready for that either. I will be fine as long as I can talk to him and know that I am going to see him again at some point."

"If you're so fine, then why don't you look it?" Ashlen asks knowing my fear before she even asks. My confessions to her the other day helped me but I can't imagine she truly understands.

"Nerves I guess. Sean brought up how to act in front of the media last night and for some reason it never occurred to me who he is until that moment. The last time I dealt with the news media was during Spencer's trial and they were relentless. Everything he did to me, they only made worse by reminding me of it whenever they could get the chance. They are the reason I had to hide in the first place, they needed a story, so whenever he asked they gave him my whereabouts. I was afraid to leave my house, afraid to answer the phone and now even though I am still hiding from him, I have somewhat of a life. I don't think I could ever go through all that again."

"But this time it's not because of something horrible that has happened to you but because of something wonderful, it's because of Sean. Is he not worth it?"

"He is wonderful, I would do anything for him including go back to therapy to help me deal with these crazy celebrity reporters," I smile feeling her reassuring hug.

"Okay let's get back to enjoying this beautiful weather." Ashlen said as we turn around only to see him leaning against a tree, watching us. "Well good morning, Sean."

"Good morning. Do you mind if I talk to Ava alone for a few minutes?" He said holding his solemn gaze on me. Ashlen agrees leaving me alone with him and the sudden awkwardness between us.

"What's wrong? Why are you looking at me like that?"

"I heard your conversation with Ashlen, not purposely, I was looking for you, and then I overheard what you said."

"I didn't say anything that would cause you to be upset with me."

"I'm not upset with you. I am concerned about you and saying you are going to go to therapy just to date me? The media scares you that much? Ava do you even understand what you're getting into with me?" Nodding I reach for his hand and seek comfort in his arms. "What are you doing?" He sighs, "Ava I care about you so much, I don't want to see you get hurt."

"I'm not going to get hurt."

"I don't know what to do, a few minutes ago I could barely touch the ground I was so happy and now I ... I don't know."

"You don't know what?" I grip his hands feeling my heart pound, waiting for the ground to fall out from under me.

"You see the runway. I came out here after I got a message from my brother, telling me my flight plans for tomorrow."

"What about me and ... and Gavin ..."

"There's a boat coming to take you to the main island so you can catch a flight home." Sean holds my face towards his and with a soft smile, he waits for me to look at him. "Ava my time with you here has been amazing."

"What are you doing?" He stands silently and I jerk my hands away from him. "I thought. I thought you liked me."

"I do! I think you're the most incredible woman I have ever met."

"Then why are you saying good-bye?"

"Ava ... I'm not saying good-bye. I'm going to let you make the decision. If you want to see me after this place, then we will." I watch his eyes turn serious as he holds me in place. "But being with me Ava isn't going to be easy for you, with your past and the reporters following my every move. They will eat up your story in a heartbeat and next thing you know you will have to relive it all over again. Every time they see you with me, it will come up. I did not even consider it until I overheard your conversation with Ashlen. He doesn't know where you are but he will, as soon as you step off this island by my side."

"No Sean, they won't be able to find me. I have made sure of it and you can make sure they ..."

"Baby you can't possibly believe that I can control what they report or when they follow me or don't. I'm struggling with this like you don't know Ava but I can't see it working so you don't end up suffering."

"We don't have to let anyone know."

"How Ava? How in the world can we possibly?"

"They don't know you're here with me now."

"So we are going to run and hide every time we want to be together. Is that what you want? You want me to sneak you in through back doors and hallways and never let you outside until after I'm able to leave?" I nod fighting my tears. "No you don't Ava! What kind of life is that? You can have so much better with someone who can take care of you daily and be there for you without all the extra eyes judging your every move." I pull away, hiding my eyes as he reaches for me and not allowing me to push him away this time. "Please don't cry."

"I care about you so much, please don't push me away."

"Damn it! Ava!" He screamed startling me. "This is why I didn't want to get involved with you in the first place." Stunned by his sudden anger I stop crying." Ava, no I mean … Fuck! I don't know what I mean." He paces away from me fisting his hair. "I want you to be happy and safe and." Swallowing hard, I watch as he paces back to me and takes me in his arms once again. "Baby you know no matter how hard we try you're going to end up hurt. That crazy fuck is going to end up finding you and all because you're with me and because the relentless photographers and reporters who want nothing more than the next big story." Sean leans down and kisses me on the head. "I have loved every second I have spent with you, even when you hated me. I want nothing more than to continue being together after this place but no matter how much we both want it to work, all I can think is that I am going to end up hurting you even more." He said inhaling deep and forcing a strong stance. "I won't do that Ava. I couldn't live with myself if I caused you that kind of pain?"

"But it wouldn't be because of you, not if it's my decision. And it is my decision and I know full well what I am getting myself into and I am willing to take the chance if you are?"

"It's an easy decision for me, my life doesn't change much at all."

"Well there you go we both made our decisions and we're not going to say good-bye. We keep casual and quiet and then maybe I can come see you or …"

Sean pulls me tight into his chest, "You don't know how many times I have thought about you coming to see me. Being able to show you my house or even take you to my hideaway house and keep you in my bed for days." He sighs with a lingering *but* hanging in the air around us. "You're going to hate me."

"Is it better to say good-bye to me or to worry about me possibly hating you one day?"

"I don't know." His honesty catches me off guard and for the first time I feel his pain.

"This is a new relationship for both of us, it's hard to say where it's going or if it's going anywhere, I understand that. But I think we owe it to each other to do our best to keep quiet and see where it goes at least. We can talk on the phone and maybe meet up at your hideaway house." I smile an encouraging smile at him, which he returns with a concerned one. "Or you could try and sneak away to see me, my house is under someone else's name. I have taken great care in making sure Spencer can never find me, if you can make it there I know no one could find you either." Holding him and kissing him, I try my best to reassure him. "Plus all my neighbors are senior citizens with bad hearing and bad eyesight and they have never heard of you or your stupid web site. So you could sit on my front porch all-day everyday Mr. Grant and they would simply think I am dating an out of work bum." I smile wide causing him to break his concern with a laugh. "Okay?" He nods reaching in to take my lips in with his.

We try to make the best of our day but no matter how hard we try the knowing sits heavy in the back of our minds. Sean tossed and turned all-night, I could feel his worry and it made me worry even more about him. And when the time came, I do my best to fight the tears, but as I watch him slowly making his way out the door, I force myself to ask, "Wait!" His sullen eyes turn to me as I take his hand. With a deep breath, "if you were me what decision would you have made?"

Before he answers I see it in his eyes and I drop his hand as he leans in pressing his lips to my forehead. "I would have said good-bye Ava … you should say good-bye to me." I push him away trembling. "It's not fair to you, my life, I chose it, but you choose to live secluded and away from the limelight. We couldn't be more opposite in the lives we lead."

"You don't even want to try, do you?"

"I don't think it's necessary, we already know it's not going to work."

"No we don't, you're just too big of a coward to even try," I smack his hands away from me managing to hold back the tears as the anger and the crushing beats of my heart fight each other for dominance. Turning away from him, "you're not worth my time. I will be better off without you in my life." Swallowing hard I fist my frustration and jerk away from his hands for the last time, "Go Sean!"

"I'm sorry Ava. You have to know how much I care about you." Pushing him out the door, I lock the door behind him and collapse to the floor, already feeling the regret.

# Chapter 14: Sean

*F*orcing my pace and the distance between us, all I can do is replay her words in my head. I do not understand what it is I am feeling but I curse everything that is carrying her away from me. I curse the island and the weather and anything else that caused me to meet her in the first place. *If she only knew the nightmares I had last night, watching her cry to me for help and never being able to do anything but watch her be tortured.*

As I sit impatiently waiting for my plane, Ashlen taps me on the shoulder embracing me with a sympathetic smile. "You know you can't do anything about your heart except follow it."

"She deserves better," I said fending off her obvious attack.

"You do too." Ashlen sits down next to me. "You know Sean, when you start letting your head dictate what you should do instead of your heart, you end up in a world of confusion."

"If everyone listened to their hearts then the whole world would be full of morons."

Ashlen laughs, "Not if they listened to what their heart was truly saying. The fools are those that force themselves to believe that their wants and desires are the same thing as what their heart needs."

"And how do you know that my heart needs her and it's not just me desiring her?"

"I suspect you have desired before, you know the difference." Huffing I shake my head at her absurdity. "Well if I'm wrong at least you will be able to go on with your life and not have to worry about her at all. If something happens to her, you will never have to know, it makes it a lot easier if you never know. You can pretend that she's perfectly happy and fine when in reality she may meet up with another Kevin, alone and no one to stop him this time."

'Ashlen! Please…"

"I'm sorry, I guess I should mind my own business. It's hard for me to believe how much had to happen for you two to find each other again and then to not even try to understand why … it's a shame." She sighs and hugs me good-bye.

Staring off into nowhere, I fight the restless feelings raging inside of me. *I know I have it. I have not looked at it since I have been here but it is always with me. Whatever it decides ...* Working my way into my bag I feel for the little leather pouch that has held my heart for some time. It's worn and faded but holding up strong. I admire it until I can work up enough courage to open it, letting the small broken locket fall into my hand. *If it's not hers then I am doing the right thing.* Staring at it, I inhale fully before turning the locket over to read the back and seeing the delicate etched letters scratched and worn but still easily legible, *L.K.* "Lillah Kelley," I whispered. I would have never imagined seeing her again. The girl that captured me from the moment I looked into her eyes and now I am letting that undeniably perfect feeling go out of fear. *I am lying to myself, I cannot go on not knowing where she is or if she is safe. At least if she's in my life I know. I should have ... I need ... her.* Standing up with the dizzying thoughts swirling in my head I finally give in and run.

My heart beats even faster as soon I see the cabin. Running up the stairs of the patio, I take hold of the doorknob with excitement. *Locked?* "Ava, open the door!" I yelled knocking and preparing to convince her to give me another chance, until I hear her crying. "I can hear you."

"I don't want to talk to you," she screamed.

I smile as I lay my forehead against the door. *Stubborn....* "Please Ava."

"No, I don't want to see you. Go home Sean."

"Ava damn it! Open the door I need to talk to you."

"Talk then!"

"I am not going to talk to you through this door. Open it!" Trying the window, I am left disappointed and even more frustrated.

"I am not opening that damn door Sean ... OR the window!"

*She is so fucking stubborn, she really needs to work on that. There has to be something I can use to pry this door open.* Taking notice of the beams above me, I make my plan. "Ava I am asking you, no I am pleading with you, please open this door or I am going to break it down."

"Sean! No! I am not opening the fucking door!" She screamed back.

"Alright then. Get away from the door!" Reaching up I grab the beam and kick the damn door in, busting the lock clear off. I walk in tall as she sits wide eye.

"What the hell were you thinking?" She yelled at me.

"I told you I would break the door down if you didn't open it." Her eyes red and strained hold the same pain I was feeling. *I want to kiss her so bad.* She gets up shoving me away from her before turning her back towards me. "Ignore me if you want but I have something to say to you, actually I have something for you, something I have been saving for a long time to give back to you." She continues to ignore me while I handle my little pouch. Taking out her locket and stretching my arm out over her shoulder, I adjust my hand in front of her face and open it to the let the locket gently fall in front of her. A sparkle forms against the gleaming metal causing her to take notice. Her gasps are broken as she takes hold of the locket and turns to me in shock. "I guess our first meeting did mean something to me too." Her eyes soften as she searches my eyes for more. "I can't let you go Ava, not again, not without trying." I said wiping away the remaining tears from her face, her beautiful blue eyes smiling right into mine. "I'm sorry sweetheart, I can't let you go." Her smile takes form fully as she rolls up on her toes meeting my lips with teasing softness and complete acceptance. I embrace her with every part of my body, feeling the same happiness I felt for the first time on that cold New York night so long ago.

ෆ෨ං

*A*fter I arrive home, I have a mix of happiness and pain. Happiness to finally be home and pain knowing she will not be here. I will sleep alone tonight for the first time in days and it feels strange.

"So I bet you're glad to be back home? Some vacation you ended up with." Ethan said with a sarcastic chuckle as if he had imagined the misery I must have gone through.

"I guess," I said staring out my living room window, watching the water crash against the rocks of my pool.

"I have your schedule here, you are set to …," I didn't here another word he said after that. It doesn't matter he's just going to tell me again the day before and again the morning of and again hour by hour right before until it gets down to the minutes prior. Ethan is wonderful at keeping my life straight but sometimes he is annoying as hell.

"Sean! Are you listening to a word I am saying?" Ethan sighs, exasperated with my obvious indifference.

"No, not really," I turn to face him confirming his accusation even more defiantly.

Ethan slaps his notebook down sitting back with a superior look on his face. "Okay, what the hell is going on with you? You have barely said a word since I picked you up. Is there something wrong? Do you need a break that bad? If so tell me and I will make sure you will be able to take a breather, I think I can free you up by December."

"I think that's a good idea."

"Really?" Ethan breaks away from his superior attitude and begins typing frantically on his laptop. "Okay where do you want to go on this breather? If I go ahead and start planning now I can have it all setup and planned for when you are ready to leave. Give me a few ideas of what you want and I will get some options together for you."

Ignoring me, he begins making notes. "Ethan you don't need to make any notes or whatever shit you do. I already have it figured out and planned."

"Hotel reservations and everything?"

"I don't need any."

"What?" He asked standing up with his arms folded, strolling warily closer to me and ready to talk me out of whatever I am planning. "What kind of place doesn't take reservations? Sean you did not buy another house did you? Because I really wish you would talk to me before you do those kinds of things. I still can't believe you bought that car, the death trap ..."

"Ethan! I did not buy anything and stop acting as if you have to baby me. I can take care of myself."

"Where are you going then Sean?"

*He is not going to believe this.* "I am going to Atlanta," I said looking back at his face to judge his reaction.

"Atlanta? Georgia?"

I laugh, "Yes, Ethan."

"I don't understand. That's not a place you usually go to relax and get away from everyone. In fact, they are almost as crowded as L.A. That's the worse place for you to go. You might as well stay here at home and save yourself the travel time."

"You might want to sit down," I said motioning to the sofas. Ethan uneasily sits while I sit across from him stretching out and rubbing my face. "I am going there to stay with someone." I pause searching for the right words and details. "Or rather, to be with someone and she lives in Atlanta so that's why I need to go there."

Watching him, I can tell exactly when things begin to click for him. "This is pretty sudden, considering you have been on a small populated, working island since I last saw you and I know you weren't thinking about this before you left, otherwise, you would have gone there in the first place. So I am wondering who in the world could you have possibly met on this island that would turn your whole demeanor and …," he said waving his hands at me. "And basically seem to have changed you completely." He pauses as he begins to laugh and relax into the sofa. "The architect? Right? The one Mom was so desperate for you to meet?"

"Yes." I reluctantly admit.

He gets up and strolls to the bar, chuckling under his breath. "So what are you going to tell Mom? She is going to be unbearable when she finds out she was right."

"You are going to have to help me with that one." He hands me a drink and sits back down across from me.

"I don't think so. You are on your own with that one little brother." He says cheerfully raising his glass to me with an annoying smile before drinking. "So?" He said motioning for me to continue.

"Soooo…? I furrowed my brows.

"Details Sean, I want to know details. I am your brother, I should get that much."

"What do you want to know?"

"Fuck Sean. Okay start with what she looks like. Don't give me that look. You don't have to give me private details just the highlights."

*Sighing.* "Okay," I sit back staring off into space, picturing her in my head and smiling. "Well she's a redhead for starters, long gorgeous soft red hair." I chuckle at the thoughts of me ever being with a redhead. Leaning deeper into my chair, "beautiful sapphire blue eyes, soft innocent face, kissable pouty lips, and an incredible body …" My smile becomes uncontrollably wide. "Long legs, great ass and perfect breasts and the cutest belly button, that I can't get enough of and so fucking smart it's painful but wonderful all at the same time and just as stubborn as beautiful." I take a drink with the goofiest smile on my face that I would not have realized if Ethan had not cleared his throat waking me up out of my fantasy. Ethan laughs at me again and I roll my eyes at his obvious enjoyment of the situation. "Don't make me get out of this chair asshole."

"I'm sorry but I have never seen you like this. You're a pile of mush, all soft and dreamy." Leaning back comfortably into my sofa, he continues to laugh. I tense, mumbling under my breath things I can do to him to get him to shut up. "I'm sorry, no more laughter I promise. So was it love at first sight? Did you run across the runway and twirl her in your arms and run every day in fields of flowers …." Within a second I am holding him down with a threat of pounding on him until he stops laughing. "Okay, okay!" He said still laughing, of course.

"You're a fucking prick. You know that right?" I said sitting back down.

"I know but I owe you. I seem to remember getting similar criticism from you, if you recall?

*I do remember and I guess he does owe me but I will never admit it to him.* I continue explaining how Ava was the girl in New York years ago but his eyes widen when I explain our living situation on the island.

"So you had sex the first night?" Ethan smiles wide at my narrowing eyes. "Oh come on get to the good part. I know you and there is no way in hell you spent that much time alone with that girl and didn't have sex repeatedly." Glaring holes through him, "you didn't? Bullshit! You described her body like you were up close and extremely personal."

"It's not what you think."

"I'm sure it isn't."

"It wasn't like that!" I yelled as he raises his hands up in defense. "Yes we had sex … eventually, and it was the best sex I have ever had in my life. There is something more though and I don't understand it right now but I'm going to try, we're going to try to figure it out but I don't want anyone to know about her." I sit up straight looking him in the eyes. "Ethan seriously no one. I don't want her to deal with the relentless bullshit she would have to go through, not yet at least, not until we know."

"I will take care of it."

"I need to get through these next few months, until I can see her again. I am going to have to get used to dating by phone for awhile. Which reminds me, do you know when you had her flight scheduled?"

He looks at his watch with a yawn, "ummm yea she should be back home within the next hour. You know I should have known as soon as you asked me to help her get home." He shakes his head at my admitting smile. "Well I need to get home myself. Thanks for the great story and I am happy for you." He paused smiling bastardly again. "I think you have everything you need for tomorrow. Call me if something comes up before I see you next."

"Ethan! I do need your help with something." I pause battling with myself. "I need you to check on someone for me." *I know I should not be asking him to do this but I have to.* "I need to find out about a man who was convicted for rape and kidnapping in New York." Ethan nods, knowing that without my even saying to keep it between us.

After saying goodbye to my brother and taking my bags upstairs to my room, I find the leather pouch and pull out her locket, pinning it to my bedside lamp. *I can't believe she let me keep it but it means more now than it ever did.*

# Chapter 15: Ava

*I* called Kyle from Miami to let him know I am on my way and promised to call when I landed. I, of course, did not once I was aware of the driver that awaited me thanks to Sean. The man gathered my bags and led me to a luxury car helping me in as he packs my bags away. He already knows exactly where to go, allowing me to sit back, relax, and drift back to my memories. Once I arrive home, the driver helps me out of the car and carries my bags to my door and avoiding my tip, again thanks to Sean. As soon as I open the door, two overzealous dogs and an anxious Kyle greet me.

"Oh my Gosh, I thought you would never come home! You didn't call and I thought for sure your plane crashed again!" Kyle rambling and panicked over me not being here. *He doesn't believe in himself enough.* Kyle is still worrying about all the things that could have gone wrong while I was away as he goes through the whole list again and again. I hug my puppies, matching their enthusiasm with a kiss on every nose and ear possible. "Oh you are both getting so big. I missed you so much." It feels awkward to be back here, in my own home. My house is not large but it is comfortable, an older house that I restored, the best part being a screened in patio containing my easel that I have yet to use. Out back is the converted in-law house, which holds my office and workspace. There is an extra bedroom on the second floor that Kyle or Anna stay in when necessary.

"So?" Kyle asked searching for some sort of answer to something.

"Sooo?" I shrugged.

"So did we get the project?" Kyle asked impatiently. "What, did you forget the entire reason you went out there in the first place?"

*Well he has that about right.* "Oh. Well, I think it's definitely in the bag." *More than you know.*

Kyle and Anna immediately broke into their customary victory dance and song. "We gettin paid … oh yea - shake it … shake it - dip it to the ground and … pose." They sang while dancing out of sync.

I laugh at the lunatics, "I hope clients never see you doing that."

"Okay, now tell us …"Anna looks over at Kyle as he nods at her in encouragement. "Did you get to meet him?"

"Meet who?"

"Who? Ava please … you know who," Anna persisted.

I breathe in deeply as they take notice and both curl up on the sofa opposite me intensely staring. "Yes, I met Sean."

"Sean? Oh, so you're on a first name basis with him already huh?" Anna asked with a giddy wiggle.

"Hold on! I have to get the wine and the popcorn," Kyle said hurrying out of the room and running back with a bottle of wine and glasses, hugging a big bowl of popcorn for us all to share.

"Okay continue. So his Mom introduced you or did you get to go to the set and meet him? Did you get to meet anyone else? Oh and did he remember you or did you even bring it up? Probably not best for you to do that, Ava," Kyle inquires excessively.

"DID you get to go to where he was living? OH his bedroom! Did you see his bedroom?" Anna asked wide-eyed and dreaming.

"Did he shake your hand or hug you?" Kyle asked.

"He wouldn't hug her Kyle," Anna scoffed.

"He might," Kyle said to Anna's disgusted expression. "Whatever. Wait, did you get to go to his house while he was swimming and see him with his shirt off?" Kyle edges closer to the sofa.

"Oh no, even better - while he was working out?" Anna nodded proudly.

"That's not better, then he's all sweaty and smelly rather than just being wet," Kyle said.

"I bet he looks incredible wet, especially his great abs," Anna gushed.

"I bet you they're airbrushed, they do that a lot now," Kyle said assuredly.

"No they don't!" Anna pouted.

"Yes they do, I read it … somewhere … but anymore you never know what they actually look like in real life. He could be only five feet tall, chubby, and balding," Kyle said sitting back and chomping on a mouthful of popcorn.

"Ava is that true? Tell him he is being ridiculous. Don't ruin this for me Kyle." Anna griped waving her finger at Kyle.

"Ruin it for you, honey, please. I wanted to go and meet him as much as you did."

"So then you admit he has great abs?" Anna asked.

"I admit nothing," Kyle cocks his head defiantly. "Until I see them in person, I will never admit anything."

Their random comments run together. I am not sure who said what or what I should even answer. I watch their banter like it is some kind of sport, waiting for the final take down so I can award the winner with an answer.

"Ava so ...?" Anna motioning with her hands to give it up.

"No, I didn't see where he lived and he's six - four, not five feet tall. Kyle you know that. And he isn't balding or chubby." I forgot myself for a second thinking about him and sigh. "And his abs are incredible and so are his eyes and his arms and his hands, oh his hands ... and his face and his lips are so ..."

"Wow Ava, he must be something. I haven't seen you like this since ... well since him," Kyle said.

"Yea Ava, it's nice to see you finally noticing men for a change."

"Thanks Anna but I have noticed men before."

"You have not."

"I have too!" I yelled.

"Who?" Kyle asked.

"I checked out that guy ..." *Ummm let's see ... crap.* "Oh! The guy at the restaurant."

"You mean the guy that sent you a drink when he saw you look at him? You nearly came out of your skin to get out of there and away from him." Kyle said as I shyly nod.

"I think our point has been made," Anna said folding her arms confidently.

"Don't worry sweetie, it's all about the baby steps. Maybe a little gawking at Sean Grant has done you some good and you can get busy with Justin," Kyle said dancing a provocative number with a smartass chuckle.

"Ava would you like for us to call Justin now? We would be happy to cover for you for one more day if you want to capitalize on your renewed sexual prowess." Anna smiles wide.

"Speak for yourself! We have been covering for her long enough. She can wait a few more days to screw Justin, besides I'm sure she needs something new and lacy to entice him."

"Entice Justin? She could wear a potato sack and say a word that sounds like sex and he would be all over her. Damn Kyle where have you been?" Anna laughs.

"I know you're right about that, that boy looks freaky too," Kyle grunted. "I like 'em freaky." I ignore his comment while the two laugh and joke among themselves. "So Ava did Sean remember you at all? I suppose not but you didn't embarrass us and remind him did you? Oh God, please tell me you did not do anything embarrassing. I know you haven't been attracted to anybody in awhile but you didn't drool on him or anything did you?" Kyle winks at me as Anna spits out her wine.

I narrow my eyes at both of them with a frustrated sigh. "NO. I did not do anything embarrassing. I think you guys should go home."

Kyle stops his annoying dancing and sits next to me. "Oh sweetie, I'm sorry I didn't mean to hurt your feelings. I'm sure you were respectable around him." He puts his arm around my shoulder jarring me a little. "So was he nice at least? Because if he wasn't I will be more than happy to kick his ass for you."

"He was very nice," I said accidentally looking into his eyes too long.

Kyle's eyebrows shoot up, "how nice was he?" I glance in his direction before returning to my boys and rubbing their ears. Kyle leans over waiting for me to look at him, after a short time he gives up and jerks my face to his looking me straight in the eyes. "Ava? No. You didn't?" Kyle releases me and begins waving his arms. "I can't believe it, of all people."

"It's not what you think Kyle."

"I'm sure it isn't. Well maybe he'll help get you over the hump …."

"Ha-ha. But it isn't …" I try to defend myself before Kyle puts his hand in my face.

"Ava please, I don't care what he said to you or how he did it but I promise you he has already moved on, probably the moment after."

"Wait! Did she have?" Kyle nods in Anna's direction. "Ava. Oh my God! You had sex with Sean Grant?"

"Yes I did and if you don't mind, it's supposed to be a secret."

"Of course it is!" Kyle exclaimed pouring himself another glass of wine.

"NO! I mean he is trying to protect me from the media and …" Kyle nods his head mockingly making me even angrier. "OH! You don't understand and if you would just listen to me for one second." Kyle stares at me while Anna bounces her interest between the two of us. "You know what - forget it. All that matters is that I know how he feels about me."

"How he feels about you? Honey he doesn't feel anything about you. He wanted to fuck you and you supplied him with the opportunity." I raise my eyes slowly up to him and his eyebrows shoot up again. Kyle slams his glass on the table, "Ava Kelly! How many times?"

Kyle's intense gaze burns my skin but Anna's wide-open mouth makes me giggle before Kyle's blazing gaze straightens me back up. "How many?" Anna asked with a sparkle in her eyes.

"I didn't exactly count. But I had a great time and he was wonderful."

"Well I hope so because that has to be the dumbest thing you have ever done."

"He didn't take advantage of me Kyle, he's not like that."

"Did you have sex with him more than three times?" I glimpse Anna's still curious expression. "More than five? Forget that ... what it look like?" My mouth drops open. "You know how big is it?" She motions her interest with her hands.

"Oh my God, Anna! What is wrong with you? Besides I am assuming she barely remembers since she must have been drunk as hell!" Kyle yells.

"Kyle why are you acting like this? You should be happy for me."

"Because I am the one that has been there through everything and now after all that - I find out you gave it up for some cheap experience with an actor that's never going to speak to you again."

For a brief moment, I worry that he might be right. "You don't know what you're talking about, you'll see." I barely finish my sentence when my cell rings, I pick it up smiling at Kyle wide. "Hi."

"Hello beautiful, I guess you made it home okay." Sean sensuous voice reassures me.

"I did, thank you for all the extra care in getting me here."

"You're welcome." A few seconds of silence and I hear him sigh deeply. "Wow, all those nights of non-stop talking and now we have nothing to say."

"I hope that's not true, we have a lot of time left to do nothing but, Mr. Grant."

"Well then I guess we are going to learn an awful lot about each other." My sigh is a little more pitiful. "Now what was that for?"

"No reason." I try to reassure him.

"Uh huh and I miss you too." I smile biting my lip, wishing I could hop the next flight to LA.

"Aaahhh there's that beautiful smile and stop biting your bottom lip."

"Well, you should stop fidgeting and tossing whatever it is in your hand up in the air or against whatever wall you don't care about." I said enjoying hearing him laugh aloud.

Before I can react, Kyle grabs my phone out of my hand and darts to the other side of the room.

"Hello, who is this? This is Kyle her best friend for your information." He pauses for a few seconds. "Yea right, I'm sure it is. Okay the joke is over, I am not playing the fool any longer. I know this is Justin and yes you and your girlfriend …" I shake my head at Kyle vehemently as I struggle to get my phone from him. "Like I said you two had me fooled for a little while but the joke is over so you can stop now." He pauses with a confident look that slowly dissipates. "Huh … oh … I am so sorry." He said handing me my phone.

I take my phone back with a growl, "are you still there?"

"I am."

"Are you mad?"

"I thought you said that Justin is only a friend?"

"He is. He didn't mean girlfriend like that." I growl again with a vicious glare in Kyle's direction. "I promise he didn't mean it like that. There is nothing between Justin and me. I promise Sean."

"Maybe I should call you back after your company leaves?"

"That may be a good idea, I'm sure they will be leaving soon." I whisper my good-bye to Sean and promise to be alone in an hour. After hanging up I smile proudly at my silent onlookers. Kyle and Anna quickly get some more wine and change out the diet popcorn for the situations more suitable delight - chocolate chip cookies, as they listen to me tell the story in detail or at least most of the details. Anna's wide eyes stay in constant awe while Kyle eases some but his concern still shows along the edges of his tense jaw. At the end, they both agree and understand the need for secrecy and even agree to help in any way they can. Once they leave, I quickly prepare for bed, making sure the phone is nearby and begin mindlessly flipping through channels until the phone rings.

"Hello?" I asked foolishly.

"Are you in bed?" The deep seductive voice asks.

I smile sinking into my soft bed. "Yes, why?"

"What are you wearing?"

"A tank top and some simple shorts, nothing interesting."

"Wrong answer."

"Wrong answer?"

"I told you Ava, no more clothes in bed. Don't make me come over there and take them off you." I can hear his smile through the phone as I tug at the seams of my clothes, missing him already.

 C3&O

*I*t has only been a couple of weeks but Sean calls every night and I make sure to be there and ready every time. When I sit back to think about it, I cannot believe that I have become that girl! The girl who waits by the phone, the girl who thinks about nothing else other than the phone call she might get at the end of the night. I would be lying to myself if I had not thought at some point the calls would stop. Some part of me waits for that day. I am not sure why it matters, there isn't anything I can do about it. Despite my worries, I still wake up every morning and the sun is brighter, the news media seems positive and even the traffic seems lighter. My focus is completely on him.

"Ava? Earth to Ava? Can you hear me?" Kyle persisted.

"What? What do you want?" I asked shaking off my daydream.

"We have a meeting in a couple of hours are you even close to ready?"

"Yes, I have everything laid out and prepared," I lied.

"Okay but we have to leave here in an hour. *You* know how bad traffic is in midtown at this time."

"I do and I … *We* will be fine." I look up at him as he glares at me with doubtful eyes. "I promise." I insisted even though I am not sure.

We arrived at the meeting on time but I winged it from start to finish. The client invited us out for dinner after, leading me to believe I did not do too badly.

"Unbelievable!" Kyle yelled. "That was not your best presentation and somehow this guy still wants to talk to us more?"

I catch a glimpse of his suggestive glare. "Why are you looking at me like that?"

"Because he stared at you the whole time. I'm not sure he heard a damn word you were saying and good thing because you didn't say shit worth hearing!"

I huff rolling my eyes, "what do you want me to do Kyle? There is nothing I can do about that."

"I would like for you to get your head back on straight so when *that* happens, like it always does, I can still say it doesn't matter because she is the best, we are the best." I try to speak but am quickly interrupted, "Ava your head hasn't been into it since you've been back. I need you here. I know you have this incredible boyfriend now and I am happy for you but I need you here." I begin to brood knowing he is right. "Honey I am happy for you, I am, but I need you too."

"I'm sorry, I promise a lot more focus and a lot more sleep." *Sighing.* "If I could only find a way to get off the phone with him and feel like I gave him something to hold on to him with, then I'm sure I could."

"What do you mean?"

"Well I feel like he is going to get tired of me, only talking on the phone all the time. I can hear in his voice how much stress he is under. There are so many reasons for him to find someone else and release all his stress and frustration. I am so afraid that if I let him off the phone I will never hear from him again. He has to be so tired of only talking. And what more can we talk about? I even told him about my pet gerbil, Ted, from when I was seven. The thing died after three weeks! There was not much to tell him and I am not sure why anyone would care. I don't have that much more interesting to say. He has traveled everywhere and has met so many fascinating people. I tell him about Ted and he tells me about meeting Clint Eastwood at some big fancy charity dinner. Seriously, it is not even close. It is humiliating. We are nowhere close to the same and I do not know why he keeps calling me every night, unless maybe he likes torture by endless monotonous conversation. I am surprised he hasn't hired someone to come out here and shoot me and put himself out of misery." I rambled while Kyle laughs at me.

"Oh Ava and you say I am too dramatic. The man clearly has something for you or he would have never called in the first place. I wish you would see yourself for who you are, any guy would kill to have you give him the time of day." I anguish a look in his direction. "Even this guy today was uninterested until you walked in and he was hooked from the moment he saw you. He could care less about what we can design for him as long as he gets to talk to you every day. And it is not only this time, it is the same way with all of our clients. You have some weird southern witchcraft charm or something." I laugh at him. "Seriously, you are incredibly talented but you could talk a gazelle into living in a lion's den. You have this way of making people feel comfortable. I don't know how you do it but it works." Kyle kisses me on the cheek holding my hand for reassurance as we drive to dinner.

After dinner is over we have a signed contract and a new client but I am not sure I want to deal in business with him. The asshole made his presence known as soon as we sat down. If it wasn't his eyes then it was his hand accidentally slipping. Within the first ten minutes, I began sweating as each breath he took echoed heavily in my ear. I could not regain my composure until Kyle took my hand and was able to mention my new jealous and large boyfriend. Once the jerk backed off, I continued into sales mode, the fastest sales job I have ever made. A bad night but is a great opportunity and this guy has connections to even greater opportunities. I set my boundaries with him and even though he crossed them a couple of times, at least I did not throw up my hands and cry. This is the game and I have to find a way to make it work and remain respectable. At least by the end of the meeting he was listening to me, actually listening and understanding my ideas. It is always a struggle but what is the alternative? Be the constant victim and never get anywhere? That is not me, no matter how many times I cringe and want to scream.

Kyle takes my hand reminding me that we both understand. It is not easy for either of us in this business but together we find a way.

Once I get home, I go through my typical routine, and then shower to wash off the day and my still present anxiety. Completely oblivious to the time, I miss Sean's call for the first time and have to call him back. "I'm sorry I was getting a shower and trying to unwind from the day." I said before he can say a word.

"What happened?"

"Happened?"

"Ava, I can tell something happened to upset you. You're stressed and tense, you always take a hot shower when you're like that."

*I can't believe he knows me so well.* "How?" I pause listening to his unapologetic sighs. "I … we had this client today and he was a bit much."

"How exactly?"

"He invited us out to dinner to discuss our ideas but I didn't or rather I ignored that he only invited me out for dinner after," I said as his breathing changes intensity. "And he made a couple of advances towards me while we …"

"He did what? Where the hell was Kyle and why the hell did you go out with this guy anyway? Damn Ava! What the fuck were you thinking?" He yelled.

"I was thinking that I need this project and that I have to find a way to get it, so I can keep my firm afloat!"

"So you allow him to do or think whatever he wants to get the job - like a prostitute?"

Anger suddenly builds up inside me. "No Sean! I thought I might be able to change his mind about us and I did. He finally saw us as a firm he needed, rather than a woman he wanted to sleep with. If I turn away every possible job that tries to look down my shirt then I wouldn't have much of a firm. I have to put up with bullshit sometimes so I can get in the door and then I can change their minds and earn their respect. I have never and I will never, do anything with someone to get a job. I would rather not have it." Pressing my hands to my face, "oh you don't understand how hard it is." Sean tries to speak but I hush him. "Do you think I feel good about it? Because I don't, I want to fight them but it is useless and it does not get me anywhere. So I play their stupid game and I find a way around it and if you can't accept that then … Fuck you!" I said releasing years of frustration.

"Ava, I'm sorry, that was a horrible thing for me to say. I didn't want to upset you but I don't like hearing things like this, you don't know how helpless I feel not being there to protect you, it makes me crazy. Tell me what I can do for you?"

"Be there for me at the end of the day."

"I'm here but damn I wish I could be there with you."

"I do too but this is good enough for now." I straighten up and clear my tears along with my frustrations. "I won't compromise who I am." I said unsure if I was talking to him or myself.

"I know and I believe in you," he said confidently, which is the most wonderful thing he can say at this moment.

# *Chapter 16: Spencer*

*H*er picture hangs perfectly square on the opposite wall, as I imagine her underneath me. Making love to her is an exhilarating feeling. My heart races and my breath heavies, as I prove my dedication to her. Her skin is so warm and comforting, I can only imagine how beautiful this moment must feel to her. I look over her to search for that love she must be feeling but once again - she denies me. She is lucky I don't strangle the stubbornness right out of her. I refuse to look at her disrespect! Racing to the wall I rip the picture back down and stuff her back into the dark box where she belongs. *Until she learns ... until she can learn who she belongs too.*

"Jefferis, you have a visitor." The guard yells, eyeing me briefly before realizing his job doesn't pay enough to care.

Shackled, I make my way to the meeting room where my mother waits for me with her usual admiring smile. "Oh there is my boy. Handsome as always." She knows what I want but she obviously can't give it to me. "Is there something wrong?"

"Have you found her yet?" I growl. Her shoulders sink as she sits back in her seat. "I assume that would be a – *no*. So why are you here then?"

"Spencer darling, I have good news. I found a doctor who is doing a study on how people manipulate others to the point of causing damage to the brain." She pulls out an article of the good doctor Knight, with his smiling face and documented reports that he says proves his theories. "Doctor Knight, believes that this damage can cause people to do things they would not have otherwise. He reviewed your file and believes what she did to you is not your fault, it is a kind of psychological torture. His new process can help rebuild the damaged part of your brain and will cure you of the torture you endured from her. He is *very* excited to meet you and work with you. He said you could be an example of why his system will work. If you let him talk to you, then he can help prove that you should not be held accountable for what she says you did. He can help get you a new trial." I stare blankly at the wall as she continues to babble on. "Did you hear me Spencer? A new trial, a chance to go free again."

"That doesn't do me any good until I know where she is. Did you talk to the investigator?"

"I did but he wants more money than I can give him. The doctor cost me ..."

Standing up, "I don't care! You find her!" I rage until she nods with understanding.

❧

*T*he supposed highly regarded doctor sits across from me, making notes as he studies my answers and my reactions to his questions. He doesn't care about me. He only cares about making a name for himself, proving that he is worthy of the acronyms that accompany his name. Nonetheless, I give him what he wants. I weaken my voice and lower my posture. I tremble at the idea of having to go back to my cell. His greedy beliefs help me control what he sees in me. "So tell me again how you first came in contact with Ms. Kelley?"

"Ava. Her name is - Ava. I don't like talking about her as if she is a stranger. Referring to her by her last name, is such a cold way to speak of someone you care for," I say gripping the chair for control. The doctor smiles and nods while making notes about my progress. Stepping back into my thoughts and memories, "she walked into the corner store where I worked. I had seen beautiful women before but when I clumsily ran into her, she asked me if I was okay. Most women yelled or smacked me."

"Smacked you? For what?" He asked.

"They said I did it on purpose to try and get a feel of them. I wasn't though. I was only trying to help them. I get nervous around women especially beautiful women. I can't help it, I become clumsy and careless. No matter how hard I try, I make a mess of things."

"What would you do after they smacked you?"

"Nothing, I apologized and walked away. I didn't want to get into trouble. Whenever they would come back to the store I would hide from them. I was afraid they would yell at me again."

The doctor looks at me with sympathy, "that says a lot Spencer. You are intimidated by women. It's not surprising you would become nervous and cause unintentional accidents. You saw these women countless times and none of them accused you of any stalking or reported you to police for any malicious intent. If any of these women can be persuaded to come forward, it might help prove you don't have a history of harming women. In fact, you run from confrontation with them, not attack them."

I nod happily in unison with him, all the while knowing, they won't find any of those women. Each one of them are lovingly buried.

"How often did Ava come into the store?" The doctor asked writing hastily in his book.

"Only that one time, I didn't see her again until she started at Columbia that following semester. I had just taken a job as part of the janitorial service there."

"So all these accusations that you followed her is simply not true, she followed you?" I nod remembering the pile of Columbia housing paperwork she had dropped after I ran into her. "And the security job where she worked?"

"I found a business card when I was cleaning one day. Someone had written that there were positions available on the back. So I looked into it and found out they were hiring in security, it paid more, so I took the job. I had no idea she would be there too." The doctor smiles happily as he takes more notes about what he believes happened.

"This is amazing, I can't believe none of this was ever brought up during your trial. Now when she would talk to you, did she ever act a different way with you than she did with others?"

"She always smiled at me. She always made sure to walk by me, wave to me even. This one time she even had this guy follow her in and harass her, to make me jealous. I told her I didn't like it, that she didn't need to do those kinds of things to make me notice her. She laughed and said I was her hero. I know she enjoyed watching me take control of the situation."

"So she likes playing games, role playing games?" I nod. "This woman flaunted her sexual relationship with her boss in front of you. Forced you to watch her bring in other men to tease you? Followed you from one job to the next until you snapped. She played with your head, like a toy for her pleasure. This woman should be here begging you for forgiveness. Ms. Kelley is obviously, severely disturbed."

"Her name is *Ava*."

# *Chapter 17: Sean*

*I* sit waiting for my next scene when Randy comes into my trailer. Randy my valuable security specialist is also my best friend and is a bit underpaid for both jobs - according to him.

"Sean. How's it going?"

"Randy," I said with a sly smirk.

"So anything new?"

Before I can answer him, Cory, one of my co-stars, comes in to talk to me for the fifth time today. "Sean," she said posing and caressing herself, as she tries to encourage me with her excessively glossed lips.

I respond with little interest or respect. "What do you want Cory?"

"I was wondering if you might have some free time tonight."

"Nope."

"What?" She asks shaken out of her sex pose. Pointing to the door, I direct her to the path she needs to take. "You are such a conceded asshole!" She yelled walking out in a huff.

"Are you crazy? She's hot?" Randy insisted.

"She isn't hot, she's an immature child, and annoying as hell." Smiling I sink back into my previous daydream. "Besides, I have better." I mumble under my breath but quickly realize I was not silent enough.

"What was that? You have better, since when? And please let me meet this better." My glowing reaction causes him to raise an eyebrow at me. "Really? Sean is in love?"

"I don't know about love yet but she is wonderful and I can't get enough of her."

"Oh I am going to have to write this down in my journal."

"Your journal?" I question with a laugh.

His smile fades from his face as he leans over to me. "Yea my journal, you got something to say about that? It helps me deal with my emotions." He said, while I make no attempt to hide my laughter.

Randy is huge but neither one of us is the least bit intimidated by the other. We trained together and know each other's tactics better than our own. We rarely get anywhere other than tired trying to fight each other, which we do on occasion, when the day becomes longer than we can handle. "I guess if you need to get your feelings out you big baby, you do what you have to," I said mocking his stature. He punches me nearly knocking me out of my chair. "Hey fucker watch it, I'll have to fire you or something."

"You wouldn't dare," he said tilting his chair back against the wall. His cockiness allows me the perfect opportunity to knock the leg of the chair out from under him, sending him hard to the floor and causing me to laugh hysterically. "Son of a bitch, Sean! Motherfucking asshole," he said straightening his chair and eyeing me with disgust.

With a girlish attitude I hunch over the table with my fake pen and fake journal, "dear diary, Sean was mean to me today but I didn't cry this time … until now." I mocked him, exaggerating my performance with fake tears.

He eyes me with contempt as I make my way out the door. "You better run." He yelled running after me.

At the end of the day, I come home and begin sorting through the stack of papers Ethan left for me. After two hours, I finally make it to my mail. Exasperated I sort through it quickly, almost too quickly to notice a small letter from Atlanta but the perfect block lettering is easy to spot. I toss everything else aside while I tear through the envelope, pulling out a short letter attached to some pictures.

*Sean, I received these from Ashlen. She didn't have your address so I am sending you your copies. I hope you enjoy them as much as I did.*
*Thinking of you always – Ava*

Sorting through the pictures, I laugh at some and grimace at others. Each time I come to a picture of her, I pause gazing over it with an extended interest, especially the one of us together dancing, looking into each other's eyes and oblivious to everyone around us. Who would have thought a single picture could brighten my entire world.

I held the picture in my hand for the rest of the night and when I went to bed, I leaned it against the lamp below her locket. As great as the picture is, it only makes me crave her more. The media is not helping me any, they are doing everything they can to match me up with whoever I breathe near. Clearly, I am not allowed to be single. If only I could tell them to go fuck off and mind their own business but instead, I have to smile and nod and pretend that I am too busy to worry about it.

CʒꙄꙨ

*M*y birthday is in a couple of days and nothing could matter to me less. I talk to her every night. I miss her more and more than I did the day before, I want to feel her next to me, touch her and … I'm becoming one horny bastard. I fear for Ava's safety when I do see her. Instead of being with her, I sit here listening to Ethan's non-stop ramblings that don't concern me or conversations we have had hundred times already. I have no idea why he is still talking. "So you have a few appointments tomorrow but not until later," he tells me for the third time. "THEN you have your birthday and the next day off. So you have quite a bit of time off to enjoy your birthday." It's dark in his car but I know he can still see me rolling my eyes. As soon as he pulls up to my door I jump out hoping to free myself before he begins all over again. "Sean, hold on I need to give you these." I wait impatiently in my doorway for him. "Here is some paperwork you need to review and sign these." He said handing me paper after paper. *Is he kidding me?* "Oh and here's your mail and your financial reports you need to look at. Make sure you review them, please."

"Ethan!" I insisted "Can't we do this tomorrow? I just want to call Ava and go to bed. Nothing else is getting through to me right now."

"No, I would rather do it now and then you can have some time to …" He said making a peculiar expression before continuing. "Relax. Remember you do not have to be in until late tomorrow and only for a little while so you can have a nice dinner for your birthday. I made some private reservations for two at your favorite place. Carlo is already expecting you."

"Ethan what the hell are you talking about? I am not going to go with Mom and I am certainly not going with you. I plan to have a quiet night at home," I said with an exaggerated sigh.

"Anyway, you are clear if you should end up with plans on your birthday," he said smiling sheepishly.

*What the hell is he talking about?* "You better not be throwing some surprise birthday party!"

He laughs directing me to my living room. "Happy Birthday, little brother."

I walk heavy-footed into my living room but before I can look up I hear a delicate, breathy and southern, "welcome home." With a sharp turn, I see her standing by the giant window, with the sunlight shining in bright behind her. I slap all my paperwork back into Ethan's chest never releasing my gaze off her. I walk slowly towards her hoping this is not one of my vivid dreams trying to fool me again. Ava stands awkwardly with her perfect smile, while her sweet dress hugs her body so gently I can barely think. Scooping her up to me without saying another word, I kiss her as I have been dreaming of doing. Ethan makes little noise as he excuses himself from my house.

"How, when ..." I tried to ask her between re-familiarizing ourselves.

"Ethan, he said it was your birthday tomorrow and that I should do him a favor and spend it with you."

"Best damn brother in the world," I whispered against her lips. "Are you hungry, need a drink, or something?"

"Well I ate already and I have a drink but I might be able to use something, what do you got?" She smiles eagerly.

"I was thinking I am kind of tired and maybe," I inhale reminding myself of her body. "Maybe we should go straight to bed tonight."

"No, I don't think so," she said with a serious expression, worrying me but then with an innocent smile she caresses my cheek. "I'm not waiting that long. I want you now, right here." Wrapping her arms around my neck an unavoidable smile creeps across my face. I look down at the sweet little dress that is about to be incredibly abused and move my hands up under it. She closes her eyes and gasps from my deliberate touch, "I missed you so much."

Lifting her up easily into my arms, I carry her by the bar and grab what I need before proceeding to my favorite big chair. Setting her down in front of me, I rip the tie of her dress as I struggle to get it off. Ripping it yet again, I forgo being gentle with it and rip the dress completely off her. Touching, gripping, and kissing her while she tugs at my clothing, jarring me this way and that, pulling my shirt off and jerking my pants open. I feel her hand take hold of me, stroking me harder until I fall back into the chair and watch her slide her panties down her legs. "You did miss me." I said pulling her down on me. She finds her perfect spot with a gasping delight. While pushing her hands deep into her hair, she rides the vibrations of her orgasm, calling out to me with the sexiest moans and sending me over the edge with hard groans of my own.

"Welcome home," she said caressing my face. "And you owe me a new dress." She laughs.

"If I knew you were waiting for me, I would have been home a whole hell of a lot sooner." Taking her hands from my face, I kiss them both. "And I will buy you a closet full of new dresses baby."

"That would be wonderful but I am a little more concerned about the condoms in your bar?"

I smile unashamed, "that's a long story but it's not what you think." She narrows her eyes at me and sits back in a superior posture. "I was having a bachelor party for one of my friends and the strippers …" *I am probably not helping myself at all with that phrase.* I peek up at her as she tilts her head. "Anyway … there were these strippers that had my friend tied to a chair and they were ... doing what strippers do and part of their act was showering my friend with these ridiculous colorful condoms. And … well after it was over, I was tired so I went to bed but before I could get up the next morning, my Mom called and said she was coming over. So I had to clean the room quickly and throw all the condoms in a drawer in the bar. It was the closest place to hide them where she wouldn't look. And I forgot about them until now." I said holding my hands out to her. "I swear."

"Okay, so what happened with the strippers that made you so tired?"

"No. You can get that out of your mind right now because nothing happened it was a long night and that was it. So you can simmer that Irish temper of yours back down." She laughs at me stroking my hair. "That's not funny, you scared me. I was afraid you were going to leave before I got a chance to enjoy having you here." I said winking at her.

# Chapter 18: Ava

*H*is blaring alarm startles us both. Removing one of his arms from around me, he reaches and slams his hand down, silencing it. With an exaggerated sigh, he slips back down into our cradling warmth. "Good morning, beautiful." He hummed in my ear. Our cuddling session doesn't last nearly long enough before he gets up to shower. I stay in bed enjoying his velvet, soft sheets and huge bed until I see his closet door still open where he hastily left it last night. Removing the comforting sheets from my still naked body, I scurry across the wooden floor to his closet and take a half step in. It is bigger than my house. It is so organized and with a seating area in the middle, as if he is planning to have a small party in his closet to simply watch him get dressed. I need to get that thought out of my mind before he catches me, besides, who would want to watch someone get dressed anyway? Suddenly I feel his hands on my waist and his lips against my cheek, I shiver from his wet hair dripping down my back.

"You cold?" He said grabbing a blanket from a shelf and hugging me tightly within it. "Better baby?"

"Yes, thank you." He motions for me to sit while he rummages through drawers and clothes, wearing nothing but a towel hanging firmly against him. *I am so glad there is a place to sit because my legs are suddenly weak.* Once he has what he needs he slips the towel off hanging it on a rack nearby. *I should probably blink.* He systematically puts on each item causing an awkward exhale from my lungs as each part of him becomes covered. *You know I do think people would pay for these seats, I would pay for this seat.*

"So what's with the seating area, do you have meetings in your closet or something?" I asked with a sarcastic expression.

"No, actually, you're the first person to ever sit in here."

"Then why have them?"

"To fill the room I guess, I didn't pick them out I had someone do that for me."

"I guess it is a big closet. Well room," I said looking around the large space, until he stuns me by his close presence.

Leaning on each arm of the chair, he smiles deep into my eyes, "do you like it?" He asked still wonderfully shirtless. Nodding I blush before I can stop myself. *So embarrassing.* "Good," he laughs with a sweet kiss before finishing getting dressed and leaving me to gawk in private. I should be back before dinner and Ethan said we have reservations at my favorite restaurant tonight."

"We are going out to dinner?"

"The owner of the restaurant is a good friend of the family and he will sneak us in through an unknown entrance to our own private patio. The food is great. You're going to love it." Taking my hand, he leads me out of his closet.

"I wasn't planning on us going out, so I didn't bring anything but I guess I can go get something?" I said while my mind works its way up to the ultimate panic level.

"Would you rather stay in?" He asked.

"No!" *Calm down Ava. Deep breath.* "I need to get something a little nicer, all I brought that's nice are ...," I said blushing and turning away from his animated expression.

"Maybe I would rather stay in then." He hums gazing over me.

I run into his arms, "Sean, no, please. I will find something while you ..." Hushing me with one finger gently to my lips.

"Shhh. I think I can help you out. I will have my sister in-law, Abbey, take you out. She'll know where you can go and get something that will suit you perfectly."

"That sounds wonderful. So we are actually going on a real date?" I said vibrating in his arms, causing my blanket to fall to the floor. Looking down over me, he inhales grasping my waist. "Don't you have to go soon?" I asked as he nods with a harsh exhale helping me cover up again.

"Our first real date, so I guess I should make sure this date is perfect for you?"

"Oh no not for me, it's your birthday." Suddenly remembering I put my hand over my mouth and look up at him in horror.

"What's wrong?"

"Oh Sean I am so sorry, I completely forgot that it's your birthday. I forgot to say Happy Birthday," I said watching his smile return.

"I will forgive you this once."

"Thank you and Happy Birthday" I said with a kiss. "I promise to do better tonight."

"I am going to hold you to that, sweetheart."

CR&O

"*H*ello. Hello?" A voice calls out from the side entry.

"Yes," I said running into the living room, happy to see a smiling face headed in my direction with her arms out to greet me warmly.

"You must be Ava."

"I am and you're Abbey?"

"Yes, it is so nice to finally meet you. I have heard so much about you."

"It's nice to meet you too."

"So. You need a dress for the night?"

"Yes, I am not sure what would be appropriate though. I guess you know this restaurant that Sean is taking me to?"

"I know everything, but we don't have much time to get done all that I want to get done." She said taking my hand and leading me out the door. Before we make it to any type of shop, Abbey takes me to a quaint café for lunch and she does not hesitate to start asking me questions. "So you like Sean?"

"Yes, I like him." I smile, careful not to give away too much information.

"No, you're in love."

"What? No I am not."

"Please, I can read your feelings for him all over your face. Besides I think it's a good thing." I stare at her curiously. "Well considering how crazy he is about you. I would hate to see his heart get broken." She looks happily at my stunned face. "Oh Ava, tell me you realize how much he loves you."

"He loves me?"

"Oh right, I forgot how these Grant boys work. Well I will tell you then, it is hard to miss his feelings for you. You should hear the way he talks about you, how much he misses you. He might not have said it to you yet, but he is, that I am positive. He has been moping horribly for the last few weeks. That's why I told Ethan we need to get you here somehow."

"You told him to bring me here?" I asked.

"He certainly would have never thought of it on his own. So you're in love with him right?"

"I think so."

"I knew it," she said pleased with herself.

As we eat, and talk about our men, we become fast friends. She told me about finding out that she's pregnant a few months prior and how nervous she is about it but that she never lets onto Ethan, because he would surely become a nervous wreck. I shared more about my feelings for Sean and anything I thought important to judge his feelings for me.

After we finish our lunch, we leave for a hidden away boutique, where a small woman seeming to be in her early 70's greets us. "Hello darling, I haven't seen you in awhile," she said to Abbey in a raspy German accent.

"I am sorry Greta but I can't fit into your clothes these days," Abbey says pulling her shirt tight to show off her small belly sticking out.

"Oh my, how wonderful! Ethan has done well." She said jubilantly kissing Abbey on the cheek. "So then what can I do for you?"

"Well Greta, I was hoping you could help out my friend Ava here, she has a *very* important and romantic dinner tonight."

Greta turns to me with her chin poked out and her eyes squinted with measurements running across her face as she scans over me. I gulp louder than I would have liked to. "How important and how romantic?" She asked with a fixated expression.

"Well we would like to make it hard for him to take his eyes off her but we want him to remember to breathe," Abbey said satisfied with her explanation.

Greta grunted once before jutting off to the back of the store. "Ah! Here it is," she yelled, as I glance over at Abbey nervously. She nods with reassurance but I am less concerned about the outfit and more so about the price, but before I can ask, Greta is back hurrying me into a dressing room and tossing me an ivory dress. I finally am able to change into it after some time trying to figure out how. I step out of the dressing room hoping I have it on right. They both smile with pride and then quickly throw shoes, underwear, and every other accessory possible at me to try on with it, until they achieve the look they are wanting. After I change back into my clothes and step out to pay, Greta hands me my entire outfit, wrapped up neatly for me.

"Good luck my dear. I think you will have him right where you want him in this." Great smiles.

"Thank you but how much …" Abbey quickly grabs my arm, pulling me away. "But I didn't pay her for any of this."

"She knows who you are going out with, Ava. Sean will pay for it and she will bill him happily."

I stop abruptly, "Sean? But … no. I can't let him do that."

"You can and you will." She frowns at my frustrated stare. "Fine. Then you can write him a check for it when we get back," She said pulling out one of the tags for me to read.

"What? This was that much?" The blood begins to rush from my face.

"Ava, it is a special occasion and you're going to look your best for him. Besides, it is his birthday and I am sure it will make his day that he could buy this for you. Trust me will you?" She insisted. "He is going to be eating out of your hands"

"He does owe me a dress, a closet full he said so I guess this would be about the same price." I quickly glance at the other tags and nearly faint. "Or maybe not." Abbey laughs and helps me back to the car.

# *Chapter 19: Sean*

*I* arrive home eager to see her but she keeps me waiting until she is ready. I can hear the anxiety in her voice as she speaks through my own bedroom door. "Okay, I'm ready," she calls out to me from the stairs. I turn and my mouth drops to the floor. She stands nervously as I gaze over her in awe and motion for her to turn for me, which she does ending it with a shy smile. Her dress is amazing, her hair hangs down her back in one big long curl and her blue eyes are sparkling with anticipation. A perfect Grecian princess, and she has me rapt. *Abbey damn you! She knows me WAY to well.* "So what do you think?" Ava asks me, not that she should have too.

I walk towards her and take her hand, kissing it gently before looking into her awaiting eyes with a reverent smile. "You take my breath away Ava." I said weakened by her presence. "Are you ready to go, beautiful?"

"Yes," she said smiling as bright as I have ever seen her. Taking her politely by the hand, I lead her to my car and spend the entire drive to the restaurant smiling ridiculously.

Pulling up to the restaurant, I hand the keys to my car over to a known assistant while Ava finds her way to my side. She takes my hand helping me forget about my car that is disappearing into the night.

Leading Ava into the already open back door, "Sean, so nice to see you again and who is this?" Carlo greeted us.

"Easy Carlo, this is Ava, Ava – Carlo, an *old* family friend."

He smirked waving me off as he takes her hand and kisses it gently, "old friend but not old."

"Do you have everything ready for us?" I asked taking her hand away from his. "And she is my date Carlo."

"Of course, follow me," he laughed motioning for us to follow him up the less than impressive backstairs but when we get to the top and turn down a short hall Carlo opens the door, "please watch your step." He helps Ava step up into the space and I watch as her eyes grow wide. It is the roof of the building and being the tallest building, in this area anyway, it is private and the view is perfect from the hill the building sits on. This secured garden area, atop the hill is where I have planned the perfect date. There are candles, delicate lighting and flowers everywhere, even a gathered bunch sitting atop a table for two. There are dozens of sunset colored, movie star roses all for her. "We received the flowers earlier and I took the liberty of putting them all in fresh vases for you, very romantic I think, yes?"

"It's perfect," Ava said glowing beautifully.

"Very good, I will let you get settled and be back soon to take your order," Carlo said.

I walk Ava over to the table, holding out her chair for her before sitting myself. "Sean this is incredible, did you do this?"

"It's our first date and it has to be perfect, right?" I asked but her lit up expression is enough to tell me all I need to know. She sits taking everything in, seemingly to notice every detail as if she is trying to memorize it to re-create it somehow when she feels the need. I begin to wonder when her last date had been. Carlo comes back to take our order and pour us some wine. Taking her hand once again, I toast to her being here, she adds to my birthday, and I add her dress with a wink. We talk endlessly, laughing about her trying to figure out the dress she has on and me screwing up my lines today by calling everyone Ava. I am surprised we have anything left to talk about but she continues. She even tells me how much she enjoyed shopping today with Abbey but she is worried about how much it cost me and offers to pay me back. "Don't be absurd Ava, it makes my day to be able to make you this happy and to see you in this dress is payment enough."

"Abbey said you would say that but I still feel like I owe you something."

"Right now, with you, is all I want." I say meaning every word.

"But I actually have something for you, well I have a birthday present for you," she said getting up grabbing something to bring over to me.

"Ava I didn't expect you to buy me anything. I appreciate it but …"

"Well I didn't buy it. I mean I bought the materials to make it," she said causing me to sit back in confusion. "When I got those pictures from Ashlen there was one picture of us that inspired me to paint again."

"You painted something for me?" I asked excitedly.

"Well that wasn't the initial intent but when your brother called about your birthday, I panicked because I had no idea what to get you and it seemed ridiculous to try to buy you something. So Kyle told me that I should give you the painting. I wasn't sure at first but he insisted you would like it, but I am still not sure."

"I'm sure I will but how did you get this here?"

"Abbey dropped it off for me," she said as her trembling hands motion for me to open it. Laughing at her nervous impatience, I hurry through the paper and my mouth drops. Stylized in her own style, is the same picture that sits underneath her locket on my bedside table. Ava somehow was able to express the emotion and bring that moment alive - the feeling I had flawlessly painted.

"It's not exactly the picture but my version of the picture. Rather my thoughts and feelings at that moment, so that may be why you don't recognize it." She said shying away from my eyes on her.

"No, I recognized it right away. Ava this is extraordinary," I said looking over at her as a single tear strolls down her face. "Why are you crying?"

"I was scared that you wouldn't like it."

"Ava this is by far the best gift anyone has ever given me. I didn't know you were so good at this."

"I get by but I do better when I get inspired by something."

Sitting the picture down carefully I then lean over the table and pull her face to mine, kissing the tear from her cheek and then her lips. "I love it, thank you." Sitting back down we toast to her beautiful artwork, plane crashes and rainy islands with no room service. After we enjoy our food, I ask her to dance and she readily accepts. I guide her to a good spot pulling her in close and move effortlessly to the music, earning a kiss with every spin and a giggle with every dip but I get her laughing aloud when I sing for her. Carlo checks on us quietly, bringing us more wine and winking at me as he leaves. I have never brought a girl here before, no one has ever been important enough to me. Sinking my head down into her hair, I listen to the flowing music as I kiss and touch her every chance I can get. Feeling more pathetic with each passing second. "Ava I …"
Suddenly I am interrupted by a loud crash when a man comes stumbling through the door. The intruder crouches down, slowly gathering broken pieces of dishes while making moves towards his bulging pocket. Eyeing him steadily I try to place his familiar face. *The door is clearly marked private and Carlo never allows anyone up here but*

*himself or some special member of his staff, all of which would be well aware of that step up.* In an instant, I find myself hovering around Ava, hiding her. "Don't speak, don't move." I whispered to her.

"Oh I am so sorry. I didn't realize anyone was up here," the intruder said eyeing Ava directly.

"I think it's best if you go," I said sliding my jacket off.

"Yes sir, I am so sorry to interrupt you and your … girlfriend?" He said standing rapidly and jerking out his camera, sending a barrage of flashes our way.

My reaction is quick, throwing my jacket over Ava and shielding her from him and his camera. Frustrated, the wiry kid runs out the door and out of sight.

"Who was that Sean, what's going on?" Ava asked with a trembling voice.

"I don't know for sure."

Carlo runs in breathing heavily. "I am so sorry, this man bribed his way in and then found the backstairs before I could do anything. I called the police but he has already run away," he said looking down in shame.

"You don't have any idea who he is Carlo?" I asked.

"No, I'm sorry."

"We need to go." I said.

"Of course!" Carlo yelled rushing out to give orders.

I call Ethan, putting him on alert. By the time I get off the phone, Carlo has given Ava some extra food he boxed up for us, along with all of her flowers wrapped tight into a paper wrapping. She looks ridiculous trying to hold everything.

"Ava you don't have to take all those flowers, I will get you some more," I said motioning to her impatiently.

"No, it's okay."

"Alright let's go," I grab my painting and escort her quickly back to my car and speed off into the dark.

"Where are we going?" Ava asked.

"I am taking you to a hotel."

"NO! I don't want to go to a hotel Sean, I want to be with you."

"Ava I will stay with you but you can't go back to my house right now."

"You are going to stay with me?" She said with tears strolling down her face.

"I am not going to leave you somewhere and then go home without you. Let me get you somewhere safe and then we can enjoy the rest of our night together." I said holding her face gently in my hand. "No reason to cry sweetheart everything is going to be fine, I promise." Once we make it to the hotel Ethan set up for us, two men usher us inside hovering close until we are out of sight and within a minute, we are secure in our own room. The events of the night and knowing we will not get to enjoy the other surprises I have for her at my house, cause me to become frustrated. Ava stands silently looking over the large room, peeking into the bedroom and at the bar before looking back my way, still clutching all those flowers. "Ava will you put the damn flowers down!" I yell at her.

"But." She said looking down at them with sad eyes.

"They're just flowers."

"But no one has ever given me flowers before," she said innocently. *Damn, I am such an ass. Of course, all those stupid flowers mean much more to her than most girls.*

"Come here," I said taking the flowers from her a set at a time and no matter how ridiculous the container I manage to find, I am able to eventually place them all around the suite evenly. Afterwards I stand back admiring my work, as does she. "Better?"

"Yes, thank you," she smiles reminding me who they are meant for in the first place.

I spin her back into my arms, "no problem. So now what, do you want to finish our dance or get comfortable?"

"It's your birthday?" She said as I play with the fabric of her dress. "No Sean, what do you really want? I mean is there something different you would like … well … for me to do?"

"I don't understand what you're asking me Ava."

"Like a fantasy, is there something or someway you have dreamed about with me or …" She shrugs looking away from me. "Or maybe with someone else?" My mind leaps to the first time I saw her naked and wet in that shower. "There is isn't there?" She asked reading my expression well.

"It doesn't matter," I said shaking my head and waving her off. "No, nothing … it's nothing." I try to kiss her again dismissing it but she is not about to let it go.

"Sean, tell me? Is it that bad?"

"No it's not that bad" *I just don't want to have to tell you how I came up with the idea.*

"Sean, I am not going to let you touch me until you tell me."
She said walking away from me and sitting down on the sofa with her
arms crossed and lips tense. *Stubborn as hell!*

"Fine!" I grimace fighting with the words.

"Tell me, please."

"I have this fantasy of you in the shower. And before you ask,
yes I came up with this fantasy because of you and no one else …
just you. There, are you happy?"

"The shower? Why the shower?" She questioned me rightfully.

I groan rolling my eyes. *Must she always ask the questions I don't
want her to? I should lie to her.* Sitting next to her on the couch
perfecting a lie I feel good until her sweet face smiles at me. "Ava
honestly you are not going to like me much if I tell you this. So I
would rather not." I said watching her puzzled expression turn to
determination.

"I promise, I won't get mad," she said grabbing my hand.

*I am such a fucking idiot.* "I saw you in the shower when we were
on the island." Her puzzled expression confirms that I blurted it out
to fast for her to understand. "The first night we were stuck in the
cabin all-night. You left the damn door open Ava! I swear I was
simply putting my clothes up so they wouldn't be in the smoke
infested suitcase anymore and when I looked up into the mirror to
clear off some of the mud from three-wheeling." I close my eyes,
"well, I saw you and I … watched you." *Like a pervert.* Slowly I open
my eyes seeing her stare at me. "Ava?"

"You watched me?"

"I tried not to but it was like I was stuck, I couldn't take my eyes
off you. I was mesmerized by you and your moaning and lathering
yourself, it was … Fuuuck." I moaned remembering it all again
unwillingly. "Then you called out to me. I tried to run away from you
but then we got stuck together for the rest of the night."

"You were mesmerized by me?"

"Hypnotized is a better word. I don't think I was breathing. I
thought about the most absurd things to try to calm back down
before you saw me like that. I was aching like hell for you at that
moment." Leaning back into the sofa with my head falling back, I let
the images run freely through my mind.

"I didn't do that on purpose Sean."

*What?* "I know that, well actually I didn't figure that out until
later but I did think at first that you did do it on purpose."

"No, Sean, the light really did go out, you have to believe me. I'm sorry."

"I know that Ava, why are you apologizing to me? I am the one that was spying on you."

She starts laughing. *Laughing? She must be in shock.* "I don't know. I guess if I had found out at the time I would have been mortified that you saw me like that but now to know that you were so excited by it that it's a fantasy of yours." She said sitting back and biting her lip with excitement, "it's kind of flattering."

"So you're not mad?" I asked watching her shake her head as I feel the weight lifting from my shoulders. "Okay. Well there you go, that's my fantasy. I hope you're happy."

"So you fantasize about watching me take a shower?"

"Sort of, it is a fantasy so I get to watch more closely and a lot more physically." Suddenly, she gets up pulling me with her, dragging me into the large bathroom where there is a large luxury glass shower. Ava pulls in a chair and pushes me down into it. She lights some candles Carlo packed in with our food. *I am either a little scared or really, really excited, I'm not sure which but I am sure as hell not moving until she says so.* Eyeing me for some awkward seconds, she finally pulls the clips out of her hair and undoes her dress, slipping it off skillfully. My breath heats up as she fingers the delicate edges of her provocative underwear causing me to move. Suddenly she puts her foot on my chest, heels still on and pushes me back in my chair. "Fuck me." I mumbled staring at her sexily clad foot and down her long bare leg.

"You stay right there," she says with her blue eyes tensed in control, forcing me to do as she wishes. Removing her foot from my chest, she turns on the shower before sitting on my lap. Her hands cradle my face as she forces my lips into motion. She strokes my tongue with hers before leaning back and unbuttoning my shirt, pushing it, along with my suit jacket off me. Gasping, I hold my breath as I watch her hair follow her down my chest and to my pants, unbuttoning carefully she moves me ever closer to ecstasy. My breathing heavy, she pulls my already throbbing hard cock out and wraps her mouth around it making it even harder.

Simply from the sight of being in her mouth, I fall back into the chair and let out violent gasps. "Oh damn! Fuck Ava!" I groan trying to get a hold of her but she pushes me back in the chair and takes her place back on my lap, rubbing her body against me and kissing me with wild abandon.

"You stay right here until I tell you to get up," she demanded.

"Oh ... kay," I breathed unsure if I am suppose to answer.

She tosses her hair back before removing her bra and while watching my unblinking eyes, she tosses it away. I lick my lips watching the last garment slide down her legs. She steps into the shower moaning as the wet heat washes over her skin and leaving the door open so I can see every part of her perfect body become drenched in steaming water. Leaning her head back, letting it rush over her just like it did the first time I saw her, running down her back, over her ass and down the backs of her legs. My chair unconsciously slides closer, as the water catches her lips. She begins rubbing her breasts together, letting the water run around and between them, down to her belly button, causing her diamond to sparkle in the water. Again, I feel my chair move closer, while the water drapes down her stomach, between her legs - I begin to shake and whimper for her. "It's okay baby." Ava points her toe outside the shower rubbing it up my leg as I sit back watching it come up between my legs.

"Ava. Please," I plead as she bites her bottom lip and motions with her finger to come to her. Breathing so heavily that I can only assume the whole building can hear me, I jump up and yank the remaining clothes off my body. Stepping into the shower with her, I feel the steam-filled water hit my skin but only recognize the feeling of her hot, bare, wet skin against my hands. I move my hands to either side of her on the shower walls and my head against hers, panting in her ear while I try to restrain myself. *My fantasy is coming true and I am going to make sure we both enjoy it.*

"So what happens next in your fantasy Sean?"

"Turn around ... and I'll show you." Slowly she turns her back towards me and I lean into her breathing heatedly. "You are so sexy." Her sharp gasps soften as I pull her hair to one side and run my hands over her body. Massaging her breasts I suck the water off her warmed, pink skin and lean her head back to my shoulder. I go deep into her mouth, tenderly stroking her tongue. Letting the lust take control, I press my palms against her hips and push myself closer to her. My hands trail down to feel her bare ass and pull it towards my erection, letting its hardness throb against her skin. "Lean over ... against the wall," I whispered into her ear. My tongue follows the water running down her skin as she does what I ask of me. I wrap my hand around her thigh pulling her leg up to the place I need it.

Holding back for a second I take in her wet body one more time before feeling the tightness of her take in my erection slow and deep, forcing soft moans from her tender wet lips. She reaches for the back of my head as I thrust and pull, massage and kiss her over and over. She moans loudly for me, gripping my hand. I hold her waist while my other hand slips between her legs to increase the intensity for her. With the water keeping our bodies hot and wet, I follow her deeper against the shower wall, fondling her lips in between gasps. Suddenly she grips me hard, fisting my hair and moaning for me loudly as I groan into the side of her neck. I lean her back a little more, watching her gasping moans intensify until I feel her tightening release and her body whimpering against mine. All I can think about is how incredible it feels to be inside of her. "Can I come inside of you Ava?" I asked hoping she will let me finish the dream. "Please, Ava," I pleaded, moaning her name one more time as she holds onto my rapidly thrusting body.

"Yes … yes, just don't stop." Gripping her tighter, our quivering bodies enjoy the filling moment with deep exhales and tender hands.

"Baby that was even better than the fantasy." Sighing I turn her back around and kiss her, holding her in my arms until she is more steady on her feet. Biting her lip she steps away from me and begins bathing and lathering up in front of me. "Oh now you are going to do that? You are killing me. At least let me help you." I said unable to control my smile as she hands over the soapy cloth. Moving my hands through the rich lather on her skin, massaging her muscles and her breasts and anything else I can get my hands on.

"My turn," she says taking control and lathering her hands over my chest and my stomach. She kisses my back before massaging my ass for some time. I suddenly feel her lips explore and her hands caress, and her tongue tease me, making me hard all over again. I watch her knowing eyes look up at me with a superior expression.

"You know this doesn't mean you win anything."

"Oh yes it does," she said provocatively kissing my chest.

"Well maybe it does," I said picking her up and forcing her back up against the shower wall. "Thank you Ava."

"For what?"

"For the best damn birthday I have ever fucking had." I smile against her lips finding my way back to where I want to be.

# *Chapter 20: Ava*

The next morning I wake up to him playing with my hair. Looking up into his gorgeous green eyes and smiling, "hi."

"Hi," he smiles back at me. "Your hair is really curly."

"It does that if I don't blow-dry it completely. I guess it looks pretty bad?"

"On the contrary it's very sexy. I have been playing with all these curls for almost an hour now."

"I don't know about sexy, you should have seen me when I was little, crazy curls. Horrible."

"I bet you were adorable."

"Adorable, yes red hair and freckles, I thought I was cursed."

With a glimmer in his eyes, he gently strokes his finger across the top of my nose. "Like these freckles? These adorable freckles."

"They weren't so adorable when I was twelve."

"You're crazy. I bet you had all those twelve year old boys eating out of your hands."

"Hardly, they always wanted the perfectly tanned blond girl." I said enjoying his tender touch.

"And now you are getting them all back."

"You are so not who I thought you were the first time I met you." I say enjoying his warmth around me.

"Well that's good, if I recall you hated me then."

"I didn't hate you, I just wanted to push you off the plane is all."

"Oh is that all, then I am glad we crashed and you were the one that had to be carried off and not me. You would have left me there."

"I wouldn't have left you, I would have pushed you off the plane or didn't you hear me?" I laugh feeling his smile against my cheek. "You are off all-day today aren't you?"

"I'm all yours today baby, whatever you want to do we can do."

CRED

𝒯he hours fly by and the sadness is beginning to set in as we snuggle in front of the picture window where he slowly starts to hum a tune. With a renewed energy, he begins singing one of my favorite songs in my ear, missing most of the words and messing up most of the song on purpose to make me laugh.

"That was horrible. I hope that was not your attempt at romance?"

Looking down at me with a hurt expression, he causes me only to laugh harder, "I thought I sounded great."

"Well don't sign up to do any musicals any time soon Mr. Grant." Without hesitation he over vocalizes the lyrics to One from A Chorus Line and controlling my body to work in tune with the lyrics of the song, laughing with me the whole way through. At the end, I look up into his smiling eyes falling deeper in love every new moment with him.

"What?" He asked.

"I can't believe how incredible you are," I said as he stiffens suddenly, taking my hands and pressing his fingers between mine.

"Ava technically I have been in relationships before but honestly, this is my first real one that I give a shit about." He hangs his head before looking back up at me. "I don't know what I'm doing here."

"It's a first for me too but don't worry, we'll figure it out together."

"And you think I'm incredible - you're amazing."

"Only to you." I said softly. *Can it be possible that love can be this intense? I want to tell him how I feel, but what if he doesn't feel the same way?* Letting go of my worries, I give in easily to his hands finding their way underneath the big fluffy hotel robe, pushing me up against the window. Without even thinking, I wrap my legs around him as I feel his hardness powerfully control me, sending me wreathing against the glass until the feeling of him rushes through my body. Collapsing in his arms, I hold on to him tight, resting my head against his shoulder. Sean carries me to bed and tucks me in tight against him.

"Randy is going to escort you to your flight tomorrow and I want you to do everything he says to do. Please listen to him, he will get you home safely, without being noticed." Sean sits up looking at me directly. "Ava tell me you will do everything he says?"

"I will," I said as he lies back down with a soft sigh.

"It won't be much longer and I will be able to come see you." Sinking deep into the soft bed, we lay silent for some time while I slowly work up my courage. "I love you Sean." I whispered listening for anything but only hearing his breathing. I look up only to see him sound asleep. *Perfect.* I kiss him gently on the cheek, "I love you so much. I wish I knew how to tell you when you're awake."

CR&ED

The next morning routines are simple but the conversations are awkward. Waiting for our rides to come I sit against him, holding his hand. I thought the first time I had to leave him was hard, but this time is much harder.

Sean's phone vibrates signaling the end of our time together. "They are going to be up here soon." Sean said standing up with me and pulling me into his arms. "I'm going to miss you." I immediately begin to feel emotional. "Don't cry please. I will see you in December and it's already October. I promise it will fly by." He said laughing slightly at my weak nod. "Randy should be here soon, make sure you do everything that he asks." He pulls my chin up to look at him. "He will make sure you get home safely but I will call you tonight to verify for myself," he said as Ethan comes through the door suddenly.

"Are we ready?" Ethan asked walking in smiling a bright smile at me before leaning over to me for a reassuring hug. "Doing alright sweetheart?" I nod to him. "Good."

"Stop flirting, Ethan." Sean said taking my hand and pulling me back to him. Ethan ignoring him shows no sign of retaliation. Another large gentleman follows Ethan in, giving Sean a quick man greeting of nothing more than a slight head nod. "Randy, did Ethan feel you in?"

"Yea he did, I will take care of her Sean. No problem." Randy said winking at me.

"Ava this is Randy, Randy - Ava." Sean said as Randy holds his hand out to take mine, his of course, wrapping around mine and probably can, twice over. Sean laughs putting his arm around my shoulder. "Don't worry Ava, Randy's big, but he's just a big brown teddy bear."

"Fuck you." Randy scoffed.

"Sean we should go." Ethan encourages.

Sean leaning down takes my lips into his innocently. "Do everything that Randy says." He whispers looking into my eyes to verify that I agree again.

"I promise." I receive another brief kiss before he exits with only a glance over his shoulder before he is gone. *I want to cry but it feels so ridiculous to do so now.*

"When I get back we are going to move fast, so be prepared." Randy grabs my bag and heads out the door. Before I know it, he is back and hovering around me as he escorts me out of the building and into a waiting car. It all went so fast I am not sure if I walked or if he carried me.

Randy seems so serious driving, watching everything around us carefully. *I hate to interrupt his concentration but I need the distraction.* "So have you known Sean long?"

"Yea, we met in the military." He chuckles, shaking his head at me. "Well you are certainly not one of his groupies, they would have known that already. Luckily, we became friends before he became the big movie star."

"So you're good friends?"

"Oh yea, he's always getting me into trouble."

"Like what?" I asked.

With barely a hesitation, "just so you know that boy has a knack for causing me hell. This one time he got me so drunk that I passed out. And the next morning? I woke up lying on the lawn of the base, in only my boxers and a cigar." He laughed. "I was woke up by a major who was none too thrilled to see me there. He kept yelling and my head was spinning. He told me I had to run in my boxers until I learned my way to and from my bed, from every possible part of the base. All I could hear the whole time I was running was Sean laughing. I didn't know where he was but I promised myself I would get him back. Especially for the plus ten days cleaning the latrine. It was awful."

I laugh into my hands picturing the scenario in my head. "So did you get back at him?"

"That's an even better story, one that I am damn sure he will never tell you."

"What did you do?" I asked repositioning eagerly.

"One night when Sean was dead tired, he was getting ridden hard for pulling some other prank he got caught doing, nothing serious but he paid well for it. Anyway, a bunch of us were all going out and all he wanted to do was go to sleep but after much persuading and pleading, he finally agreed to come out with us. He was so exhausted it didn't take much of anything for him to pass out … right on the bar." Randy shook his head laughing. "I mean he was out cold. We were going to take him back but on the way I got a better idea." Randy snickered to himself before he finally got a hold of himself. "Anyway, I put him in a bed with a woman, a large drunk woman, who had been hitting on Sean for months and he wanted nothing to do with her. I don't think that woman bathed ever."

"How did you do that?"

"Oh that crazy, drunk, smelling like ass, woman was walking home when we passed her on our way back. We gave her a ride and then we stripped him of everything but his boxers and put him in her bed, she cuddled up, right next to him and went to sleep. Damn that woman could snore."

"And he didn't wake up?"

"Not right away but we had barely made it out of her drive when he came blasting out of her house. I think he beat us back. That boy could run." Randy said laughing hysterically.

"Was he mad?"

"Oh hell yea, furious." He said laughing harder. "When he finally calmed down I asked Sean how he woke up." Randy dances in his seat laughing. "He said." I roll my eyes waiting for him to calm down enough to tell me. "He said he woke up from the smell, looked around and then saw her toothless smile and ran out of that house never looking back. To this day I still tease him that she had her way with him and that somewhere out there is a toothless, smelly little Sean, he hates that. I named him woolly mammoth junior." He continues laughing wiping the tears from his eyes.

Laughing at his over enjoyment, "so you and Sean are pretty good friends?"

"Best friends. When I got out of the military, he hired me right away. It's a good job too. I get to travel and do many things I would not have otherwise and meet a lot of interesting people. Plus, the pay is great but don't tell Sean, I tell him I'm under paid so he doesn't expect me to start doing his laundry or something. And not to mention the girls are …" Randy pauses glimpsing my suspicious expression.

"So Sean has had a lot of girlfriends, huh?"

"Ummm, not really, I mean he's dated girls and has had I guess what you would call a girlfriend now and then but he has never really been serious with any of them. If they threaten to break it off with him, he lets them walk and doesn't give them another thought. Now you on the other hand have done some crazy things to my man."

"What do you mean?"

"Well for starters he has never asked me to protect anyone before, only him." He said. "He really cares about you and I have never seen that kind of emotion out of him. Whatever it is, you make him try harder and want to be better. I haven't ever seen any girl even come close to getting him to do that." Overwhelmed, I lean over and kiss Randy on the cheek.

"Thank you," I said as Randy glances over at me gulping with a blushing nod.

# Chapter 21: Sean

*A*fter being out late at a charity event, I decide to sleep in, that is until my phone rings. While still groggy I grab my cell, rubbing my face clear to read the number. *Ava?* "Everything okay?" I asked, feeling the smile slowly come across my face.

"It's not Ava, although it probably should be," a husky voice said.

"Who the fuck is this?" I asked.

"Justin, a friend of Ava's."

"Is Ava alright? What's going on?"

"She's fine and I would like for her to stay that way," he said with a tone that wakes me up instantly. "Sean, I may not know you but I know your type. You think you can walk in and out of her life, expecting her to wait for when you are ready to see her again. Is it not enough that you are screwing everything on the west coast you want to make your way to the east coast as well? Leave Ava alone Sean, she's too good for you." Justin said preparing to end our conversation there.

"Don't you dare hang up motherfucker," I said pausing only long enough to make sure he heard me. "You don't know me so I would appreciate it if you didn't classify me to some group of your choosing. Contrary to what you may think, I am not out to hurt Ava and I have been thinking of her from the beginning and I will continue to do just that. So while I appreciate your concern for her, I think your jealousy of me is clouding your judgment."

"You care about her? You are so full of shit! You know you don't give a DAMN about anyone but yourself! You smug son of a bitch, YOU leave her alone or else!"

Standing with fists forming, "or else what?"

"Try me pretty boy but I don't think you want to go there with me."

"I will be right there, or hell I will send you a first class ticket to my front door. But you should take in some sights before you show me your sweet skills because I doubt you will get a chance after."

"I'll show you skills. Send me the fucking ticket son, I can't wait. I also can't wait until Ava sees you for what you are."

"And what's that Justin?"

"Nothing but a bored rich boy looking for a flavor of the month to get him through until the next one speaks to his cravings."

"You don't know what the fuck you're talking about, so why don't you hang up and go find some girl of your own and leave mine alone …"

"YOU'RE GIRL!" He laughed. "Fuck you! Let me tell you something! Ava, as far as I'm concerned, is fair game and since she's met you it only makes it that much easier to make her mine."

"OHHH, *I have* to hear this."

"You're never here, Sean. You're not here to hold her when she's upset after a bad day or enjoy her smile when she knows she's hit on a great design. But I am. Every time she needs someone I'm here, holding her and fighting off those scary dreams of hers. She needs more than a phone call and I am the one that is able to give her more. Sooner or later, she is going to realize whom she needs and it is not going to be some Hollywood pretty boy who only sees her when his schedule allows. Who do you think she's going to choose Sean?" He huffs, "you know what it doesn't really matter because I am going to be here no matter what." Justin inhales obviously feeling proud of himself.

"I'm not letting her go and nothing you do or say is going to change my mind."

"Well you've been warned. For now I am going to continue my quest for Ava and since I see her everyday it shouldn't take me long to work *you* out of her mind. Have a good night Sean." He hangs up abruptly.

"Son of a bitch!" I scream before rushing to call Ethan to change my schedule.

CXEO

*M*y remaining event has been cancelled, which gives me the opportunity to leave town earlier than expected. My reservations are booked for Atlanta, seconds after knowing. This is going to be the first time I see where she lives, how she lives and I am more than curious after all of our conversations. "You're going to have a heart attack before you ever get there, not to mention you're driving me nuts. So stop fidgeting!" Randy glares at me.

I huff staring out the window as the Atlanta skyline approaches. No one expects me to be here. Ethan has someone impersonating me booked on another flight and to a much likelier place for me to be. I am hoping that the prying eyes will be too busy searching for me far away to ever consider searching for me here. They have been following me even closer since that kid released the pictures from the restaurant. You could not see Ava at all but that is just making them all the crazier.

As soon as I get off the plane, I jump into the waiting car. My heart beats faster with every house that passes. "So are you going to tell her?" Randy asked.

"Tell her what?"

"Tell her that you love her."

"I don't know what you're talking about?"

"You don't? I knew it, you're looking for a reason to change your mind about her? Keep running Sean and you will lose her for good."

"That is not at all what I'm doing and I think it is a little early to be talking about love."

"No, it's not." He says assuredly.

"Well I thought I loved Rebecca and I told her in the first few months and what a mistake that was. I'm not doing that again."

"Rebecca was a psycho and low class, Ava is certainly not Rebecca. Thank God. I hope I never have to see that crazy witch again."

I give him a harsh look, "I thought you liked her?" He shakes his head shivering ridiculously. "Well no matter, I'm taking it slowly with Ava. Especially with her past, I don't want to introduce her to my media obsessed life until I know for sure she's the one for me." Randy rolls his eyes while munching on some chips. "Shut up, and stop rolling your eyes at me. You know I hate that. Besides, that crazy fuck that hurt her is still trying to get out and pleading to be able to see her to make an amends. My people intercepted countless letters from his mother that were supposed to go to her by way of her grandparents' house. Supposed apologies, but they are nothing but a lunatics attempt to keep hold of her."

Our driver slows, pulling in next to a quaint cottage home. With a smile I cannot hide, I get out and tip the driver before sending him on his way.

"I don't think you should have sent the driver away Sean, I don't think anyone is home." Randy said looking over the surroundings.

"I know. She's at a meeting all-day today."

"Then why did you send the driver away?" He said waving his hands in the direction the car left.

"Calm down we are going to wait for her."

"Outside?"

"No, of course not, in the house."

"And how are we going to do that?"

"I know where she keeps a key in case she locks herself out." I feel behind one of her rain gutters and pull out a metal box with a key inside.

"Okay Romeo, now let's get inside. It's cold out here."

Making our way to the door I can feel Randy hovering over me the whole way. "Do you mind backing up a bit? We're not on a date here."

"Then hurry up and open the damn door. It's cold out here." I put the key in hearing it click along with some other strange noises. "What was that, I thought you said she wasn't supposed to be home?"

"She's not supposed to be. No one is." I said turning the knob when I hear … sniffing? "It's just her puppies," I smile relieved.

"Puppies? I don't like dogs Sean," Randy said backing up.

"Relax, they're probably no bigger than the palm of your hand, nothing to worry about." I open the door slowly and big snarling noses start trying to force their way through. The enormous faces begin barking and growling in an amazing display of fearlessness. I shut the door back quickly, backing up a couple of steps before searching for Randy, who is now standing on the other side of the street. "What the hell are you doing?"

"No way Sean, no way!"

"No way what? I'm sure they are friendly once you get in."

"Hell no!" Randy yelled folding his arms and shaking his head.

"I tell you what, I will stay here in the front and you sneak in the back and maybe we can trap them in some room. We'll confuse them." I say with confidence.

"What kind of crazy are you trying to sell me? No way in hell am I going in that house!"

"Well what are we going to do, sit out here until she gets home?"

"I don't know but I do know I'm not going in there." Randy insists.

"Maybe they are not as big as they look?" I said as one of them jumps in a nearby window, snarling and barking.

"I have seen horses smaller than that Sean."

"Stop shaking your head, it's annoying." I sit down on the steps listening to the two snarling dogs protesting our presence while Randy carefully sits down next to me.

"Great plan Sean, let's get here early and hang out on her porch and wait for her for … how long?" He asked in a sarcastic voice.

I cringed at his question, "I'm not sure, an hour or two."

"It's December Sean."

"I know!"

"I can't believe you didn't know about those beasts in there."

"We talked about her dogs but she always calls them her babies, or puppies and so I assumed they were small."

"All this time and you have never talked about what kind of beasts they are?" I shook my head at his disgusted expression. "What did you talk about then?" A smile slowly grows across my face. Randy huffs, rolling his eyes. "So what were you planning anyway?"

"Well I thought we could get here early and I could order some food and light some candles, send you off to the bedroom out back." He huffs immediately. "It has satellite TV and its own kitchen, you will be fine you big baby"

"And then what?"

"And then I would arrange all the …"

"All the what?" He asked as I look down the road and away from him. "What did you do?"

"Nothing."

"Sean what did you do?"

"I might have ordered some flowers and other stuff for her."

"How many flowers Sean?"

"Well I wasn't sure how big her house was and I know how much she loves getting flowers. Do you know that I am the first guy to ever give her flowers?" I smile at his unamused expression.

"I am calling the driver back," Randy said pulling his phone out.

"No, no we can't because we have to be here to receive them or they won't come back," I said as vans begin to pull up.

"Oh you didn't." He said watching my innocent smile turn to pleading forgiveness. Randy tried to talk them into coming back but they have to deliver them all, plus some extras. By the time they finish, her entire porch, steps and our laps are filled with flowers, balloons and one extra large teddy bear. We look ridiculous. I am holding flowers and a stuffed bear that sits nearly as tall as I do. Randy holds all the balloons with his flowers and a scowl a mile long. "I hate you Sean." He said as I laugh. "No, I really hate you."

"Well at least the dogs seem to have calmed down. I don't think they want to kill us now."

"I think they're trying to decide what seasoning they are going to use on us." Randy looks behind us. "Hey big dogs, white meat tastes better!" He yelled nodding as if he has gotten me back. Laughing I settle against the bear making myself as comfortable as possible.

We wait as car after car slows down to look at the two fools on the porch. One nice old lady even makes time to walk by and tell us she doesn't think Ava is home. Randy thanks her for pointing out the obvious and luckily she is hard-of-hearing and walks off smiling when we nod and wave at her. Finally, Ava's car pulls up, slowing before turning into the drive. I sit up straight watching as the car doors open and a man gets out the passenger side, while she gets out the driver side smiling beautifully and looking incredible. My mouth waters watching her approach.

"Congratulations Sean, I think you surprised her. I bet she never thought she would come home to see this," Randy said.

"Welcome home," I said beaming.

"What are you doing here?" She laughs taking in the entire scene, searching for her way towards me.

"Waiting for you to get home," I said helping her over some of the flowers.

"I can't believe you're here. I thought …"

"I wanted to surprise you."

"Surprise!' Randy said sarcastically.

She laughs as she manages her way into my arms. "Best surprise ever," she said, kissing me and allowing me to express a superior smile in Randy's direction.

"Why are you out here, why didn't you use the key?"

"We tried, but …."

"Your so called puppies turned out to be man-eating bears," Randy continued.

"Who Rondo and Prince? They're sweethearts they wouldn't hurt a fly. Simply play ball with them and they will love you to death." She grimaced at the phrase. "Well you know what I mean." Randy backs away from the door as she lets the two beasts out to sniff us.

"Let them get to know you, they really are sweet," Kyle said. I stood up trying to be still, as he walks over to me. "Boys go play! Hi, I'm Kyle." He holds out the one free hand he has, the other holding a bag of groceries. I greet him respectively and he shakes his head. "Wow! I mean I know all about you but it's so unreal that you're here. I mean wow."

"Kyle will you help us get this all inside?" Ava asked while examining her porch before glancing up at me with a smirk. Shrugging I turn to see the other fool standing in the middle of the yard like a statue and still holding balloons while the two dogs stand at his feet, pawing him for attention.

"Ava, can you call your dogs?" I laugh.

"Boys come." They follow in after her at once.

"The coast is clear you big baby, you can breathe now." I yelled to him.

"I hate you Sean." He said looking both ways before he enters the house.

Once we put up the flowers, I explore her warm and cozy place, looking at pictures of her grandparents, friends, and her dogs – there are many of those. Then one framed, sitting right on her mantel where you can see it from anywhere in the room is the same one I put under her locket. I pick it up daydreaming back to our island. Suddenly the front door opens and I turn right before a short, brown haired woman runs right into me. She looks up smiling joyfully, "oh sorry," she said as I take hold of her to steady her. "AHHHHH!" She screamed. "Oh my God!" She screamed again and vibrating. I take a few steps back from her, putting my hands up in defense.

"Anna!" Ava yelled running over to grab her.

"Sean, this is Anna." I put my hand out cautiously to shake her trembling hand. Taking my hand she begins to giggle hysterically.

"Nice to meet you - Anna."

"Yea … uh huh, I mean you too."

"Are you alright?" I asked wondering if Ava invites mental people into her home often.

"She's okay, she's going to be okay," Ava said escorting her away from me.

I sit down near Randy who is eyeing both dogs sitting patiently at his feet, one of them with his paw on his leg and staring at a ball resting in his lap. "I hear if you play dead they will get disinterested and leave you alone."

"Shut up Sean," he murmured motionless.

"You should feel honored. They don't let just anyone play with that ball," Ava said from behind us.

"Yea, they like you, their favorite ball and everything, how sweet." He glares at me as he mumbles terrible things he is going to do to me. Once the smell of dinner gets to me, I get up to go see who is cooking. I pass Anna carefully since she is still giggling and approach Ava. She chops some vegetables before throwing them in a steaming pan. "Are you cooking?"

"I was planning to make dinner for Kyle and Anna anyway, so I added a little more for you guys. I hope you like it?"

Walking up behind her I wrap my arms around her and kiss her neck and her cheek before resting my head against hers, "I'm sure it will be wonderful." Sighing happily, she leans into me holding my hands to her. "I think everyone should leave now." I whispered as soft and as deep into her as possible. Suddenly, she stiffens pulling away from me and directing me to Kyle and Anna who are staring at us wide-eyed. "Okay, well do you need me to do anything?"

"No, I think Kyle and I have it," she said as Kyle waves some kind of cooking utensil at me. "So sit and relax, watch some TV if you like," Ava said, grasping my hand one more time before shoving me off.

I walk into the living room and sit down talking to the boys. "Randy watch, when you talk to them they look like they're listening to you." I turn to the dogs, "you guys want to go play?" I asked as they both cock their heads at the same time. "Did you see that? Cute as hell, huh?"

"Yea ... real cute. They're going to kill you in your sleep tonight, you know that, right?" Randy said, not at all impressed.

"Are you guys going to kill me? I know stupid question right, you guys love me already." I throw the nearest toy I can find and watch them slip and slide all over the hardwoods to try to get to it first. I laugh until I hear someone laughing behind me, turning I see only Ava watching me. For whatever reason I earn a kiss bigger than the welcome home kiss. I need to figure out what I did so I can do it again.

When we sit to eat, it is clear the empty seat next to Ava is for me. The food is wonderful and luckily easy to eat with one hand since my other is holding Ava's and even though it is obvious, no one is commenting on it. They do, however, tell me stories that are embarrassing her relentlessly.

"Oh and then there was the time she told us we were going to the spa." Kyle exclaimed.

"No Kyle!" She tries to persuade him with her anxiously, shaking head.

"Oh I am telling this one because he should know this about you. She's a liar, Sean. I'm telling you if she ever tries to tell you she is taking you somewhere like a spa for instance and she insists on driving, don't believe a word she says." Kyle animatedly tells his tale.

Ava stares down into her lap. "Why?" I asked lifting her chin with my finger and brushing the back of it across her velvet face.

"Well. One day Ava comes in and tells us she has an exciting surprise for us, you know for working so hard and …" He turns to look at Anna.

"And being such great friends," Anna added.

"Yea that, so she told us she was going to take us to this spa … in Kentucky. Now I had never heard of such a spa but what do I know, I from Georgia. So we got all excited, packed and even got up early so we could get there by what we thought was check-in time."

"Where did she take you?"

"To a basketball game!" Kyle exclaimed crossing his arms.

"You like basketball that much?" Randy asked.

"Ava here, is a huge basketball fan," I said remembering her playing on the island and our almost first kiss.

"Oh yea, she made us walk *forever* in the cold too," Kyle added.

"It wasn't that cold," Ava said shyly.

"It was February Ava. Then we had to sit through this game. We had to check into some hotel that was not a spa at all and nowhere close to where we had to endure that torturous sport. The worst part is they barely had decent room service."

"But I took you guys out horseback riding the next day."

"It was Febr … u … ary!" Anna spoke up.

"Alright, I'm horrible, a horrible person but I couldn't find anyone to go with me, and I knew you wouldn't go if I asked you," She said pitifully as she fumbles with her napkin.

Pushing her fallen hair out of her face, I lean in kissing her on the cheek. "I would have gone with you baby," I said enjoying her smile at me.

"Ohhh, that's so sweet," Anna said, gushing, causing me to blush and then to get annoyed by Randy smirking at me.

"Well I don't want you to think she is all bad Sean or at least she isn't totally evil. She did eventually pay for us all to go on a cruise a few months later."

"Thanks Kyle," she smiled at him.

"You're welcome," he said kissing her on the other cheek.

"Okay, I think it's time for me to go," Anna said looking at her watch.

"Oh yea, you can still take me home right?" Kyle followed as Anna nods.

"You know I think I am done for the night as well. Ava, Sean said you had some place for me to stay?" Randy asked.

"Yes, I think you will like it, it's in the in-law suite in the back. Most of it is my office but the whole upstairs is an apartment with satellite TV and everything. There is a full kitchen and a bathroom. I will show you."

While Ava leads Randy out back and the other two leave for home, I grab my bag and search for her room. I assume the location and know I am correct by the softness of the room. It even smells like her. I breathe in, laying my things down in a corner before looking at more pictures.

"What are you doing?" She asked coming up behind me with her hands making their way up my chest.

"Looking at your pictures and I was right by the way."

"About?"

"You were super cute," I said pointing to her in a picture.

"I was five, everybody is cute at five."

"Not that cute," I said, kissing her blush and feeling the usual electric current run through my body whenever I am near her. Despite the warning that her clothes are difficult to get off. I still have her undressed in seconds and making my way to an enjoyable night. I did not realize how much I have missed her.

# Chapter 22: Ava

*I* awake to darkness, chilled air, and warm arms as I feel the rise and fall of his chest against my bare back. I do not want to get up but I know the choice isn't mine to make. So giving into my fears, I squeeze out from under his arm, pull on my robe, and cautiously walk through the house. Holding my breath, I open the back door and let the boys outside while I stand stiff watching the yard, the light, the shadows from the moon and listening for anything … but there is nothing.

"Ava?" Gasping I tense my back up against a wall before realizing it's Sean. "Sorry I didn't mean to scare you?"

"It's okay, I guess I was deep in thought."

"Deep in thought about what?" I shake my head ignoring his question. "I watched you Ava. I watched you get up trembling. When you let the dogs out you watched every shadow without taking a breath. You don't feel safe here?" *Safe? The place doesn't have anything to do with it.* No matter where I live, he still could find me. No matter how much my doctor tells me what happened to me, won't happened again. I can't help see him around every corner or within every shadow. It is, after all, not the man but the piercing echoes of his voice that haunt me still. "He's still in jail you know?" Sean said.

"How do you know that?" I asked pushing back from his chest.

Sighing and fumbling with my fingers, "my father handled business for many important people Ava and they are more than willing to help my family out whenever we ask, so I asked for the information. I have someone keeping me informed on his every move. I promise sweetheart, I only did it to make sure he never hurts you again."

"So you know everything?" He stands tall and silent. "You know everything?" I asked realizing my biggest fear about seeing him has come true.

"Yes, I saw the whole case file, transcripts from the hearing and even details of his daily records in prison." Sean confessed shamefully.

"Even the pictures they took of me and …"

"I wasn't trying to invade your privacy, Ava. I didn't know anything like that would be in there." He said rubbing his face. "Ava, damn, for what he did to you, I could kill him myself. Please don't be mad at me." His voice breaks as he reaches out for me, "you can trust me, you know. You're not alone anymore, I'm here and I will always watch out for you." Sinking deep into his strong arms I do feel safe and loved.

附

*T*he screaming alarm brutally disrupts my perfect dream. I retaliate harshly before trying to untangle myself from him, making sure to kiss every part that I have to move away from me. I manage to get halfway up before he pulls me back in, smiling his sexy, I am too cute for my own good smile. "Hey, I have to get up and get some work done today, remember?"

"Call in sick," he said roughly against my lips.

"Don't you think they will get suspicious?"

With his eyes still nearly closed, he shakes his head. "No? Sean you know better" I said laughing harder as he holds on to me tighter and more determined to convince me. "You have to let go. I'm sorry but I have to work and you are going to have to stay here and be a good boy."

Growling at me, "your bed is too small."

"My bed is too small?" I asked narrowing my eyes at him.

"I like big beds that give you plenty of room to …," he said pulling me back in and maneuvering me around to some secure spot that he can manage me in. "Big enough, to you know … to do things right." His warm lips move up my neck while his hands pull my legs up around him.

"Sean, I can't get a bed any larger than I have, it won't fit in my room," I squirm escaping his grasp.

"I will get you a bigger room and then a larger bed."

I lean into his face quickly kissing him. "No, you won't." I say before running off to shower, he follows soon after. "And you are most certainly not taking a shower with me, Sean Grant." His hurt expression nearly causes me to feel bad until I realize his career choice. "No Sean!"

"Why not, I like taking showers with you," his bedroom eyes working me hard.

"Because I will never get ready and get to work."

"Fine, can I watch then?" He asks smiling wide.

"Get out," I hiss at him. Trying to fight my smile, I shut the door in his sweet face and laugh when I hear him doing the same. After getting ready, I find Sean sitting at the bar, drinking his coffee. "Are you hungry?"

"Too early for food," he said as I take notice of his drawstring pants and nothing else. I stick some toast in the toaster and pour some cereal before moving in beside him. Taking my hand in his, we kiss and get a little closer.

"You guys can stop being so damn obnoxiously sweet, it is too early for that," Kyle demanded looking half-asleep as usual, when he and Anna arrive for their typical morning breakfast. "Oh good somebody has the coffee already made." Kyle said taking notice of Sean's cup. "Thank you," he says to Sean's half nod back.

"Ava, cereal?" Anna said mummy walking towards the kitchen.

"On the counter."

"I guess I should go check on Randy." Sean kisses me once before walking out the door and taking the boys with him.

I watch him walk away only to turn back around to see Anna and Kyle doing the same. "Hey!" I yelled breaking their gaze.

"If you want to keep us from staring then you might want to tell him to wear a shirt," Kyle said.

"And some underwear," Anna whispered into her cereal.

"Anna!" I yelled.

"What? The man has been blessed - so I am looking. Sorry. But really, it's hard not to look at him." Anna grunted.

"Find a way. At least you stopped giggling at him," I said taking a sip of Sean's coffee.

"Yea Anna you were embarrassing last night," Kyle bumps her playfully.

"Me?" She stands up straight with her chin out but we do not budge in our statements. "Okay, I will try to behave but I'm not making any promises. Oh Ava! Do you think you can get Sean to let me go to one of those celebrity parties? Maybe …"

"No! Absolutely not! We are not even seeing each other according to the outside world. I certainly can't have him setting you up with some kind of freaky celebrity fling."

"It doesn't have to be freaky, unless that's what they are into." Anna shrugs.

They both perk up immediately when Sean walks back in. "How is he and where are the boys?" I asked.

He smiles devilishly and shrugging. "As soon as I opened the door they ran in and got into bed with him. I guess they like him."

"You're cruel," I said as he sits back down beside me. I don't think men ever grow out of their little boy games. They mature and find ways to make you not care or forget completely, if they know what they are doing and possibly your own name too, if you're real lucky. *I'm feeling very lucky these days.* I smile hoping no one notices but he does and is smiling at me knowingly. *What, does he read minds or something? That could be embarrassing.* I roll my eyes away from him. *Cocky bastard.*

"Okay, let's get going. We have so much to do and I would love to get out of here early today and I know Ava feels the same way. Right?" Kyle raises his eyebrows at me.

"Let me get changed and I will be over in a few minutes."

Suddenly the boys are by my side. "You are an asshole Sean." Randy said followed by Sean's hysterical laughter.

Shaking my head, I make my way through my closet. I have to meet with a client today so I pull out one of my favorite outfits and slide on some of my favorite heels and admire them on my foot. I find the right jewelry and finish my hair, then begin the custom twisting and turning in front of the mirror and decide I need a different pair of underwear. I pull out a more suitable pair and push my skirt up, slipping my others off and my new ones on when I hear a gasping grunt. I turn seeing Sean watching me from the bed.

"I could have helped you get that … off." I throw the ones I took off at him, earning a desiring wink.

"How long have you been there?"

"You're fun to watch get dressed, almost as much fun as watching you undress, pink underwear today … mmm." He crawls over to me grabbing my butt and twirling his tongue in his mouth. "Must be a special client?"

"Behave," I said smacking his hands.

"That's going to be hard knowing what's under there. All that lace and pink and …." He smiles.

"Try. Please." I kiss him quickly and release his grasp, sprinting out before he can catch me.

"Good morning, Randy." I said laughing at Sean just missing getting a hold of me.

"Morning." Randy said eyeing Sean and rolling his eyes at him.

"There is plenty of food Randy, help yourself." Sean sits down watching me with his eyes, driving me crazy and he knows it. "So what are you boys going to do today?" I asked trying to hug him from behind to keep away from his hands.

"Not sure, although where is your Christmas tree?" Sean asked pulling me around into his lap.

"Oh I haven't had a chance to get one yet," I giggled struggling with his hands.

"Well then that's what we are going to do today," he said kissing my cheek. "Unless you would rather me do something else to you?" He whispered.

"We are? Where the hell are we going to put it?" Randy interrupted looking around at the flower-filled room. "Can't we just stack some of these flowers in a tree formation and put a star on top or hell let's tie the balloons to the top. I think there's a star on one of them?"

"We will get you a tree today, baby, if we may borrow your car?" Sean asked, laughing at me still fighting his wandering hands.

"You may. Now stop before you embarrass Randy."

"He knows when to leave," he smiles wide ignoring Randy's huff.

"Nice Sean. Now I have to go ... now," I said pushing away to his immediate sadden face.

# Chapter 23: Sean

*A*va obviously loves her car, not a speck of dirt or anything out of place. Randy and I drive around the area until we find a place with a lot full of trees and void of any people except one bear of a man working the lot.

"Can I help ya?" A voice called out.

"I would like the best tree you have."

"How tall you looking for?" He said spitting off to the side.

I looked back at Randy only to receive a shrug of his shoulders. "I don't know what do you suggest?"

He laughs at me shaking his head and mumbling something under his breath. "How tall are your ceilings?"

"My ceilings, nine or ten feet?" *Hell if I paid attention.*

"Follow me." He sighed. "Alright I would say this baby right here is your best bet."

"I'll take it."

"Do you want it delivered or do you want it tied to your pretty little car?" He said motioning towards Ava's car.

I eye him to back off before my good mood diminishes. "Delivered will be fine, thank you"

After we buy the tree, Randy convinces me to tour the city some before heading back. As it turns out, we stop only once more to pick up some Barbeque for Randy, the Alabama boy. When we arrive back, Ava's client has already arrived, discouraging my hopes for a private lunch. Randy lays out the food and huffs at the dogs whimpering at his feet. "I don't think so dogs, you're not getting a bite of this."

"This is good."

"I told you. Damn this is one of the things I miss the MOST."

Leaning back with my sandwich I take notice of Ava's client sitting with Kyle, both watching Ava as she talks to him with her hands passionately and glasses on. Her every move is impressive.

"You know if I wasn't enjoying this food so much, I might be offended."

"What can I say? She's amazing."

"She's amazing and you are in mad love my friend."

"Would you stop with that love shit? I'm happy and there is no reason to screw that up right now." As soon as I see Kyle walk out of the office with the client, I wrap up the rest of my food rapidly. "Don't eat my other sandwich I put in the refrigerator, I am going to go see if Ava has any decorations for this tree that's coming." I run out the door before Randy has a chance to respond and enter her office quietly.

"Did you get me a tree?" She said smiling at me from the corner of her eyes, while I try to sneak up on her.

"I did." Surrendering and taking hold of her. "Is it okay I'm here?"

"A few minutes might be okay."

"So what were you presenting today?"

"He found an existing warehouse that he wants converted into a Jazz bar," she said pulling out the presentation boards to show me.

"These are good, Ava," I said realizing it is the first time I have gotten to see her work.

"Thank you, but you probably should have looked at my work before you hired me."

"I guess you do work for me."

"Yes sir. So are you happy with the service so far?" She leans up against a table eyeing me seductively or at least in my mind she is.

"Mostly."

"Is there something I can do to make you happier?"

I check one more time to make sure we are alone before turning back to Ava and lifting her onto the table. With her glasses and her hair pulled back, she is irresistible. "I want to feel like I'm your only client." Running one hand up her leg, the other intertwines in her hair, I nose her glasses with a wanting smile. "These are sexy by the way." I said maneuvering between her legs causing her skirt to push up her thighs as I caress her sides gently. "And I like this sweater, it looks nice on you."

"Sean, I can't right now."

"Why?" I asked moaning against her cheek.

"Because if I do this now I may not be able to get any work done today and Kyle will kill me if I leave now."

"Come on, it's lunch time. You have to have a break right?" I said kissing her neck down to her breasts that I manage to expose fully.

"No," she said breathing heavily and causing me to smile.

Feeling my success, I help her off the table and take her hand guiding her into her office, immediately pulling the blinds and shutting the door, locking us in. Whispering in her ear, "am I your best client?"

"Yes," she says pulling me in close.

"Prove it."

# Chapter 24: Ava

*I* knew when I left him, there is no way he is going to get that tree the way I want it but maybe I can try and let it go this once. Right now, I have to try to put the tree decorating and the memories from being laid out on my desk out of my mind so I can work. Kyle and Anna are still smirking and laughing at me. If we had any hope that we had fooled anybody it was erased as soon as we walked into the house.

*I can still see Randy's knowing expression as he spoke. "Next time, make sure the blinds stay closed so no one else can see." Randy said relaxing confidently.*

*Sean and I both jump looking back at the perfectly secure blinds. We breathe a sigh of relief before we realize we had confirmed their suspensions. "Asshole." Sean said glaring at him as Randy smiles wide.*

With only an hour left in the day I dive into some plans on my computer, trying to concentrate when Anna comes running into my office with panic clearly overtaking her usual joyful expression. "What is it?"

"Guess who just pulled in?" She said with half a step and a whisper.

"I don't know? Who?"

"Jusss … tinnn," she stressed wide-eyed. "Ava! With Sean here, do you really think it is a good idea? How is Sean going to react to him? Or Justin to Sean?"

"I don't think it's as bad as you are acting Anna. Justin and I never had anything between us other than friendship and Sean knows that already. And, I have told Justin all about Sean and he is happy for me. I admit they weren't too keen on each other at first but I think they are both over all that now."

"Sure that's all fine and good in your little fantasy world that you have created but in reality you have two men who both are clearly in love with you. Men have fought for fewer reasons," Anna said animatedly.

"Oh don't be absurd," I said waving her off.

"Am I?" Anna said planting her hands at her sides.

Kyle suddenly pops his head through the doorway. "Ava get a clue, there is going to be some bloodshed if you don't do something quick."

"What would you have me do?"

"Keep them apart, head off Justin before Sean sees him, and then keep him from the house before he sees Sean," Kyle said exasperated as if I should know this already. *My first real boyfriend in ... well ever and I am supposed to be an expert already?*

After thinking for a couple of seconds, I meet Justin at the door pulling him into my office and away from the windows. My watchdogs keep the perimeter under guard to shout out warning signals if need be.

"Hey beautiful," Justin said picking me up and hugging me in his usual way.

"Hey sweetie let's talk about … things," I said hiding my concern from his obvious curiosity.

"Okay, but I brought you those plans you wanted and I wanted to hear about your meeting today but I'm also hungry as hell," he said gesturing towards the house. "Mind if I go grab something real quick first?"

"Can it wait? I'm anxious to tell you about the meeting."

"Sure but I think we will need the plans, let me go get them."

"We'll get them!" Kyle and Anna chimed in a little too enthusiastically.

Justin looks at them suspiciously but pulls out his keys and throws them to Anna. "O … kay." Justin chuckles and turns towards me with a curious expression. "I don't know what that's about and I don't care if you come have dinner with me. It is almost time for you to finish up here and you still owe me a dinner anyway.

I nod knowingly as I struggle to think. "Yea, ummm. So how …" I hesitated hearing the phone ring. *Damn.* "Give me one minute," I said holding up my hands to hold him in place like one of my dogs.

"No worries, go ahead," he said stretching out in my chair.

I pick up the phone and quickly become involved in the conversation before noticing that Justin does not wait long. When I finish my phone conversation he is already halfway to the main house. "Oh no." I watch Justin stop halfway, cocking his head to one side and turning to look back at me with understanding before walking eagerly into the house. Hanging up and as natural as possible,

I walk through the door unsure of what I might be walking into. *Silence.* Good I think, but after a second glance, I realize that it isn't so good after all. While Justin is helping himself to everything in my kitchen and smiling way too much, Sean is standing in the middle of the living room eyeing Justin with a snarl and tensed fists. Randy however, is merrily hanging lights on the tree seemingly enjoying the awkwardness. *Great.* "So." *Which name do I say first?* I battle in my head trying to decide if it matters. "Justin did you meet Sean and Randy." Sean turns to me with harsh eyes. *Clearly, it does matter.*

"No, I assumed he was another stray you sought to help out by paying him to put up your tree. I thought you could do a lot better but you're always a sucker for the less fortunate looking, Ava." Justin said casually walking to my side and taking support from my shoulder. "So you're the actor my girl has been talking about."

"Your girl?" Sean snarled at him.

"Oh hold up, that's just what I call her. No reason to get defensive son."

"Can you please be good and go eat your sandwich?" I nudge Justin in the side hard pushing him away to go sit and eat his food.

"Oh yea, I found this incredible barbeque sandwich in the refrigerator." Justin smiles taking a huge bite out of the sandwich with an obvious grin. "I assumed you didn't want it Ava, it's not anything like what you would normally eat anyway."

"Justin I think that was Sean's."

"Oh shit, I'm sorry. What did you get full after your salad?" Justin laughs.

Sean smiles and I run to him expecting the worse to come out of his mouth. "No," Sean says looking down at me. "Ava kept me busy through lunch helping her in her office – it was pretty hot in there."

"Sean." I strain through my teeth at him.

"But don't worry about it I would rather have my time with her than a sandwich any day," Sean caresses and holds me tight to him.

"Well I don't know about her office but it sure is hot in here." Justin said watching me shake my head at him. "No, it's definitely hot, maybe it's you, but I don't think I can take it like this." Removing his shirt, Justin rubs the back of his neck, showing his pride for his bare, muscular body. Glancing at Sean's intense expression, I quickly look down at my feet, surprised by my enjoyment of his obvious jealousy. "Will you look at me, I am a mess.

Damn construction site. I'm sorry Ava would you prefer me to shower in your bathroom again before …" Anna and Kyle enter stumbling over each other while checking out the surroundings, trying to catch up with the events.

"It is fine in here, right Sean?" I asked watching a slow smile take form on his face.

"No, Ava, I think he's right, it is a little hot in here," Sean said removing his shirt, apparently another challenger in the newly battle of the bare chests. Only I find myself squeezed up against this one in a protective ownership form.

"Oh wow! I am sooooo glad we didn't miss this," Anna whispered to Kyle excitedly.

"Ummm, Justin brought me plans to look over for the new project that I showed you this afternoon, Sean."

"Oh yea … the project you showed me right before our private meeting in your office." He said playing with my sweater and kissing me, all the while watching Justin's reaction carefully. I kick him as subtly as I can. "Owe!" He yelped in surprise.

"Stop it."

"No worries Ava, you know how actors are, all fervor, and not much substance to back it up."

Sean lets go of me lunging in Justin's direction, "you want substance? I'll show you substance."

Justin at once meets him eye to eye, "let's go pretty boy."

"Stop it!" I move between them, putting my hand on both of their hardened bare chests. "You're acting like children."

Justin grabs my hand kissing it, "sorry beautiful, you're right"

Sean forces a smile taking my hand from Justin and hovering over me once again. "Sorry baby, you're right." He said staring at Justin as he kisses both of my hands with a debonair attitude and humored by Justin stomping off back towards his sandwich. "Come here, look what we have done for you so far." Cradling me in his warm arms, he shows me the Christmas tree that is nearly completed.

"Oh Sean, it's beautiful."

"You like it?" He whispered in my ear sweetly.

"Yes, it's wonderful."

"And this is how you want it, right?"

"Well you might want to move it out some from the corner so it becomes a bigger presence." I said feeling his hand tense against my stomach while Justin laughs.

"I told you so son. I know how she likes it!" Justin yelled out excessively pleased with himself.

Grimacing and realizing what I have just done, "you did a great job picking it out Sean, I love it. Thank you. You are sweet to do this for me." Jumping into his arms and taking in his lips forcefully, I make sure to balance the scales back towards Sean's happiness.

"You're welcome, anything for you."

"Are you ready to go over those plans?" Justin barked.

Sighing as Sean glares, "sure why don't you go ahead over and I will be there in a second." I nudge Sean to get his attention back on me.

"Sure, Randy … Pretty Boy." He nodded towards them each lingering on Sean's tense expression before he leaves. Justin chuckles to himself while holding the door open for Anna and Kyle.

"Sean." I said pulling his face down to look at me. "I shouldn't be long and then we can finish the tree together, okay?"

"Why don't you let Kyle go over the plans and you stay with me?"

"Do you not trust me? I am only going to be a few feet from you, nothing is going to happen."

"I know but I want to spend more time with you," he whimpered.

"That's not it, you're jealous."

He pulls away from me huffing and rolling his eyes. "You're crazy, I don't trust that guy is all."

"You are jealous, I don't care what you say."

"I am not …," he tries to protest.

"Yes you are Sean, as soon as you saw him walk through the door like he owned the place you were ready to rip him apart. All because you're j …e …a … l …o … u …s, jealous," Randy sung ignoring Sean's evil glares at him.

I put my arms around his neck, kissing his snarled lip. "I am going to finish up some work and then I will be back to spend time … *alone* with you?" I kiss him once more before escaping his grasp and walking out the door.

Back at the office, I give Justin the meanest look I can muster. "Oh come on, he's a big boy, he can take it!"

"Justin that was uncalled for. You could have made that a whole lot easier on me."

"I'm sorry Ava. I promise I will be a good boy from now on."

"Uh huh. Come on, let me see what you have." Getting down and into the drawings Justin moves in close to me.

"Justin!" I snapped.

"I'm just trying to get a better look Ava, calm down." Justin stays clear from me for whole five seconds before he is back to caressing my arm.

Jumping away from him, "why are you acting this way?"

Standing back on his heels and huffing, "I don't like *him*. AT ALL!" Justin glances over my shoulder suspiciously. "I like pissing him off."

I turn seeing Sean eyeing him through the window. "Would you please let me make my own choices?"

"He's not right for you! He is never going to be able to give you what you want Ava!"

"And you know what I want!"

"I do," he said confidently.

"And what's that?" I asked glancing over at Kyle who is trying to ignore the argument.

"Ava! Are you that blind? Do you think he is going to marry you, have children with you?" He waves his arm as if displaying some storyboard I cannot see. "Build some kind of life with you?" I put my hand up to my mouth suddenly feeling nauseous and have to shake my head carefully. "I'm wrong? That's not what you want?" He said strongly.

"No you don't know him, you don't know … him," I said as tears start to form in my eyes.

"I'm sorry Ava, I don't want to hurt you, but I think you are living in some dream world right now."

"Why don't you let her enjoy her life?" Kyle stands up in protest while Anna comes running up to comfort me.

"Justin do you think now is the best time to talk about this?" Anna said calmly.

"Oh I got it now! So, we should wait until she gets deeper involved with him and after he leaves her… THEN we say something?" Justin mocked harshly.

"Do you all think this?" I said surprised by their eyeing one another and ignoring me.

"Ava, no, I mean who knows what can happen," Kyle said.

"Sweetie we think he's wonderful and he obviously cares for you. You shouldn't think too much about it, be happy, who knows what can happen," She said pausing and sighing.

"You're all crazy. He's going to leave her, and then we're all going to be left picking up the pieces."

"She should enjoy the time she has with him!" Kyle exclaimed.

"Enjoy the time she has? Are you kidding? And what will that mean when she is crushed by this fucker, when he leaves her for someone new and then she has to watch him all over the place with some Hollywood slut? Not to mention, that crazy ass who is constantly trying to find her? Which is surely going to happen because of that little bitch she's seeing in there," Justin exclaimed animatedly.

"I don't think Sean is going to let that happen, he seems to care about her," Kyle tried to reason, while my head starts to spin.

"Oh how fucking wonderful, the asshole cares. He isn't going to care too much when you are ready to get married Ava or have children or have any type of long lasting life together. You're going to always be waiting for him ..."

"Stop! Just stop, I am happy for the first time in ..." *Whoa.* Suddenly the world goes sideways and black.

# *Chapter 25: Sean*

"**O**h shit!" Suddenly Randy's eyes go wide. "Ummm Sean, whatever you do, you need to remain calm." Not understanding his sudden concern, I turn and see Justin carrying Ava to the house with Kyle and Anna following close behind.

"What the hell did you do to her?" I yelled forcing her from his arms to mine.

"Nothing," Justin insisted.

Laying her on the sofa, "Ava, what happened?"

"I got dizzy is all," she said trying to get up.

"No, lay still and I will get whatever you need."

Anna approaches Ava with a cold cloth, "here sweetie."

I stand up and rage at Justin, "I think you need to go!"

"You don't tell me anything!" He yells back into my face.

Kyle jumps between us, "I think Ava would be better off if we gave her some space to feel better, right Justin?"

"I want to make sure she's alright." Justin says a little calmer.

"Anna, I don't feel so good," Ava cried out grabbing hold of Anna who quickly helps her up.

"I think you need to go," I eyed Justin with contempt.

"I said I want to make sure she's alright first."

"You can go, I will make sure someone calls you if we need you." I said with a pleasant smile.

"We huh? *We* were all here before you and believe me son, *we* will all be here to pick up the pieces after you." Justin pokes me in the chest.

"You don't know anything about me." I push him away from me.

"Wow that's funny, that's exactly what she said, and I don't believe either one of you," he gets in my face and I respond equally.

"Okay gentlemen I think it's time to break this up," Randy forces his way between us.

"Don't worry about it Randy, he's just mad that she chose me over him. I get it, not that it has happened to me before but I get it."

"Oh Sean Grant, what a brilliant and promising actor but too bad you make such a horrible boyfriend and an even worse future husband. Ava must be nuts." My smile disappears as Justin's smile returns even brighter. "She hasn't talked to you about this at all, has she? Figures. This *relationship*, is going to be over before I even thought. Nice knowing you Sean. I think I will leave, tell Ava I will call her later. Oh and by the way … Sean … if you don't mind, watch yourself on the way out of her life because if that crazy fuck finds her because of you? Well let's just say you better expect a visit to your front door." He said grabbing his jacket and walking out.

"Thank goodness it's Friday, you people make me want to drink heavily," Kyle exclaimed collapsing on the sofa.

"You good?" Randy asked.

"Perfect," I said through my teeth, walking away from everyone to find Ava. Before I can get too far, I am met with Anna coming from the bathroom and trying to stop me from going any further.

"Sean, she is really sick." I walk around her finding Ava crumpled on the bathroom floor.

"Baby are you okay?"

"Yes," she whimpered.

I pick her up off the floor, tuck her safely in her warm bed and make my way back to the living room where I find Anna and Kyle making dinner and Randy playing with the dogs.

"How is she?" Kyle asked.

"I put her in bed but I think she's feeling a little better now. What happened?" Kyle and Anna look at each other ignoring my question. "What happened?"

"What do you mean?" Anna asked innocently.

"Something was said to her to make her so upset. So what was it?"

Kyle looking down, "Justin."

"Justin said what exactly?" Feeling my fists form and my body tense, "never mind I already know don't I?" Kyle nods. "We have barely been together long enough for anyone to judge how long or short our relationship is going to last. We certainly haven't been together long enough for Ava to even consider me Daddy potential. This whole thing is absurd."

Anna laughs. "You don't know much about women do you? She has never actually said anything specifically about you but that is exactly what she wants. We can only assume that since you're her first real boyfriend in … a long damn time that she has become a little more hopeful about the potential than she should."

"If you only knew what she's been through, I mean really knew, then you would understand why I worry so much." Kyle said watching my reaction.

"I know everything Kyle, more than even you."

"You know?" Kyle questions while I nod sheepishly. "How? Because there is no way she told you."

"No, I took it upon myself to find out and yes, she knows this already. I don't want to hurt her Kyle, I want to protect her as much as you do."

"Then make sure you consider her before you do anything. You two could not be a worse possible match considering. As soon as the press finds out about you two, they will make her life hell bringing all that up again."

"They're not going to find out."

"How long can you hide Sean? Sooner or later, someone is going to find out and then what? Have you even considered it?" Kyle asked sighing with a defeated frustration. "Forget it, it's too late anyway."

After long pauses and awkward stances, I am finally left standing alone and confused. Settling into the sofa, I stare at the television while my thoughts wander elsewhere. *I don't know what I was thinking, I should have let her go on the island. There is no way we can get out of this now without trouble.*

"Hi," she whispered, sneaking into my lap and warming me up. "Thank you for putting me in bed."

"You're welcome," I moan into her fragrant hair. "Feel better?"

"Yea I became a little dizzy, tired from fighting with Justin I guess. I wish you two could get along."

"Sorry, I don't think that's ever going to happen." Her sweet smile, beautiful blue eyes and admiring touch continues to hold me captive and reminding me why I disregarded all those reasons to let go of her in the first place. After a few minutes with her, again, I ignore my better judgment. "So what do you want to do tomorrow beautiful?"

◌⃰

**O**ur first full day together is at the park with the boys. Ava was worried that I would not be able to go out in public with her but I wore what I could to disguise myself and few even bother to look our way. We become comfortable, ignoring the world around us. It is easy laying back and enjoying being with her, playing fetch with the boys. It is a perfect day and again I find no reason, to ever leave her and I am starting to wonder if I can give her what she needs.

As I lie here in bed, tracing her body gently with my fingers, she sleeps soundly on my chest and I struggle to search for anything that can make ... us ... possible.

CROS

**O**ur second day, is baking day, we are making Christmas cookies and candy, while watching old Christmas movies. I made sure to let her know that I would prefer to be naked doing it but she said it was not a good idea to cook naked, you might burn things you treasure. I am sure she is right but when she accused me of having no control around her, I took offense. I am determined to prove that I can easily deny her and prove I can work around her with no attempts at all to encourage her to take her clothes off. Although, I have considered asking her if I can spread the chocolate all over her body so I can lick it off. Now that the cookies are lying out to cool and most of the candy has been set, I decide to let my achievement be known with a mocking strut. Ava not amused, walks out of the kitchen in a huff. Whistling loudly to make sure to drive my point home, I continue with my victorious acts until she reappears in a frilly red and white checked apron and nothing else. Choking on my merry tune, I immediately feel aroused. I watch her dance around happily with her bare ass and her tits bouncing freely against the barely there apron. She brushes by me sliding her fingers down my arm and I gasp watching her go on as if she doesn't know what she is doing. *Two can play this game.* I find another apron for myself, a plain white one. I take everything off, tying it around my waist and letting my bare chest show proudly before proceeding to the kitchen where I enjoy watching her eyes widen at the site of me. *Oh! She is SO mine!* Grabbing a spoon of chocolate we had made, "so is this done?" I hold it out so she will have to look at me.

Joyfully she turns and without hesitation walks up to me, takes hold of my hand, sticks her tongue out and moaning, licks my spoon, "mmm yea. Its sooo ... done." She smiles seductively walking away from me with her perfect ass hanging out below the tie and ruffles. *Done? I am not giving in first, despite my enormous hard on.* Without even a glance in my direction, she diligently cleans up the leftover mess from our cooking. *Now she is ignoring me again? I don't think so.*

Tossing the spoon and moving behind her I lean in, "do you need any help with that?" Making sure she feels my breath against her ear and my respect for her, hard pressed against her ass. She breathes in so deep I assume I am about to win this game but she manages to be unaffected by me and walks away.

"No I'm good, thank you though." I narrow my eyes at her. *She is going to break, she has too!* Devising an even better plan, I begin to move into position but then Ava leans over with her legs slightly spread to put dishes in the dishwasher. My jaw drops, my body begins to shiver, and with my hard on pointing the way, I move forward. Suddenly she glances over her shoulder at me with a knowing smile. *Damn she's good.* Turning away and trying to maintain control, I hold tight to the edge of the counter and hear her get into the refrigerator and begin spraying something. *I am afraid to look.*

"Sean, I think I missed," the southern temptress whispered.

*I'm breaking and I'm starting to pant uncontrollably, whatever you do DON'T look at her.* "Missed what?" I asked focusing hard in the opposite direction.

"Ohhhh look." Instinctively I glance over at the counter in front of her seeing a can of whip cream. *Fuuuck.* I close my eyes tight, trying to block her out. "Sean," she moaned causing a twitch in her direction. *I have to look.* I open my eyes and agonize over her biting her bottom lip and standing with her tits hanging out with whip cream on her nipples and her apron barely hanging on her hips. *Fuck me!* She walks towards me knowing she has me. "Will you get it for me?" Forcefully, I shake my head at her teasing eyes while looking her up and down, sliding my hands off the counter and aching to touch her.

Imagining that sweet cream on my tongue, I begin licking my lips. *I really like whip cream.* "Fuck it, you win." I surrender, grabbing her hips and swirling the cream right off her nipples with my tongue, making sure I do not miss anything. "Oh baby you don't know how hard it was to hold out this long. I was about to bend you over that table and take you when you got into that dishwasher," I moaned continuing to enjoy myself.

"I'll let you, if you tell me who won again."

I pause watching her continue to tease me right into her control. "You win sweetheart, you win." She smiles taking my hand, leading me to the table where I bend her over in front of me, taking only a second to take her in before finding my way deep inside her. Wrapping my arm around her waist, I massage her breasts while searching for her mouth. Listening to her moans with each push and pull, I fight my desires to let go and fuck her like anyone else and forget who she is.

Refocusing I slow my pace until she reaches behind me fisting my hair. "Fuck me, Sean," she pleads repeatedly, groaning and wanting it as much as I do. "Fuck me!"

Upon that request, I lose it, bending her over completely and slamming into her with no words, only harsh gasps and pants, gripping her until I come. Pure pleasure and no emotion. I had not had that since I met her and I hate myself immediately afterwards, especially when I start to feel her trembling. "Why Ava? Why did you want me to do that to you?" I turn her around trying to intersect her view but she avoids me, breaking my heart even more. She is in shock and it's my fault, "I'm so sorry." I said trying to comfort her as best I can. "I don't like treating you like that, Ava, I feel guilty."

"Why? I told you to, I wanted you to … I thought …"

"You thought you could handle it?" She nods and I clench my eyes shut, hanging my head in shame. "Ava, I can fuck anyone, I don't want to fuck you. I wouldn't be here if I just wanted to fuck. Why did you want that?"

"I thought that it would make you happy and maybe you … I don't want you to think I'm boring," she said tears still running down her face as she hides from me. "You didn't try anything while we were cooking and I was afraid you were becoming …"

"YOU told me not to Ava! It's not that I didn't want to but I was trying to respect you."

"I know, I'm sorry." She covers her face crying. "I know you're going to have to leave soon. It's hard not knowing when I'm going to get to see you again. I want to do everything possible to make you happy so you will want to come back."

"When I come back it's not going to be because of sex. I love being with you, you make me feel good about myself. You make me feel incredible, not because of sex but because you smile at me or you laugh at my stupid jokes. You make me feel like you care about me," I said wiping a tear from her cheek.

"I do care about you."

"And I care about you, probably too much because you drive me insane sometimes." Sighing I pull her to me. "The teasing was so incredibly sexy, Ava," I said flicking her chin up with my finger until she looks at me. "But next time when I win, we do it my way, okay?"

"But what if I win again?"

"Not going to happen," I said feeling better as her smile reappears.

"Well I was going to suggest the shower if I win." She said standing on her toes and emphasizing with a kiss.

"Well it won't matter who wins then." I smile giving her a tender kiss on the lips.

CR&ORD

*T*oday she wants to go ice-skating and as always, I give in easily to her. I again cover up to hide who I am but again no one is paying attention, so I shed some of it. As soon as we enter the ice rink Ava begins slipping and sliding. I have done this many times growing up so it is not anything new for me. She, however, is not good at all. "Why would you want to go ice-skating? You are not at all good at it?" I said wrapping my arm around her waist to keep her from falling.

"Maybe I am only pretending to be bad so I can be close to you?"

I laugh, "I don't think so; you are clearly bad at this."

"Whatever," she said trying to do it on her own but quickly falling and pulling me down with her.

"No, you're horrible. I think I should put your picture up and make sure they don't let you in here anymore."

"Fine, I'm not good at this one little thing. Besides how was I supposed to know you would be good at this? I was hoping to get a chance to laugh at you falling."

"Excuse me, but I am from New York."

"New York, I thought you said you were from London?"

"I moved from London to New York when I was young but either way ..." I say as she slips and falls against me. I laugh pulling her back up, "have you still not done your homework? I told you sweetheart, click on the tab that says, *Interesting Facts about Sean.*" I laugh as she rolls her eyes at me. "Now watch where you are going before you knock down some poor unsuspecting person." I pull her to me to protect her and everyone else. *I don't think she is even trying.*

She continues laughing as I keep trying to let her go but again she begins to fall and again I reach out for her pulling her back into my arms, enjoying her huge joyful smile. "Silly girl, I think you actually knew I could skate."

"Maybe," she said smiling suspiciously. "Well, I am a member of the Sean Grant fan club." She opens her jacket showing a shirt underneath with my picture on it and I immediately laugh aloud. "So I read up on you, you know, *Interesting Facts about Sean*." She wiggles in my arms, "and did a little shopping too." She winks at me.

"Why are we here then?"

"Silly boy, so you will have to hold me and never let me go." I lean in taking her lips in mine. "You are the most beautiful, intelligent and clearly ...." I stop short, noticing something out of the corner of my eye.

"What is it?" She asked looking back in the same direction.

"We need to go right now." I rush off so fast that I nearly carry her off the ice, driving us back watching every shadow and car that passes us.

"Sean you're scaring me, what did you see?"

"Nothing. I'm sure I overreacted but it is probably best we get back anyway."

I reassure Ava again that everything is fine before she falls asleep and as soon she does, I sneak away to make a call. "Ethan, I can't be sure but I think I have been found."

# *Chapter 26: Ava*

𝕿he morning approaches with a new awareness. I can barely make it out of bed before getting sick again. Luckily when I make it back to bed, Sean is still sound asleep. I crawl in next to him huddling close and under his warm, protective arms. *I hope the next few months don't continue like this, I am already feeling sleep deprived.* By morning, I awake to an empty bed and to only slight nausea, for now at least. I decide to shower before I see him, to stall. Telling him is not going to be easy and besides I have not confirmed with a doctor yet. If not for Anna's quick math the other day I might still be in the dark, he has clouded everything in my life. With concentrated steps, I make my way to the living room finding Sean standing in front of the television with a serious look. "Sean, I need to talk …"

He jerks his head in my direction, "don't come in here!" He quickly flicks off the TV with a sharp gasp.

"What?" He continues to avoid my eyes. "WHAT?" I jerk the remote from his hand, turning the television back on.

*"Ava - she is very special to me and I to her and as soon as I get out I know we will be together again. I love you Ava - And I forgive you."*

"That was part of an interview with Spencer Jefferis from earlier this morning. Mr. Jefferis is currently serving his sentence in a prison in upstate New York. It is expected that Mr. Jefferis will be released soon for a new trial after defense attorneys have submitted new evidence in regards to Ms. Kelley's role in her alleged abduction." The smug uncaring reporter continues on about how Sean has been seeing me for an unknown amount of time. "I end this report asking you - what do you think? Do you believe Ms. Kelley is manipulating Mr. Grant as she did Mr. Jefferis or is she an innocent victim that will soon be added to the list of Sean Grant's ex-girlfriends? Let us know what you think." Spencer's face flashes on the screen again with his words being repeated, once again. *"… will be together again."*

I barely notice Sean turning off the television as the impious voice echoes over and over in my head. The next thing I know, I am waking up in bed again and finding Sean sitting in a chair next to me with his luggage packed and sitting at the door. "You're leaving me?"

"If I leave now then we can squash a lot of this media attention before it grows anymore."

"They already know about me Sean, what difference does it make now?"

"They don't know where you live or where you work. That's why they are allowing him to talk because they are searching for you. You did a real good job hiding yourself but it will not take long for them to find what they need to get to you. If I leave now, you can still have a reasonable life here."

"Without you?"

Shaking his head in frustration, "you are purposely not hearing me right now. You are so fucking stubborn. I am not leaving you Ava. We can be together again when things die down. You can come to LA again or better yet, I will take you to my house in the Keys. No one will be able to find you there."

"I don't want to hide anymore Sean. I'm tired of hiding. I want to show *him* especially that I'm not scared anymore and I'm not going to let him control my life anymore."

"Ava I don't think you understand how harassed you will be." I focus on him strong. "Okay fine, let's go out right now and announce to the world we are dating. And then when I have to leave to do another film, you can stay behind and deal with all the reporters and cameras in your face asking if we are broken up, am I cheating on you, or how you feel about some co-star that I was seen hugging or some shit. Our relationship will be so heavily scrutinized, because you are news baby and combining my celebrity status on top of that ..." Frustrated he shakes his head harder. "This is the story of a lifetime for them. Not to mention, they will give him a voice and not just the one time. They will keep on and on and on until everyone has analyzed every possible angle, until people are sick to death of hearing it. Until we are so beat down and tired over it all, that we can't even stand the sight of each other. You don't want that Ava, trust me." He said approaching me with a tender touch.

"I can handle it Sean. I know I can. I have even been seeing my doctor again and she says ...."

Taking my face gently into his hands, "baby, there is nothing I would love more than to show you off to the world but trust me you don't want this and you're not ready to handle it. You faint every time you get upset. How do you think you are going to handle the madness that is going to come at you?"

"But Sean the fainting has nothing to do with me being upset. It's because …"

"Ava, stop. It's not a good idea right now. Give it a little more time and then we can let everyone know our way and on our terms."

"But Sean, I am stronger than you think I am. I know even my own friends think I cannot handle it but it is not true. You haven't even noticed …"

"Noticed what? That you get up in the middle night making sure he isn't trying to get in somehow?" Pushing his hands away from me, I step away from him. "Don't look at me that way Ava, you know it's true."

"You don't even know the progress I have made, have you even noticed that I'm not having the nightmares anymore?"

Sean glares at me sideways, "none at all?" Jumping up I try to walk out before he pulls me back to him. "Ava, baby, I am trying to protect you, to take care of you and make sure no one hurts you."

"So you're taking care of me by forcing me to watch you say that I don't matter to you."

"Whatever I say is for your own safety Ava, I'm not going to mean a word of it."

With tears forming and my legs threatening to give on me, "do you love me?" His jaw drops and his once tender hands become rigid. "It's a simple question Sean, that's all I want to know. Do you love me?"

"I don't think that's relevant right now."

"I think it's the most relevant question there is right now," I said staring at his twisting and fidgeting figure. "If you can't answer that, then there is no need for any of this other conversation."

"What are you saying?" He asks stepping back from me.

"I thought it was pretty clear. You either stay here with me proving to me that you do love me or you leave and prove that you don't."

"Are you making demands on me now? We have only been dating for a few months. Now you are demanding me to tell you how I feel about a relationship that I have had to keep hidden from everyone? I have to go home *alone* and treasure the few minutes I get to talk to you on the phone before I go to bed. I have to know how I feel about that? I don't Ava! I'm sorry, I am not going to give you any false hope when I am still trying to figure it all out. I care about you and I don't want anything to happen to you – that I know!" Sighing he steps towards me and caresses my face, "please understand sweetheart."

This time I step away from him, "I think you better figure it out quick Sean. Or else."

He narrows his eyes at me, "or else what?"

Taking in a deep breath and searching for the strength I need. "If you leave me today then …" I swallow hard on the words that are choking me on their way out, "then don't come back. Don't call me, don't write, and don't even attempt to talk to me if we happen to run into each other again."

"AVA! You can't be serious. What is wrong with you? This is not like you at all," he yelled as I fight back the tears.

"I'm sorry Sean but I want a family, I want to grow old with someone and have babies with them." I focus on him hard. "I want a family of my own, I don't want to run and hide with someone who doesn't even love me. I think maybe this relationship …"

"Don't Ava." He interrupts me causing tears to well up in my eyes. "Don't you fucking do this."

"You know it's best. The relationship has gone as far as it can go and it's time for both of us to realize it and move on." I turn hiding my anguish from him. "You have plenty of girls that will be a much better fit for you and I have …" With a deep breath I raise my chin, "and I have Justin. He is a better fit for me and for what I want."

"If that's what you want, I'll go." I nod before he can say another word while trying to reassure myself and him with my stiff posture. "Then I will go, so you can get on with your life … with your new man." He leans in tight to my ear. "I'm sure he will be more than happy to fuck you the way you like. I know I enjoyed myself," he breathed harshly.

"Get out!" I spin around directing him to the door, only to come face-to-face with him, seeing his pain and feeling mine. "Get out. Go home Sean." My legs giving on me once again, I grip the nearby chair and try to hold myself together as he storms off grabbing his bags, cursing under his breath the whole way.

03&0

**R**andy waits outside at the car as I stand by the window hiding behind the drapery, glancing out when I think no one is looking until Sean comes storming up the walk. I move away quickly, raising my chin and forcing my conviction to the surface when he rushes through the door. "Last chance, sweetheart. You still want to end it this way?" I nod softly, glancing at the walls around him. "Just remember you're the one that did this." I close my eyes hard only to be shaken back by Sean's hands on my face suddenly. His lips crash to mine, "you're upset, I get that. I don't want to leave you but please understand I am doing this for you. Call me when you calm down and want to talk."

"No. You're doing this for yourself. You are doing this - so *you* don't have to answer uncomfortable questions. So you can have me, without having to deal with all the issues that come from being with me." His warm eyes quickly change as I confront him with the truth. "I can handle Spencer, I have handled him, and I ... will continue to handle him for the rest of my life – without you."

With a snarled lip he steps away from me, shaking his head. "By the way, Justin can't possibly satisfy you like I do." He said glaring at me as he approaches the door, tossing an autograph picture of himself on my sofa. "For your scrapbook."

*I have to do this. I have to. It's for the best.* Gritting my teeth and fisting the back of the chair, I watch him walk out the door. "Sean!" I yelled, surprising myself even more so, than him. He takes a step back in, waiting for me to respond with eager curiosity. "I'm ... I am ... I really wish you the best and I always will ... think of you fondly."

Sean nods with an exasperated exhale, "you as well Ava," he said slamming the door shut, jerking my heart out of my chest and smashing it to the ground.

# *Chapter 27: Sean*

"**A**re you going to be okay?" I give Randy a half nod while staring out my window still dazed. "Do you want me to stay here with you?" Shaking my head I still feel numb. "Are you sure because …."

"Go. Please. Go," I said waiting for the door to close before making myself a drink, my first, but over the next few days it will not be my last. My days have turned into weeks as my silent phone becomes a haunting reminder. *I hate her. I wish I had never met her.* "Fucking Bitch!" Throwing my glass against the wall, I watch it crash into pieces while the alcohol rains down, hypnotizing me into my chair and letting the deadness take me over.

"Sean!" My mother continues screaming through my house until finding me, drowning my issues. "What are you doing? Drinking? Give me that." Taking my drink from my hand, she grips my face hard. "I can't believe my son is sitting here, in the dark, hiding from life. Sean!"

"What Mother!"

"Get yourself together!"

"What do you want?"

"I want to know what happened with you and Ava."

"She doesn't want me anymore?"

"I don't believe it. What did you say to her?" Twisting my head away from her grip, I manage to get up and stumble back to my bar. "You must have said something." *It has to be my fault, obviously.* "You need to go to her and tell her how you feel, that you made a mistake and you are sorry?"

"She turned *me* away mother or did you forget that?"

"You have made a mistake letting her go. This decision is going to haunt you, mark my words."

"Go away mother." I close my eyes tight and luckily when I open them again, she is already on her way out the door. As much as I hate fighting with her, I know she is right about one thing, I need to get up and stop hiding. Ava would have called by now if she was going to.

Over the next few days I try to get back into a routine. Ignoring the numerous reminders of Ava that haunts me throughout my own home. It all seems to work until an alarm I had set for her birthday goes off, causing me to crash all over again. The pain overwhelms me right to bed, into dreams of her. *Always of her. It is maddening but yet I would go crazy without them.*

"Sean! Sean where are you?" Ethan yelled.

"I'm up here," I said roughly and unsure if I really know where I am.

"Damn you look like shit."

"Thanks."

"Get up and take a look at this. Here are some possible projects for you, I thought maybe it might get your mind off of things."

"Ethan," I said pushing the papers away from me. "I need to know she is okay at least. Can you make sure of that, without her knowing?"

"I can do what I can but I won't invade her private life for you."

"That's all I want." Taking the papers and rubbing my eyes to focus, I know my brother is watching my every move as if I am a wounded child. If he only knew, he would understand a little more than what he is at this moment. I can still remember when I found the beautiful necklace with the antique locket. I had put a picture of us from when she was here within it, scaled to fit perfectly. I did not get the chance to give it to her before I left Atlanta. It sat for days staring at me. I must have picked it up a hundred times at least, threw it in the trash almost as many but eventually that damn alarm went off. Yesterday, I had it wrapped in a velvet box and sent it to her with her favorite flowers. The note attached was simple, no more than, *Happy Birthday - Sean.* I am not sure she will ever open it or even accept it but maybe if she sees it … she will forgive me.

A chilling breeze blows through my windows, blowing the papers around my room until one floats down in front of me. I pick it up and read the description before handing it back to Ethan.

"This one," I say to Ethan. "This is the one I want."

"Sean this is a secondary roll, it's not even the roll they are offering. You should read the rest of the script, read the roll I am suggesting before you decide." Ethan narrows his eyes at me, confused by my decision.

"It's the one I want Ethan."

"You don't even get the girl, you lose the girl to the leading man."

"Perfect," I said walking away ignoring his judging eyes.

⊂ℬ⊃

*I*t does not take long before the contracts are signed and the time comes to pack my bags and head off to the location in Ireland. The countryside is beautiful here, giving me some hope that I can drown my memories. The movie is taking months longer due to weather, script changes and other complications and of course, I'm miserable. The first chance I get for some extended free time, I take it. After hours of seeing the usual sights and using the known roads, I take a detour and get lost deep into the country for hours. I come upon an old cottage overlooking a lake, surrounded by lots of lush land and mountains. The empty old stone home is being over taken by wild flowers and deep green ivy but still, I am speechless.

"Can I help you sir?" A voice said coming out of nowhere.

I turn, seeing an old man struggling his way towards me. "I'm sorry, I didn't mean to trespass but when I saw this beautiful place I had to stop."

He nods with a shining smile. "Yes, it is a special place," he said gazing over it with obvious fond memories.

"Would you happen to know how old the place is and maybe some of the history?" I asked, relaxing as the old man smiles happily.

"Oh yes, I was here when this place was built. The couple that built it lived here for many, many wonderful years. "Tá mo chroí istigh ionat" they always said to each other." Leaning into me he whispers again, "tá mo chroí istigh ionat". They shared one heart and it was only able to beat when they were together." The old man looks up at my curious expression. "Come, come see," he said waving me to follow him. I walk with him to a rock within the overgrown wild flowers, where he pulls back some of the growth to reveal the names Finn and Nora with the words, "tá mo chroí istigh ionat" underneath.

"What does it mean?"

"My Heart is Within You." He said with certainty of the words meaning.

"That's an interesting story."

"Oh the story is much more interesting. You see Nora's father was strong, powerful man and abusive. He did not like to be disobeyed. When her father found out about them, he made a deal and traded her for more land. She was shipped away overnight. Finn assumed her to be gone forever, promised to another man." The old man shakes his head with a groan. "Horrible time. Finn searched for her for some time before finally giving up. Assuming she had moved on, he traveled from place to place trying to run away from the memories of her, never worked, of course." He pauses grimacing a smile. "If he had only known that, *the stubborn mule* had jumped out of her transport and had been searching for her way back to him." He chuckles with an exasperated sigh. "It was on a cold, rainy day when while they both were trying to take refuge from the rain, found each other and at once *their heart* beat again. Never looking back they escaped from her father to here." He waves his hand over the place.

"That's some story," I said raising my eyebrows.

"Ahhh it is, but it is the truth. You can deny love but you can't deny your heart." I give him a respectful smile before sighing at the sight of the old place. "You have such a love?" He asked, although it seems as if he was making a statement. Not that it matters, I do not have an answer for him. "Hmmm, well you will find her again Sean, and then your heart will beat once again."

I turn to say something to him but as quickly as he appeared, he is gone. I stand in place for some time trying to recall when I told him my name. My strange encounter with the old man sends chills up my spine, forcing me to go straight back and to bed for some obviously much needed sleep.

After a few more days, filming begins to pick up again and so does my energy, so much so that I have even taken notice of a British actress that made a point to flirt innocently whenever she can. Her sweet approach always makes me smile.

"Sean," Nicole said cocking her head with a provocative gaze.

"How are you today, Nicole?"

"Better now but I could be even better if you have dinner with me tonight?" Most men would have agreed without question to the beautiful blond but I hesitate.

There is nothing more I can do about Ava, it has been months and she has yet to even respond to my gift. She has obviously moved on and so should I. "What time?" I asked. My inner turmoil continues for the rest of the day into the night but I still pick up

Nicole and we have dinner at a place she recommends. The dinner is wonderful and the conversation is decent. She is charming, beautiful, and eager for us to be alone. At the end of the night, I take her by the hand and escort her to her door hoping for more than a kiss. I am sure she wants the same but I am not sure if I am able to overcome the voice in my head.

She leans in close to me. "So do you want to come in?"

Leaning against her doorframe and staring into her smiling eyes, I stop myself again. "I don't know."

"You don't know?" Huffing she dismisses my indecision and presses her lips against mine.

Taking hold of her aggressive hands, I gently pull away from her. "Good night, Nicole," I said walking away. By the time we finish shooting, Nicole begins speaking to me again but yet I still board my flight home leaving her number behind in my hotel room.

০৪৩৮০

There is not much to do when I get home from filming. I try to keep myself busy and distracted but I am becoming anxious and wanting to get laid more than ever. *It should be easy*, I thought, walking into an old hangout and drinking immediately to work up the courage needed. Within minutes my ex, Courtney approaches, which should not be a surprise since we did meet here.

"Sean, I haven't seen you here in a long time."

Looking over her slutty outfit, I immediately have to fight my temptation to run. *I need this. I just need to get her to my house before she talks too much and annoys me into changing my mind.* "Courtney, you look good," I said forcing a smile and focusing on the goal.

"I know," she smiled appreciatively. "So, you here alone?" I nod silently. "Are you going home alone?"

I take another drink nodding, "unless you want to change that." She melts into agreement. I call my driver and hurry her to the car. As soon as I shut the car door she leaps on top of me, grinding down hard and barely giving me a chance to breathe, while I repeat to myself, *I need this*. Once we get to my house, I push her up the stairs to my room, we kiss and grab at each other the whole way. I am pulling Courtney's clothes off as she kisses my neck, pulling off my shirt, watching her take her underwear off, while I strip down to nothing. I kiss her and she kisses me back, rubbing the back of my head and positioning her legs around me. My dick is hard as hell and in position when she begins kissing along my jaw line, "ohhh Ava." *Unfuckingbelievable!*

"Who did you call me?" She asked pushing me off her. I shake my head. "Sean?"

"Give me a minute," I snapped while walking to the bathroom. *Unbelievable. I am not doing anything I haven't done before her. Why is it so hard now?* Splashing some water in my face, I continue to argue with myself.

Courtney begins pacing with a loud impatient huff. "Hey what's this?" She called out. "Is this you? It is, but who's the girl?" I lean out to see her holding the painting that Ava did for me. I forgot about it, never bothering to hang it up and never bothering to move it from the spot I had left it, after I removed it from my sight. "Are you okay?" She tenses as I approach her.

"You need to go Courtney."

"Why," she squeaked. "Sean? What is wrong with you?"

Silently, I help her out of my house and safely home. *It has been more than a year. How can one girl do this to me?* I crawl into bed next to the painting, unwilling to touch it.

# *Chapter 28: Spencer*

**T**hanks to Sean Grant there has been renewed interest in me. This new interest has brought in a reporter that is now working behind the scenes to raise money for my cause and provide services I wouldn't have had otherwise. My newly provided, well-paid attorneys are frantically working on my appeal. They say it looks promising, considering how much improvement I have made under Dr. Knight's care. All I have to do is be the man they want to see, the man they want to believe that I am. Innocent and weak, I beg and pray for help in every interview I have with them. I plead until they see the tears in my eyes, until they feel the pain I desire them to feel. "Ava is the love of my life, I can't dare go on knowing she is angry with me. I know she still cares for me. If someone would only help me talk to her then I know she will forgive me. If only someone would help me, I know I could convince her that it was all done out of love. My poor Ava, she is obviously ill. She needs psychological care and I want to help her get that care. I want to be there for her – *forever.*"

"Mr. Jefferis, your story is unbelievable. I can't believe after all that you have been through, that your only concern is for the woman that put you here. I want you to know that I will do everything in my power to get you out of here and make sure you have the opportunity to face Ms. Kelley and let her know how you feel. I have made some calls to some friends of mine and they assured me that you will be getting a new trial. Your attorneys are filing papers right now to have you released until the new trial. Now we are going to need to keep this quiet so we don't have to run into any unnecessary walls." Proud of himself, and anticipating the interview of a lifetime Mr. Brinkman sighs with happiness. "So if all goes well Mr. Jefferis, you should be walking out of this prison within a few weeks. How do you feel about that?" Mr. Brinkman said with his glowing teeth shining expectantly.

This man disgusts me, I crave the opportunity to slit his throat and watch him bleed. Sitting back with an easy smile, "Mr. Brinkman, all I can say is that I can't wait to have my life back. It will be so nice to walk out of here and see my mother and actually hug her. I can't wait to drive a car or eat a steak."

"Do you have any dreams that are little harder for me to help you with?" Brinkman laughs.

"Oh … I have all kinds of dreams. I can't wait to have a farm full of cattle, a house far from nosey neighbors, three sons and a little girl with red hair – just like her mother's."

# *Chapter 29: Sean*

Christmas Day and I managed to get up early and drag myself to my brother's and surprisingly I am glad I did. Playing with my nephew all-day has helped me forget all my issues. I even changed his diaper, several times. He is a constant mess, I am not impressed with that at all but he is cute as hell and I love him despite his lack of much hair and teeth. When he fell asleep for the night, I find Ethan out on the deck, staring off into nowhere.

"You know, I never thought I could love anyone this much and Abbey, she is so amazing with him." I listen to him go on and on with so much love and compassion for his family, like nothing else matters to him other than them. "Don't worry Sean, it will happen for you one day."

*I wonder if it will, if I even want it to.* Without warning, the image enters my thoughts abruptly, she is beautiful and humming to our baby, swaying with him in her arms. *Sigh. Damn I want it to be true. I must be out of my mind for even considering such a thing.* Shaking it off I return to reality, "so where is Mom anyway?"

He laughs, "I think she has a new boyfriend."

"Really?"

"She came by this week to take Collin out for a special day with Grandma, spoiling him rotten with toys galore. Then she said she couldn't be here today because she had important business to attend to, so she had dinner with us last night and left this morning."

"She stopped by to see me the other day and said she wasn't going to be around but I didn't think anything of it. Why did it make you think she has a boyfriend?" I asked him watching him laugh to himself.

"No, it's the man's voice in the background whenever I call her."

Looking over at him wide eyed, "are you serious?"

"Yes, it's hilarious. Especially if you try to call her out on it, she's a horrible liar," Ethan laughs harder.

"I would love to hear that," I said leaning back in my chair with a wide smile of my own.

"You have to catch her at an odd time but usually she answers without thinking to go somewhere private first. She would never make a good spy, she's so obvious, and she thinks we are oblivious to everything." Suddenly a huge Cheshire grin comes over his face. "You want to call her now and see?"

"Do you think she's with him right now?"

Ethan nods, "sure it's Christmas Day, where else would she be?"

"Let's do it"

Making ourselves comfortable and joking about the man our mother is possibly seeing, we hover over Ethan's phone. "Okay now stop laughing," Ethan said putting his phone on speaker after dialing Mom's number.

"Hello Ethan," Mom said obliviously happy.

"How are you doing Mom?"

"Oh I'm fine. Merry Christmas, I love you."

"Merry Christmas to you and we all love you too," he said, winking at me. "So what do you have planned for the day?" I listen hard for a man's voice, smiling expectantly.

"Oh not much, probably hanging out at the spa all-day getting facials and such, you know."

I almost laugh at the ridiculous lie, until I hear dogs barking and playing. "Mary this is so cute, she is going to look so adorable in this." Immediately I stand up straight, listening even harder than I would ever think possible.

Grabbing the phone with a fierce intensity, "Mom, where are you?" Silence. "Mother tell me where you are!" I yell.

"Sean - Merry Christmas," she sung.

"Sean!" The voice said before something crashes hard.

"Sean are you still there?" My mother nervously asks.

"Mother, where are you?" I ask with an angered determination.

"What do you mean? I am in my room watching TV."

"Mother, the TV doesn't talk back to you or say my name."

"Oh you must have heard it wrong, funny how things travel over the phone. You know once…"

"Mother, I want to know why you are with her?"

"With who Sean?"

I begin to shake with anger and confusion. "Mother!"

"Oh Sean, I have to go. My room service is at the door. I will call you later. Good-bye sweetie, I love you." The phone goes silent while I stand stunned.

"Was she with?" Ethan asked.

"Yes."

"Why is she with Ava?"

"I don't know," I said still shaking.

"What are you going to do?"

"I thought you had someone watching Ava, how did you not know this?" I lean over at him angry.

"I have someone watching out for her, not reporting to me on her every movement. I told you I wasn't going to pry into her private life and more importantly I didn't think you wanted to know."

I begin walking in circles rubbing my head, "I need to go to Atlanta."

"Are you sure?"

"Yes, get me a flight out as soon as possible."

"Okay," Ethan says with an awkward glare.

♋

The day after Christmas and I have so many questions and so many I am not sure I want to ask or know. The biggest being, will I be able to leave her again, even if she wants me to? My flight is too short for me to arrange my thoughts and the drive to her house is even shorter. I grab my bag with a shaky tension before heading towards her door. I knock hearing scuffling and whispering on the other side. The boys look out the windows at me, not barking but whimpering for me. *At least they didn't forget me.*

The door flies open and my heart pounds as I stare down at the feet of my greeter. "Sean," a surprised voice said. *Justin.* My hopeful heart stops for good when I see the baby in his arms with soft red curls. "I guess I should have known you would show up eventually. Of course, it would have to be my day to baby-sit. You might as well come in." He motioned for me to come in and for some reason I follow him, even though my mind keeps screaming at me to leave. *I hate him, I could knock the hell out of him right now.* "So I guess you finally wondered what your mother has been doing here all this time."

"What the hell is she doing here?"

He laughs, still holding the baby while I take a second look at her. She is beautiful and there is no question that her mother is Ava.

I close my eyes hard, looking away from her. "Well you know she always liked Ava. And when Lillah here was born there was no getting rid of her then."

"Lillah, that's her name?"

"Ummm yea, it was Ava's mother's name." *I know that already, prick.*

"She's beautiful," I said without looking at him or her.

"Yea she is, oh I'm sorry. Here." He lifts her towards me.

I wave my hands up high at him, "no, that's okay, I only want to talk to my mother and then get out of here." He looks surprised. *He is an asshole.*

"Really?" He makes a strange expression before his phone rings. "Hi baby, well I'm baby-sitting. You are. Well I don't know what I can do." Justin looks up at me smiling sheepishly. "Actually baby, I will meet you in thirty minutes. Yea, I know. No, I have someone perfect to watch her. Okay, I will see you soon. That was my fiancé. She is registering for gifts and is all upset about choosing the right plates or something, I don't know. Anyway, since you are waiting for your mother, you wouldn't mind watching Lillah would you," he said putting the baby in my arms before I have a chance to protest. "I didn't think so." Justin puts on his coat and heads for the door.

"Wait, you are going out to meet Ava and I am supposed to watch your … her baby while you're out looking for china?"

He turns laughing at me. "Wow! Sean you really are clueless. I thought you were just a real asshole but I guess that makes me wrong. Ava will be happy to hear that, she always likes being right."

Shivering at the sound of her name coming from his mouth, "so you are going to meet … her?"

"No, Sean I am going to meet my fiancée, Holly."

"You have a baby with Ava and you're marrying someone else?"

He laughs again, "Sean as soon as you left I admit I tried. I tried like hell to get her to forget about you, especially when I found out about Lillah." He shakes his head looking down at his feet. "I even booked a flight to LA ready to kick your ass. But in the end no matter what I did to you it wasn't going to make any difference, she is always going to love you. So, I finally gave up and found someone else. And believe it or not, I couldn't be happier."

"And your baby?"

Justin laughs. "You know you're right, Lillah is beautiful," he said staring admiringly at the baby in my arms. "She looks so much like Ava. Well except for her eyes, her eyes as beautiful as they are," he says with an expression I do not understand. "Those eyes … well they look exactly like her father's." He walks halfway out the door before stopping again." Oh and Sean, my eyes are brown." He smiles arrogantly before walking out.

With his words still lingering in the air, I begin piecing together the fragments to try to make sense of it all but everything keeps coming back to the baby in my arms. I pull her away from my chest and then I know. Staring into her beautiful green eyes, my tension lessens and my heart suddenly pieces itself back together, only stronger. "Hello Lillah, my sweet girl," I said as she puts her little hand to my face as if she knows who I am already. Kissing her hand, she giggles, making her father the happiest man in the world. "I'm sorry sweetheart, if I had known I would have been here sooner. You forgive me?" I kiss her sweet rosy cheeks and become overwhelmed as the understanding races through my head. *You're why my mother is here … Lillah. My child. My daughter. Her granddaughter.* It is almost too much, I would have never thought Ava capable of keeping a secret like this. Swallowing hard, I change my concentration back to my daughter, watching her take hold of my fingers while the warmth embraces me. She is so beautiful, she even has Ava's sweet pouty lips that she frequently pushes into a breathtaking smile, and I am falling in love with her already. I'm in awe watching her, ten toes, ten fingers … I continue to count, going through the complete checklist. Checking her little chubby legs and arms and her little chubby belly, while she giggles and holds tight to my fingers. She is perfect, I am in love, and this love is easy for me to understand.

As the day goes on, I realize my daughter is as stubborn as her mother. *I am in trouble for sure.* I also learn the way she cries when she is hungry, the way she is cranky when she needs to be changed or the way she rubs her eyes when she is tired. At the end of the day, I cradle her in my arms, rocking her to sleep before putting her in her crib and watching her sleep peacefully until I hear a car pull up. I jump to the window to see my mother walking in with food bags. *Now maybe I can get some real answers, more answers than I even knew I needed.* I grab the baby monitor and pull the door shut before walking into the kitchen as my mother lays out takeout and not taking notice of me at all.

"Mother?"

She jumps slightly but does not seem to be surprised to see me. "Oh Sean, you scared me, you shouldn't do that." She continues to unload food and setting the table, even kissing my cheek in the process. "I hope you're hungry, we have plenty. I think my eyes were bigger than my stomach."

"Mother, you're not at all surprised to see me?"

"Oh Sean, I'm your mother. I know what you are going to do before you do."

"How is that possible? Actually never mind that. Why are you here?"

"You know why or haven't you met your daughter?"

"I have been with her all-day but that doesn't explain why you would go behind my back and …"

She turns abruptly taking my face into her hands. "Oh honey, if I had any other choice I would have never done it this way, but Ava was so sure you wouldn't want her. I'm not sure why but she was sure and that was the only way she would let me stay in her life was if I promised not to tell you."

"You knew we would call, you knew I was listening and would hear her. You knew I would come here, didn't you?"

She smiles, "I knew as soon as you heard her voice you wouldn't be able to stop yourself. Well I did not tell you but I was not about to keep her out of your life, so I had to think of something. If you would have only gotten back from filming sooner, you could have been here for her first Christmas. It takes time planning something so skillfully. And well I guess I should give Abbey some credit too"

"Abbey knows?"

"Yes, if it wasn't for her I would have never been able to prepare before you and Ethan called me. She also might have called and told me your flight schedule too." My mother winks with a smile.

"Well now, Ethan thinks you have a boyfriend."

"He does, how silly."

I lean against the counter watching her with narrowing eyes, "you do have a boyfriend, don't you?"

"Sean, you should sit and eat."

"So who is he?" I asked sitting across from her.

"He's a doctor, he is in charge of the hospital where Lillah was born. He was very kind helping us keep it quiet, who she was and whose baby she was having." I look down considering that latest news being released. "I didn't want you to hear it that way."

"So he's nice?"

"He's a gentleman." She beams.

"Well I can't wait to meet him and thank him, of course."

"Well enough about me, isn't she beautiful," she said grasping my hand?

"Lillah, yes, she is – very actually."

"What do you think about her?"

"Mother you already know. She had me from the moment I looked at her and knew she was mine."

"Oh I wish you could have been there when she was born, it was something."

"You were there?" I asked with great interest.

"Oh yes. I had to help Ava, she needed me, despite her protests to the contrary. Sean that girl is so strong and independent, fearless. You should have seen her eyes light up when they put Lillah in her arms. It was a beautiful sight. I was glad if you could not be there, at least I was for you. Oh I must show you these …" She hands me a book and I open it looking at pictures of Ava pregnant, more beautiful than ever. The last few, are pictures of her with Lillah, after she was born but I stop at one of Ava rocking Lillah to sleep and wearing the locket I sent to her for her birthday. I remove the picture unable to understand why.

"I would have been here." I whispered to the picture.

"I know dear," my mother said kissing me on the head.

"When did you know she was pregnant?"

"I knew something was not right but I didn't know exactly what it was until I came to see her. She tried to hide it from me."

"She should know better than to hide anything from you."

She winks, causing me to laugh. "So I asked her and when she didn't answer, I knew. I told her I was going to tell you. And the panic across her face was … it was like she was afraid of you or at least that's what I thought at the time. Now I think it was more that she was afraid that the media would crucify her and Lillah. She was trying to protect Lillah. By keeping her a secret from you, she was able to keep it from everyone else."

"I would have protected them both."

"Sean all she knew was that you were leaving her behind and didn't think enough of her to fight for her." With a defensive posture, I start to protest but she halts me easily with a motion of her hand. "I know but that's how she saw it, you didn't tell her how you feel. What would you have thought? She thought she was just another girl to you."

*How in the hell could she not realize how I feel about her?* "Where is she?"

"Spending the day with some friends. She should be home soon. She does not get out often, and since I knew you would be here today I thought it best if I talk to you first and allow you some time with your daughter.

"Does she know I'm here?"

"No, I told her that you didn't hear her. You should have seen her face when I said your name and she realized you were on the phone. She froze, dropping everything, breaking a dish and spilling food everywhere. The dogs loved it but it was a mess. She was a bigger mess. It took me some time to get her to calm down. I made sure she went out tonight. She needed to shake off that ridiculous trance she has been in since hearing your name."

"What are you going to tell her?"

"Tell her? Oh honey I am not going to tell her anything, you are."

"Me?" I asked not understanding her reasons for everything.

"I am going to leave you here and let you two work it out. I have plans anyway." She looks at her watch, "oh and I am going to be late if I don't hurry." Suddenly she gets up and begins gathering her things. "Darling will you clean this up when you're done, I don't want Ava to have to deal with anything more than necessary. She doesn't get much sleep these days." I nod while she kisses me on the forehead. "Good luck, and make sure you listen before you respond. Be patient with her," she said with her motherly finger pointed in my direction.

I clean up everything as asked, considering all that has happened and all that might. During my time alone, I make some decisions about my life and take out my phone making some necessary calls. My life is going to change dramatically and so is hers whether she likes it or not. I check on Lillah one more time before taking a seat facing the door and turning off most of the lights. I want to see her first, I want time to react properly, after of course, I enjoy seeing her again. I do not have to wait long before I hear her car. Watching the door closely as it unlocks and opens, she walks in sending my heart spinning towards her. She shuts the door and takes off her coat, shaking her hair out from being inside it. She is as beautiful as she is in my dreams and with my wide smile taking over my face, I am glad I allowed myself this moment. Refocusing and reminding myself of my anger, I lean down putting my elbows on my knees, watching and waiting.

"Mary, I'm sorry I took so long I ...." She said turning and seeing me immediately.

"Hello Ava," I said as calmly as I can but with probably a little more anger than my mother would have liked for me to.

She watches me carefully seeming unsure if she should move, I give her time to decide. "Sean?"

"Yes. And please keep breathing. I don't want you passing out on me right now."

She starts trembling, "why are you here?"

I got up helping her to a seat, feeling the twinge of excitement in my veins as soon as I touch her. *Damn she still makes me crazy.* "Sit down, please."

"Sean, why are you here?"

"I heard your voice when I was talking to my mother. I wanted to know why she was with you. I could not for the life of me figure out why she would be here. The project long done and built, there was no reason for her to be here. I just couldn't understand. So I came here to see why."

"Lillah," she whispered.

"Yes. Lillah. She was to say, at the very least, a surprise for me."

"I'm sorry ..."

"What are you sorry for Ava? Are you sorry you never told me you were pregnant or because you never told me about my daughter?" I said continuing to watch her face carefully, as my anger starts to show through even more. "Or because I found out?"

"I guess all that," she said playing with her hands in her lap.

"I don't understand Ava, why wouldn't you tell me?"

"I know it wasn't fair not to give you the option but I wasn't sure what was best for her or you or me. It was all so much to take and when I tried to tell you, you wanted to leave," she said with a quivering lip. "You left, you didn't even try to find another option to stay with me."

"I was trying to protect you." I stressed.

"Protecting me, by leaving me alone to face it by myself? Your protecting was you running away and I wasn't sure if I would ever see you again."

"I thought the sooner I left you, then the sooner they would leave you alone. I did not intend on never seeing you again. It killed me to leave you!"

"I had to change my number twelve times! That bastard called me over and over and the police couldn't figure out how he was getting my new number. I finally gave up my phone entirely and used Kyle's when I needed it," she said trembling.

"I had no idea, if I had I would have stopped it."

"How? From California … Ireland? How would you have stopped it Sean, you weren't here to do anything? Hate me if you want but I did what I had to, I protected our daughter the best way I knew how, getting as far away from you as possible."

"So you are going to blame me forever? You wanted to keep my daughter from me to get even? Is that it Ava?" She doesn't answer. "That's it. You wanted to get even with me, punish me for something I did not even know anything about. You pushed *me* away Ava, I couldn't help you if you wouldn't talk to me."

"It wasn't to get even. I saw how they treated me and I was afraid that I wouldn't be able to protect her and I wasn't sure you would be around to do it yourself. I'm sorry, I did what I thought was best. When your mother showed up, I knew she would somehow let you know. As scary as that was, it was also a relief because then it wouldn't be up to me to decide, to make ether the right or the wrong decision."

"Okay, well now I know and I am not going to let anything happen to her."

Her soft expression calms me, "you've seen her?"

"Yes, Justin left her with me all-day."

"Justin told you?" She asked with alarm in her voice.

Huffing I force a laugh, "sort of. He's still a jackass by the way." She looks at me surprised by my harsh words. "He made me spend time with her and figure it out myself. She has my eyes."

Ava smiles beautifully, "I thought I was being punished seeing you every day. But she is so wonderful, I couldn't dare hate her for reminding me of you."

"I know, I fell in love with her instantly. She's as beautiful as you are."

Ava instantly turns away from me, "she does have a way of melting your heart doesn't she?"

"She does despite her mother's stubbornness."

"She has your temper though." She says facing me with superiority.

I furrow my eyebrows at her, "what temper?" With a satisfactory grin she walks away from me again, "what temper, Ava?"

"Sean please, you know you have a temper especially if you don't get your way, harmless but frustrating."

With a roll of my eyes and a huff, I stiffen, watching her laugh at me, "maybe sometimes."

"Wow you spent the entire day with her by yourself? I should go check on her."

"Sit back down, she's fine. I have been helping with my nephew quite a bit lately. I know what I am doing."

"Are you sure?" She asks insultingly.

"Yes, and now I guess I know why Abbey was so insistent on me learning how to change a diaper." I said narrowing my eyes at her, causing her to laugh. "I've missed seeing you laugh."

Jumping up and nearly running away from me, "are you hungry or thirsty or something."

"No, I ate with Mom but a drink might be good."

I follow her closely into the kitchen, leaning in against the counter and gazing over her, while remembering every desiring softness. "So when exactly?" I asked as she hands me a glass of wine with a questioning expression. "Do you know about when Lillah was conceived?"

"I think it goes without saying that it was your birthday. The shower would be my guess since that was one of the few times we didn't over exaggerate the protection."

"Aaahhh the shower, that was a great night," I said glancing back at her with a wink. Ava backs away with a hard gulp. "So when did you know?"

"Soon after you got here. The fainting and being sick. Anna suggested it and with the dates, I assumed but I did not confirm it until after you left. I did try to tell you but you wouldn't let me talk. You were so hung up on the media finding out about me, you weren't hearing me at all."

"I was so worried about you. I thought you were being affected by what was going on, and all I could think to do was get away and take all the problems with me. I didn't want to leave, I just didn't think you could take much more. I was scared of what it might to do to you."

"I told you. Or rather I tried to tell you that I could handle it."

"How Ava? You aren't used to the media and you don't need that fucker interrupting your life anymore than he has."

"SEAN, listen to me. I could, I can handle it. I have been seeing a doctor that has helped me tremendously. You didn't even notice that I didn't have one nightmare while you were here."

"But Kyle and …"

"All of you are all the same, you don't listen to me. You are so hell-bent on protecting me, you did not stop to think how best to do that. And leaving me alone was not the best way."

Carefully moving behind her, I lean over her shoulder and whisper in her ear, "I'm sorry but I did miss you ... so much." She smells so good and her skin is so soft, I cannot help let my mouth linger against her skin and pull her in close to my chest.

Shockingly she pushes away from me, "I'm sorry, I didn't miss you at all. I mean at first I did but after awhile it got easier."

With an assured approach I move back to her, feeling her so close that we both let out a soft moan. "Really?"

"Yes."

"You don't think about me at all anymore?" I asked nosing her earlobe.

"No … not really," she breathed.

I run my finger down her neck feeling for the chain, pulling it out slowly and dangling it in front of her. The locket I sent to her for her birthday shines brightly in front of us both. "Not at all, huh?" I open it seeing the picture I put in of us together on one side and a picture of Lillah on the other. With a reassured smile, "you love me still. I know it."

Jerking the locket out of my hand, she sprints away. "You know I probably should try to get some sleep, she … Lillah gets up early," she choked out with a rough voice. "And. You need somewhere to sleep and I haven't prepared the guesthouse."

"The guesthouse, no I'm staying here with you and Lillah."

"I guess I could make up the sofa for you," she said glancing at me, waiting for me to protest.

"That will be fine," I said reluctantly.

After we say good night I watch her walk away into her room, even the boys leave me to sleep with her. *Clearly, I am the only one in the doghouse tonight.* I am able to fall asleep for a few minutes before Lillah wakes me up crying. I respond to her cries only to find Ava already soothing her back to sleep, swaying her hips and humming softly to her, just like how I had envisioned her, only better.

"Did she wake you?" She whispered after catching me out of the corners of her eyes.

"Yes, but it's my job to get up and check on my little girl, right?" I watch her fight her smile as she comes out of the room, shutting the door behind her and pushing me to back me up.

"She's fine, a little upset is all." She looks everywhere but up at me.

Moving slightly towards her and taking hold of Lillah's door. "Are you sure she is okay?"

"Sean, I just got her back to sleep" She puts her hand on my chest and I smile taking hold of her hand, only to have it jerked away from me.

"Are you sure she is okay - Ava?" I run my fingers through her hair.

Trembling she puts out her hands almost touching my chest again before she pulls them back. "Yes. She just wakes up and gets upset."

"I think I should check on her anyway," I say, easing myself against her stiff stature.

Looking up at me suddenly, "Sean, I said no!" Without hesitation, I take in her bottom lip with mine, caressing her mouth and encouraging a response. Taking hold of her waist, I kiss her until she finally kisses me back. As I run my fingers through her hair, I rub my tongue against her lips and she opens her mouth for me responding equally. She moans, increasing my excitement so I pick her up and carry her to her bed, following her down and in. Her lips taste so good, and her skin feels so incredible. I begin moving my hand to her shirt, grabbing the edges and pulling it up until she stops everything. "No Sean. No I can't."

"Why?"

"I can't do this with you again!" She runs out of the room twisting her clothes back into place.

Running after her, I pull her back to me. "Ava, I know you want me."

"It doesn't matter what I want. It's not right, we are not right."

"Who says?" I ask taking her arm to stop her from walking away but she pulls away and runs from me again. I find her pacing with fisted hands and wiping away tears. "Ava I have missed you more than I could have ever imagined, please don't push me away."

"I have heard you say that before Sean and it's not good enough. I want more and I don't think you can do that. No, I know you can't, you won't."

"Ava, please don't," I said as fear begins to take over my emotions.

"Don't worry, I won't keep Lillah from you." She paces away from me. "Maybe your mother can come and get her and take her to you."

"What are you saying?"

"You know custody details," she said looking everywhere but at me.

I shake my head, "I'm not letting you go Ava, not this time."

The tears begin to stream even more down her face, "you have to, it's better for both of us, and you know it." Ava continues to hold me back from her.

"No it's not, Ava."

"Yes it is, besides I'm over you and I don't feel the same way anymore."

"That's not true, I see it in your eyes. The way you kiss me and the locket Ava, you could have thrown it out, not wear it."

With her usual stubborn attitude, she ignores everything I am trying to say and turns her back to me. "It is and I want you to find another place to stay first thing tomorrow. I don't want to see you again after tonight." As soon as the words leave her mouth my whole body begins to shake until I break. Falling to my knees, I push my hands over my face and over my head, tensing every muscle. I can feel her eyes on me, "Sean!"

I shake my head, refusing to hear another word of her denials, while tears form in my eyes. "Ava please don't do this." Swallowing hard, "don't Ava, I need you. I can't let you go. I won't." I look up at her and see her face frozen in shock. Focusing honestly on her, I take in a deep breath searching for the words, the only words that have a chance to persuade her. I lick my lips before breathing, "I love you Ava. I love you. I love you and I don't want anyone else but you." But she doesn't move. *No. She can't!* Trembling, I crash into my hands and pray to God that it isn't too late, until I feel her push my hands away from my face.

"I love you too, I never stopped. I'm sorry, I wasn't sure," she said fighting her own tears. "I had to make sure that you won't ever leave me again."

I wrap my arms around her as she collapses into me. "Why do you have to be so damn difficult? You could have asked me, I have wanted to tell you for a long time." I kiss her everywhere I can. Looking into her eyes again with a smile, "I love you Ava."

"And I love you," she said reviving my heartbeat again.

# Chapter 30: Ava

*I* am waking up in his arms again and I have no desire to ever move away from him but our daughter has other plans. She has begun whimpering already, following it with soft crying. One … two … three … and now the screaming. She is impatient and demanding as hell, like her father.

Sean wakes up with a look of shock, "what the fuck!"

"That would be your sweet little girl, I told you. Now get up."

"Are you kidding it's …," he begins searching for a clock, "the sun isn't even up yet."

"It's getting there, now get up." He quickly covers his disgusted expression with a pillow, wrapping it around his head as Lillah screams even louder. "No Sean, you are going to get up. I did this for months without you and now you are going to get to experience all the joy too. Now get up!" I said taking the pillow away from him and smacking his perfectly bare hind end, after he rolls over into my pillow. "You go get Lillah and I will get you some coffee going. Okay?" I asked grabbing the baby monitor and waiting for his response in the midst of his grumbling. "OKAY?"

"Okay," he growls with a lazy smile. As I fix his coffee, I hear him over the baby monitor go into her room. "Lillah honey, I love you but come on, Daddy needs sleep. Mommy makes me crazy and I need a lot of sleep in order to deal with her all-day." She quiets down as soon as he begins talking to her. *Great, a Daddy's girl already.*

Sean walks into the kitchen with her in his arms, smiling innocently. "Sean, I have the baby monitor you know?"

"You do? Oh no Lillah, Daddy's in trouble now." Sean still half asleep, approaches me with a gentle kiss. "I love you," he said before making his way to the sofa with coffee in hand.

Taking the seat next to him, I pick up Lillah and adjust to feed her, all the while waiting for a smartass comment from Sean. Instead he pulls my hair out of the way for me, rubs my neck, and watches us admiringly. "You need me to get you anything?"

"I'm good right now, thank you" *I cannot believe how amazing he is being.*

"If you need me to warm those up for her later, let me know." Catching his expected wink, I see him laugh to himself while I roll my eyes. *He thinks he's funnier than he is.* "Where are the boys?"

"They don't get up this early."

"Oh hell no, they don't get to sleep in, Rondo, Prince come." Nothing, Sean calls them again and still nothing. Sean smirks at me as I laugh at his failed attempts. "Squirrel!" He yelled and suddenly the house starts shaking as they both come scrambling on top of each other with twisted ears and eager anticipation for the squirrel that is nowhere to be found. Sean doubles over in laughter watching them search high and low.

"That was mean." Sean continues laughing as he lets them outside to verify the missing squirrel.

"Mean or not, it was funny as hell."

"I am going to go get her changed and cleaned up, don't go anywhere I will be back and it will be your turn to entertain her." He smiles but when I finish both Sean and the boys have gone back to bed. With a frustrated growl, I stomp my way to the bedroom, put her right on his chest, and just as I had hoped, she commands his attention immediately. "Your turn," I said cheerfully.

He forces a smile through his tired expression. "Thanks," he growls picking Lillah up and kissing her cheek. I hand him some toys while I crawl into bed myself.

Watching Sean play with Lillah is a sight I never thought I would get to see. I always wondered if we be any good at it. "You're so good with her already."

"I have had some practice but I'm sure you are still better."

"I don't know about that, I'm so tired all the time that I'm not sure I am good at anything anymore."

"Well now you have help, so you can get some sleep. Is there anything else you need my love?" He smiles wide at me.

"Right now sleep is the only thing I can think of but I will let you know." I smile happily before kissing his scruffy, morning face.

"Well have you thought about where you would like to live?"

"Live?" I look at him, puzzled to why he would ask such an odd question.

"Ava, you know we can't stay here." With his usual demanding attitude, he ignores my obvious disapproval over his statement. "It's not safe for you here. Eventually it's going to get out about you and Lillah and then we are right back where we were before I left the last time."

"But what can we do about that?"

"I want you to get yourself and Lillah packed up and then I am going to relocate you to a safer, more secure place."

"Sean!"

"Ava, I am not going to argue with you about this."

"Where are we going to go?"

"I called my realtor yesterday and he is sending someone over to help us get set up in a rental place until I can find us a permanent home."

"Why can't we stay here?"

"There is no security here and there is no way to have any real security here."

"We could put in an alarm and a fence or something …," I plead with him.

"Ava. Damn it, no. Please for once don't argue with me?"

"But I love this house."

"I know you do and I'm sorry you have to leave it but there is no other choice."

"Isn't there?"

He looks at me with a stern confidence. "*No.*"

"But Sean."

"Why are you so stubborn?" He pauses looking down at Lillah and calms. "I am not going to argue with you. You are going to need to do as I say. I'm sorry that you have to leave your house but there is no way I'm going to put either of you in danger by letting you stay here. Now please don't stress me out anymore by arguing with me about it." He stops when Lillah becomes determined for his attention, throwing her fists in the air crying. He looks over at me with his eyebrows furrowed and tensed. "Now there are two of you to drive me crazy." I bite my lip to keep from laughing. "It's not funny, Ava."

"Okay so I will move but when?"

"We should have a place in the next couple of days."

"That soon?" He nods and I look around my house that I love so much, "but what do I do about my house?"

"You can sell it I guess."

I pause somberly. "I know, I can sell it to Kyle and then we can still have the office here." I smiled with excitement.

"No, Ava"

"Why not?"

"You can sell the house to Kyle, give it to him even but you cannot come here and work every day. You need to get an office in a secure building, somewhere where you have to have an appointment to get in."

"Sean that's ridiculous. What am I going to do when I need to go to a client's office that's not so secure, are you going to have me followed by some armed guards?"

"That's not a bad idea."

"Sean no. I won't do it."

Leaning over he takes my hand, "Ava if you can promise me that you will be careful and think about where you're going and whom you are meeting with, then I will back off on the guards. I will back off some on the office but it still needs to be in a building that has some sort of security. Okay?"

Considering what he could demand to put me through, this seems doable. "Okay." I smile at him earning an appreciative kiss. Lillah simultaneously begins to demand Sean's attention be back on her. This one time, I let her have her way. Feeling my heavy eyes once again, I lie back within my pillows and blankets and close my eyes for a few seconds. When I open my eyes again, I am confused by the sun's position, even though I am slightly dazed, I know it is later than it should be. I do not hear Lillah and I do not see or hear Sean. I focus hard on the numbers of the clock ... *I slept for 6 hours? I missed most of the day.* I stumble out of bed running to Lillah's room, finding Sean rocking Lillah to sleep. I step inside quietly but the boys' excitement towards me alert Sean to my presence. "I'm sorry, I didn't mean to fall asleep."

"Don't worry about it, I was able to get a couple of hours too."

"Thank you." He smiles back at me with a wink, causing my legs to suddenly quiver. "While you are taking care of her I am going to go get a quick shower." I said scrambling backwards. I rush to shower before starting my juggling act to find the perfect outfit, fix my hair, makeup and find the perfect underwear, all I hope, before he can take notice.

"Ava?" Sean called out to me as I stumble back to him, still adjusting my clothes.

"Sorry I had to change after my shower," I said hoping I am not being too obvious but still being sexy enough that he will want to try. His slight smirk tells me nothing but that he is curious to my sudden weirdness. Lillah thankfully is kind and falls asleep peacefully, allowing us time to make dinner together rather than having to order out. Sean lights some candles without me even suggesting, and it is all I can do not to scream for joy and attack him. I sit down with no hint to my ulterior motive and watch his body move. With every bite, every twist and thrust of his tongue, every flick of his fingers and every gaze in my direction until suddenly he gets up and sits right next to me.

"You look too good to be sitting over here all alone," he said taking my hand in his.

"Did you get a chance to talk to the realtor today?" I asked him while enjoying the tender circles he makes on my hand.

"Yes, she brought some options over."

"So you found a house for us?"

"A rental yes but I am still working on somewhere permanent. I should probably also tell you there is a photographer coming over."

"A photographer?"

"To photograph us for a magazine."

I jerk my hand away from his. "Sean why would you do that? And without asking me?"

"If we take the pictures ourselves then we can beat the reporters from trying to get the first scoop. It will cut down on the craziness and make it safer than trying to hide Lillah and you from them. Once they find out, they will be relentless until they get what they want, this way we beat them to the punch. Believe me I wouldn't do it if I didn't think it was for the best, sweetheart."

"Why didn't you do that before, when it was just us?"

"I didn't know where it was going then. And you were right, I was scared to answer questions about us. I was scared that it wouldn't work and then it would be my fault for putting you in the limelight again and then not be able to give you anything in return for the pain it would surely cause."

"And now you know. Where we're going I mean?" I said staring at my plate and pushing food around with my fork.

Sean, using one finger pulls my face towards his. "Ava, I know exactly what you want and I want the same. All I ask is for you to give me a little time to do it right. I love you more than I can tell you and I'm not ever leaving you or Lillah again." Pausing he kisses my hand. "Let me ask you the right way, you deserve it," he said with his tender green eyes melting every part of my body. I grasp his hand on my face, nodding as he touches my lips softly and follows with an excelling breath. "You know, you're a pretty good cook, I would have never guessed that about you."

"Why is that?"

"Because when I first met you I got this impression of you being so uptight that you ate frozen dinners, so none of your food would touch." He smirked.

I eye him with disapproval, "ha-ha! Well you know what? When I first met you I thought you were so full of yourself, that you had mirrors covering all your walls and ceilings, so you could continuously look at yourself," I said proudly.

"What? You did not."

"I did, I even imagined that you hired somebody just to walk around with a mirror for you."

"That's absurd," he said shaking his head at me with a mocking smile.

"I know but I thought you were," I said cocking my head to one side.

"You know if someone told me then that you would end up having my child, I would have thought you must have taken advantage of me in my sleep."

"If anything sweetheart, it would have been the other way around. You were after all, the one gawking at me while I took a shower."

"Mmm … the shower," he moans staring off into space with a goofy smile. I kick his chair to bring him back to me. "That wasn't nice," he scowls.

"You're sitting there fantasizing about me, right in front of me."

"So? It has been a long time. Damn Ava, I haven't had sex since you."

My jaw drops, "you haven't been with anybody else … at all … since me?"

Shaking his head, he looks at me from the corner of his eyes. "I did try once. I went out specifically trying to find someone to get you out of my head. I brought her home and had her in my bed and then …" He grimaces as if he is remembering something horrible.

"Then what?" I asked facing him fully.

"Then right before anything could happen, I called her your name."

"You didn't?" I said trying hard to hold back my laughter.

"I did and it was my ex-girlfriend, so you would have thought I could have remembered her name."

"What did you do?"

"I kicked her out and then went to bed alone and pissed off."

"Pissed off at whom?"

"You."

"Me! Why?"

"Because I couldn't get you out of my head. It had been over a year and I still could not get you out of my head. You don't know how frustrating that was."

"So no sex with her, just kissing?"

"Yes, but in some fucked up way, I thought I was kissing you. I don't know why, you kiss way better than her."

I smile, "really?"

"Don't get cocky, but yes." He pushes his plate away and leans on the table as he watches me finish. "I assume with Lillah and all you didn't get much dating in either?"

With a hard gulp, I force a reassuring smile. "We should get this cleaned up so we can relax," I said taking our dishes to the kitchen quickly.

"Ava?"

"Hmmm."

"Tell me you didn't have sex with some other guy?"

"Sean, you know I am not good with new men touching me like that."

"I did."

"Yes, but you're different."

Sneaking up behind me, he waits for me to face him and hovers over me so I cannot escape his intense stare. "Ava, what aren't you telling me?"

I shake my head but he is not buying it at all. "Well I might have gone on one or two dates, after Lillah was born. People set me up trying to make me feel better. You know because I had a baby and I wasn't sure if I still looked attractive to anyone. I went out only to make myself feel better. That's all." I slowly look back up into his concentrating eyes.

"You went on two dates?" He looks at me as my eyes, tell the truth. "Several?" He gulps. "You didn't?"

"NO! I couldn't. I wouldn't. It really was nothing, some of them were terrible but they made me feel like I am desirable and that is all I wanted, I promise. They would try to kiss me and I always maneuvered away. It was frustrating for them, and most never called me again after the first date."

"Most didn't?" *He would hear that.*

"One guy did. I met him at the grocery store, he is sweet though."

"He picked you up at a grocery store? Did he know you have a baby?"

"Well I had Lillah with me, he thinks she is adorable. He reminds me of you. Except he is young," I said wishing I could take it back. "Well he's only been out of college two to three years, he's twenty-three at best."

"You went out with someone younger than you, *a lot* younger than you?"

"Hey, watch it! He is nice, he goes running with me and helps me at the gym. He says I have a better body than any of those girls there." His eyes intensify. *He deserved that one.* "But nothing happened." I smile innocently at him.

"What's his name?" He glares at me as I try to speak. "What's his name, Ava?"

"Tad, why?"

"Tad? What the hell kind of name is Tad? Never mind, he sounds like a loser," he said waving off the idea of Tad. *Now would be a good time to shut my mouth and agree.*

"Yes he is, feel better." With a simple look, Sean lets me know that it was a stupid question and walks away from me mumbling under his breath.

"I can't believe you went out on dates."

"Well you kissed and tried to sleep with your ex-girlfriend."

"No, I tried to fuck her, nothing more."

"How is that any better?"

"I don't know, it just is." He said taking his wine and going into the living room to sit down on the sofa, still mumbling under his breath.

*Great now he's in a bad mood and I am horny as hell. Surely it won't be too hard to get him to refocus.* I turn out the lights in the kitchen, leave the candles still burning and walk in front of him while he sits, leaning on his knees, and still mumbling under his breath. I take the opportunity to quickly undo the last couple of buttons on my shirt. I barely show my diamond which he specifically asked for me to put back in last night. He is still not paying attention, so I undo a couple of top buttons too. *To hell with it, go for obvious. One more button with an inviting stance.* But he continues to grumble. Rolling my eyes … *idiot, if he would only realize I am throwing myself at him. He was begging me last night and now he doesn't even see me?*

I grab his hands and pull them to my waist. "What are you doing?" he asked ridiculously.

"Sean, pay attention to me. It already happened and it's not that big of a deal."

"It's not?"

*He is so insanely jealous.* "It's not! I thought of you on every date and the whole time wishing it was you instead." *I give up.* I let go of his hands and put my own on my hips, "Sean! Get over it! Honestly, we could be having a real nice night and you are dwelling on some guys that aren't even here, that don't mean anything to me." I keep huffing until I feel his hands glide up my legs to my thighs and abruptly reach around to grab my behind and pull me to him. He traces around my diamond with his tongue, causing me to lose my breath as he pulls up my shirt kissing my stomach, sucking and exhaling lightly against the wetness he creates on my skin. Standing up in front of me, he pulls off his shirt and throws mine behind me, snapping open my bra, he tosses it aside. His mouth with eager massaging moans, takes hold of my naked breasts. Holding his head against me, I close my eyes and enjoy the feeling of his mouth. I remain standing as he unbuttons my jeans, pulling them down until his tongue can reach underneath the edge of my panties. Muffling my excitement, I suck on my fingers, watching as his lips brush against me briefly. I catch sight of his cocky smile, the smile that can make any woman tear her clothes off for him and I am no different. Using his palms held out wide, he slides my panties slowly down my legs leaving me nude and wanting in front of him. Sean glances up at me once before moving in and with simple movements of his tongue, he does all the right things while I keep my fingers tight in my mouth. *Panting.* He gently spreads my legs further apart, while I fist his hair. Naked and vulnerable, feeling his tongue, his fingers, and lips graze against me repeatedly, until my moans become satisfied whimpers. His cocky smile finds its way back to my lips.

"I wanted to show you my appreciation for dinner."

"What about showing your appreciation for having your child?" I asked jokingly.

"Oh I'm going to take care of that right now, baby," he said picking me up in his arms and carrying me to bed. Watching me with his sex driven eyes, he slowly removes his pants, reducing my patience completely. I reach out eagerly, pushing his pants off him. Seeing how hard he is, I take hold of him feeling his pulsating growth between my fingers until he pulls my hands away and climbs in on top of me. Placing his hands to either side of me he opens my mouth with his, "say it; tell me what you want." His tongue touches mine lightly. "Say it," he said against my lips.

"I want you … I want you inside me." I begged feeling his hands slide along my legs pulling them up around him.

"I love you." He said focusing on my eyes and giving me what I want. I wrap myself around him kissing his toned chest, sucking on his delicious neck, and finding his perfectly soft lips as he pushes in even deeper than the previous. Our breathing rough and rugged, our hands grasping and massaging, "let go Ava. I want to hear you let go, I want to feel you," he continues to whisper in my ear, seducing me into ecstasy until my toes curl and I feel him growing larger inside me. He groans deep into my skin, "that's it baby." I arch my back against him, gripping him tight as the sensation shakes me and controls me into my release. Groaning he continues, whispering, gripping my thighs tight, and building me up again.

I grip the back of his neck, unsure if I am going to explode in pleasure or pass out in his arms. "Sean, please!" Rocking his body back and forth, again and again, faster he pushes until – climax. He slows with our release, shivering to the end. Exhausted and relaxed we end the night curled into each other, using our old rule, of no clothes. "I love you so much," I smile finding my place within his arms as he whispers the same.

CR&EO

*I*t is amazing how quickly things can change. Sean has permanently relocated to Atlanta and surprisingly so did Ethan and Abbey. Neither thought twice about moving. I assume to get away from the Hollywood lifestyle that neither enjoys. Mary practically lives here already with her new boyfriend and Randy always follows Sean, and he is especially excited about being closer to his family in Alabama. While Lillah and I, are moving into a much larger lifestyle, one I am not sure I am ready for. Sean helped me pack the house and Lillah's things especially. I left some furniture for Kyle, who is ecstatic about moving into my little warm house. I try not to concentrate on leaving my home and to be excited about the other parts of my life but Sean has caught me a few times saddened, by the memories I am leaving behind. He tries to make me feel better and I always pretend that he is, despite my anxiety about my new life. However, he did give me one last memory, the day Tad stopped by to see if I wanted to go running with him.

When I heard someone at the door, I was a little surprised at first but then I realized the day and the time. I tried to get to the door without alerting Sean but he caught my expression and cut me off.

"Who's that?" He asked judging my reaction suspiciously. I shrug, unsure if I can get out believable words. Furrowing his brows at me, "sit. I'll get it darling." I thought at first to fight him but something told me that it is not worth it. As I sit, I watch him walk to the door, still judging my facial expressions until he opens it and sure enough there stands Tad, all gloriously built and decked out in his adoring, running clothes, cute as ever. Mr. "Boy Next-Door" at his finest.

"Hi, is Ava available?" He asked without any concern.

"Not anymore," Sean said coolly as he shut the door in Tad's face.

"Sean!" I stood up running towards the door, surprised by his rudeness. Sean grabs me and throws me over his shoulder, taking me to my room and tossing me on my bed. He positions himself around me so I cannot move anywhere. All I can do is look into his eyes that are intent and questioning. I lie back trying to look innocent.

"Ava that was not the guy you led me to believe he was."

"No?" I asked innocently.

"No," he said roughly.

"I said he was young."

"Ava ... that is not a guy that would be fine with just talking."

"I said he is sweet."

"Sweet doesn't make a guy want to keep coming by and still not be getting something in return?"

I fumble my fingers around the covers on the still unmade bed, "I didn't have sex with him Sean, and I resent the accusation."

"I'm not accusing you of anything. I'm asking what you did to make him return," still sounding like an accusation.

"Maybe he thinks I'm pretty?" I shrug.

"Pretty? Ava you're beautiful and I have no doubt that he thinks that but that still doesn't explain his persistence."

*Sigh.* "I kissed him or rather he kissed me when I wasn't expecting it and …" *I am not sure the next part is entirely necessary.*

"*And?*" Sean asked with wide-eyed curiosity.

"And he grabbed my ass and got a quick hold of my chest in the process. It was completely innocent and nothing else happened. I got nervous as usual and excused myself from the situation gently." Sean gets up, stomping his way back towards the door. "Where are you going?"

"I'm going to break Tad's hands."

I jump quickly onto his back. "Sean no, it was nothing. I thought of you the whole time and he wasn't even close to as good as you." He smiles a little too easily. I slide off his back looking at him closely, "oh you did that on purpose!"

"Maybe, but at least I know I'm better," he boasted.

Giving him the angriest look possible he laughs at me and caresses my face "Oh kitten, don't be mad. It only makes me laugh harder."

"It's not funny, Sean."

"You should have seen that guy's expression when I shut the door in his face. It was hilarious!"

"That was not nice."

"I wasn't trying to be."

"You know since your mother took Lillah this morning I was going to let you shower with me but now I'm not." His laughter stops abruptly when I grab a towel and huff in his direction before walking into the bathroom.

"Ava, now that's not nice."

"Too bad, you need to be punished," I said holding my head up high and ignoring him purposely. I turn on the shower and strip my clothes off while hearing him approach from around the corner. "Don't you dare come in here Sean Grant," I said hearing him laugh. Stepping into the shower, I let the water wash over me for a few seconds before feeling his hands and caressing lips. *I love teaching him a lesson.*

CR&O

*T*he days have flown by and the packing was completed before I wanted it to be. We have moved out of my perfect little house and into a massive, more secure house. It is big, modern and has everything and nothing smaller than my old bedroom. I am afraid I will lose my daughter in her own room. Most people would be ecstatic but it is not me, the big white fortress swallows me whole. I pretend in front of Sean, showing him no sign of how much I hate it, telling myself it does not matter as long as we're together. I am too happy to worry about where we live. However, my nightmares have returned and I'm not sure why and I am not going to tell Sean until I know. I am sure they will go away as soon as I get use to my new life. Besides, even if Spencer manages to get out of jail, there is no way he is going to be able to get to me in this house.

Tonight, Sean has agreed to make up for my struggle by taking me out on a date, my way. "So, where are we going beautiful?" I direct him to the Varsity, so we can eat junk food and people watch from our car. He is skeptical but proceeds without questioning. We park as far away from the restaurant lights, order our food, and then relax watching the unique people coming and going, talking and laughing about all the crazy things we see. We decide to leave the restaurant soon after a drunken man tries to urinate in the parking space next to us. Sean ushers him to move on and we head off to the movies. I pay for the tickets, the popcorn, and the sodas and am excited about doing so, making a point to dismiss the cash he tries to hand me. "You are so damn stubborn," he said putting his arm around my shoulder.

"I know but I'm having fun."

"Good," he said leading me into the theater with his head down under his baseball cap. I swore no one knows me anyway, so I don't bother hiding. Sean made it clear that he is not happy with that decision. When the movie is over, we mix into the crowd rushing to get out. No one is paying attention to anyone, including us. Once we get outside, we see a crew of guys dancing and stop to watch them from the back of the crowd. I lean into Sean's chest enjoying our time together until he tenses up. "We need to go," Sean said suddenly taking my hand and leading me off in a mad sprint. He rushes me

232

through the crowd and towards the car, pulling money out of his pocket and throwing it into the dancers' box as we pass. I am not sure why he is in such a hurry but I know enough not to question. We are almost to the car, when I hear someone call out his name.

"Sean!" A low squeaky voice called out again.

He tenses up on my hand as the voice becomes closer. "Sean!" I look out of the corner of my eyes seeing a young girl chasing us down. Sean is careful not to run from her but continues to get us as close to the car as possible. She reaches us leaping to tug on his jacket. "Sean, can I get your autograph?" She asked shrugging her shoulders. She is around seven or eight and cute with her glasses and big smile.

Sean stops at the car. "Sure sweetheart."

Her mother runs up on us, breathless and distraught. "I'm so sorry, she got excited and ran off before I could get a hold of her.

Sean waves her off, taking the pen and paper from the flustered mother, "no problem, what's your name?" He asked crouching down to the little girl's size, causing her to become ecstatic and barely able to stand still.

"It's Candice. You know my friend Lydia is going to be soooo jealous." She wiggles, exaggerating her hands and expressions.

"Oh yea and how old are you Candice?"

"Seven. I knew it was you as soon as I saw Ava, Candice said as Sean looks up at me. *I am never going to hear the end of this one.*

Sean hands her the piece of paper and pen back to her, "okay Candice you have a goodnight?"

"Wait, can I ask you a question?" Candice tugs his jacket again. Sean nods. "Are you going to marry Ava?"

He smiles crouching back down to her. "Do you think I should?" He asked glancing up at me before giving her a serious look.

"I guess so, she is pretty and seems nice. She lets you hold her hand in front of people, so she must like you a lot."

He laughs, "I agree."

"So you are?" She persisted.

"Candice, that's none of your business," her mother chastised her.

"No, it's alright," he said before whispering loudly in her ear. "I'm going to ask her to marry me soon but don't tell her, it's a surprise."

She smiles wide back at him and then me. "Okay!" She yelled gushing.

"I know this might be too much to ask but would you mind taking a picture with her?" Candice's Mom asked.

Sean agrees picking Candice up in his arms as her eyes grow wild. Her mother takes the camera from her father, who is exhaustively running up on us.

"Wait Mom, we have to get Ava too!" Candice yelled. Sean grabs my hand pulling me into the photo with them. After they take a couple of pictures and thank us, Sean puts the young girl down watching her smile wide, up at him and pushing her little glasses back into place. Her mother swiftly takes her hand and escorts her and her smile back to their car. Sean waves back at her once more before helping me into our car.

While Sean maneuvers us out of the lot, I stare at him admiringly. "What?"

"You were so sweet to her. You made her day, Sean."

"She was a little girl Ava, what would you have me do knock her to the ground and step over her?"

"Well I didn't expect you to be so gentle and caring towards her, especially after you had us nearly running from her."

"What must you think of me? Besides, I wasn't running from her, I was trying to get away from the crowd of people before her and her mother caught up to us."

"You were so obnoxious when we met, I guess I assumed you would be similar with others."

"I thought you were some crazed groupie, who was trying to get to me through my mother. I wasn't interested in encouraging that any."

"Well that was still sweet." He reaches for my hand kissing it softly. "Sean what about her question?" I asked biting my lip.

"I was wondering how long it would take you to ask that."

"Well then I have asked it, so…"

"So when am I going to ask you to marry me?"

"Actually, I was more interested in you saying that you were but either or both answers would be good."

"Ava you know I love you and I can't imagine anyone making me as happy as you do. So yes, I do want to marry you but I told you I have a plan on how I want to do it. So if you can be patient with me, I promise I will ask you. Soon."

I smile at him. *Crap! Am I blushing? He's laughing at me, so I guess I am.* "I think I can be good with that." I said simply turning my red face away from him.

"If you want, I will take you to pick out a ring?"

"No ... no that's okay, I would rather it be a surprise. I don't care about the ring."

He looks at me in shock, "you are not normal at all. Most girls would be all over the ring part."

"I trust you, you did get my locket." I pull it out to look at it. "Plus, I like the idea of being surprised." I said relaxing into my seat more and staring out the window to try to hide my ridiculous smile. "Sean?"

"Hmmm."

I scoot over to him and kiss him on the cheek. "Thank you, this was the best, normal date I've ever had." He smiles his sensuous smile with a wink.

# *Chapter 31: Sean*

*A*va's bright smile and dreamy-eyed reflection makes it hard not to pull the car over and propose to her right now, but she deserves perfect and that is what she is going to get. We arrive home, with Ava still in her enlightened mood and me still amused by it. Suddenly I realize something different about her.

"Ava, you haven't been getting up in the middle of the night have you?"

"No, I haven't for some time. Once I met you, I became more determined than ever to be normal or as close to, as I can possibly be. I tried to tell you before you left that I was getting better. I wasn't perfect yet, but I was trying." She said bringing my guilt to the surface once again. "I became even more determined when I found out about Lillah. I wanted to make sure I was going to be the best mother I could be for her."

"You are," I said grabbing her hand and pulling her into my arms.

☙❦❧

*I* have to return to Ireland soon, as I was asked to be in a British film when I was there previously. It is different from my usual. This time I get to play the seductive evil killer but I die early on, since the movie is more about the small town I committed the crimes in. No one believes I am actually dead and therefore, is haunted by my character until they go insane. It is intriguing, and at the time that I agreed to do it I was looking for any kind of distraction. Now I am wishing I hadn't. I asked Ava to come with me but she is busy with work of her own and cannot afford to take the time off. So to make up for my soon to be absence, I am trying to spend as much time with her and Lillah as I can. Ava tries to ease my guilt but her sadness is apparent every time I mention it. It is the night before I have to leave and after we put Lillah to bed, I put Ava to bed. Lillah was kind enough not to wake up during our grand send off. I am concentrating on memorizing every detail of us together to take with me. However, Ava seems intent on making the night last as long as possible by asking me random questions and talking about the most absurd things. "What are you doing? You're not even making sense now." I asked her with a questioning expression.

"I don't want you to go, I'm sorry. I'm trying to be supportive and understanding but instead all I can do is ramble hoping the night won't end."

"I don't want to leave you either but this is my job and I'm going to have to leave sooner or later. I am going to miss you every time I have to go." She leans up hugging me tight as I rub her bare back. "I will be back annoying you before you know it." I said kissing her weepy eyes, "be careful while I'm gone, don't let anyone in the house you don't know and don't go anywhere without Kyle or someone with you." She mocks me while nodding. "I have a right to be worried and you know it. If I hear anything about him, I am coming back here to get both you and Lillah and we are leaving the country. I don't care how much kicking and screaming you do." I said hoping she understands my concern. "Oh and there has been a reporter calling Ethan to try to setup an interview with you. I told Ethan to tell him no. So if he somehow gets a hold of you let me know and I will take care of it." I said, thinking nothing of it, until I notice her tension and long silence. "No Ava." I groan at her.

"But Sean, maybe I should do it."

"What? Why?"

"Because I get tired of hearing things made up about me. Like I am an alien, trying to possess your body with my alien husband." I hide my mouth with my hand trying not to laugh while recalling that magazine picture, it was funny as hell. "I know it won't stop all the ridiculousness but maybe it will, at least give me a chance to give my side of what happened … they got his."

"I know they did but are you sure you would want to bring all that up again?"

"I think it will be good for me to let it go and move on - for good. Does that make sense?" She asked working her southern sweet magic on me.

"I guess so but I worry that it might not turn out like you want it to."

"Ethan can help me make sure they ask only certain questions and we can ask to see the final edited version to make sure it's agreeable."

*Wow, she pays attention to me more than I realized.* "Okay, but make sure you talk to this person and you feel comfortable with him first. There are others to choose from you know?"

"I will, I promise." She smiles kissing me again. "Thank you for understanding and … I love you."

ೞ౫౨

*I* don't like leaving my girls behind but Ireland is as beautiful as ever and the movie is going as scheduled, so the days are going by fast. I spend most of my free time communicating with Ava and Lillah through the computer in my hotel room. The rest of my free time, I spend purposely looking for the little old house I found the last time I was here. I am not sure how I found it the last time, so it is difficult to find it again. Luckily, I finally found some locals to help and after explaining the details of the house, I find it. This time I take the time to walk the grounds and look through the house before that same little old man reappears out of nowhere.

"You are back," he said startling me again.

This time I know I am not sleep deprived, so I am hoping I am not crazy and talking to myself. "Yes, I was curious."

"How is your heart?" He asked.

"She's wonderful, and waiting for me at home."

"Ahhh that's wonderful news," he said with not an ounce of surprise in his voice.

"Why do I think you knew that already?"

He smiles sheepishly, "you like the house?"

"A lot actually. I was hoping it would be for sale. You wouldn't happen to know who I could talk to about it?"

"I do."

"That would be great. I know Ava would love this house as much as I do."

"This is the man you should see." The old man holds a piece of paper out to me and I take it from him reading the name, number and an address of a local man.

"He owns the house?"

"He will be able to help you." He insisted.

"Thank you."

"You're welcome," he said looking suddenly concerned as to what sounds like whispers coming from behind me. "You are heading back home soon?"

"Yes, this Thursday, why?" I asked when the whispers from behind me become more frenzied. Soon as I turn, they go silent. I look back at the little old man who is suddenly staring fixedly at me.

"Five o'clock Thursday, no later in getting home," he said with no sign of a smile.

I laugh, "Ummm, okay. Why is that?"

"You know what to do Sean. You can save her." I hear the whispering from behind me again and turn but again they go silent and when I turn back, the old man is gone too. *Shivering.* Not sure I want to live with ghosts but something is drawing me to this place, despite all the weirdness around it. I get back into my car reviewing the piece of paper the old man gave me and program the address into my GPS following its direction attentively. The directions lead me to a small old shop in the town nearby. I park the car eyeing the old broken down place carefully before deciding to get out and go in. Once inside, I take in the crowded space of antiques and odd pieces, of all sorts.

"Can I help you?" The man said with a stiff posture as he looks me over.

"Yes, I was told I could find a man named Deaglan ...?"

"That would be I, Deaglan Quinn, what can I do you for?"

"I was curious about the old house on Glendon Hill?" I asked becoming more at ease as he does.

"Curious, or interested in purchasing?"

*Nothing like cutting to the chase.* "Purchasing." Deaglan pulls out an old book of information about the house and bargains a good price on the land and house. He even tells the same story of the original owners that I heard from the old man but when he shows me pictures of the couple, chills go up my spine. I recognize *him* immediately. I read the names below the picture realizing he never did tell me his name, Finn and Nora Glendon ... 1902! My legs become weak and I forget to breathe until Deaglan laughs.

"So you have met them?" He asked with a superior smile. I hesitate to answer, unsure whether to admit to my delusions. "You're not the only one."

"Well that's ... reassuring."

"Don't worry they're harmless, nosy but harmless. Angels making sure their property is taken care of, I suppose." I smile even though chills are still rushing through my body. Deaglan exits to the back to make copies of the information for me, while I lean on the glass in front of me reviewing the items within the case, and that's when I see it, Ava's ring glaring at me. When Deaglan returns, I have him take it out for me.

The bright, sparkling ring has a beautiful softness to it but the center stone holds it position strong and defiant. I negotiate with Deaglan for the ring and return to my hotel eager to finish this movie and get back home to Ava and Lillah. It is all I can do not to tell her everything when I speak to her at the end of the night. Luckily, she reminds me about her interview with a reporter named Cole Brinkman and we spend most of our time discussing the interview instead. She seems nervous but excited about the opportunity, so I promise her I will try to make it in time to be there with her. Although I am sure I will be late, I have plans to see a house that I hope will become a permanent place for us to live, getting Ava out of the white fortress for good. It is the perfect time to see it while she is distracted, so I can surprise her later.

∞

Once I arrive in Atlanta and make a quick call to Ava to let her know I made it okay, I approach Randy, enjoying my car a little too much. "Who said you could drive my car?" I asked him with a cold stare.

"If you want me to pick you up in style then you need to let me have a car. Besides Ava said it was okay."

"Oh now, what Ava says goes?"

"When it's what I want to hear," he smiles wide.

"That's what I thought," I said taking my keys from him and climbing into my car to drive, despite his huffs. I drive straight to the prospective house to meet the realtor. As soon as we pull up to the gate, I know it is the one. As we tour the home, the warmth of the house embraces me and reassures me even more but the wooden bridge over the organic pool with the fully-grown trees surrounding it, gives me an idea. Everything is perfect, even the master bedroom has skillfully designed double doors leading to its own personal patio that overlooks a beautiful garden and stream. A fireplace in the bedroom and bathroom and most importantly … a large separate shower for two, as well as, an exceptionally large bath. There are several extra rooms for my office, for Lillah, a gym, plus additional rooms we may find we need later, like room for a least one more little brother or sister for Lillah, if not a couple. The house flows effortlessly, as it embraces the environment surrounding it naturally, it is a perfect combination of her and me. I tour Randy around with me explaining every detail.

"I like it, I think you're right she is going to love it. There is even room for the boys to run," he said as I stare at him in amazement.

"Yes, there is. There is a great tree to put a swing in for Lillah. There is even a huge in-law house out back which part of can be turned into a studio for Ava and the other part into a game room for us … after hours," I said nodding with him in agreement.

"Do you have the ring?" Randy asked. I pull the little intricate box from my pocket and open it. "Wow! Now that's nice."

"Now that I have the house for us, I can propose properly."

"You've been waiting to give her a house? Trust me Sean she knows you have money. You don't need to impress her with it any further."

"I'm not trying to impress her asshole, I'm trying to give her the perfect night. Proposing in our house, the house we are going to raise a family in." He looks at me with a blank face. "I'm trying to be romantic … fucking sentimental and shit." Staring at me and still possessing the annoying blank face. "Damn, are you doing this on purpose?"

He starts laughing. "Yes, I get it. It is a great idea, making your first memory here your proposal. I get it."

"I was beginning to worry about you."

"Yea, whatever. Hey can we stop and get some food after?"

"As soon as I sign the paperwork and get everything I need." I said thinking it would be just that simple, however, the paperwork takes longer than expected. I could have counted the seconds, by Randy's sighs but now I am even starting to get anxious. Eventually all the paperwork is completed and the keys and codes are handed over. I take one last look around our new house, envisioning my plans for tomorrow night.

"I'm hungry, can we go now?"

"*Yes*, we can go," I said listening to the bear like growl coming from Randy's stomach. "So what is it you want to eat?"

"I don't know what time is it?" He asked rubbing his stomach.

"What time is it? What the fuck does time have to do with food?"

"Because Sean, traffic, I would like to go to one place in midtown but if it's close to rush hour, I'd rather not."

I check the time, "it's 4:25, so rush hour for sure," I said suddenly remembering Ava's interview today. "Actually, can we pickup something close to my house? I want to be there before Ava's interview gets started. I am sure she's nervous."

He shrugs, "are the boys there?"

I stare at him in amazement. "No, they're at my Mom's with Lillah, so they're out of the way."

"Alright," he sighs pouting.

"What is with you and the dogs suddenly?" Randy huffs ignoring me. We stop by a restaurant and while Randy goes in to get the food, I stay in the car and try calling Ava but it goes straight to her voicemail. I check the time again, 4:40. *I wish he would hurry I would like to get out of here before traffic gets any worse, it's almost 5 and traffic gets even....* The realization begins sending strange waves of uneasiness through me. I stare at the time until I remember the conversation I had with Finn and my heart begins to beat in triple time.

Randy jumps in the car with an armful of food, "okay I got you ..."

"We need to go," I said trying to remain calm since I don't understand what it is I am feeling.

"Why what's wrong?"

"I'm not sure but I have to get to Ava ... by 5:00?"

"What?" He asked even more confused than I am. My phone begins ringing and I reach for it too quickly to keep Randy calm.

"Can I call you back Ethan, I'm trying to get a hold of Ava?"

"Sean. I didn't know until just now Sean, it was unexpected for all of us." The regret in his voice begins to make my hands shake. "Spencer Jefferies was released from prison yesterday." With my heart halted, he continues. "A reporter apparently hired an attorney for him and he's getting a new trial. As if that wasn't bad enough he was granted bail and it was posted. He hasn't been seen or heard from since." *I can't breathe, as I listen to the words.* "I'm sorry Sean, it was all done under the radar and quickly. The police think he is in Massachusetts somewhere, he used to live there with his mother."

I shake my head unconsciously, "he's in Atlanta."

"I wouldn't worry Sean, he would need a lot of help to get down here and find her this quickly."

"He got it Ethan … from us."

# *Chapter 32: Ava*

$S$ean arrived back safely and I am hoping he finishes his errands earlier than expected for more than one personal reason. My interview is today and despite his encouragement, I need him here. My daughter, my dogs and everyone else including my comforting boyfriend is absent from this white fortress and I do not know whether to wish for the time to fly by or to slow down. Even my hot shower is not helping, all I can think about is the questions, my answers, and the responses to them. I take my time getting ready, checking, and triple checking my entire look, marking off my checklist that Sean's stylist gave me. I look sophisticated but alluring which is how the professional put it but I feel like an idiot and I hope I am not being a fool. My consistent pace becomes more agitated, until I force myself to sit down and not wear out the floor over something so unimportant. Now I have to sit, watching the devilish clock, dance around in its concentric circles, flashing its brilliant numbers around the room … *4:15* … 4:16 … 4:17. Finally, the gate security calls to let in the reporter. I begin shaking harder but with a nervous breath, I allow them in despite them being over an hour early. Their truck drives up in an instant and Cole Brinkman, the reporter is at my door even faster. He seems nice but eager. Both Ethan and Sean talked to him about what was allowed to be asked and what was not, and both were reasonably happy with him.

"Hi, Ms Kelley," Mr. Brinkman said with his hand held out and his smile blinding me.

"Ava," I said shaking his hand.

"Ava, great," he said loudly as he follows me in, outwardly checking every inch of the white fortress. "I'm so happy you agreed to finally do this Ava. Are you ready to get started?"

"I think so but honestly, I am a little nervous."

"No reason to be nervous, we will go slowly and take breaks whenever you need too, I promise." He said, feeling righted in putting his hand on my back and sending chills through my body for the first time in awhile. I nod as he introduces me to his cameraman,

Joseph, who is nervously hurrying his equipment into place. It is only the two of them, a small crew it would seem but I do not know enough to be certain. "Sooo, Sean will be here soon? He's scheduled to come back from Ireland today, correct?"

"He is on his way, he has some errands to run before, but he should be here soon," I said watching him form a restrained smile.

"Well let's get started and maybe we can be finished before he gets here." I look at him oddly. "I mean that way it will be ready for him to review and then we can get out of your way and let you two enjoy your night together." He expresses his minor reassurance, with an overbearing hover around me. "Okay Ava, if you will take a seat here, then we can get started." I sit checking the rhythmic, radiating numbers once again ... 4:30 ... 4:31, my hands continue to shake. The lights come on and the crude set is in place. Cole sits near me, suddenly placing a microphone on me himself, while jerking the piece into place, he nearly causes me to come unglued. Joseph gives Cole a cue and Cole's smile takes form once again. He introduces himself, then me and dives right in with questions. He asks me about Sean and I first, how we met, do we plan on getting married, when did I know I was pregnant, which is a question he is not suppose to ask. No questions in regards to Lillah, other than she exists. I eye him silently and he moves on. "Do you believe Sean is in love with you?"

"Yes. I do," I said hesitantly, unsure why he would ask such a question.

"So I assume you are equally in love with him?"

"Of course, he's the love of my life."

He smiles mockingly, "that's wonderful. And did you ever imagine that you would be involved with someone like him?"

"Someone like him?" I asked.

"You know what I mean, a celebrity, someone who can provide you with everything you could ever want."

"No. I would have never imagined falling in love with Sean and he is all I have ever wanted. He doesn't need to provide me with anything else."

I watch carefully, taking notice of his suspicious eyes seemingly circle me into a corner. "Weren't you worried that your past might hurt your relationship with him or is it that you used it to make him feel sorry for you?"

"No!" I demand staking my ground and steadying myself for the fight.

"No? A man was convicted of raping you, although he claims that it was consensual."

"That's absurd." I huffed at him.

"It is? You did get into his car, didn't you?"

"He kidnapped me and held me hostage for days. He tied me up and beat me viciously. The very idea that he thinks it was consensual, proves how crazy he is."

"So you think he should have pleaded insanity?"

"No, he knows what he did and he knows it was wrong." My body begins to shake in rhythm with my hands. *4:45 … 4:46, please Sean hurry.*

"How do you respond to his repeated requests to talk to you?"

"Why would I want to talk to him?" I question nervously.

"He has seen many doctors that say he is telling the truth about what happened, he even passed a polygraph test. He just wants to talk to you and try to clear things up with you, so you both can go on with your lives."

With a harsh chuckle, "I don't believe it. He wants only to hurt people."

"Hurt people or hurt you?"

"Both!" I yell back at him.

"Would you ever consider letting him apologize to you?"

"No, I don't want to see him ever again."

"Well then maybe Ava, it's you that enjoys hurting people. He says you two had a secret affair and that he went temporarily crazy, when he discovered you were sleeping with your boss. Are you sorry for what you did to him?"

"I never had an affair with him and this interview is over!" I stand tugging at the microphone frantically.

Immediately Cole stands up taking hold of my arm. "Please Ava, I'm sorry. This is my job and I promise I will change the questioning but I have to ask what others are thinking. It doesn't matter if they like me, but so far *you* are doing wonderful." He said as I check the malicious ticking clock again … *4:53 …* exhaling deeply I ease back down. "If you had a chance to say something to him what would it be?"

"Nothing," I nearly whisper knowing that this interview is never going to make it to air, once Sean see's it.

"Nothing at all?" Cole asked surprised. I shake my head, biding my time and glancing over at Cole as he licks his lips and adjusts his tie, while a familiar evil sensation slithers its way back to my spine. "What would you say if I told you I have a connection to Spencer Jefferies right now and he can hear and see you right now?" Cole said leaning in closer to me.

"I would say you better get the fuck out of my house!" I yelled, standing immediately to get away from him and his camera.

"Ava." A chilling voice calls out from behind me and with a slow easing turn, I see his large domineering stature standing in front of me. Within a fraction of a second, the fear I once thought long gone, shackles me in chains once again.

"I told you to stay in the truck. We were going to do this through video until we were sure," Cole said as Spencer's gaze stays focused on his long awaiting target.

"You don't tell me anything," Spencer growled.

"What did you say to me?" Cole stands up confronting him but is easily thrown back. Joseph tries to step in and get control of the situation but is met with a gun to his chest and in that split second, his focus is off me, so I run. A gunshot rings out from behind me, halting my breath and my movements briefly. Guilt ridden, I look over my shoulder seeing Joseph writhing in pain, mouth to me – "Run." I force my legs to move without looking back but catching up to me quickly Spencer closes my options off, circling me like prey with his wild black eyes and his gun waving at me.

"Stay away from me," I said searching for a way out.

"You don't love me anymore Ava? I love you, I still believe in us. I knew we would be together again one day," he said as I close my eyes trying not to give into my fear. Shaking my head I maneuver away from him, as he dances around me - enjoying his game. I decide to inch my way to the wall that holds my only hope. "Don't even think about it Ava, you do and I will kill you right here," he said with his fiendish grin.

"You know you won't be able to get out of here," I breathe in deeply, watching him almost break out in laughter at me.

"Oh Ava, I am going to get out of here and I'm taking you with me. We can build that life that we always dreamed of having together. You know you love me."

"I don't love you. I love Sean," I say watching his expression intensify and his posture sink down into his chest. "I had his child you know."

"Shut up."

"I'm going to marry him and I'm going to have more of his children."

"SHUT UP," he growls with rage, fisting his way closer.

"No! I love Sean and I'm going to build a life with him, not you."

"SHUT … UP!" He yells closing his eyes, rubbing his face with hardened breaths while I rush for the alarm on the wall, setting off the screeching siren. Before I have a chance to relish in my small victory, he takes a hold of me. "You stupid fucking bitch!" He yelled, jerking out every ounce of fear within me into a terrifying scream. He begins to drag me towards the door and I fight him with every step until he throws me to the ground, kicking me and punching me with wild rage. With every hit he makes to my body, he beats out another ounce of energy and once he sees my surrender he picks me up and moves swiftly towards the door again. "Don't worry, you'll heal after we get home."

"NO!" With one desperate kick, he drops me, leaving me crawling, and kicking my way out of his reach, until I feel the blow whipping my head hard to the floor. As I lay crumpled on the ground and screaming in pain, he turns me over and climbs on top of me. "Is this the way you want it! Really? Fine with me. Let's go out in a blaze of glory together then. But before we go, let's have one last beautiful moment. Let them see us die in each other's arms, like it is meant to be."

My eardrums burst as my echoing screams reach their limit. "Sean," I cry.

"Stop saying his name," he growls in my face.

"No, I love him not you, I love Sean, and I had his baby not yours." I watch him snarl as he stands shaking and gripping his crimson face. "He makes love to me over and over. We laugh at you together." Spencer begins spewing unrecognizable words at me, with vigor. "Do what you want to me but it won't change anything." I smile feeling my strength return as I stand slowly. "I will always love Sean and I will always detest you. You're a fucking loser!"

Spencer lets out a trembling scream and fires his gun at me, hitting me and forcing me to the ground with my head spinning. "He's never going to touch you again," he said as I hold my wound tight. Forcing me up and into his arms, he holds my head to his, pushing the gun to the edge of my ear. "I won't let him have you. Even in death, you will always be mine. We are going to die together.

I found you first," he sears into my face. My jaw is locked open, as I fight for breath. Staring at the joyfully dancing devil, swirling its triumphant numbers in my face … 4:59 … *5:00*. With a last breath, I call out for Sean and with a loud exploding crash, I hear … the shot.

# *Chapter 33: Sean*

*I*magining the worst, I cannot drive fast enough. "Sean! What the hell is going on?" Randy yelled.

"Spencer Jefferies was released on bail and they can't find him," I said watching his eyes widen, obviously still not understanding my fear. "The reporter that bailed him out, is the one that is meeting with Ava right now." Now my fear becomes clear as it washes over his face. "Take my phone and keep calling her until she answers."

"I keep getting her voicemail Sean," Randy said continuing to dial and I continue checking the time with my heart pounding harder and harder against my chest with every minute that passes … *4:50 … 4:51 … 4:52* …. Once we are near the house, I can hear the alarm blaring verifying the worst of my imagination. With the iron gate in sight, I race towards it; not waiting for Boston, our gate guard to open it wide enough for my car. He meets me at the gate looking beyond stressed, but hearing Ava's screams I ignore Boston and try to get to her but I am stopped hard by Randy. "No Sean, you don't know what's going on."

"Mr. Grant I tried to call the house but no answer and I heard gunshots." Boston said vibrating.

"Did you call the police?" Randy asked trying to hold on to me. When I jerk my arm from his grasp I see his gun under his jacket.

"Yes, they are on their way," Boston says easing his stress some.

"Randy give me your gun," I demanded holding my hand out to him.

"Sean no, the police will be here and you should let them handle it." I wave my hand out towards him, demanding him to give it to me. I can barely breathe as I listen to Ava's screams, I continue to wrestle with Randy, only to be stopped by a single shot hushing her screams. Eager to hear her again, I wait only a second more as even her screams would be welcomed now.

"What time is it?" I yelled.

"What?" Randy yelled back in confusion.

"What is the fucking TIME?" I screamed at him.

"4:59!" Randy yelled back, preparing to fight me to keep me from running into the house.

"Give me the damn gun!" Not waiting for his permission, I reach into his jacket and take it from his holster. Randy screams at me as I run to her. With a sharp gasp, I hear her cry out my name. *She is still alive.* With that knowledge, I crash through the door seeing him holding a gun to her head. Stunned he moves, foolishly allowing me a split second without the gun to her head and without hesitation, I aim and shoot knowing exactly where I need to put the bullet. The gun in his hand crashes to the floor a split second before Spencer's lifeless body. I do not even take a breath before running to her and grabbing her before she collapses. I fall to the floor holding her, "Ava?"

"Sean? He's here … you have to …"

Shaking my head, "he's dead Ava. He's dead." She stares at me for a few seconds before she calms. "Are you hurt?" She nods looking down.

"He shot me," she said pulling her hand away from the bloody mess.

"You're going to be okay, I promise. The police are on their way and we will get you to the hospital and get you taken care of." Taking my jacket off I wrap it around her shivering body. "It's going to be okay, baby?"

"I love you." She says over and over.

"Not as much as I love you." I kiss her gently.

"I'm so tired Sean, I fought him so hard. I really fought him this time."

"I know sweetheart but you need to stay with me for a little longer and then you can rest for as long as you want too." *I made it by five she was supposed to be all right, stupid fucking ghost better have not got the damn time wrong.* Watching her struggle to keep her eyes open, "baby do you know I found the most beautiful place in Ireland?" I said caressing her cheek softly. "I think you're going to love it but I am going to need your help." Tears well up in my eyes as she stills. "And you will never believe this but it has ghosts there and they are a little too friendly but …," I said trying to laugh and jarring her enough to open her eyes to me again. "Ava, don't you die on me. Don't you die on our daughter. We need you." I said holding her tight in my arms. I yell for someone to help her but every sound I make, seems as if I am in a vacuum. *It's not real, this isn't real.* The police come rushing in, holding their guns at me but I won't let go of her.

"No! He lives here!" Randy yelled.

The sirens come blaring up the drive. "Ava, the ambulance … they're here. They're going to take care of you," I said as she lies limp in my arms. Tears streaming down my face, I reluctantly release her to them and before I know it, they sweep her up and out of my arms. I steady myself eyeing her blood on me before running into the ambulance after her. Taking hold of her hand, I kiss her on the head and watch her eyes open and search frantically until I make sure I am in her view. "Ava," I struggle to speak her name. "It's okay, I'm here, and I'm not leaving. Please don't leave me, Ava. I need you." I pause clenching my eyes and gripping her hand tight. "I love you too much for this." Her eyes close again, even though she is being poked and stuck by the meticulously calm EMT. Fiercely fighting the tears, I caress her face, "keep your eyes open baby." She jerks her eyes open faintly before they fall closed again. I cannot stop my tears any longer and bury my head into her hair while holding her hand tight. *I can't lose her now. I have so much to tell her … to ask her.* I swallow hard and feel for the little box in my jacket that is draped over her. "Ava, I love you," I breathed softly in her ear. "I found the perfect house for us. It's everything we've been looking for." Opening the box, "I have a ring … I have your ring, sweetheart." Warming her hand, I kiss it gently and place the ring on her finger. "Marry me Ava. I love you." Her eyes close and I kiss her lips, quietly praying. We reach the hospital and they rush Ava in, stopping me at the last door. I watch her disappear in silence, as the door shuts in front of me.

"Mr. Grant can I get you anything?" The nurse asks, approaching me with tender hands and a concerned look.

"No, I'm fine," I said with no feeling or idea of what to do next. I sit fidgeting and becoming more impatient with each passing second, when the nurse comes back pushing water and some aspirin at me. "I said I'm fine," I snapped as she raises her eyebrows and holds strong in her persistence of the aspirin. "I guess I will take the aspirin, thank you." It does not take long before my entire family and all of our friends show up to our little personal hospital living room. Waiting for me to break, they all stare at me with their concerned and worried faces. *If I have to wait much longer, they may get their wish.* With a sharp creak and an abrupt slam against the walls, the doors open and my head jerks up to see the doctor coming in. Stepping to him quickly, I meet him more than halfway.

"Looks good. I think she's going to be fine, we'll know more over the next few hours but I don't think there is anything to be concerned about." He smiles reassuringly. There is a collective sigh within the little room.

"Can I see her?" I asked determined.

He nods, "sure, I will let her nurse, Pamela know." He nods again before exiting to somewhere unknown.

I take the time to say good-bye to everyone, promising to call with any news. After everyone leaves, my pill-pushing nurse enters with nothing close to a smile, Pamela I assume. "We have her settled in a room but if you don't do exactly as I ask at all times," she said pointing her finger at me sternly. "I will throw you out, do you understand me?" She emphasized with extreme clarity. Too scared to speak, I simply nod. "Okay then, follow me." Once we reach Ava's room, Pamela turns to me again, "you better behave. I am only going to warn you this once," she said with her angry finger nearly taking out my eye. Pamela leads me in and I find Ava attached to every machine possible. Taking her hand that now holds my promise to her, I make myself comfortable near her. "I am going home for the night but I will have them bring in some food for you."

"I'm not hungry," I said ignoring her huffing.

"I said I am sending in some food for you and you're going to eat it, my rule. Are you breaking my rules already?"

"No, I will eat every bite."

"The sofa pulls out into a bed. I laid some sheets on it for you to make it up, I will be back in the morning," she said as I force a smile at her. "I better not hear that you caused any trouble." She eyes me sternly before leaving. Someone does bring some food and I do eat, not a lot but enough that I think it will satisfy. I try to stay near Ava but manage to be in the way every time they come in to check on her. Eventually the sofa becomes more inviting than the hard, awkward chair and that is where I wake up the next morning, with the sun shining brightly in my eyes. I jump up worried about the time, when Pamela comes walking through the door and looking at me disapprovingly, again. "Oh so you decided to wake up. They said you were being stubborn about sleeping. You know if you would have gone to bed at a reasonable time, you wouldn't have missed most of the day."

"It's not that late," I said wishing I hadn't when I see the fire shoot out of her eyes at me. I make my way back over to Ava reaching for her hand. "How is she doing?"

"She is going to be fine," she said confidently. "We cut down on her pain medicine, so she should be waking up here shortly. She will be groggy though. Do not let her talk too much, she needs rest. I will be back to check on you two a little later and make sure you are still following my rules."

"Pamela, she is going to be okay?"

"She's going to be fine and back to keeping you in line real soon." She forms a weak grin before walking out with authority and chastising some other poor soul that happens to cross in front of her.

Pamela sent in food for Ava, and me. *She is so sure of herself.* I turn the TV on to check out the media craziness over our drama the day before but luckily Ethan has managed to keep that reporter's video out of their hands. I am not sure how he managed it but I am extremely grateful. With a sigh, I flip through channels trying to find something a little less dramatic.

"I like that show," she said, so softly I barely heard her.

I jump up with a mouthful of food and spit out nothing but indiscernible words that make her laugh. Swallowing and laughing myself, "hi beautiful, how are you feeling?"

"Fine," she answered roughly.

"You're not fine, you will be though. Right now you need to rest."

"Are you okay?"

"I'm fine. Especially now that I know you are going to be okay."

"Lillah?"

"She's perfectly fine. She is at home with everyone we know and the boys too. All waiting for you to come home."

"Can I go home today?"

"No," I laughed at her.

"Sean, I think it will be …"

"Don't you say it will be fine, the answer is no. Besides your nurse will have my head if I even consider it."

"She's scary huh?" She asked as I nod with a frightened look that makes her laugh again. "Sean?" She says looking up into my eyes. "Will you hold me?" She asked scooting over in her bed.

"You're going to get me in so much trouble."

"You know you want to." She teased.

"I will as long as you stop talking and rest and eat some when you can." She nods and I move in carefully beside her, sighing happily, as she curls up into my arms.

"Oh hell no! You get out of that bed and mind your own business." Pamela comes in yelling and pointing her angry finger all over the room. Ava pouts and gives Pamela a harsh stare of her own. "Oh, so she is the real stubborn one. Well I am going to tell you what I told him, there are rules here and then there are my rules, and those are the only rules that matter. Do as I say and we will all get along and live happy lives. You can do all that nasty stuff once you are out of my hospital." Pamela pushes Ava's food to her, insisting until Ava agrees, giving us her angry finger one last time before leaving.

"Umm Sean," Ava asked, staring at her ring on her hand. "Did we get … engaged and I don't remember?"

"Not exactly, I mean yes, but that's not how I planned to do it, it was in-the-moment type of thing." I said shaking my head, hoping that she will understand. "I do have a plan to do it better, so ignore it for now, if you will."

"Do you want it back?"

"No it's yours, unless you want to give it back?" I said smirking at her sparkling eyes.

Turning her hand in the light and smiling enormously at the large brilliance on her finger. "No, I think I'll hold onto it, I don't want you to think I don't want it or anything."

"You like it?" She bites her bottom lip, nodding with a shy happiness. "I knew you would. Okay, now eat so you can get out of here and I can propose to you properly," I said brushing my lips gently against hers. I know I should calm down but it is nearly impossible to keep myself from crawling back into the bed with her again.

# *Chapter 34: Ava*

*A*fter being released from the hospital, I find out Sean has moved us all into his mother's house until we can find another place. He is afraid the white fortress memories will be too much for me to handle, but I think the memories are too much for him but I am not going to complain. As far as the other participants in the nightmare interview, they are dealing with their own ordeals. The cameraman is still recovering but is suing the reporter and his studio for forcing him into the situation. Ethan found somebody in the police station to accidently lose the video of my interview. Cole confessed to helping Spencer get bailed out and to helping him get to me. He said he thought Spencer was going to apologize and try to make amends, never imagining he was crazy enough to do what he did. However, the judge was not sympathetic to his pleas and convicted him of assisting Spencer in his crimes. A minor roll but he still got more than enough time to please Sean and that is good enough for me. The media ate up Sean's hero status, which the police have repeated continuously in interviews but because he still blames himself for not seeing it coming, Sean has refused any interviews to discuss it.

I am suppose to take it easy for a few weeks but I understood that to mean, do whatever you want until you can't, that is until Sean caught me running and playing with the boys. Thankfully, he corrected me on my misunderstanding right away. When the doctor finally gave me the okay to return to life as usual, I made him put it in writing because I know Sean will not believe me and as expected his suspicious eyes do not disappoint. "Here," I said pulling out my doctor's note for him.

"What's this?" He asked taking it from my hand and gazing over my posture with distrust. "What did you do, steal this from his desk and write it yourself?"

"No smartass. I let him feel me up and look at me naked. Then he was more than happy to do whatever I asked."

"Funny," he said with a soured expression.

"I think so," I said happily.

"So I guess this means we can get a little closer and …" Sean takes hold of me and trails his mouth up my neck.

"Sean I can't do this in your mother's house, it's too uncomfortable."

"I promise you, it won't be the first time I have had sex in my mother's house."

"Is that supposed to encourage me?" I huffed pushing him away.

"So what I am supposed to do, wait until we have our own place?"

"Yes, how much longer can that take anyway?"

"Hmmm, actually I do have a place I wanted to show you when you felt ready. I'm not sure if it's the right place but …."

Eagerly jumping into his arms, "where? Can I see it now, or tomorrow? When can we move in?"

"Whoa, hold up. Tonight no, tomorrow maybe, I will make a call and then let you know. Let's look at it first, then we will go from there … okay?" Sighing I reluctantly agree. "Baby, it's only one day, surely you can wait one day."

CA&EO

*I* wait the one day at work, trying to not think about it but only managing to drive Kyle and Anna crazy until Sean calls. He rambles on about how he cannot be there because of an important party for charity. For that reason, Ethan is going to take me on his way back from a meeting of his and we will meet up with Sean and Abbey at the party, after I see the house. I do not remember Sean telling me anything about a party but when I arrive home, I find a beautiful jade green dress waiting for me with a note:

*Wear this dress tonight for me and I will be sure to find you.*
*I love you – Sean*

The dress is sleek and simple as it falls down my body, showing every curve under it. Deciding to keep it simple, I let the dress be the focus and add the jade combs to my hair that Sean had gotten for me in Ireland.

Ethan arrives right on time as always, and like a perfect gentleman he takes my hand and leads me to his car. The ride to the house though is strangely uncomfortable. Ethan is unusually quiet even for him, luckily, my mind is so filled with anticipation that I can barely concentrate on anything else. We drive into the quiet area of trees and I edge to my seat as a house appears delicately lit up on its edges and the setting sun begins to highlight the grounds surrounding it. Within an instant, I feel at home. Ethan pulls to the front, helps me out of the car, and escorts me through the unlocked door. "The door is unlocked? Is someone here?" Ethan smiles without another word and guides me in until we see candles and hear music. I turn to him in shock and he hands me a key. "What's this?"

"You look beautiful Ava, I can't wait to call you my sister," he said taking my hand and pressing his lips respectively against the back of my hand before exiting.

Stunned and confused, I turn my attention to the music outside and follow the sensuous vocals until I come to a trail of rose petals leading out the backdoor. The backyard is lit up with more candles, while gentle sounds of a pouring waterfall flow into a nature driven organic pool of more floating candles and petals. Butterflies begin flying through my body as I take notice of someone coming over the arched wooden bridge. The darken shadow approaches and stops short under the light, leaning against the bridge with one perfect rose in his hand and a devilish smile fighting to take form. *I am not sure if I should run to him or wait.* My body is so overwhelmed with emotions that I am speechless. I watch him in his perfect debonair tux, one hand in his pocket and the other grasping the rose's stem gently while he focuses his attention entirely on me. *Perfect,* I think as a tingly sensation begins to work its magic through my body.

"You're late," he said.

"Am I?"

"Yes, you were supposed to be here weeks ago."

"Something came up."

"Sorry to hear that. I hope it worked out alright."

"It did. Luckily I was rescued by an incredibly handsome man," I said watching him move leisurely towards me, licking his lips as he scans my body.

"You didn't fall in love with this hero did you? I would hate to think I missed my opportunity."

"Well I am sorry to tell you but I am deeply in love with him." He reaches for me as his eyes and hands touch me so appreciatively, I have to tell myself to breathe.

"And who is this man?" He whispered against my lips.

"I think you know already," I said to his reemerging smile.

"I might have an idea or at least I hope it's me, after all I did buy you a house."

"You bought this house?" I said suddenly wide-eyed.

He nods, "do you like it?"

"You know me well enough to know that I do." He smiles playing with the strands of my hair against my face, his fingers caressing my cheek as he does so. I feel for the stem in his hand and take hold.

"No, you can't have this yet," he said lifting my chin with one finger. You have to answer a question first. After all I don't have a ring to offer you since you wouldn't give it back."

"I can give it back … for a moment, if you like?"

"Not necessary. I got it handled if you let me." His eyes staring so deep into mine that the best I can do is, a barely motioning nod. "I'm going to do this right Ava." I bite my lip, fighting my watery eyes as he drops to one knee and takes my hand, nudging me with a tender touch on my palm. My heart speeds while an invisible cloud holds my body up. *Oh please breathe, you can't pass out now.* "Ava, you have changed my life in ways I could have never imagined. In ways that I didn't even know possible. I was in love with you from the first day I met you, I just didn't know it. You are the smartest, most beautiful, sexiest, athletic, sports fanatic I have ever met." I laugh, making him smile. "I love every minute of my life with you and I'm miserable every minute without you. You gave me the most beautiful child in the world and I hope that you will give me more. It would be cliché to say that I am lost without you and I am found with you, so I will just say Tá mo chroí istigh ionat … My Heart is Within You and only you Ava." Concentrating deep on my tear filled eyes. "Ava Kelley … will you marry me?" *How does he expect me to respond when I can't even breathe?* My mind continues to race as I look into his waiting eyes, smiling an uninhibited smile.

"Yes. Yes, I will marry you," I managed to choke out.

He stands up handing me the rose and tenderly taking my lips within his. "I love you, Ava."

Smiling up into his green eyes, I can feel myself floating into a happiness I never thought possible for me.

*It is all a dream come true, at least, it is my dream come true.*

# *Preview of Reckless*

**W**ith our honeymoon barely behind us, we are off to LA for some events Sean is required to attend. The most important to him a dinner meeting that he is reluctant to tell me everything about.

"Are you okay? Should I even be going with you to this meeting?" I asked him, trying to bring him out of his trance.

"I have to tell you something. This is a project with a lot of potential, it's with an old friend that I haven't seen for some time." Sean takes my hand. "I didn't want to take this one at first but after I talked to Joel and reviewed the script, it is incredible. It is a great opportunity for me and we will be filming near Atlanta, so I can be home every night," he said with a nervous smile.

"Why do I feel like you are trying to talk me into something?" I asked warily.

"I'm not trying to talk you into anything. I am trying to explain why I want this project to work out, why I am so excited about it. It is an unbelievable script Ava and the character is perfect for me. Joel wrote the script about his Uncle, a daredevil of sorts who lived life to its fullest but damaging himself and many others along the way. His father is backing it but only if I play the lead and I will only do it, if you agree. So, it is important that you come with me. There is more to tell you but I want you to hear about the project first, so you can hear it with an open mind before I tell you the rest."

"Stop, if it's what you want to do, then I will support you." I receive a weak smile from him but he is still not at ease. We arrive at the restaurant before anyone else and still in our honeymoon frame of mind. I barely have time to enjoy the peacefulness before a woman comes from out of nowhere screaming Sean's name and jerking him from me like he belongs to her. Another man wanders in casually behind her, seemingly unconcerned for her odd approach. Sean introduces them as Joel and Rebecca Castor but I learn quickly that they are actually his ex-best friend and his ex-girlfriend, whom he almost married. Sean apparently was not expecting her and fidgets awkwardly throughout dinner while I sit watching them discuss the details of the screenplay. She, however, ignores the conversations, flipping her hair and giggling at everything he says or does and touching him every chance that becomes available. Whenever I attempt to speak, her cold eyes silence me. Making no attempt to be my friend, she does everything possible to achieve Sean's attention, above and below the table. With a confident smile, I kick her leg away from his, making sure my heel forces her foot down to the ground, drawing my line deep into her skin. With my position clear, the she-devil wickedly smiles her way across the line and demands to play opposite Sean as his lover in the new movie.

I spent the rest of that night unsure how to respond. I sat in silence, suspiciously learning everything I can about the two people that are going to invade our peaceful life. The movie is as my husband said, a wonderful opportunity and I had no intention of denying him that opportunity but if I had known that night, what I know now. If I had only known that an ex-girlfriend's advances towards my husband are nothing, compared to the evil that awaits us during the making of - "Reckless."

www.ingramcontent.com/pod-product-compliance
Lightning Source LLC
Chambersburg PA
CBHW072212170626
46813CB00003B/910